ALY BECK

Cover Design: Artista Grafico

Dev Editing: Steph Rawlins

Editing: Jenni Gauntt

Formatting: Jenni Gauntt

Tropes

Secret Girl/Secret Identity
Hate to Lovers
Second Chances
Mafia
Mystery

Blurb

My name is Olivia Viotto. And five years ago, I was murdered by my three best friends.

Only, they didn't finish the job. Now, I'm back as an undercover agent, eager to tear their world apart.

Confronting my past was never on my to-do list. Neither was going undercover as a man, returning to my hometown, or unraveling the skeletons in everyone's closet.

But here I am.

Five years ago, I died.

Almost.

How's that phrase go? What doesn't kill you makes you stronger.

So, I got stronger.

From the fiery remains of tragedy, a guardian angel saved me, resuscitating and bringing me into the underbelly of a super secret government agency, where I healed my body and mind.

Yet the scars of that night never faded.

For years, I trained and brought down the bad guys. One person at a time.

Now, it's their turn.

My ex-best friends.

Huxley. JJ. Mack.

The three boys I loved with all my heart who betrayed me in the worst possible way.

My mission?

Go deep undercover, posing as a new male student named Oliver. Watch my ex-best friends. Infiltrate their frat to become a member and earn their trust.

Because something fishy is happening at Greenwood University.

Murder. Mayhem. Missing people. The list is endless in a sea of snakes.

Until it all goes impossibly wrong. My identity and life are at risk every step I take, and the bad guys are closing in.

I'm forced to lean on the very people I swore vengeance on.

Nothing is ever as it seems. Lies are everywhere.

But I'm here to uncover it all.

The deceptions that bind us, rewind us to the past, where faulty hearts were bruised and broken through trickery and lies.

OLIVIA

"WHY?" I CROAK, KEEPING MY GAZE FORWARD INSTEAD OF on him.

My uncle.

The reason I'm here.

Thick sheets of rain pour down as the dark clouds open above us. Every inch of my clothing sticks to my flesh like a second skin and I shiver, staring down at the stones sticking out from the muddy earth. The scent of nature surrounds me. Mud. Leaves. Rain. A hint of lilacs blowing in the breeze mixed with the moisture.

My eyes squeeze shut. The frigid water serves as my baptism. A renewal from the naive girl I once was when I was seventeen. The girl who blindly followed her three boyfriends around like a puppy on a leash, lapping up everything they gave her.

Until she couldn't any longer.

Because she died a miserable death. Betrayed by the very men who held her heart in their palms.

Her blood stained their fingers.

Now, she's the girl buried six feet deep beneath my soaked boots, stuck in the ground with only a grave marker, etched with her name, to remember her by.

Olivia Viotto.

A familiar stranger. A girl I once knew and used to be.

But not anymore.

I'm not *that* Olivia anymore. I'm not the girl with stars in her eyes and dreams at the tips of her fingers. I'm twenty-two years old now. An adult. Someone who lives in the real world where evil is around every corner and everyone is out to get you.

Even your best friends.

I'll never be that hopeless Olivia Viotto again. She depended on too many people to help her get through the day.

Not anymore.

I'm the new and improved me. Agent Seven with Veritas. Fighting the good fight against the evil forces, like the men from my past.

My friends. My father. Mafia and gang leaders.

A flash of lightning streaks across the raging sky, illuminating the vast graveyard and matching the torrid emotions swirling inside me. A thunderous boom immediately follows, rumbling the ground beneath my feet.

My fingers curl at my sides.

Breathe, Liv. You have to fucking breathe through your nose and out through your mouth. Don't think about it. Don't imagine their faces on the last day you stood hidden in the woods watching them grieve as the old me was lowered into the ground.

It was all a lie. Everything we had together. The love. Laughter. Emotions.

How could they lie to me so well?

And I was too dumb to see anything before it all came crashing down.

I heave a breath, panic clawing deep in my chest, anxious to leave and make me spiral into the abyss, like it's done before. I can't go back down that road again. It brings nothing but unanswered questions and heartache.

Why are we here? In my former hometown? Why did he make me come back?

I never wanted to step foot in this town again. Ever. I've made something of myself. Something big and meaningful.

I've created the new me.

I ground myself, keeping my mind in the present. Instead of the vivid past attempting to pull me back. I'm fighting against the memories attacking me from all sides.

I swallow my emotions, taking stock of my surroundings. Greenwood Cemetery. One of the oldest cemeteries in California. Rumored to be haunted by pirates and other residents of the past.

At least, that's the rumor.

Headstones line the slightly flat and hilly grounds for miles. A large black iron fence encompasses the area, keeping the dead inside and the living on the edges.

The only buildings around this area belong to Greenwood University, sitting a hundred feet from the east side of the property.

My dream college as a kid. *Our* dream college. It was always a part of the plan we came up with. Go to college. Get our education as we continued to work for Franco.

Then we can disappear and start over somewhere far away from here.

I accomplished that. But did they? Have they successfully left Franco behind yet?

I'm drawn out of my thoughts when movement on the edge of the cemetery catches my eye. Someone is slinking through the shadows with hunched shoulders and their head hanging low.

What are they doing out here?

I narrow my eyes, but through the darkness and rain, I can't make out their facial features. I home in on their heavy footsteps sloshing in the mud, getting closer and closer to us.

I put my hand on my hip, reaching for the weapon that's

always at my side. My fingers hover, ready to grab and strike if they're a threat against us.

The figure abruptly stops fifty yards from our location, freezing completely. With nothing more than a loud huff of breath, they turn on their heels and hightail it out of sight.

They saw us.

"Someone is here," I mumble to my uncle, who silently stands beside me. No doubt watching the retreating back of the stranger.

"He'll leave," he mumbles unconcerned. "He always does."

My brows furrow when I turn to look at him, but he shakes his head—not elaborating. So, I don't ask like I've been trained to do.

By him. By my father. Both Viotto men, both incredibly different, but the same.

My entire life has been a quiet existence. My father, a mafia leader, raised me to keep my mouth shut. Don't ask stupid questions or you'll find out the answers through fists and menacing words.

All very educational, if you ask me. I mean, I learned to keep my lips tight and my eyes down around my father and his abusive ways. So did my mother and my sister. We were all under his thumb and oppressive ways.

But I never thought it would follow me into adulthood, to my job.

The moment I stepped foot into the Veritas bunker where I trained, I found out the same rules applied. It's do as I ask and never question my authority. Half of me understands my Uncle Jonathan's demands. But the other half—my rebelling half—wants to beg for answers. Especially right now, as I watch the shadow retreat from us, getting further and further away until they're nothing more than a blip in the darkness, becoming one with it.

Who is this mysterious person who seems to make a consistent appearance here? And how does my uncle know about him? Has he been staking out my grave for…whatever reason?

"Why are we here?" I softly ask, letting my words hang on the thick raindrops continuing to pelt us.

My Uncle Jonathan shuffles beside me, putting a hand on my shoulder. He squeezes, bringing my gaze to his hardened eyes. Lightning flashes above our heads again, my muscles tensing in response.

The brief flash highlights the sparkle in Jonathan's eyes. He knows something I don't. Seems fitting, though. He's the head of Veritas—a secret government agency. And me? Well, I'm the agent beneath him, doing his bidding. Happily, though. This job gives me a purpose after my life went up in smoke five years ago.

Don't think about them. Don't do it.

"I wouldn't have brought you here if I didn't think you'd be up for the challenge, Agent Seven." His voice dips low, and he opts to use my Veritas number instead of my name.

He means business now. There's no questioning his motives or talking back. I am his agent. Not his niece.

My back straightens immediately, wiping away my emotions. As Agent Seven, I am unstoppable.

Trained to take down mafia leaders, gang heads, and CEOs on the bad side of the law. Corruption. Deaths. Cults. You name it. Our organization does it. *I* do it. I'm one of the best agents in our division. And I love every second of it.

"Yes, Agent Zero." As I acknowledge him, lightning flashes again, raising the hairs on my arms as it quickly strikes a tree in the woods surrounding the area.

I blow out a breath as the thunder rumbles deep and low, vibrating my fucking bones. Everything inside me begs me to run for cover and hide in the darkened SUV parked beyond the towering trees as unwanted memories trickle through my mind and flash before my eyes.

But I stand firm. Just like I did five minutes ago.

Since I was five, thunderstorms have been the bane of my existence, and standing here in the midst of it isn't helping the irrational fear unfurling inside me. It's happening all over again. The night I spent with rain pouring over my head as tears mixed with the pelting water and I had nowhere to go. No home to seek shelter in. Two parents who didn't give a shit if I was out in the cold, begging for mercy.

Because my own father kicked me out of our home the moment the storm started to teach me an important lesson. Whatever that was.

I squeeze my eyes shut, ignoring the wind whispering through the trees, carrying faraway voices from my memories. If only I could forget.

"Count the time between the lightning flash and the thunder, Trouble," Hux grins, peeking out the window of our elaborate tree house nestled deep in the woods, hiding us from the raging storm that came out of nowhere.

"I'm still scared," I whisper, scooting closer to him and grabbing his hand. "Hux, what if...." The tree falls. Or a tornado comes through. Or the wind makes it impossible for me to make it home before my dad knows I'm gone.

If he knows I've snuck out, he'll brutalize me. Or worse, throw me in the dark basement with no food or water and force me to stay there until he sees fit.

But this is worth it. The time lying in the treehouse with Hux, safely tucked in beside him. He's my protector.

I trail off when his moss green eyes sparkle with mischief. "Livy, you're ten. You can't be afraid of storms forever. Besides, you have to learn how to ride them out." His grin does little to soothe my anxiety. His low chuckle fills the space before he grabs and pulls me into him. The faint scent of Christmas spices fills my nose, and my body relaxes. "No matter the storm, I'll always be your fighter."

I wish I hadn't believed him so hard throughout my childhood and teenage years. It would have saved me this misery piercing my heart and cracking it more at the thought of him and his sparkly green eyes.

Huxley. My former best friend and my ultimate betrayer.

He didn't act alone, though. No. They were like the three musketeers. Always together. They were all complicit, standing around me with the knife in their hands as they slashed my throat and left me burning in the embers of my home with the bodies of my sister and mother.

Sophia Viotto. Espie Viotto. Olivia Viotto.

Now, we're nothing more than a memory etched into marble. The only one missing is my traitorous father, Raphael Viotto—the man who took off the second he knew a storm was coming for us and left my mother, sister, and me to die for his crimes.

Whatever they were.

"Your mom and sister were good people, Liv," Jonathan whispers, clutching my shoulder and pulling me from my thoughts.

If he only knew.

"Yeah," I croak, shaking the emotions from my voice.

Standing out in the open, breathing in the same air as that night that I fled while hanging on to the last thread of my life, has my arm hairs standing on end. My heart sings in my ears, blocking out the storm brewing around me. Absent-mindedly, my fingers trace the scars lining my face, traveling to the one that should have ended my life—across my throat. I swallow the lump lodged in my esophagus beneath my fingertips.

I wasn't supposed to come back to Greenwood, California. No matter what. Jonathan made a promise to me after he found me clinging to life with burns on my face, neck, and shoulders. Injuries courtesy of the fire that took my home, my family, and almost my life. I was barely recognizable, gasping for breath in a secure hospital room, far away from the public eye. No one knew I was there, except for Jonathan.

Somehow, I defied the odds and got out of my home before it collapsed, taking everything with it. Including the bodies of my mother and sister. That was almost me. I was teetering at Death's door, lightly knocking, looking for entry.

Except I made it out. Death's door never opened, granting me solace. Instead, I was thrust back into a painful existence.

And the worst part of all? I have no idea how I made it out alive. My last thoughts were filled with darkness. A void before me.

But somehow, I woke up in the hospital with my uncle at my side, begging me to stay alive and granting me a new life without all the pain from before.

"I'll never make you go home," he whispers, clutching my hand as I fight for my life. *The machines beep above my head and an IV drips into my veins.* *"You have a new home with me and Veritas."*

"You broke your promise," I mutter, not bothering to look at him again.

I can't.

Or the tears burning the backs of my eyes will fall. I can't have that. I'm strong. Stronger than my tears and emotions. I could yell until I'm hoarse and my throat is raw. I could punch him in the throat and knock him to his knees.

But I can't. Won't. I'm too frozen by the reality of my situation. I'm back in my own personal hell.

The place I fled from with my life barely intact.

Greenwood, California almost killed me.

My stomach sloshes, threatening to spill its contents onto the grass above my grave. *How fitting to puke on my eternal resting place.*

Hold yourself together. You don't know what he wants or expects. This anxiety could all be for nothing.

Yeah, right.

"I know," he says solemnly, digging into his pocket and retrieving something. He clicks the end of his flashlight and points it at the names, illuminating them. "I know I promised you that you'd never have to come back here. Even in the line of duty. You know I wouldn't have brought you back here unless it was important, Liv."

And there it is. The kicker. The case. He's about to rock my world and push me off my axis.

Fuck.

I lick my lips. Of course, he wouldn't harm me by bringing me here. Right? He's been in the line of duty under Veritas for years now, conducting investigations on the world's worst people who seem to slip through the cracks. In fact, every agent beneath him has the same job—going after the bad guys. We're the Dexters of the world, minus the serial killer part and tying people to metal tables with plastic. Although, my roommate Jordy might fit that part. He's a goddamn psycho. But with his background, that's easy to come by.

You see, the agents of Veritas are all connected by terrible pasts and deaths that didn't take. We're all ghosts in the eyes of society, making us the perfect spies. No name. No face. We're no one.

Olivia Seven. Agent Seven.

The number at which I arrived on their doorstep.

My new name. New me.

"Has Franco finally gone off the rails?" I quip softly, internally cringing at the sound of his name rolling off my tongue after years of not saying it.

The ringleader. The master of the fucking gang that believes Greenwood, California is theirs to fuck with and manipulate.

And the mastermind behind my death.

Nathanial Franco. Scumbag extraordinaire. Gang leader.

Hux, JJ, and Mack's foster father, who collects children to train and fill his ranks.

Also, Franco is my sperm donor's former employer. I've been waiting to get my hands on him and show him what a knife in the back feels like. Maybe throw a little fire in there, too. He'd probably like that.

Those thoughts only cross my mind when I'm lying in bed and staring at the ceiling while plotting his demise. I've imagined his death a million times over at my hands.

Only, I never imagined I'd be back in his territory—a literal walking dead girl.

"The facts of the case are something we shouldn't discuss out in the open," Jonathan says, clicking his flashlight off and shoving it back into his pocket. "They're protected details no one but you, Agent One, and I will be privy to."

"So there *is* a case here." I swallow the information down, digesting it as his hand falls off my shoulder.

I almost fall over, blowing with the howling winds that whip through the multitude of large oak trees creaking from the pressure.

He just confirmed my suspicions with words. If there's a case here, then he needs me to be strong and level-headed.

Easier said than done.

A heavy sigh rocks through him. "I've rented us a suite at the Greenwood Grand Hotel downtown across the river."

I whip my head in his direction, but he holds up a hand when my mouth falls open, ready to retort. Driving here for the day is one thing, but staying through the weekend? That's a whole other story.

"You're in no danger, Liv. Remember, you're dead in his eyes." He cruelly gestures to the darkened headstone etched with my old name. "You're here." He flops a hand at my gravestone carelessly like it isn't a stab to my heart.

Yes. I'm dead in the eyes of everyone I've ever known. A ghost walking the streets with no true identity.

And maybe that's what kills me the most.

"He could recognize me, Sir," I say more forcefully than I intended, almost spitting every word.

Fortunately, the man who reluctantly gave me life taught me a long time ago to hold my tongue and emotions.

"There's no room for your weak tears, bitch. You should have been a goddamn boy. Then you'd be fucking useful." My father, Raphael's, words from years before continue to haunt me long after being in his presence.

"And Raphael?" I gag out his name, barely containing the trembles rocking through me.

I haven't seen or heard from my father since two days before all hell broke loose and we lost our lives. He could be dead. Alive. Hiding. The list is endless.

All I know is that he knew something was about to happen and fled without warning.

Coward.

"Unknown," Jonathan says, shaking his head.

"How, after all these years? You can't just disappear..." I trail off, rubbing my temple with my soaked, pruny fingers.

"We have ideas." That is all he says when he turns on his heels and takes a few steps away from me. "Let's get out of the rain, and we'll discuss the difficulties of this case tomorrow."

Every case I take comes with difficulties. Life-ending possibilities. It's the joys of working for Veritas and putting myself into these situations.

"Give me a minute?" I ask, gesturing to the graves.

He nods, handing me the flashlight and wandering through the shadows toward our SUV waiting on a gravel road.

Lightning flashes again and thunder rumbles in calling, shaking the ground, and the trees sway in the frantic breeze as I fall to my knees, unable to hold back my emotions. I'm alone now. Able to process the situation without him watching over me. I'm fucked. Truly fucking fucked. A heaviness settles on my chest. A shriek rests in my throat, ready to release into the storm and carry it away.

All the anguish I've pushed away. The betrayals. My old life and memories.

I'm about to face them head on, crashing into them without a choice.

It's been taken from me.

Mud soaks through the dark denim clinging to my skin. My fingers curl in the wet grass, yanking at the blades until they're pieces in my grip.

"I will avenge you," I whisper, tossing the grass over my sister's grave. Tears pour out of my eyes, finally escaping the hold I had on them and mixing with the rain. "I will make them fucking pay for what they did to you. And Mom. And me," I murmur, running my fingers over my mom's name over and over again, smearing mud across the marble. "I will bring them to their knees for ever doing this to us." I hang my head, sucking in several breaths into my aching, tight lungs. "And you," I say to my name, clicking the flashlight on and lighting it up one last time. "We will make sure they never hurt anyone ever again." The light moves across the surface of the marble, finally landing on the inscription I didn't catch before.

Olivia Viotto - 17 years old. Gone too soon. But always in our hearts. 224.

"224, Trouble," Huxley mumbles, gently kissing my lips as he hovers above me. "Today. Tomorrow. Forever."

"224. Always," I breathe, closing my eyes when he enters me for the first time. I choke out a breath, digging my nails into his shoulders.

"Fuck!" I cry out when thunder rolls through the clouds, blocking out my frantic cry. "Fuck!" I shriek, throwing my head back and embracing the water pelting my face.

Rage like I've never felt before swirls like shadows in my chest, clawing up my throat and infiltrating my brain. It sinks its nails deep into my brain until I'm no longer in control of myself or my actions.

I let the ghost nestled deep inside me free from the tomb she's lived in for all these years, where I've hidden my resentments and murderous plots. All the anger. All the fucking grief. Everything I endured and felt unleashes from the depths of my fucking broken soul. Howling in pain.

Everything moves without my say so, moving on autopilot, connecting my aching fists and stinging hands to the marbled gravestone displaying my name and the number I never want to set my eyes on again. My hands burn like fire roaring under my flesh, angrily vibrating when I smash the butt end of the flashlight into the numbers on my grave marker. Over and fucking over again.

224? 2-2-fucking-4!

Our special phrase. Our numbers! Something we created as children. Carved into trees as a symbol of our undying love and devotion.

And he etched it into one last fucking thing.

How fucking dare he utters those words to me and then do this! And leave his mark when he's the one who fucking helped to end me.

"Fuck you, Huxley! Fuck you and your words! Fuck you and your fake love," I gasp out, smashing it over and over until the flashlight resembles a mangled mess and I'm left panting for air.

I sink back, heaving a breath and holding the remnants of the flashlight in my hands. Fuck it. I toss the pieces into the grass, and I clutch the long strands of my hair, gently pulling until the pain helps to relieve some of my building panic. Maybe I'm not strong enough to survive whatever Jonathan has up his sleeves. Maybe I'm the weak little bitch my father thought I was, losing myself to tears and emotions and everything in between.

"Don't show your emotions," my father sneers at me, exposing all his rotting teeth. "It's the Viotto motto." Viotto motto, my ass. Every time he lashed out in anger, he showed his emotions for the world to see.

I fall back, letting the mud and grass cushion my fall. It knocks more air from my lungs, but I don't care. Breaths continually shudder through my chest as my fingers dig into the mud again. I feel it. The cold, wet dirt. It brings me back from the brink of whatever I unleashed.

I close my eyes when the raindrops flutter across my face, leaking down my chin and into the grass. Mud still soaking through every inch of my clothes. But my give-a-damn button is busted beyond repair. Replaced by a tingling numbness working up from my toes to the top of my head, stealing my raw emotions and hiding them away.

"Fuck," I mumble, shaking off the slight chill piercing through my clothes and sitting up to assess the damage I inflicted.

I trace the scratched number—224. No longer legible. Or from what I can feel. If I hadn't smashed the flashlight into smithereens then I could see.

Goddamn it.

I hang my head again, pressing my dirty palms into the cool, wet surface.

I am here. I am in the rain and soaking wet. I force myself to feel the clothes clinging to my skin and the squish in my boots before I lose myself to the nightmares of my past.

"No more freak out," I whisper through the pounding of the rain. "It's done. You're over it. You're dead. They did this. And now, if you have to see them again, you'll be fine. No matter what," I whisper to myself repeatedly, despite the dread building in the pits of my stomach. Fuck. "You have to be okay. Okay? Just... keep your head up," I murmur to myself like I've done in the past.

If I hold these feelings in for too long, they eat away at me until I explode. And it's never a good thing when I let it all out in my rages.

Case in point—my poor headstone. Something I'll have to check on at a later date in the sunshine. Maybe no one will notice. It's not like I have anyone left to visit my remains. My mom and sister are beside me. My father never cared for us despite having us around.

And Hux, JJ, and Mack? They're the reason I'm here.

I finally pull myself together and wipe the tears and rain from my cheeks, and I stand tall over the graves at my full height. It's odd standing above them when they're dead and below, and here I am, the *lucky* one who made it out alive. Somehow. I try to tell myself I'm here for a purpose. That I escaped everything for the greater good.

But right now? I don't fucking see it. Sure, I've saved countless lives and put away the worst of the worst in Veritas prison, but at what cost?

I place my hand on top of my grave again, almost reluctant to leave this piece of me behind. Something in the center of my chest pulls at me to stay when I peel my eyes open, and my knees nearly buckle again when lightning flashes above me, lighting up two small objects I somehow missed on my first inspection.

"Got you this," JJ mutters, shoving a small box with a red bow into my hands. His cheeks redden, and his eyes fall to the ground.

"What is it?" I whisper with a grin, unwrapping the box quickly. "Oh, JJ," I murmur, pulling out the small charm bracelet with one charm dangling from it. A silver lighthouse with two red stripes at the top. "It's beautiful." Tears threaten to spill from my eyes when he shakily takes it from me.

"It glows in the dark," he whispers, clasping it on my wrist.

I throw my arms around his neck and pull him close. "Thank you."

"We'll fill the bracelet up with more charms. More lighthouses, so you don't forget that you have a bright light in here," he whispers directly into my ear. *"You're my Spitfire."*

A small lighthouse charm sits beside a shiny, dark rock on the top of my grave. Two gifts. From two people who have no business stepping foot here and mourning my loss.

Water droplets roll off the sharp edges onto my grave marker. It threatens to take me out again, forcing me to relive more memories I've shoved into a black hole of no return. I've been so successful for so many years in holding myself together.

But in one night, it's being unraveled.

Without hesitation, I grab the rock and charm, examining them at eye level. When the lighting isn't streaking through the sky, they are almost invisible in my hands. But the weight of their gifts left behind remain in my hand.

"Fuck you, Mack. Fuck you, JJ!" I whisper at the rock and charm before throwing them as far as I can. With the darkness, I don't see where they land, but I hope they never make it fucking back. "Fuck you for your lies. Fuck JJ for his lies. Fuck Huxley for everything. I hope you all rot in hell."

Fuck them all with a hot branding iron straight to the asshole.

With that, I turn on my heels and stomp through the mud with slight satisfaction thrumming through me. A heavy weight rests on my shoulders, pulling me down into the depths of my pain. I'm drowning in it as it surrounds my being and clutches me in its grip.

But I shake it away, shoving everything about tonight into the back of my mind in a secure black box that can't be broken open again. No more. I can't go through life holding onto this pain and letting it chip away at me piece by piece. If I'm not careful, I'll have no identity when it's done with me.

I return to the SUV and slam the door behind me. My body

sags into the warmth of the seat, and exhaustion pulls me under, draining the remaining dregs of my energy from my body.

"Did you get out what you needed to get out?" Jonathan asks, handing me a small hand towel he gathered from the back seat.

I nod as I wipe the wetness and mud from my face and hands, keeping my eyes forward. No matter the freak out I just went through, I don't want to show him the evidence in my eyes.

"It's okay to be emotional, Olivia," he says, pushing the car into drive. *Yeah, fucking right.* The Viotto's entire existence has always been–*Don't show your emotions. Don't be a fucking human.* And here, my uncle—a Viotto by adoption—is saying the complete opposite. "Feeling nervous and terrified to be back here is okay. It's a normal part of being human." His gaze soars through me, practically burning a hole through the side of my head.

"I'm fine," I say with a slight shrug.

I don't know who I'm trying to convince—me or him. I'm beyond not fine. I'm fucking fried. I need to unwind. I need a drink, a game of pool, a swim, or a really good fuck to get my mind out of the darkness pulling me under once and for all.

"Mhmm," he hums unconvinced, pulling out of the cemetery and heading straight through Greenwood.

I sigh, leaning my forehead against the window, and stare at the lights blurring by. Pirate-themed casinos line the main strip of Greenwood, lighting up the visitors spending their money and never winning a goddamn thing with the walls. A long time ago, despite the laws forbidding gambling in casinos in California, Franco found a way around it. Laws? What laws? Franco doesn't abide by them. He simply greases the palms of the commissions in charge and gets whatever his heart desires. Someway. Some-how. They've built it up and never looked back. Never having to follow the rules. But when has he? He commits crimes every day under the watchful eyes of the law, and no consequences seem to find him.

I think it's about time that changes.

"He's expanded," I say, mentally counting the brightly lit casinos.

"Indeed," Jonathan agrees. "He's somehow been able to open at least thirteen more casinos, despite the laws, in a small time period but still owns the largest casino in the region. He's made Greenwood a destination for gamblers and vacation goers." Emerald Cove was the first place I learned about when I was a kid. Hux, JJ, Mack, and I snuck in there all the time and snooped. Hell, Franco even put his foster sons and me to work there. Illegally, of course.

"He's also made Greenwood a paradise for all things seedy, and the criminals are flocking here in waves." Well, that's nothing new. Greenwood has always been a haven for criminals. Even when Franco owned one large casino and a criminal enterprise.

The SUV travels over a large bridge overlooking the Greenwood River, flowing through the middle of town. When I look out the window, I'm smacked with the memories of our time, walking by the river and picking up rocks that Mack swore he loved to collect. He always gave me the shiniest one he could find.

"For you, my lady." He bows like a gentleman, sporting the familiar lop-sided grin and holding out a beautiful, shiny black rock. His shaggy blond hair blows in the slight breeze.

"It's beautiful," I say, pecking his cheek. "Thank you, Mack." He beams, blushing from my kiss, and nods.

"There will be more where that came from," he says, shoving his hands in his pockets and taking a few steps. "I'll always find you rocks, Livy."

I guess he really meant it when he said he'd always bring me rocks. Why, though? It doesn't make sense to me. I don't understand why the three of them have stamped their presence on my grave like they own me.

They don't.

Not anymore.

"That's nothing new for him," I say, shaking my head. "Franco always had his hands in other business ventures, except the skin trade." Thank fuck. For such a piece of shit, he drew the line at trafficking people in his city. Hookers, though? Well, that's a different story and is highly regulated by Franco himself. "His casinos are where he launders his money."

Jonathan hums in response, pulling into the parking lot of the Greenwood Grand Hotel near the middle of downtown. People walk the sidewalks, heading in the direction of the shiny casinos on almost every corner. No matter the time of night, Greenwood is alive with bustling citizens and vacationers.

"You're sure that it's safe for me here?" I ask reluctantly, eyeing the people milling outside.

Franco could be around the corner ready to finish what he started with his boys in tow.

If I'm in Greenwood, then I'm not safe.

"Even if they walked by you, Liv. They wouldn't recognize the woman staring back at them. You've grown since then, and your features have changed." What he's not saying out loud is the plastic surgery I had to obtain after the attempt on my life from my friends and their psycho foster dad altered my look a bit. "Now, why don't we go to sleep? In the morning, I'll brief you on the case. Okay?" He doesn't offer anything else when he gets out of the car, pops the hatch, grabs our bags, and stands beside my door until I emerge.

I cast my eyes to the ground when I grab my suitcase from him and follow him into the lobby of the massive hotel where we stop at the front desk. It's not a place I'm familiar with, but I know Franco has spies on every corner of this town just waiting for something suspicious to happen. I'm even more surprised my Uncle Jonathan isn't hiding his face from the cameras and people around us. He may not look like my father in the least, having been adopted into the family at a young age, but he's still his youngest brother—the only Viotto to not take a slice of California for their own and build a mafia empire.

"This way," Jonathan says as I follow him to the elevators. We travel to the top floor before entering a suite with two bedrooms, a kitchen, and a living room.

"Damn, you went all out," I say, wheeling my suitcase into the first bedroom I see.

"We'll be here through Sunday night, Liv," he says, making me stop dead.

"S-Sunday?" I ask, abandoning my suitcase and coming to stand before him.

"Tonight, we'll rest. In the morning, we'll eat breakfast, and then I'll completely brief you on the mission." It's odd he's giving me this much time to come to terms with where I am and what I'm about to do.

Technically, I could refuse. I could walk away and tell him to go fuck himself and that I'll never stay in this god-forsaken town again.

"Get some rest, we'll talk over breakfast, okay?"

I nod in response, watching his retreating back as he goes into the other bedroom with his suitcase and shuts the door, leaving me to my own crazy thoughts that I don't want to drown in. Fuck that. I'm not drowning tonight. Well, not in my misery. Maybe in a small bottle of vodka or whiskey from the snack bar conveniently located in our room. So what if they charge us an enormous amount of money?

It's what I have to do to survive right now.

OLIVIA

MORNING FOR ME COMES TOO QUICKLY, LEAVING ME UNRESTED and hungover. Way too hungover. I swear a small band plays inside my brain with booming bass and screaming lyrics.

Fuck.

Who knew two small bottles of booze could turn into ten small bottles and get me completely drunk off my ass. The upside is that I was more relaxed than I've ever felt and practically melted into the bed the moment my head hit the pillow at 3 am.

The downside is, I tossed and turned, wanting to puke my brains out the moment the sun rose and peeked through the windows.

And the worst part? I'm aching to do it all over again when I realized what city I woke up in.

Greenwood.

So much for a good start to the day. But what else do I have to do? Jonathan is going to hole me up in this hotel room until we hopefully leave on Sunday and I learn my fate. Dread sits heavy in my stomach at the prospect. What will my uncle have me do? I have an inkling, but I don't want to believe it. Not yet, at least.

"Good morning, Sunshine," Jonathan quips when I zombie

walk out of my bedroom and slump at the small, round table near the kitchenette. "Or should I say, good afternoon?" He smirks, checking his black wristwatch and chuckling at the time.

Two P.M.

Whatever. I needed the rest. Despite my shitty sleeping situation.

I wave a hand. "There's nothing good about this morning or afternoon," I groan, rubbing my temples, willing my damn hangover to go away.

I need fucking coffee inserted straight into my veins before I can even think about our discussion.

"How about some coffee while we wait for room service to drop off the French toast and eggs I ordered you?" It's like he read my mind. Of course, he's my uncle. My family.

Jonathan wasn't around much when I was a kid. I have vague memories of him visiting my dad, playing poker with the other Viotto brothers, and drinking into the night. Something changed, though. Maybe it was when Jonathan got into the military, trained, and was forced overseas for an extended period of time. It must have changed him and his mentality. When he came back around, he was a completely different person. More rigid. Calculating. No longer the carefree, youngest Viotto son.

After his stint in the military, he was assigned Veritas—a secret agency—and was outcast from the Viotto family forever. A man in a government agency wasn't welcome in the criminal underworld of California. They all turned their backs on their brother, keeping him out of their businesses.

So, he did the same and stopped attempting to speak with them.

Well, until he came and saved me. My question has always been, why, though? Why save me? I was a part of that world my entire life. Of course, not by choice. I was forced into it. But then Jonathan stepped in, helping me recover and treating me like the daughter he never had. Unlike my own father, who split the moment trouble was on the horizon. I guess he learned his lesson after attempting to overthrow some of his brothers and take their territory. After that incident, he was cast from the family and came to Franco to work by his side. And then? Well, I haven't seen or heard from him in over five years. Good riddance. I hope I never have to lay eyes on him ever again.

I peek an eye open the moment Jonathan sets down my coffee cup in front of me, and the smell of Southern Pecan Coffee hits my nostrils. It's heaven in a cup. Also, very suspicious.

He's never this nice in the morning. Or ever, really. He's buttering me up for the slaughter.

"You're being awfully suspect. If I didn't know any better, I'd say you're trying to butter me up for the big case reveal." I narrow my eyes, zoning in on him as he casually refuses to look me in the eyes.

He doesn't say another word; instead, he ventures back to the coffee pot and makes another cup for himself before sitting down across from me.

"Now, why would I need to butter you up?" he asks, arching a brow.

"Because you know being back here is a goddamn nightmare," I grumble, sipping my coffee before I chew him out. The moment the sweet pecan hits my taste buds, I sigh with satisfaction. God, it tastes just like the pecan pie my mama used to make. "Besides, you never buy me my favorite coffee. You said it tastes like ass."

He scrunches his nose, putting his cup on the table. "It's not awful," he grumbles, getting to his feet as a knock sounds at the door and our food is wheeled in on a fancy cart with covered dishes. "Thanks," Jonathan says, slipping the girl twenty bucks, and she retreats. "Now, let's eat, and then once you're human again, we can talk."

We quickly and quietly eat our breakfast at the table. My

mind goes in circles on what he's about to say. He's not usually this cryptic about the details. Never worried about telling me the truth. Right now? He's avoiding it at every turn. Delicious breakfast? Check. My favorite coffee he never drinks? Check. What's next?

This could be something small or something so big, it sets off my career. I've always been a dutiful soldier, investigating every case they put me on with enthusiasm.

Well, mostly.

"You're going to East Point Prep as an undercover student. We've been tracking murders, and it's coming from inside the school. Cult-like activities are happening. Live streams on the Internet. We're having a hard time tracking them. They're sophisticated," Jonathan, AKA Agent Zero, demands of me.

There's no asking me if I'm ready for my first mission out in the field. I've been training through my entire recovery. Faster. Stronger. Smarter.

"Yes, Agent Zero," I say, lifting my chin.

"Here's your assignment paperwork. It will have an outline of what's expected of you. Your cover name. Your wardrobe. Names of everyone we need you to get close to. And finally, your list of suspects."

I nod, flipping through notes. "Espie?" I question, swallowing hard. "You want me..."

"Your mother would be honored if you used her name." He gives me a stern look, folding his arms.

But I see the affection in his gaze. He always loved my mom, even though she married his idiot brother on her own accord. For the most part, Viotto's take arranged marriages. But not Raphael Viotto. Nope.

"It's a way for you to be close to your past and a name you know. Later in your career, we'll give you challenging identities."

"So, I'll be back in high school?" I wrinkle my nose at the

thought. The last time I was in high school was with them. They protected me from everyone in Greenwood.

My first case in the field was solid. A bit of a shit show in some areas, but I made good strides toward my overall goals as an agent. From that point, I was in the field for months at a time, going from one job to the next. There was no stopping me.

Well, until...

I cringe, thinking about my last disaster of a case.

"Liv?" Jonathan questions, putting his plate back on the cart with a worried expression.

I shake those thoughts from my head. "I'm fine." My new mantra to get through life.

How ya doin, Liv? I'm fine. How's it hanging, Liv? I'm fine and fucking dandy. All day. Everyday. Forever.

At least, I can pretend.

"How many little bottles did you manage to consume last night?" he asks, sitting and sipping his coffee again, giving me a judgmental glare.

Prick.

Is it frowned upon to injure your superior for daring to speak and ask questions so early in the morning? Yeah, probably. Plus, I'd be down an uncle and friend. I don't have many of those lately. Well, Jordy. But he's a completely different story.

My uncle may not be my full-blooded family, but he's been there for me when no one else has. Hello, six other Viotto uncles who I haven't seen in over seven years. They didn't even come to my funeral. Maybe because we were ousted like my father. Even though we didn't turn our backs on the family. Whatever. Jonathan has been nothing like his brothers, and I'm thankful for that.

"Just a few," I say, shoving the last piece of French toast into my mouth without telling him it was about ten. "Now, can we talk about the case?"

"Is the curiosity killing you yet?" Yes, yes, it is. I'm more curious about what I'm about to face than anything ever in my life.

"Maybe." I shrug, drinking the rest of my coffee, and setting the empty cup on the table.

Finally, the caffeine spikes through my veins, and my hangover slightly lessens. Only slightly, though. It still bangs around in my skull, making bed seem more and more appealing. I wonder what my uncle would do if I stayed in bed all day to recover?

"Are you feeling more human now?" Jonathan asks, eyeing me cautiously.

No. I'm definitely not. But fake it til you make it and all that jazz.

"Definitely less zombie-like now." Anticipation runs through me when he nods and reaches for what I can only hope is my newest case. If I don't find out soon, I'm going to claw his damn eyes out. On second thought, I might need more damn caffeine for this.

Jonathan nods and retrieves his laptop and a manila envelope from beneath the table and sets them in front of him. "Greenwood has had some massive changes over the past five years since you've been gone. Franco has expanded his empire into a multitude of casinos, amassing a net worth of over thirty million dollars." He slides the folder to me. "These papers contain your undercover ID."

I swallow hard when he doesn't let the paper go. "What exactly aren't you telling me?"

"Four years ago, Franco and a couple stakeholders heavily invested in Greenwood University. So much so that he's now on the board of trustees."

I tense. "Okay... Why did he do that? I'm assuming there's a reason he would invest in something so... normal."

"Strange, right? Why would a gang leader invest in education and become a vital part of running it?"

I swallow hard, sitting on the edge of my seat. Where is he going with this?

"Why?"

Jonathan sighs. "That's where you come in. There are several unknown aspects of this case and investigations that need someone in the middle of it."

"And that's the case?" I ask, crinkling my brow.

I don't really understand what he's saying.

"Yes," he says, nodding. "We need someone on the inside of this institution. In the classes and frats. We need you to be in the thick of everything, observing Franco's moves and anyone else that might be involved with him. The University is ringing alarm bells left and right, but we're not sure what exactly is happening there. We want you to observe and take notes on the people important to that place."

Sweat trickles down my neck. My stomach swishes from the nerves. *Anyone associated with him.* That means *them*, too.

"Okay? So, you're sending me to college to keep an eye on the institution itself? Or Franco?" His name leaves my lips in a whisper as my hope dwindles down the drain.

College, I can do. Easy peasy. I already graduated from my online classes with a bachelor's in criminal justice and cybersecurity. But doing it in my former hometown with my ex-best friends and murderers lurking around somewhere, probably running parts of their foster father's enterprise by now? Much harder.

"Both? Sort of?" he says as if it's a question, cringing slightly.

"Both..." I trail off breathlessly, groaning at the hangover banging inside my brain again.

"Something else is going on within those walls. We believe Franco has created some sort of initiation of sorts and is siphoning off college students to fill his ranks and push his control outside of Greenwood. He's building something, Liv. We just don't know what, yet."

I rub my temple. "I mean, every leader in the history of leaders pushes the boundaries of their gangs, mafia, or whatever. What's different about this?" Literally, nothing except that he wants to torture me by making me come back here. Ugh. I squeeze my eyes shut, throwing up a bazillion walls in my brain. I can't think about the upcoming case or who could be involved.

"It's the fact that Franco has never attempted to step out of his comfort zone, until now. By investing in the college, Franco has extended invitations to other gangs to join."

"Another gang?" I ask, quirking a brow.

"Yes. There are multiple gangs residing on campus now, each living in their own quarters, presenting themselves as frats for the student body to join." Jonathan only nods when he turns the computer screen toward me. "But the main adversary is them. The Shades, as we call them."

"And what do we know about them? Or any of them?" Sometimes it's tiring trying to pry information out of his elusive ass. He's as tight-lipped as he was when he was in the special forces and learned how to keep everything inside. Something he tried to pass down to us in our training when he took all of us in and expanded Veritas.

"Absolutely nothing. We simply have their names, but nothing more. They're elusive and hiding a lot of what they do from the public eye." Jonathan slides me a sheet of paper, listing off five gangs living on campus. Some I've heard of. But others? Not a clue.

"Helpful," I grunt, glancing at my empty coffee cup and wishing it would refill itself. I was right, I need more caffeine to survive this conversation. "I'm assuming this is all a part of my assignment when I go there?" I raise a brow.

"Indeed. This will be your most complicated case yet, Liv. There will be a lot of moving parts you need to keep your eyes on. But we trust you to fully immerse yourself and get the job done."

"What's the bottom line of this mission? The main reason you're sending me here?"

"We want eyes on Franco and his..." his lips roll together, and my heart drops into my stomach. I know exactly what names are about to fall from his lips. "And his sons, Huxley Crewes, JJ Jones, and Macklyn Owens."

My heart drops into my burning stomach and dissolves completely at the mention of them.

My jaw clenches as my fingers tighten around my coffee cup. I'm way too sober and hungover to even pretend I want to jump headfirst into this mission armed with nothing but a *keep an eye on the people who orchestrated your murder*.

No matter how much caffeine runs through me. It'll always be a fuck no from me. Fuck them. They can die under Franco's thumb. No matter how much I want to put Franco away and watch as he rots in Veritas prison, I won't willingly walk back into the lion's den.

"Y-you... Y-you want me to-to..." My tongue sticks to the roof of my mouth. "Find someone else," I demand rigidly. "Ask Jordy!" I basically shout, losing myself to the panic clawing inside of me. "He'd love to do this." That's not an understatement. When I finally opened up to my loud and crude roommate a few years ago, he finally understood my story. And in return, I understood his.

When I left Greenwood with burns on my body and a slit across my throat, I promised myself I'd never fucking come back. Why would I? My best friends betrayed me in the worst way possible because their foster father told them to. They stood over me as I begged for my fucking life and... they ended me. Now, I have to face them? Be back in their sights when all I want to do is fucking run and hide and never show my face here again.

Jonathan watches me sympathetically. "I know, Liv," he says softly.

But his voice doesn't break through the emotions clawing at my throat. It does nothing but make it worse.

How can he even pretend to know? Sure, he caught me when I was broken, put me back together, and gave me this life. But he wasn't there to watch the demise of my family like I was.

"Olivia," he says, standing and stalking toward me. A heavy hand lands on my shoulders, attempting to ward my panic away. "I told you one day you'd have to face the hardest job of your career, right?"

I suck in a breath, trying to pull the oxygen into my burning lungs. "Yes," I croak through the panic.

"This will be your most difficult case yet. You'll be facing what no one else has faced within Veritas before. Their past."

"Why does it have to be me?" I whisper in defeat, exhaustion sweeping through me. "Why?"

I don't want to see them. I don't want to look into their eyes and know they're the monsters I left behind.

"I'll tell you the truth," he says, leveling me with a stern look. "You're the only one who can infiltrate his gang, Liv. You know the ins and outs of his operations. You were there. No one else can possibly predict his next moves. You can."

"I don't know shit about that!" I cry out, breaking his hold on me. "I don't know how he operates!" I throw my hands in the air, huffing.

"My brother worked side by side with him for years when the Viotto's turned their backs on him and forced him into alliances with Franco. You were there. You lived on the grounds. You watched your father."

"I watched my father do a lot of shit, Jonathan, like when he beat my mother to a pulp for talking. I watched my father lock me in the basement when I was an inconvenience. I watched my father put bars on my windows so I couldn't escape the hell he put me through. I watched him favor some strange kid over his own daughters. I watched him do a shit ton, but being by Franco's side was not one of them." My chest heaves by the end of my tirade, and I shake my head. "I don't know what my dad did with Franco or what plans they made for the future. Whatever it was, my dad screwed the fucking pooch and got us all murdered." Or at least, that's the running theory I have. Why else would he disappear right before we all died?

"Except you," Jonathan says lightly.

"Yeah. And what good did that fucking do, huh?" I toss my arms in the air.

"You're such a strong woman, Liv. You've grown so much since the first time I saw you. I know this hurts. But you survived for a reason, and I think it was for this. To bring Franco down. Isn't that what you want? To put the man down that fucked your family over and eradicated you?" He rants, shaking his head with more emotion than I've ever seen cross his face.

He rarely shows what he's feeling. Despite his words from earlier telling me that it's okay to feel, Jonathan locks everything up tight behind the indifferent facade that he shows the world, because he has to. He doesn't allow himself to get emotionally invested in our cases. It's only facts with him and nothing more.

"You don't even know how much it hurts," I say, putting a hand on my chest and rubbing the ache festering beneath my flesh. "You're asking me to step into the lion's den with my murderers. And who is to say they won't recognize me? I haven't changed that much. No matter how much you remind me of my plastic surgery and skin grafts. I still have the scars of their betrayal lining my fucking face and the biggest one across my throat!" I shout, pointing to the various scars snaking across my cheek and neck. They are still raised, the ridges feeling like a giant wrinkle that refuses to be smoothed out, but they are no longer angry and red. Now they are a shade slightly darker than my skin, but still a prominent feature on my body. They let the world know I went through some bullshit and walked out the other side as someone new. "Besides, only men can get into Franco's gang." Unless you're one of the wives or a hooker, there's no way they'll let me within ten feet of their organization.

"No. You're right," he says, taking a step back. All the emotions displayed before vanish into thin air like they were never twisting his expression. "Liv, I can't imagine how it feels to think about seeing them again. But we need you. The fate of Greenwood needs you. The people of this town need you. This is a heavy investigation, and you're the only agent I trust with it."

Fucking bastard. Fuck him. Fuck all of this. He can get on his knees and beg me to do this stupid case, but I won't. I won't walk the same grounds as the people who threw me away like trash.

I wipe my eyes, stepping back from the table and him. "Listen, I'm not feeling well. I'm going to go anywhere but here."

I only make it a step when Jonathan stops my retreat and squeezes my arm.

"Liv, they won't be able to recognize you," he says, pulling my gaze to his. His eyes plead with me to hear him out. "Read your cover story. Thoroughly, and we'll discuss this later. Okay? I'll give you time to process." He steps back, eyeing me like I'm a wounded animal. Before I can process, he hands me the large manila envelope, thick with papers.

I don't bother with a response as I snatch the envelope and head into my room, slamming and locking the door behind me with a huff. Childish? Yeah. But I'm not feeling hospitable at the moment. I need this time for myself. To analyze what he's going to make me do.

Maybe I can run away. Change my name and identity. For real this time. Start over in a small cabin in the woods with three hunky mountain men who bend over backwards to make me happy.

Ah, the dream.

Reality crashes down on me again when I sit on the bed, rubbing my temple, and glaring at the envelope mocking me in my hand. If I open this, my fate will be sealed. There's no going back or running away. If I leave it on the bed, sneak through the window, and hightail it out of here…

He thinks the boys won't recognize me. That six feet of dirt and a headstone carved with my name is enough to erase the girl they permanently left behind.

That they won't look into my eyes and see her. *See me.* The girl they betrayed without a backward glance. The one they left to bleed out while gasping their names with desperation and begging for mercy. The one they left behind in a house swallowed by fire, silencing me.

Forever.

But the soul lurking beneath always remembers, holding the weight of everything they've endured and that was taken from them.

And mine?

Fuck.

Mine knew them. Loved them. Trusted them with my entire being when I shouldn't have.

Until the moment they slit my throat, laughed at my pain, told me I was worthless, and watched me fall into a pool of blood, choking on their betrayal.

I gave them everything. My loyalty. My love. My fucking soul. And what did they do? They stomped on it. Crushed it beneath their knives and turned everything we once had to ash.

So unless Jonathan has a miracle up his sleeve, I'll never be able to stare my former boyfriends in the eyes without giving away every single detail of my past and pain. It'll blaze through every stare until they take notice.

They'll know by one look who they're staring at.

Fuck.

I run a hand down my face, aching for something to take away the pain that encases every molecule in my body.

I can only be strong for so damn long before I break further than I was before. I can only stuff down the despair of my past for so long before it bleeds through my veins and infects me with the memories of the boys I loved the most in this world.

I sit on the edge of my bed, staring at my shoes. Silent tears fall from my eyes, cascading down my cheeks and falling onto my hands.

For years, I've built myself up as this badass chick who can take down a fucking cult, for fuck's sake. Without blinking an eye, I can strangle a fully-grown man, and it's lights out. I can shoot like a professional assassin.

But this?

Having to suck it up and be around who I hate the most has my stomach turning and bile rising in my mouth.

I want to run.

JJ smiles at me when he whirls me around. His golden brown eyes sparkle in the dim sunlight barely filtering through the forest that surrounds us. Our paradise.

"Caught ya," he chuckles, pushing my back into the thick bark of the tree.

"Yeah? And what are you going to do about it?" I taunt, tilting my head, goading him into doing something for once.

This is our game. They chase me through the woods, laughing until they wrap their arms around my waist, push me against a tree, and take my lips with theirs.

But never more. I'm aching to feel their hands dance across my flesh, burning me and marking me as theirs.

"Dangerous questions," Hux whistles, putting his arm above my head and leaning against the tree.

"So dangerous," Mack chuckles, boxing me in from the other side.

"I'm so scared," I quip breathlessly.

Hux bites his bottom lip. "How about we take a tour of the treehouse?" He raises a brow.

My brows raise. "The treehouse, huh?" It was our meeting place when I snuck out of my room to get away from all the fighting and to run from my own abuse.

"Yes," Hux agrees, taking my hand in his and leading me away from the other two as they trail behind. "You're not scared, are you?" He peeks over his shoulder as I snort.

"Scared of what exactly?" I raise a brow.

"When I fuck the life out of you for the first time."

I rear back, heat blooming across my cheeks and down my neck. "You... You want to...?"

He stops dead, pulling me into him and gently kissing my lips. "You're ours, right, Trouble?" He murmurs my nickname against my lips like a sin laced with a promise. Of what? I'm not sure. But I'm eager to find out.

Shivers fall down my spine. Goosebumps form on my flesh when his pupils dilate and a smirk pulls at his lips.

"Yes," I say without an ounce of hesitation. "I'm yours. 2-2-4."

He smiles. "2-2-4."

"So, what are we waiting on?" Mack quips, smacking my ass. "Let's go get naked and..."

"Macklyn," I groan, pushing him on the shoulder. "Be romantic or something."

"Romantic," he scoffs. "I'll show you romance, Buttercup." He winks at me, giving me a shit-eating grin.

"I'm so convinced," I jest, poking his pec, and he grabs my finger, squishing me between him and Hux.

"You will be convinced, baby. We'll prove to you just how romantic we can be." He kisses the tip of my nose.

I blow out a breath, trying to shake the memory from my mind. Fuck that memory. Fuck that day.

Fuck it all.

I tear into my new identity with force, almost shredding the large envelope.

My eyes scan the sheet of paper, and my brows furrow. Jonathan's words from before ring in my mind. *"They won't recognize you."*

And now, I see why.

Oliver James Davenport. Male. Parents deceased, living with Uncle Jonathan in East Point, California. Birthdate, December 24th. 22 years old.

Not Olivia. Not even a woman.

Mother fucking fuck.

I slam down the paper on the bed more forcefully than necessary. Yeah, they won't recognize me at all. And they'll definitely let me into their gang if I play my role right.

Because I won't be a woman trying to seduce them into bed with me.

I'll be Oliver fucking Davenport.

A man in disguise.

A secret fucking girl.

OLIVIA

You know, I've watched the movie *She's the Man*. Many times over. Want a live reenactment line by line? I'm your girl. Hell, I've even read a few good books on the subject. Girl binds her breasts, dresses in baggier clothes, and infiltrates a prep school or goes undercover to solve a murder. Or whatever her reason may be.

Now it's my turn.

Apparently.

I didn't bother confronting Jonathan when I ran out of the hotel like my ass was on fire. Not after studying my newest case for a few hours until the sun was slowly setting in the sky and going over every word in the document. Nope. I didn't bother to stop when he called my name, begging for me to come back and talk about it. Fat chance, buddy. I hightailed it out of the hotel with rage in my throat and my fingers curling into fists.

I need time to swallow everything that's happened today. Between being back in Greenwood without warning and standing above my own fucking grave to this. This is the pivotal moment in my life where I have to choose if this is what's right for me. This case? Facing my past?

My phone buzzes on the gray and white granite bar top, taking my mind off the mental crisis brewing inside me.

JONATHAN

We have a lot to discuss when you get back. I understand you're feeling a lot. Take your time, Seven. But I want you to keep in mind that by going through with this case, you're in line for a raise and promotion. You've worked hard these past few years...

OLIVIA

Thumbs up emoji

Is it a dick move to send my boss who is trying to console me the thumbs up emoji instead of speaking to him like a big girl? Yes. There's something deep in my gut that's nagging at me to run away from this place and never come back. Change my name again and disappear.

Nothing about this feels like a good idea. Not at all. How am I supposed to be a completely different person without someone getting suspicious? What about showers or bathrooms? What about my period? Cramps are the worst. And mine? They try to kill me every month despite the birth control I'm on to help them. Fuck. I didn't even ask about getting my own private apartment on campus.

Fuck.

I'm so fucked.

I've been deep undercover before. It's nothing new to me. Last year, I was dressed as an eighty-seven-year-old woman living in a nursing home while investigating the nursing staff and attempting to find a serial killer. Pretending to be an older woman was difficult. The disguise alone made my skin itch with the enhanced wrinkles, wig, and glasses capable of recording my every move for Veritas to watch. But I made it through. I caught the culprit, and she's now rotting away at Veritas' prison.

So, why should this be any different? I won't be playing Ethel May, a widowed old lady. I'll be Oliver Davenport, a male student at Greenwood U.

I run my fingers over my forehead, so lost in thought, I don't even see the bartender set down the drink I ordered after coming inside the packed bar.

"Give me your most expensive, top-shelf bourbon, whiskey, scotch, or whatever. I'm not picky at the moment." I slid him a hundred-dollar bill for his troubles, and he delivered.

My gaze wanders over the industrial-style bar with its exposed beams and heating ducts crawling across the ceiling. Soft lighting hangs over leather-backed booths and oak tables lining the outside of the perimeter.

This place wasn't here five years ago. I'm sure of it. In fact, I'm sure this used to be a part of the Greenwood Medical Group. An entire block of walk-in doctor's offices for the folks of Greenwood. And now? Gone. Replaced by something that could bring money to this tourist-heavy area. My entire walk from the hotel led me into the heart of the city. Flashing lights from the theaters, casinos, bars, and strip joints lit up the night. People from every walk of life roam the streets with smiles on their faces and booze in their veins.

Seems to me that Franco has made this town into everything he ever talked about. A way for him to extend his wealth.

Including this bar.

Patrons of every demographic pack the place, chatting while eating dinner and drinking. Some play pool at the back of the bar under softly lit lamps and quietly whoop in excitement each time they sink a ball. Some play the mini gambling machines to the left of the pool tables.

Everyone's having a good time and enjoying this city. Everyone but me and my miserable ass.

Ugh.

I want to bang my head against the bar, but that would bring attention to me. I'm trying to be good and keep a low profile, what with the undercover mission coming up and all.

"Looks like you could use that," the bartender says, tapping on the swirling granite bartop a few times.

"You have no idea," I groan. "This has been one of the worst days of my life."

Not an understatement. Although, I think technically dying and then being brought back to life is number one on my list. The pain of my recovery from the burns covering my flesh after their betrayal was enormous. How does one recover from that, though? After witnessing your friends surrounding you and holding you down so their father could cut you up and deliver the final death blow. Through bleary eyes, I watched as they poured gasoline through my home, over my mom and sister's bodies, and then they lit the match, dropping it into the liquid without sparing me a glance.

So, yeah. I'm a little bitter that I have to be back here. And fucking heartbroken I'm about to step into their paths again.

"Well, you're in the right place, then. Holler if you need anything," he says with a smile as he drifts away toward the other end of the bar.

"Will do," I mumble more to myself, staring at the amber liquid glistening under the low lights. Three ice cubes clink together the moment I take another drink, relishing in the burn of straight bourbon running down my throat.

"It was the aliens!" a drunken voice rings out, filling the bar with his desperation from across the way. He dismounts his barstool and pulls up his shirt for the man sitting beside him to see. "See! I have the scar to prove it!" he shouts frantically again, drawing more eyes from the patrons around the entire bar. I shift on my barstool, eyeing him critically as I sip my drink, attempting to numb myself from the pain festering inside.

So much for a chill environment.

Maybe going to such a public place wasn't my brightest idea. But I needed somewhere to go. Somewhere to forget myself in.

Maybe find someone who will help with that. I'm not picky at the moment.

I just don't want to feel the sorrow sitting low in my chest, pressing on my heart. I want the numbness to consume me so I forget about them. My past. My everything. I don't want to feel the rage beneath my skin or the fear hiding in the back of my mind.

So, I take another sip of my liquor and focus on the stocky man across the bar, showing the long scar below his left ribs. I cringe when tears spill out of his eyes, and he huffs, sitting back down the moment a security guard comes into view, staring him down with narrowed eyes.

"Earl," the bartender chastises impatiently. "We've talked about this before." I can't see the bartender's face, but I hear the tension leaking from his words. "You can't spout your delusions in my damn bar. It's bad for business. So, you either drink your beer or Eugene will see you out the back door."

Harsh. Earl has obviously had a little too much to drink by the sway of his body and the glassiness of his eyes. In fact, his head barely stays upright, flopping around every time he blinks. Someone needs to escort the poor man home and put him to bed before he overdoes it.

Earl frowns, pulling his shirt down over his belly. "Why won't anyone believe me? It happened! I swear it was the aliens. There was a beam of light and probes, and this!" He points to his stomach where the fresh scar would be, but it is covered by his shirt. "They took parts of my liver," he slurs, slumping more.

"Earl," the bartender sighs, nodding at the security guard who reluctantly waltzes over. "I'm going to ask you to leave now and kick you off the premises for thirty days. I can't let you scare away business."

Earl grunts when the security guard lifts him off the stool by his upper arm and escorts him away from the bar, down a hallway until they disappear from sight. Once the commotion dies down, the bartender shakes off the interaction and goes back to checking on everyone.

I down the rest of my drink and slide it forward, catching the bartender's attention.

"So, you here for the slots?" he asks curiously, as he pours me a new drink and sets it in front of me.

His fingers tap the bar again, drumming a few times. A heated hunger swirls in his eyes as he looks me over, stopping at my chest before meeting my eyes again. A red tint takes over his cheeks, and he clears his throat when he discovers he's been caught peeping.

"That's what most everyone is here for. Gambling for the weekend and stopping here to drink and eat." He waves a finger around, gesturing to the other patrons.

Interesting. Greenwood used to attract a lot of big players. Franco loved bringing in mafia, mob, and gang leaders from all over the world to create alliances and forge new business. It must have paid off with how much he's expanded. That's how he convinced my dad to work with him, at least, I think. One second, we were on our knees, begging for another chance in the family after my father attempted a takeover on his brother's properties. The next, we were in our van and heading for Southern California, landing here in Franco's arms—per my uncle's request. It was the stipulations they placed on us. Earn your way back into the family's good graces by submitting to Nathanial Franco and his syndicate while gathering insight into how he runs things. Somehow, Franco accepted us. Offering lodging, jobs, and a more stable life than I ever had.

Well, kind of.

I shake my head. "Not the slots or casinos. College," I say, using as few words as possible.

"Oh," he says with a nod. "Greenwood, then?"

"Yup. Starting my senior year there, hoping to graduate and move on." Not a lie, but not the full truth. But I need to do a little recon on Greenwood to understand what I'm fully getting into. "How about you? You ever attend?" I sip my drink when a lopsided grin passes over his lips. His shoulders relax, and he nods.

"Bachelor's degree in business," he says, holding out his hands. "I've always been interested in this space and mixology. So, here I am."

"Oh? Nice. So, you own this place?" I raise a brow.

"Yup. Getting my degree was the best. Greenwood is pretty amazing, too. Lots of opportunities, internships, and…" he leans in slowly before lowering his voice. "Connections."

Well, color me intrigued. This conversation will prove fruitful in my recon. It never hurts to understand what I'm about to walk into.

"Connections?" I whisper. "What kind of connections?" His eyes dip to my breasts again and then back to my face.

What a transparent idiot. He probably wants to take me home and fuck my brains out. Not a bad idea. But with him? Eh, I don't know. He's not really my type. I'm more into the dark and dangerous. You know, men who shouldn't get my engines going, but do. But I could gather more information about Greenwood U and the town from him without offering him a piece of my pie.

He grins. "I can tell you later, if you want? I have an apartment in the basement." He shrugs, averting his eyes as a blush covers his cheeks.

Ah. There it is. So bold.

"Maybe," I say, downing my second drink. "Another? I bat my eyelashes, luring him in further.

Oh, yeah. The liquor is definitely working through my veins and impacting my inhibitions. Whatever. This is what I wanted. A reprieve. A moment where nothing matters.

"Yeah," he says, brushing his fingers against mine when he takes my glass. "So…" he trails off, his entire body stiffening at the jingle of the bell above the door.

A hush comes over the bar as two sets of footsteps slowly walk past and lean against the bar. Danger wafts from the two newcomers, pulling me in like a moth to the stupid flame.

Yeah. That's more like it. That's my type. All tall, dangerous, and could probably snap me in half. Fuck. I should cut myself off now before I climb either of them like a tree. Or both at the same time. I'm not picky. God, they're mouthwatering and delicious.

I need to stop drinking.

I shake my head and clear my rampant thoughts. Yeah, I've definitely achieved numbness and slight horniness.

It's been a while, okay? I'm a woman. I have needs.

The bartender quickly drops off my drink in front of me, but doesn't hang around to offer me any more heated looks. He stands rigidly in front of the two men, waiting expectantly.

"Hey, guys. All good?" he barely croaks, nervously twitching when the tallest man shifts on his feet. "Can I get you anything?" Worry rests in his tone now. Like he's about to be under attack, and if I didn't know any better, I'd say he was reaching for something beneath the bar for protection.

And Jesus. I mean, I see why. They're tense. Brooding. Looking like they could reach down the man's throat and pull his heart out. I quickly push my hair to the side of my face, attempting to hide myself from the newcomers. But I check them out as much as possible. If the bartender is shaking in his boots, maybe these two are people I should keep an eye on.

Damn it. Consider my interest piqued. First, the alien man who disappeared. Now, Viking and his familiar assistant.

Greenwood is a goddamn poison.

My back straightens as the massive man's muscles ripple when he leans forward. Viking man. With his long blond hair, hitting his shoulders. Muscles for days. Dimples on his cheeks and piercing blue eyes. And a towering frame.

Fuck me.

No, seriously.

If I ever thought about losing myself to anyone—it would be him. It's unfortunate, though, that the man accompanying him is someone I used to know. Someone I crossed paths with many times over the course of my childhood. Jackson Wilder. AKA my ex-best friend—Mack's—slightly older half-brother.

Great.

At least I know the name of one of them. But Wilder, as he preferred to be called, never hung around for too long. He lived in the shadows, just trying to survive. He was only twelve months older than Mack, but the two didn't get along. Ever. They were cats and dogs, always at each other's throats. Something I had the pleasure–or not so pleasure–of witnessing. Their hate for each other was visceral, which to me was odd. They were supposed to have each other's backs. They were family, after all.

I swallow hard, side-eyeing the Viking as he grins at the bartender. Now him? He's new, yet slightly familiar. But where have I seen him before? That's the question.

"Just here for a drink, Nick. Maybe some pool." The Viking grins, dropping his voice low. "You don't mind, do ya?" He cocks his head like an innocent puppy, but seems to be anything but.

Nick visibly swallows hard, eyeing the Viking and Wilder. "No, man. It's all good. Just no issues."

"Now, why would we walk into your establishment and cause issues? We're good boys. Right, Wilder?" The Viking slaps Wilder on the back three times with force, but Wilder doesn't flinch. "Besides, we're all on the same side, right?"

"That's right," Wilder says in a low voice. "We're good people, Nick."

"See? We're good. Now, how about a round for the bar, huh? My treat!" He throws his hands up as the entire establishment cheers in thanks.

I don't take my eyes off them as they stand together. Wilder peers around the bar, looking for something.

"And you're sure, Nick. That you haven't seen her?" Viking pulls out a large missing person's poster from his pocket and slides it forward on the bar.

Nick sighs, picking up the picture while shaking his head. "Sorry, Malic. I haven't seen her. I told you before when you dropped off the other posters." He gestures toward the darkened hallway with a grim expression, highlighting the corkboard filled with papers and Meredith's large missing person poster attached to it.

Malic's smile doesn't budge. "Did you take a nice, long look at my sister? Hmm?" He points to the picture a few times. "Her last known whereabouts were here at your fine establishment. 5" 6'. Brunette. Probably wearing her nursing scrubs."

Missing sister, huh? This bar must attract all kinds of weird vibes. I wonder if she had a run-in with the aliens, too? I snort to myself, downing the rest of my final drink. No more for me. That's enough for the evening or I won't make it back to the hotel in one piece to confront Jonathan on his bullshit.

"I told you before, Mal. She left alone, and I didn't see her again. You can't keep coming in here to badger the customers, either." The same security guard from before steps forward, raising his brows.

Real intimidating, buster. But I don't think you're having the effect you want.

Malic tilts his head back and laughs at the guard's attempts to intimidate him. Yeah, I don't think anyone could make him leave or feel scared.

"Funny. No one else has seen her either." Malic taps the bar a few times. "Maybe put that picture on your bar to remind your regulars that she left here and disappeared. And we'll add some to your corkboard." He gestures to his left, toward the dark hallway Earl left through.

From the sharp tone of his voice, I can tell it's not a gentle suggestion. It's a *'you better fucking put her picture up or I'll stab you.'* And damn, what a show that would be.

Nick swallows hard and nods, pinning the missing person's picture on the small register at the center of the bar. See? He got the message loud and clear.

Maybe this Malic person is more than talk and intimidating looks. I peek at him, taking in his features again.

"I hope you find her, Mal," Nick says, filling two glasses with dark beer. "Meredith was a good person."

Sweat drips from Nick's temple, slowly trailing down his cheek and dropping off his chin. I tilt my head. Even in my condition, AKA, halfway to drunktown, I notice the word he used. Was. Was a good person. As if it's in the past tense.

But why would Nick phrase it that way? Unless he knows something he's not telling Malic.

My heart kicks up, knocking against my ribs. Well, this place got a whole lot more interesting. Not saying that I want an innocent person to have disappeared.

I expect something from Malic. A reaction of some sort to the phrase Nick used, but the big lug doesn't budge or ask questions. Well, not how I expect anyway. I guess I'm trained to suss out the bad guys and listen to their phrases and watch their facial expressions. More than the average Joe does, anyway.

"More than good," Mal barks out, curling his hands into fists. "Pure. And my only goddamn family. The amount of holes I'm going to drill into the person who took her…" he trails off, grinning maniacally when Nick goes pale and shakes, setting the glasses down. "Wonderful hospitality."

And with that, Malic sits at the bar beside Wilder, quietly discussing something as Nick backs away like a cornered animal. I swear his eyeballs nearly pop out of their sockets and roll on the floor when Malic eyes him again with that smile. Ugh. Shivers roll through me. There's something about that grin that sets goosebumps rising across my flesh. Good goosebumps? Bad goosebumps? I haven't decided. Perhaps it's the booze talking. Or the cobwebs collecting in my lady bits. Either way, this man is affecting me. More than anyone has in a very long time.

I can't suppress my smile when Nick scurries out from behind the bar without fulfilling the round of drinks Malic ordered for everyone. Including me. Not that I need anymore. But still. Suspiciously, Nick heads toward the same dark hallway Earl left through earlier. A door slams. Footsteps echo from somewhere, and then, he's gone. Coward. He's probably running off to clean the piss from his pants. Or maybe he's calling someone to let them know Malic is onto them.

Either way, I need to follow the slimy fuck and get some answers from him. Too bad I don't have access to wherever he went. Fuck. I should get another drink and mind my own business. I have a case in this town, anyway.

But what if it's all connected?

Something strange settles heavy in my gut. This entire place reeks of corruption, and something beyond strange is happening. In this bar. In this fucking town. But what? I don't fucking know. Something stinks, though. And well, I'm going to sniff it out.

I make mental notes of all the chaos I've collected after having two drinks. That's all it took to interest me. How pathetic. I want to go all detective and start asking questions, but if I'm supposed to live here soon, I can't draw that much attention to myself.

Whatever.

I quickly text Jonathan through our secured messages and relay the information. If it's pertinent to the future, then so be it.

"Need another?"

My gaze snaps to Malic, suddenly sitting close to me. When did that happen? And where the fuck did Wilder go? He leans his angelic face, dimples out in full force, on the palm of his hand eyeing me with hearts in his eyes. Fuck. He can't look at me like that. It's ridiculously illegal, and I'm too tipsy to stop myself.

Down girl.

"You need a bell," I huff sarcastically, pushing my glass away. If I drink another, then I'll do something I regret. Or not-so-regret? I haven't decided. "And no, I'm good." I should get up and leave. I shouldn't count the freckles dotting his nose and forehead, or recognize the fact that he's barely blinked. Is that even possible? Why aren't his long, luscious eyelashes moving? Does his eyeball hurt with all that air?

Wait, what am I thinking?

Shit. I shake my head, catching myself staring again. Walk away! Don't fall deep into his crystal blue eyes that look like the ocean dancing in the sunshine. And nope. It's confirmed. The man isn't blinking. I kind of want to poke his eyes, but I refrain from the impulse, much to his amusement.

He chuckles, taking my glass and inspecting the dribbles at the bottom. Leaning close, he sniffs the contents and grins more.

"Stagg. That's high-class. Top shelf. High proof. And I bet it's warming your belly right now." His eyes linger on my abdomen as he sizes me up.

Well, that's very forward of him. But also, is it hot in here? God, I'm playing with fire and about to be burned. But like, it doesn't feel like a bad thing.

For far too long, I've played it on the safe side, barely toeing the line. I'm a good soldier for Veritas, sticking with the rules presented to us. As a teenager, I broke every rule there was. Sneaking out, risking my neck to see the boys I loved.

But right now? Fuck. Right now, I want to break every damn rule in the book to satisfy the fire under my flesh, begging me to extinguish it with this massive man beside me staring at me like no man should.

I'm so fucked.

Malic eyes my glass with renewed interest, licking his lips as he moves the small droplets of liquid at the bottom.

"It was a bad day. Needed to take the edge off."

Every breath in my lungs pushes out the second Malic lifts my glass above his parted lips, dumping the dribbles and back-wash into his mouth, getting every last drop. It shouldn't look so sexy to see his tongue swipe along his bottom lip, making sure he gets it all.

Is this his version of flirting? Fuck. I think he's a psychopath. But also. It's working.

What does that say about me?

Malic carefully sets my glass back on the bartop with a satis-fied hum. Speaking of hums, I swear something vibrates straight through me the moment his gaze reconnects with mine. I'm no longer staring into the vast ocean, dancing in the sunshine. Nope. I'm gazing into the lust-filled eyes of a man who could probably break me in half.

"Why was it so bad?" he asks innocently as the corner of his lips tilts into a salacious smile filled to the brim with so much heat, a sweat breaks out across my flesh.

Well, until I remember why I'm having such a rough day.

Oh, I don't know, because I landed here in Greenwood against my damn will, where my stupid uncle took me to my own grave and forced me to stare into the eyes of my name. Oh, and then, he told me I would go to college here and parade around undercover as a man. Meaning, I need to cut my hair, bind my breasts, and wear baggy clothes.

Just another day of undercover work.

Malic moves impossibly closer, brushing his arm against mine. My body lights up like a damn firework erupting and heating my flesh.

Bad day? What bad day?

The heat of his stare, watching my every move, has me wishing for another drink. Come on, Nick. Come back and refill my empty glass that I don't really need refilled—the same glass that Malic made out with and took like he owned it.

Like he owned me.

I lick my lips, attempting to ignore the heat brewing between us. "Just a bad day." I shrug it off because I can't give details to him.

"That's a shame," he mutters in a low tone, brushing against my arm again. "What could make your day better?

Every hair on my body stands on end with anticipation. My muscles lock up, and my breaths freeze in my lungs as Malic touches me again and again. His warm fingers work up and down my jean-clad thigh. I swear tingles erupt under his heated touch, getting closer and closer to the promise land.

Is this how it feels to be picked up at a bar? The rush of knowing that in two point five seconds, this stranger will be inside you? Excitement races through my veins, and the rules of Veritas tick off in my brain.

Yeah, I think I'm about to take a walk–or fuck–into the wild side.

"There might be something," I basically croak, trying to talk through the lump lodged in my throat.

"Well, I…" Malic trails off when a commotion erupts behind us and two men start throwing punches, stumbling from their booth and heading in our direction. My entire body tenses the more they punch and the more blood rushes from their noses and split lips. The urge to jump in and break them apart has me eager to leave my seat.

But I don't have to.

For the first time in almost five years, someone fights for me.

Malic loses the lust in his eyes and stands tall at my side, cursing at the idiots coming our way. Malic growls, stepping into the line of danger when they run into the barstools beside me. Or would have, if Malic hadn't been guarding me with his life.

"Back the fuck up!" he roars, pushing the two men to their

asses as the security guard rushes over. "Don't fucking touch her or come near her again. Or you'll have me to fucking deal with," he growls again, standing above the bloodied men.

"M-Malic! We're sorry," one of the men quivers, staring at Malic with wide eyes before they're carted off and booted out of the bar.

Jesus.

Don't fucking touch her. His words ring in my mind when he comes to stand beside me again, without missing a damn beat. His elbow leans on the bar, and he leans in close again–a breath away. A kiss away. A...

Well, fuck.

He hypnotized me again with the lust twinkling in his eyes. Maybe he sees the effect his protection has on me. Or maybe he wants to make my day better. Whatever it is, my body is on board and possibly my mind, too.

"That was close," I breathe, licking my lips again.

"It was," Malic mutters, watching my every movement again.

More sounds happen around us, filling the bar with yells and claps. But we don't bother to take our eyes off each other.

"So, you've had a hard day," he begins, leaning in more until his face is a millimeter from mine again. "I could offer to make it better."

I lean my head on my palm, watching when his sparkly blue eyes find mine. "What exactly are you offering?" I know exactly what he's offering, because my body buzzes with the need to let him fulfill that promise. But it strikes me odd that a man who was so hellbent on finding his sister's whereabouts would all of a sudden want to take me back to his place and get down and dirty.

But the sizzling chemistry between us is undeniable. I've never met another person alive who ignites something so deep inside me like the three boys I loved before. This feeling, though? It's more intense. Like he belongs to me and I to him.

But that's silly right? This is just my body betraying me in the worst possible way after a sexual drought. Right?

The grin that stretches across his face has goosebumps spreading across my flesh again.

"A ride?" He lifts a suggestive brow.

"A ride to where?" I ask as innocently as possible.

He leans in further until the warmth of his breath brushes down the skin of my throat. The smell of his cologne ignites my senses. Heat boils in my stomach, growing hotter and hotter until sweat trickles down my back.

Fuck.

I've never had this reaction to anyone before. Let alone a probable psycho who will eat me alive. I guess this is what I asked for, though, right?

Numbness. Forgetting. Setting me on fire. Breaking the rules.

"If you follow me, I'll show you," he murmurs in my ear as his lips brush against my skin, lingering for far longer than necessary.

Pulling back, he watches my dazed expression with satisfaction. And then, he holds out his hand, suspending it in the air.

He's giving me a choice.

Walk away from his offer or stay and get fucked.

OLIVIA

As his hand stays suspended in the air, awaiting my answer, I know exactly what I want to do.

Fuck the consequences. Or the shame. Or whatever will follow me in the morning when I'm staring at the ceiling of the hotel.

I'm staying.

Malic leads me down a long, dark hallway—the same space Earl was led down and never returned from. I note the doors we pass: an office, another office, a supply room, a men's bathroom, and a basement door. Because despite my current predicament of temporary horniness, I'm still a government agent on a case.

Yeah, a case of getting dicked down. I wave off my pesky conscience and turn off my brain. Here's a big, tall mistake waiting to fuck me in…. I pause when he turns the knob of the women's bathroom at the end of the hall. *Okay, then. This will be fast, dirty, and just what I need.* I let him drag me inside without a fight as he checks the three separate stalls and comes to stand in front of me after he's satisfied the room is empty. Odd for a women's bathroom, but I shrug it off and lose myself in the intensity sparkling in his eyes. The lust glazing over the perfect blue of his irises. So perfect, I could get lost in the vastness of it.

He takes me in. All of me. From head to toe. Only stopping

on the heaving of my chest, concealing the frantic beating of my heart against my ribs.

A lump forms in my throat, nearly seizing my voice.

"So?" I rasp out, aching to get this show on the road.

Without saying anything, his fingers brush against my cheek, tracing the small imperfections of burns covering my flesh. His only response is the lifting at the edge of his lips, forming a smirk that could burn the panties off any normal woman.

Including me.

For one split second, I think about running in the opposite direction. This man is dangerous. Alarm bells ring in my mind. I could go back to my bed at the hotel, use my fingers, and come to the almost hook up in a bar bathroom. But then he utters a challenge, cementing my decision.

"You won't run from me again, will you, Little Ghost?" he murmurs, so close to my face that his breath brushes against my flesh, sending shivers up my spine.

My brows furrow in confusion at his question. "I never ran," I say, breathlessly taking him in. Again his pupils dilate dangerously black like he's imagining what's to come.

Same, Malic. Same.

Wetness coats my panties as an unmistakable ache pulsates in my core.

"As long as we have that settled," he says, reaching behind him and locking the bathroom door. Sealing my fate and separating us from the noisy bar continuing their night, none the wiser that we're about to create something magical in the bathroom.

I don't have time to overthink what he asked. Or even contemplate if I'm doing the right thing. The second the lock clicks into place, he's on me and pushing me up against the bathroom sink.

The heat of his skin sets me on fire, and I nearly explode when his lips press into mine hurriedly and hard. So fucking hard, we're nearly knocking teeth. Hands explore my body. Squeezing. Groping. Exploring places no one has touched in months. Fuck. Maybe even years.

Something crackles around us, the air thickening with every labored breath I try to suck in.

"Fuck me, already," I hiss between breaths.

I arch my back when his fingers find my hair, yanking my head back, and forcing me to look directly in his lust-filled eyes dripping with an unsaid promise of what's to come.

"You're in charge, Crumpet," he whispers with a slight smirk. "You tell me what you want and I'll say, 'as you wish'. I'll crawl on my hands and knees to you and worship every fucking inch of your body until only you are satisfied."

I blink several times at the intensity in his eyes. He's serious. Every word he says, he fucking means it. Holy shit. This man is going to tear me the fuck apart, and I think I might enjoy it.

But just for tonight.

After this, Olivia disappears and Oliver steps into her place.

"Fuck me, Malic," I challenge, sucking in a breath when he gives me a tiny nod.

"As you wish, Crumpet," he murmurs just above my lips, forcefully spreading my legs apart and around his body. "I'll fuck you. I'll do anything for you. Always..." he trails off.

My brain wants to conjure something smart to say, but I'm too distracted by the tickling sensation of his fingers working down the front of my shirt, heading lower and lower until he stops at the button of my jeans, hesitating.

"Tell me what you want me to do, Crumpet," he rasps, pulling on the waistband of my jeans several times.

I suck in several breaths, my mind finally going blank from all the anxiety and stress holding my head beneath the waves in my mind, drowning me.

"I don't want to think," I rasp, practically begging for him to take the lead. "I want to feel. I want to...I want you to fuck me!"

I nearly beg. I'd get on my knees at this point to release the orgasm building and building in my core.

I groan when the button of my jeans rips open and nearly tears off.

"Oh, God!" I moan, attempting to arch my back when his fingers dive into my panties and pound into my eager pussy, dripping with need.

"Good." His shuttered breaths come out in pants when he pumps his fingers inside me. Over and over again. His thumb brushes against my clit, eliciting fireworks behind my eyes and moans from my throat. "That's one," he whispers, pumping his fingers a few more times before removing his hand.

"One?" I question with furrowed brows, focusing on the way his eyes light up at the sight of his glistening fingers in the poor lighting of the bathroom.

"One orgasm out of...." he draws out, leaving the answer to be determined, and shrugs once before sucking my cum from his fingers with a satisfied groan. "Yeah, I need more of that. Let's get these pesky pants off you."

I don't argue when he pulls my pants down and tosses them over his shoulder. Or when he peels my panties off and does the same with them. I don't even argue when he lifts my shirt and bra up and latches onto my nipple, swirling his tongue around the hard bud.

"Fuck." I try to stifle my cries as he works my nipples into a frenzy, sending heat to my core. "If you keep that up," I trail off, barely breathing when he lifts his head and connects his gaze to mine.

"Will you come again?" he questions curiously, licking his lips.

"Maybe." I'm not even sure it's possible. Can I come again in such a short time without being fucked? Well, I don't have to question it for long when Malic drops to his knees, getting eye level with my pussy.

"Hmmm. Look at that pretty, dripping pussy. Is this all for me, Crumpet?"

My lips move and sounds escape me, but no true words form when his tongue swirls around my sensitive clit. I moan. Loudly. But I don't give a shit at this point. I wind my fingers through his long blond locks and hold him there as I grind against his face, moaning as he brings me to another orgasm.

My body sags against the mirror behind me. How can I go on? I think he's orgasmed the soul from my damn body.

Worries? What damn worries? I don't have those anymore. I've truly achieved what I came out to do—forget everything. It's just me and Malic.

"Even better straight from the tap," he quips, licking his lips. "I could live on my knees for you, Crumpet. Just snap your fingers and I'd make you come any time you wanted. As long as I got to be the one to do it."

There's a possession in his tone as he says the words. A deeper meaning that rests beneath them. Something he doesn't have the right to say.

This is one night. One time. Nothing more. Nothing less.

A fog forms over my mind. Yeah, I'm way too gone to question his words or motives.

Heat fills my cheeks when he steps forward, finally unzipping his pants and revealing the biggest dick I've ever laid eyes on. Thick veins protrude from the base of his cock, leading to the reddened tip, dripping with precum. His large hand wraps around his thick length, slowly pumping up and down.

Jesus. That's not going to fit.

He doesn't take his eyes off me the whole time. It's like he's committing this act to memory, so he'll never forget the night he fucked some random chick in the bathroom.

"Tell me what you want, Crumpet. I'll give you the fucking stars or the heart of anyone who harms you," he rasps, taking one step forward and kicking his shoes and jeans off. "Tell me you want me."

"I want you," I say without hesitation, sucking in a breath when he stands between my legs.

Don't think about the damn heart comment. Just open your legs and let him pound you so you forget yourself and your name.

"I want you, too. So, fucking badly," he groans, dragging my ass off the counter and holding me as I dangle there. "Always have…" he trails off breathlessly.

"Prove it," I goad.

"As you wish, Crumpet," he says with a slight smile, leaning over me. "Guide me into you."

Reaching down, I gently stroke his cock, wrapping my fingers around his pulsating appendage. A deep groan vibrates through his chest when I put his tip at my entrance. He doesn't move. Doesn't push forward as his breaths pick up and his eyes squeeze shut.

"Push forward," I practically beg, needing him to be fully seated and bottoming out.

Slowly, with measured precision, he presses inside me. Inch by miserable inch. Stretching me until my back arches and my toes curl.

"Fuck!" I rasp out, digging my nails into his shoulder and leaving my mark on him.

The lust in his eyes intensifies when he finally bottoms out and my pussy flutters around his thick length.

His mouth pops open and breaths pour out at a rapid pace. But his eyes never leave mine, committing me to memory. Heavy hands land in my hair, tangling the strands around his fingers.

"Better than I imagined," he practically chokes out, putting his forehead on mine. "So much better than my fantasies."

But I ignore his words, focusing on the fire rapidly spreading through my veins.

"Keep moving," I beg, panting when he surges his hips back and forth, jostling me on the counter. "Yes," I moan, as his hands caress every inch of me, finally landing on my clit. I don't protest, even when it's so sensitive I want to back away. His fingers twirl around it with heavy pressure, going in circles until I combust, clamping down on his cock.

"Fuck," he gasps out, tightening his hold on my hair until his mouth sears against mine and our tongues mingle.

His breaths rush out, brushing against my cheek when he stops all movement and simply stays where he is as his cum coats my insides.

Wait...

"You didn't wear a condom?" My eyes snap open, all the pleasure leaving my body at once, like ice pouring over my head.

It's too intimate. Too much between strangers in a bar.

Panic swarms me at the thought of... well, anything! STDs. Pregnancy. I mean, I'm on birth control to help level out my damn periods, but still. You never know.

"Don't worry, Crumpet," he whispers, running his lips down my jaw, nibbling and begging for more as he thrusts inside me again. "I'm clean as clean can be, and I want to go again." He thrusts forward again with a groan.

But that's not happening. He sounds so confident in his answer, but I don't trust it.

Not one bit.

I slump, pushing at his chest until he takes a step back, taking his dick with him. He eyes me with a smile gracing his lips. Seeming more relaxed than he was at the bar.

"I'm glad you're clean," I groan, hopping off the counter, grabbing my discarded jeans, boots, and panties, and immediately go into one of the bathroom stalls. I quickly clean up, throw on my panties, and zip up my pants, coming to a stop in front of him. He watches my every move, taking me in with a weird level of interest.

"I am," he says, tilting his head. "Are you?"

I blink several times. When exactly was the last time I got laid, anyway? I shake my head. I can't remember. Apparently, I was going through a drought. A big, long drought of no sexy time, and Malic filled my cup.

Now, it was time to make my great escape. Far, far away from here. With the clarity this gave me, I'm ready to face Jonathan and this case head on. Well, maybe.

"Of course," I say, making a move toward the door. Unfortunately, I don't get too far. He grabs my arm firmly in his grip, stopping me short and pulling me close to his warmth.

I freeze at the feeling of his hands on me. Excitement bursts through my veins again, but I shake it off. I can't fall into his trap again. I can't let him rock my world a second time, no matter how much my body begs for more of him inside me. Not to mention the orgasms. I shudder at the thought. Could I really go for two more soul-splitting orgasms?

Yes. Yes, I could. But I have a job to do. Responsibilities to fulfill. And as much as I want to live in this fantasy land with Malic, I need to go back to the hotel.

Gently, I remove his hand from me, and he pouts. Actually fucking pouts, but respectfully takes a step back. But those eyes? Oh, those eyes never leave me, taking in their last fill. A shiver works its way down my spine, begging me to reconsider round two. Just looking at him and the way he looks at me, like I'm the sexiest woman he's ever laid eyes on, does funny things to me.

No one has made me feel so damn desired in so long. I internally shake my head, getting a better grip on myself. This has to be the post-sex fog. Where's my clarity, damn it? I got off three times, I should have a clear mind and make good decisions. Starting with walking away and making my grand escape before I let this psycho lure me back to his place.

"Until next time?" he asks with the tilt of his lips and hope in his tone.

Fat chance. I'm a one-time kind of gal, especially in this town. Besides, I can't get too attached. To anyone. The last time that happened, it went up in flames. Literally.

"I'm leaving on Sunday." This version of me, anyways.

If he is around, he'll never know it's me. Hopefully, he won't be anywhere near Greenwood U. I can't have him sniffing me out for another amazing round of amazing sex. Fuck.

"To where?" he inquires, stepping closer. "Can I come? Follow you there? I can live in your closet. Just feed me and let me eat you for dinner and…"

I startle. Wait! What kind of dinner are we talking about? Like between my legs for dinner? Because that doesn't sound half bad. I can see it now. Me spread out on the dinner table with Malic between my legs, and maybe Wilder watching from the shadows with… I wrinkle my nose at the thought. Why did my mind go there? Wilder is an asshole. Always has been. Especially with Mack. But fuck that guy. You know what? Fuck them both. I don't need to dip into any more insanity.

Well, more than I already have.

"No," I say, shaking my head.

The last thing I need is Malic living in my closet, begging for bread and pussy on the regular. What the hell did I get into bed with? Or… on the bathroom counter with? Jesus. I was right before; he is giving major psycho vibes. But damn, he was good. Too good. Almost hazardous for my health. He reminds me of my cousin Jericho's little friend, Arrow. Now, he's a true psycho. Except Malic is more. There's something deep in his eyes, giving him away.

I remove my hand, revealing a pout on his lips. "How can I keep you if you're leaving?"

Whoa. Keep me? Yeah, time to get the hell out of dodge and

vacate the bathroom before he drugs me, takes me back to his bedroom, handcuffs me to a radiator, and never lets me go.

Just as I'm about to open my mouth to retort, someone pounds on the bathroom door with force, shaking the wood and threatening to ram through.

"Malic?" Wilder grunts, knocking viciously like the big, bad Malic would find trouble in the women's bathroom and wouldn't be able to handle himself.

"Bummer, Crumpet. Looks like our time has come to a dreadful end," he sighs, grabbing the front of my shirt and bringing me forward. Before I can breathe, his lips are on mine, leaving their mark. "Until next time," he whispers with a promise—Or threat? I'm not entirely sure, and releases my shirt. "Now, if you'll excuse me. My keeper and I need to have a few words."

His keeper?

Also. There won't be a next time. Not now or ever.

Malic unlocks the bathroom door and swings it wide open, revealing Wilder standing on the other side with his fist raised. An unlit cigarette hangs loosely from his lips as he narrows his eyes on Malic and then on me. His storm grey blue eyes check me over from head to toe, scrutinizing my wrinkled clothes and hair.

I frown, running a hand down my shirt and straightening my appearance up. I'm sure once I walk out into the bar, they'll know exactly what we did back here.

"Malic." His chest heaves with a big breath, concern crossing his features. Well, until he turns to me again. "And..." he trails off, looking at my disheveled shirt and messy hair. He visibly reels back, the cigarette dropping to the ground.

"Wilder. You're interrupting," Malic grumbles, waving a hand. "Go back to..."

"We need to talk. In private," Wilder rushes out, interrupting what Malic was about to say, which is fine because I'd rather slip away from here and go back to my hotel.

Malic immediately straightens, losing his cool demeanor.

"Do we?"

Wilder rolls his eyes and plucks his cigarette off the ground. "I wouldn't have said it if I didn't mean it."

Oh, snarky.

Malic's eyes focus on Wilder's hands, but I don't catch it as I slip between them. Eager not to get caught in Wilder's gaze and be recognized. Not that he would ever recognize me. My name is on a gravestone, after all. I'm dead to these people. But that's the last thing I need. Not to mention, Wilder was never my biggest fan whenever he popped up to make Mack's life miserable.

"Uh, thanks for that," I say, shrugging lamely before walking away like my ass was on fire.

I quickly dart into the darkened hallway, my heart in my throat pounding viciously as I make my escape. I only breathe when the bathroom door shuts and the lock clicks into place, locking both of them in the women's bathroom.

Weird.

Their harsh whispered words leak through the door, but no matter how hard I try to make out what they're saying, I can't.

Bummer.

I sigh, slowly walking down the hallway that never seems to end. I pass door after door again.

I wonder if Wilder went and beat a little sense into Nick. It would make sense. Wilder always lived on the opposite side of things. Mack lived with Franco, who took him in. Wilder lived with their drug-addicted mom.

"Fuck," Mack mumbles, putting his arm over my shoulders as the last bell of the day rings out. Kids pile out of the school at an alarming rate, racing to their vehicles in an attempt to put Greenwood High in their rearview mirrors. I don't blame them. School sucks and all that. But it's kind of a reprieve from home.

My brows furrow, following Mack's gaze at the edge of campus. Wilder. He's leaning against the school sign, eyeing the traffic with a lit cigarette—or what I can assume is a cigarette—between his lips. Puffs of smoke roll over his head each time he takes a breath and blows it out. All without using his hands.

"You think she's okay?" *I mumble, sticking close as we come to stand in front of him.*

Mack's mom may still be alive. But she's a walking zombie. She only lives for the heroin in her veins and nothing else. Not even the many boyfriends she keeps on rotation. Hell, she couldn't do it for Mack and Wilder when they were kids. It's a miracle she stayed somewhat sober to even have them.

Wilder throws his spent cigarette on the ground and stomps on it with a sigh, running his hand over his shaved blond head.

"What's wrong now?" *Mack asks, tightening his hold on me protectively.*

"No hello, brother? How is everything?" *Wilder scoffs, rolling his eyes. He reaches into his pocket and pulls out another cigarette, putting it between his lips, but doesn't light it.*

"Not when you only come to see me when something is wrong with her. What did she do? Overdose again?" *Mack asks, shaking his head.*

"You're a little shit," *Wilder grits out.* "None of this would have happened if you hadn't run away."

"Run away? I was taken away, asshole!" *Mack hisses.* "I gave you an out!"

"And gifted to a goddamn gang leader. Tell me, how's the work? Huh? You're the reason she is the way she is. It's because of him," *Wilder accuses, throwing his arms around.*

Mack gently puts me behind him and stands nose to nose with his slightly older brother.

"You're blaming me for her bad habits?" *he grits out, pushing his face harder against Wilder's.*

"I'm blaming you for being a pussy and abandoning your

fucking mom and family," Wilder hisses, pushing Mack in the chest.

Fuck. I've seen this a million times before. He only comes around when something is wrong to push Mack's buttons.

And always succeeds.

Mack stumbles back a few steps, turning bright red. His fingers curl into fists, and I know he's ten seconds away from throwing fists.

"Just say what you need to say," I say, stepping out from behind him.

Wilder snorts. "Oh, look! Your little girlfriend is here to fight your big, bad brother." He rolls his eyes, stepping back. "You're not worth it, Macklyn." He turns on his toes, taking a few steps before stopping and looking over his shoulder. "She's missing, by the way."

"Missing? What's new?" Mack scoffs, taking my hand. "Don't come back until she's dead."

"Don't count on it, dickbag!" Wilder shouts, putting his middle finger above his head.

I blink back the memory as I stare at the woman's face pinned to the business corkboard in the hallway of the bar, getting lost in the similarities. She's smiling at the camera with long brown hair and crisp blue eyes.

Missing. Meredith Monroe. If seen, please call Malic at 554-425-1933 with information. Last seen at X Marks the Spot. A week ago.

This damn bar.

I wonder what it is about this place? Earl was suspect. And now, there's a missing girl from this location?

I guess I need to bring this up to Jonathan face-to-face. Maybe it's connected to Franco and his bullshit gang. He's never above removing problems from the world. Except, Meredith doesn't look like a problem. Neither did Earl. Okay, except for his disruption. He seemed like a drunken old man spouting off about weird aliens.

I pluck the missing person's paper off the cork boards. The board is filled with business cards from local landscaping, casinos, and other businesses in the area. Community events like the blood drive hosted by the bar at Greenwood U line the board, hoping to attract the people of this town.

I shove the missing person's paper into my pocket with a sigh. If anyone can solve the mystery of the missing sister, it's me... if I have time.

"He's back. Again!" a frantic voice echoes through the hallway, coming from... Well, I'm not sure.

My brows furrow as I look around. Malic and Wilder haven't said much since they locked the bathroom door. Or, they've kept their voices low enough that I can't hear a damn thing anymore.

So, that leaves one of the many offices. Or the basement. Nick did say he lived down there.

Another muffled voice comes from... wherever they're hiding, but I can't make out their words.

Dangerous? Yes. If they're up to no good and stealing girls, then I'm a prime target. But I can't leave without sticking my nose in it. Who knows, it could be something juicy and interesting. Maybe I could convince Jonathan that this is what I need to focus on.

"Yeah, I..." I recognize Nick's panicked voice immediately the further I walk, hiding in the shadows. "Sir, I..."

Sir? Well, that tells me he's working for someone. Another gang, possibly? The options are endless.

I stop outside the basement door at the very end of the hall, holding my breath. Yeah. This is where Nick's voice is drifting up from. It's too bad his voice isn't coming through anymore. I slump. Now's my chance to make an escape. But I'll keep this place in mind whenever I go undercover.

MALIC

"MALIC." WILDER'S VOICE BARELY PUNCTURES THROUGH THE euphoric fog taking over my brain. I swear, everything slows down, taking my manic thoughts with it.

Who would have guessed that I'd find the love of my life sitting in a bar? Certainly not me. Or Wilder. Judging by the way he's looking at me with twisted brows and lips, like he can't wrap his peanut brain around the fact that I had sex in the bathroom. Or sex at all.

The memory of her eyes on mine finally after so long, has my dick rising again. Down, boy. We'll have her again. It's not like she can run from me. Ever again.

I scratch my chin. Fuck. Was my flirting okay? I've never done that before. Never had any sort of interest. In anyone. Ever.

It was always her.

My one and only obsession.

My little ghost.

I smile more, watching her through the door. Or, I would if I could see her. I know she's there, though, like an invisible tether running from my chest to hers.

She's mine.

"Your smile is fucking terrifying. Are we setting someone on fire?"

I whip my gaze to Wilder, who stares at me expectantly like he's spoken words and I've gotten too lost in my thoughts. I mean, setting someone on fire would be most enjoyable. Hearing their screams and smelling the flesh burn as it drops from their bones. Ah, it's good times, especially if they deserved it.

Actually, that gives me ideas. Whoever harmed Meredith will meet a grisly end. Not only will I drill holes throughout their bodies, but I'll light them on fire from the inside out.

But no. This smile is all for her. Olivia. My little ghost. She unknowingly signed our marriage license the moment my dick entered its home. And to think, if I hadn't seen a lonely girl at the bar who looked vaguely familiar, I wouldn't have wasted my time.

But it was the scent of her hair that pulled me in, reminding me of all the nights I watched from afar... And then got close enough to touch her while she slept. If her father thought the bars on her windows would keep her inside. Well, he was wrong. It also didn't stop me from crawling through her window and watching as she descended into dreamland. Her scent engulfed me in her presence. Even now.

I had my doubts as I crept along the bar, watching her closely as she stared at her drink. Then I saw them. The scars lining her throat. An injury that should have taken her from this world.

But it didn't.

Because she's stronger than she gives herself credit for.

And now she's back, haunting me all over again. For five years, I've waited and waited for her return. Who can truly walk away without getting vengeance against the ones who did them wrong?

No one.

I knew she'd be back. But I didn't know she'd haunt me so soon.

"You're not paying attention to anything I'm saying," Wilder grunts, waving his hand in front of my face. "Pay attention, Mal. We're here for a reason."

Right. A reason.

My brows furrow until I find my boxers and pants bunched up in the corner of the bathroom and pull them on.

"I am." I grin, zipping up my pants. It's bad etiquette to let your dick hang free in the middle of a conversation. Even though he barged in on my personal time. I think her juices are still clinging to my cock.

I'm never washing him again. Not until I get my hands on her again.

Wait a damn minute. Her words from our conversation ring through my mind.

"She said she's leaving. How am I supposed to find her again if she's leaving?" I growl, gritting my teeth, momentarily forgetting what I planted on her.

A tracker.

Something that will help me watch her every move from afar. I've waited patiently for her to return. Now, my little ghost won't be able to slip between my fingers again.

My shoulders ease. Only slightly. Wilder, who wants to lose a hand, stops my movements. I jerk back from his hold, glaring daggers. He sighs and puts his hands up in surrender.

"Mal!" he barks out, looking me up and down. "Focus! And..." He pales slightly, taking in my wild hair and wrinkled clothes like what I did finally caught up to him. "You actually did it, didn't you? Holy shit. You... And her... and..." His head whips back and forth with his lips popped open.

Honestly, I thought my dick hanging out would have been his first clue. Or maybe the satisfaction on my little ghost's face when she rushed out of here. Or maybe even the stench of sex. Isn't that all a huge red flag waving in his face?

He's really losing his edge.

"Careful, you might give yourself whiplash. Do you want all

the sordid details, Wild?" I grin again, but it melts from my face. "On second thought, no details." I can't have him poking around in my newly awakened sex life.

But only with her.

"Mal. You…"

"Gave it up?"

"But…" Wilder shakes his head. He knows all too well that I've never done the deed. I barely tolerate being touched. As to why now? Well, that's my little secret. "I thought you were…" Asexual. Had no interest in either gender? Well, think again. That's what he thought for all these years we've been buddies. I've never looked at anyone with sexual interest.

Except her.

"Moving on…" I say, waving a hand. My keeper can't stop looking at me like I'm some sort of anomaly standing before him. His lips flap open and closed, but no words come out. Huh. I've finally accomplished shutting him up. Interesting. He always has something to say. Even when we were broody teenagers, coming together because of our boss. We didn't start off as friends, but now he's my best—maybe only—friend. We've worked hard together, running errands and jobs for the boss man.

"Boys," Boss Man says when we enter his office. His dark, lifeless brown eyes sparkle with a knowing glint and his mouth tilts into a pride-filled grin as he leans back in his leather chair behind his desk.

"Sir," Wilder says, tightening his shoulders.

He's still new in these parts and hasn't quite figured out how to react when the boss man stares him up and down with a hard-ened expression. Gone is the smile and the pride. Now, he wants the information.

"The job is done," I say cooly, shoving my hands in my pockets with a grin.

I feel Wilder's gaze on the side of my face.

Did we fuck up the mission? Oh, yes we did. But we rectified that mistake by taking out some witnesses. Wilder had a little panic attack, and I had fun digging holes. It was like throwing potatoes into a barrel. Easy peasy.

And the best part?

No one will ever know.

"I'd love to know about the three bodies you buried." Boss Man leans back in his chair, steepling his fingers expectantly.

Well, then. I take that back. He did find out. Now, which one of his goons followed us like a babysitter? I bet it was that fucker Chris. Or Curtis. Or Cunt. Whatever his name is, he's on my shit list.

My eyes dart to the smug asshole in question standing in the corner of the room. I was right. It was Chris the Cunt. I grin, envisioning his death at my hands. I'll take him to my playground; AKA the basement of the gym we help clean for the boss man. The very place I'm allowed to live out my wildest dreams. Cutting off ears and noses and making our victims scream and blab about the bad things they've done.

Oh, the joy it brings me.

"They were witnesses," Wilder says, shaking his head. "We didn't have a choice."

We really did. We could have opted to walk away. Or just scramble their brains. Wilder voted for that. I, on the other hand, voted for mayhem. Oh, and lots of death. Besides, we couldn't have three people walking this earth knowing we sold weapons to our newest allies. Nope. That's on the hush, hush. Boss Man thinks we need to keep all our allies a secret. I concur. But it's nice to see Wilder having my back.

He's not too bad, after all.

"They had to die," I say proudly, smiling at him again.

"Dude," Wilder breathes with disappointment.

"No, I want to hear this," Boss Man says, getting to his feet with a stern expression. *Even if he buries me in the backyard for my murderous plots, this was all worth it. I only feel bad for Wilder. Poor guy. He doesn't deserve all that.*

"They were witnesses to our crimes. They could have exposed our newest alliance with..." *I lean in a little further toward him.* "You know who," *I whisper.*

"Ah, yes," *Boss Man nods a few times.* "That wasn't mentioned." *His eyes cut to Chris the Cunt, giving him a scathing look.*

"You told me to..." *Chris explodes. No, literally. Blood splatters everywhere, leaving him an empty shell of a human bleeding on the floor.*

"Fuck," *Wilder hisses, gagging and turning away.*

Me? Well, I watch as the life drains from Chris the Cunt's body, grinning as Boss Man tucks his gun into his jacket with a sigh.

"Let's have dinner and the both of you can go over every detail of what happened. Including the parts he so helpfully left out." *He gestures to the motionless body on the ground, sitting in a pool of blood.*

Beautiful.

"What did Nick have to say?" I gesture to the blood lining Wilder's knuckles. He's never afraid to get bloody and dirty for the ones he loves. Like my sister. Me. And our family we've created.

Wilder licks his lips. "He didn't say shit. But I did get this." He holds up a memory stick, twirling it between his fingers in victory. "Surveillance video from that night." Well, that's a new lead. They haven't been very forthcoming whenever we've sniffed around.

I guess violence really is the answer to our problems. Next time, I'll burn this bar to the ground with Nick and whoever else is in here tied to the bar.

Alive. Screaming. Begging for me to stop. Oh and there goes

my dick. Getting hard and ready to go again at the thought of destruction and death. This is new…

"Hmm," I say, rubbing my chin. "Let's go find my sister then." Meredith. Her name sounds in my mind. This is why I'm here at this shitty excuse for a bar. They're capitalizing on my enemies' casinos and local hotels. Hoping to make enough money to stay afloat.

Fucking Nathanial Franco. He's taken over the city, snatching up any sort of real estate he can get his hands on and building casinos to enhance his cash flow behind legitimate business. And his three foster sons–Huxley, JJ, and Mack–are by his side, stealing what doesn't belong to them.

Fuckers.

I will take down their kingdom piece by piece and burn them, too. Huh. Fire sounds mighty handy right now. I could just toss it on everyone and win the game of life.

This town has only had Franco and his gang running things for so long, providing jobs and financial security. Well, within the next year, that will be changing. Boss Man has a massive takeover plan, and I can't wait to execute it.

Too bad Meredith isn't the only person who has gone missing after visiting this place. It seems Franco might be up to something more than casinos and ruining more lives than he already has.

I'll be back.

I grin when knocking sounds at the bathroom door and a drunken girly voice carries through the solid wood while urgently pounding against it. Right. We're in the women's bathroom. Or perhaps my ghost came back to visit and tell me she's back for good.

I don't think she knew who I was. But I knew who she was.

"Hey! You can't lock this door! I have to pee!" a heavily slurred female voice says on the other side, pounding harder.

Sobs pour from her lips, which is usually music to my ears. From my enemies only, though.

"That's our cue. Let's go home," Wilder says, tucking the memory stick into his jeans pocket. "Can't bring any more attention to ourselves." He gives me a look. A very judgmental look.

He's just jealous I lost my virginity in a bar bathroom and didn't discuss it with him first. He's my keeper, after all. He feels entitled to my life choices and decisions. Of course, Boss Man appointed him to that position basically from the beginning, knowing I'd go off the rails and murder a few people. Whoops.

"Home…" I trail off when the door swings open, revealing a woman with furrowed brows and a reddened face. She doesn't ask questions, barging past us and into a stall, muttering to herself.

I follow Wilder out into the darkened hallway, looking around. Her perfume hits me immediately, mixed with our combined scent. She was here, standing in this spot. I stop, inhaling her until it dissipates.

Something happens behind my rib cage. My heart. It pounds with exhilaration. Ready to track her down and take her again. Maybe keep her. Tied to my bed and never let her go.

Our history is rich. Combined. Only, I don't think she had a damn clue who I was.

Even better.

The fog my ghost left behind lifts. Rage consumes me, drowning out the creaking of my black heart.

Meredith. Her picture on the corkboard has disappeared. I want her front and center every time someone passes down this hallway. I want them to look at her and take notice.

Now, she's gone.

I swivel my gaze from left to right. There's nothing here. Employee-only rooms line the hall. Rooms I'll upend when no one is looking.

X Marks the Spot is ground zero. I'm sure of it. Only, I don't have any clues except Meredith and her disappearance.

"It's gone." I point to the board where millions of business cards sit untouched. But my sister's face and missing poster have disappeared. Much like her physical self. I frown. I know I put it up here a few days ago when we came in. It was there when I dragged my little ghost to the bathroom. And now?

Gone. Missing. Disappeared right under my damn nose. I always promised to protect her after I found out she existed.

And look, I failed.

Wilder sighs, reaching into his back pocket and taking out another flier, and sticks it on the board again. The same flyers we made. We had to. The police in this town are useless. Deep in Franco's pocket. Well, some of them anyway. Others are in our pockets. But it's been a long, hard fight to get Boss Man where he is.

I trust no one with this task. Not the police—they weren't helpful. Not Nathaniel Franco and his fucked up army. They're probably the reason she's gone. Hell, I hardly trust the man I pledged my undying loyalty to. My boss.

Only Wilder has my trust.

I barely trust myself in most cases.

Life is funny like that.

Trust is non-existent when you grew up as unstable as I did.

Just ask the woman I murdered as she begged me not to. Wait, you can't.

I shake my head, ridding my mind of the past.

"We have a small lead. We'll find her, okay?" Wilder slaps my shoulder a few times and pulls away with realization.

"If we don't…" I trail off as we saunter through the loud bar unnoticed.

"They'll face our wrath, Malic." He raises a brow when the warm August heat hits us square in the face.

That they will. They'll meet the maniac bubbling beneath my flesh, aching to take his frustrations out on unsuspecting faces.

"How about a welcome back event?" I hum, following him to our vehicle.

Wilder nods. "You want everyone to be invited? Even... *Them*?" His nose wrinkles at the thought of Franco's special sons. His brother, Mack, included. Who knew two brothers with half of the same blood rolling through their veins could hate each other so much?

"Especially them," I chuckle, slamming the door shut.

Visions of slamming my fist into their faces and watching as they bleed come to mind. Hate isn't a strong enough word for what I feel for the bastards in line to rule this town.

Huxley. JJ. Mack.

They can all burn with this place once I'm done with it.

They may be playing pretend at Greenwood U until they are needed to continue the family business. But what they don't know won't hurt them.

They know we're here. They know the gang we represent. They know us by name. But the game we're playing?

They don't have a fucking clue.

It's time to knock some crowns off three princes' inflated heads.

"There's fucking nothing there," Wilder says, slamming his laptop shut and tucking it under his arms. He flings the memory stick across the room, slamming it into the wall.

Indeed. There wasn't a stitch of a clue there on the surveillance footage. Just Meredith walking out of the bar with no one at her side. Or behind her. Or in front of her. She was alone. Happy. Smiling, the entire time while she drank at the bar. Nick, our overly friendly bartender, paid special attention to her. But nothing suspicious. Or out of the ordinary.

It's fucking frustrating.

Meredith went to the bar to meet some friends. They left ten minutes before her, and then, she ceased to exist. If only we had footage from the outside of the building from the casinos across the street.

Easier said than done, but we're working on it. Gathering more information and waiting for them to send us the intel we paid for on the down low. Patience is a virtue. But not in my case.

My fingers curl into fists. A heat works up my neck, spiking rage through my veins and pumping hard.

Meredith is out there somewhere. Alone. Possibly hurting. Dead. Kidnapped. Anything is possible.

My eyes screw shut. Feelings bubble inside me, almost pushing through the numbness and fog of my mind. Why can't we find her? What's the point of being in our position if she slipped between our fingers like sand?

We're fucking useless to her. Unless we get ahead of the game.

Wilder paces, shaking his head. "Every fucking clue is a dead end. She can't have just disappeared!" he shouts, throwing his fist into my bedroom door.

Well, that will leave a mark. On him. On my door.

For several seconds, he stands with his back to me. Heaving breath after breath until he walks out with a grunt.

He'll be back.

Heavy footsteps pound down the hall until Wilder's bedroom door opens and slams shut. Shuffling happens between the walls. No doubt, setting his laptop down and collecting the cigarettes he refuses to smoke.

I sigh. My mind immediately wanders to Meredith,

wondering where she is and who took her from me. She is innocent. She has no association with me or the company I decided to keep. All for the sake of survival.

Guilt eats away at every molecule inside me.

"We'll fucking find her," Wilder grunts, leaning in the doorway of my room with an unlit cigarette resting between his lips. Always unlit now. "I'm still waiting on Bobby to get back to me with more surveillance footage from the casino across the street. If he doesn't text me back soon, I'll track him down at the fucking horse races."

See? I knew he'd come back.

"I got the word out about the fight," he rumbles, shoving his hands in his pockets. "And I know just the assholes to call out." He smirks when his phone vibrates in his pocket, and he pulls it out, typing something quickly.

Even though the Coliseum is basically run by the three idiots we hate, anyone can create a fight night to their liking, with or without their approval.

Like we just did.

"That was quick." I raise a brow, taking out my phone and peering at the small announcement on our university's slam page.

A place for students to write their dirty little secrets and unburden themselves anonymously. Like fucking *Gossip Girl.* Not that I've watched it or anything.

No one knows who runs it. I mean, I have my ways. I could find out in a heartbeat. But I won't. It's the quickest and easiest way possible to spread the word about parties, fights, and events.

In our case. A welcome back punch fest. Blood for blood. Broken bones for broken bones. All on neutral grounds. Animosity be damned.

It's music to my ears.

Fight. First Friday after students return. Coliseum. Midnight.

If there's one thing I can say about Wilder, he's efficient. But I know he needs this as much as I do.

The blood, crunching bones, and the thrill of whooping some ass.

I'm getting hard thinking about it. I blink several times, staring at my dick rising in my jeans. Well, this is quite the new adventure for me. Thanks for awakening, Big guy.

And it's all thanks to her.

But you can deflate now. We'll save all that for another time.

Wilder grins at his phone, putting the cigarette behind his ear. Relief seems to spill over his features, and he loosens up. Obviously, he got what he wanted.

"Hux says he'll fight you. Gladly, if I'm quoting him." Wilder rolls his eyes. "I'll beat Malic's ass any day of the week." He mocks Huxley fucking Crewe's voice.

Cocky douche.

My teeth grit at the thought of him. It's his fault. All of it. And I can't wait to beat his face in. Just like last time.

Hux doesn't stand a fucking chance against me. I'm undefeated, underestimated, and his ass-beating has been in the works for years now. He may have done something heroic a few years ago, but that doesn't excuse who he is now.

"And for you?" I ask, leaning back on my queen-sized bed with my hand tucked behind my head.

Wilder shoves his phone away, knowing what I'm asking. It's the question I ask every time we line up fights, which happens at least twice a month. It's for our sanity. And the campus. They pick an opponent, and we facilitate the ring. It's a win-win. Plus, it draws a crowd and money.

"The day that asshole gets into the ring with me, is the day Hell freezes over." He flings a hand recklessly. "Mack's a pussy. Always has been," he practically spits his brother's name out like a curse.

"So who then?"

Blood soars through my veins the more I think about the upcoming school year at Greenwood U and the fights that will ensue in our Coliseum overlooking the ocean. A piece of Greenwood living in the infamy of the pirate who landed here on his last leg.

"Whoever shows up," he grunts, shrugging.

"You hear about the grand party they're throwing?" I ask, yawning.

Wilder puts the cigarette between his lips again. "Who hasn't heard about it? No one is even on campus yet and it's the talk of the fucking town." Not to mention, they throw it every year. It's a tradition of sorts. Only, the masses don't realize the meaning behind the charade.

"How about we have our own?" I grin.

"One of our own, huh? New recruits?" Wilder raises a brow with interest. Parties aren't usually his scene. He'd rather hide in the shadows with an unlit cigarette between his lips, watching people.

I nod.

"See who is interested. Boss said it would be good for us to branch out. Maybe ruffle some feathers," I chuckle. "New blood and all that."

We may have our own organization and frat house near campus, but we're always looking for new people to pledge to our cause. We've been secretly growing right under Franco's fat nose for years now. It's about time we come out to the world as serious contenders.

Now the kings of campus will know we mean business.

There's a new leader in town and has been for years. He's ready to play ball and fight against the heirs of Greenwood. Oh, and their scumbag father.

Wilder makes his exit. No doubt, sauntering into his room to stare at the walls, rethinking all his life choices. And Meredith, of course.

As for me, I sit back in my bed, pulling out my phone and one lone photograph I've kept since I was fifteen.

She sits there, not bothering to smile at the camera. Staring straight into the lens. Into my fucking soul. I sit beside her. Timid and shell-shocked, staring straight ahead like I hadn't witnessed multiple atrocities the night before I met her.

She was clueless. Yet, welcomed me without question.

"My Little Ghost," I murmur, running a finger over her face. "You've returned from the dead."

Well, not technically the dead because she was never there. She survived. I saw it with my own eyes. The world may think my little ghost is a decaying corpse resting under six feet of dirt with her name etched in marble, but I know the truth.

Me. Her. Him.

"And I'll stop at nothing to follow you to the ends of the earth." I smile at my phone, noting the blinking red dot near the Grand Hotel.

"Gotcha."

And then my smile slips when the dot blinks out, and she disappears from sight.

"Motherfucker," I hiss, nearly throwing my phone into the wall. But I stop myself. It's my only lifeline to Meredith. She could text or call at any moment, begging for help. So, I refrain. For now, at least.

"I found you once, Little Ghost," I murmur to myself with a sigh, climbing off my bed and sitting on the ground.

OLIVIA

"THAT'S A TRACKER," CARTER grumbles through the video chat with a sneer.

No shit, Sherlock.

He's always so lovely to talk to. But as my correspondent and the only man on earth I trust with technology—trust should be used loosely—I had to call him at five in the morning to get his opinion.

"Tell me again how you found a tracker in your jeans?"

I run a hand down my face, sitting on the edge of my hotel bed. The tracker in question is fully submerged in a glass of water at my bedside. Hopefully broken.

The psycho from the bar.

He said he wanted to come home with me and stay. I guess he meant it.

"I plead the fifth." No way in hell am I telling that asshole how I ended up fucking a stranger in the bathroom while he was on the hunt for his missing sister.

"You hooked up with some fucking rando at a club or bar, didn't you?" That little weasel. How in the hell does he know?

"That doesn't matter."

"Obviously it fucking does, Olivia," he snorts, rubbing his temple.

"Fine. I hooked up with some rando at the bar, and he put a tracker on me for some reason." Because why wouldn't he? That's all I seem to attract these days. Psychos.

Ugh.

"Fucking shit," he growls. "Just send it to me. I'll take a fucking look at it and see if I can find out who owns it."

I've known Carter for almost two years now. Ever since my first case out in the field, where I went undercover as a girl named Espie and infiltrated East Point Prep. Talk about an experience for my very first step into what the underbelly of the evil world had to offer. And boy, was that place crawling with evil. Teachers taking advantage of their students. An evil cult taking students and using their deaths for money. The list goes on.

Carter was smart back then. Like *'owns his own company in his senior year of high school'* smart. And now? The man is a damn genius. Grumpy as fuck, but smarter than anyone I know. That's why my uncle is so damn interested in bringing him into Veritas and making him an agent. Carter can track anyone. Hack into anything he sets his sights on. Although, I keep that tidbit to myself, because of legalities and all that jazz. So far, Carter has only agreed to help me on the side without Jonathan's knowledge.

"You're such a peach so early in the morning," I quip, shaking my head. "I'll send it today."

"You on another case?" He narrows his eyes at me through the video call.

"Until you have full clearance, you know I can't tell you." I stick my tongue out at him, earning a huff.

"Yeah fucking right," he grunts. "That'll never happen. I've got too much shit on my plate."

Right. He's running his company from a small home office while the rest of his brother-husbands or boyfriend-in-laws or whatever he calls them attend college. His main focus is his girlfriend, Kaycee. I don't understand how she or any of them put up with his grumpy ass. But somehow they do. It's a mystery to me. But whatever. Who am I to judge?

One day, I know he'll join the dark side with me. He's already done so much for me since he agreed to take my calls and help.

After hanging up, I lie back on my bed and close my eyes. There's so much about this town that has my heart in my throat.

But for now, I need to rest before Jonathan confronts me with the rest of my mission.

I groan, covering my face with my hands as the sun peeks through the curtains. Without opening my eyes, I can tell it's high in the sky. But damn. Everything hurts. And I might be dying.

It's been hours since I took my last sip at the bar, and I neglected to drink any water before calling Carter and lying down.

I'm never drinking again.

Okay, that's a lie. A big, fat lie.

Alcohol is my vice of choice. The crutch that guides me through the darkness I'm stumbling through every day. Along with my job, it keeps my mind off my past.

Well, until now.

I flinch when something wet drips on my forehead again and again. I swipe at whatever is touching my head.

"You need to wakey wakey, Livy Poo!"

My eyes fly open at the sound of my Veritas' partner, Jordy's voice. He grins above me with disheveled blond hair and sparkling light eyes. Then I see the water slowly dripping from the water bottle clutched in his hand.

"What the fuck?" I hiss, shoving his face away and sitting up. "Water, Jordan? Really mature," I huff, shaking my head.

"No one said I was mature," he giggles hysterically.

"Never said you were, you overgrown child." I pout, wiping the water from my face.

"Aw, Livy. You love me so much."

"That's a lie, and you know it. More like barely tolerate you because I have to!"

Once upon a time, when I joined Veritas, Agent Six, aka Jordan Van Horn, was assigned as my partner. We roomed together in a bunker deep in the ground. Where we lived, ate, and breathed training day in and day out. Living there was like being in college for spying. Going to class. Whether it was combat training, marksmanship, or psychology courses to better learn the human mind.

We did it all. Together.

Jordy was my accountability person. My roommate. My goddamn pest. But also, my best friend. My brother. Someone I could trust with my life. I love him with all my heart, but that's the extent of our lives together.

"Barely tolerate? You wound me. Deeply," he quips, holding a hand over his heart.

"Wait. What are you doing here?" I ask, looking around the barren hotel room.

When I snuck back in last night after the bar, using the access key, everything seemed normal. The light from Jonathan's room seeped from beneath his door, and the sound of his fingers clicking away at his keyboard rang through the hotel room. I was glad he wasn't out and waiting for me when I came back.

But now, I know why.

He intended to leave me the second I closed my eyes. I feel it in my bones. He's gone and has sent Jordy in his place. Maybe because I like Jordy better at the moment.

Jordy gives me a megawatt smile. "Jonathan said you might

need some help today. Uh... coping with you know... your newest assignment." He cringes, nervously waving his hands around without making eye contact.

"Great. So, you know what I'm getting ready to do." My shoulders slump, and my eyes squeeze shut. I'm one day closer to my new destiny.

It feels like I'm in some sort of weird reality. Tomorrow, I won't be Olivia. I'll be Oliver. A headache forms in my skull, and I know I'm about to have the longest day of my life with only a few hours of sleep.

If Jordy is here, that means Jonathan has brought reinforcements to prepare me for my mission.

"Exactly." Jordy grins, snapping his fingers. "That's why I'm here. I mean, I am the perfect male specimen to help you become... well, me."

I groan, tossing a pillow at his face. "You're not the perfect male specimen." Cocky dick.

"Pfft. Am so. Why else would I be here to help you into your new wardrobe and cut your hair?" He wiggles his brows playfully and then stops at the look on my face. My fingers weave through my long strands. "Livy, I know what it means to you." Yes. He does know.

He's probably the only person on the planet who's broken me open and seen the ugly underneath. All my scars. My nightmares. Everything I can't say aloud.

Jordy may be my pest, like a little brother who pokes at the bear too often and way too hard, but he's been my best friend for years. Others in our division at Veritas thought we were rolling around in the hay and getting frisky. But that's never been us. He's my family. The only family since my world burned to ash.

The only person besides Jonathan I grew to trust.

"I told you not to call me that." Because *he* called me that. Livy. All through our time together. Now, the nickname brings nothing but rage through my veins.

My eyes refuse to focus on anything else but the window illuminated by the sun. Its rays bounce through the glass, lighting up the room with its good morning.

The bed dips beside me, and Jordy sighs, putting an arm around my shoulders and pulling me close.

"This is why I'm here. He said you disappeared yesterday afternoon into the late night and..." He sniffs my hair, recoiling from me with his mouth open. "Holy shit. You disappeared to get laid!"

I frown, pushing him over. He cackles, holding his stomach.

"Wait until the others hear about this. Oh my God, Liv!"

"Go home!" I hiss, shoving him completely off the bed until he lands with an umph.

"Can't," he wheezes, staring up at the ceiling with a grin. "Was it good? The dick? Wait, I don't really want to know." He wrinkles his nose in disgust.

The best ever. I don't think I've had an orgasm like that since... Well, never. Too bad Malic was a certified stalker who put a tracking device on me.

"No. We're not discussing this." I frown, sniffing myself and blanching. Yeah. It's the smell of sex, booze, and terrible fucking decisions. "I'm going to take a shower. Then we can do... Whatever it is you're doing here."

I stand, making my way to the bathroom, but Jordy's voice halts my retreat.

"I'm here to help you become your newest assignment. That's all." He sounds so earnest and quiet. Like he knows exactly what's going through my mind.

"And what is your case?" I ask, peeking over my shoulder.

His lips purse. "Some art thief, thirty minutes from here in the big city. After I escort you to your living quarters, I'll be on my way." He shrugs, turning to his side and propping himself up on his elbow. "I'll be close if you need me. I'm just a phone call away."

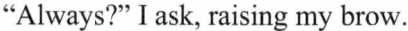

"Always?" I ask, raising my brow.

"You know it." He nods. "Now, go get naked and clean the sex from your body. You repulse me." He fakes shivers and laughs when I flip him off.

See? Like a damn annoying brother.

"He left?" I ask again for the millionth time since I got out of the shower and met Jordy in the small living room. Even though I knew the moment Jordy was hovering above me with water in his hands that Jonathan had abandoned me, I still needed to confirm.

Delicious takeout boxes are strewn on the coffee table, wafting their smells throughout the room. My stomach rumbles, but ash rests on my tongue.

Jonathan left. Without a goodbye. Without divulging more on my newest case. Just poof! He had to return to headquarters for a newly inducted agent. And left me here with Jordy. Why did he abandon me in my time of need? He knew this was hard for me, but instead, he turned his focus to someone else.

It's never me.

"He must trust me or something. Asked me to escort you to campus tomorrow." Jordy tries to keep his voice playful and even, but I feel the doubt from here.

"His trust is awfully misplaced," I groan, running my fingers through my long strands, savoring the feel of them between my fingers.

"Are you going to be okay with this?" Jordy softly asks, taking a bite of his quesadilla and slowly chewing. "I mean it's one kick in the ass to have to confront your ex-besties, who I can kill by the way." He raises his eyebrows when I snort. "But having to go undercover as the opposite sex." He whistles, swallowing his bite. "That's a lot. So, spill your thoughts, buttercup. Tell Jordy your woes."

"My woes," I quip mockingly. "I've dressed as everything under the sun while undercover. Old women, hookers..."

"Even I wanted to fuck you, oomph!" He hisses when I throw a cup of queso at him. "You're lucky the lid was on. But fine, continue." He waves a hand, studying my expression. "You'll do just fine, Liv. You're one of the best agents out there. Besides me, of course. I'm number one." He wiggles his brows.

I laugh, shaking my head. "Sure, Jordy. You're number one."

I'm absolutely terrified to walk into this mission. It's not the undercover status I'm scared about. I don't even mind that I have to wear men's clothes and parade around campus as the opposite gender.

It's them.

Facing my ex-best friends who watched the life drain from my eyes and left me to die in a fiery tomb has my stomach turning.

"I want to bring them down so badly. I want to watch them on their knees as they beg for their lives." Like I did that fateful night.

"I think I just popped a chub. Keep talking dirty!" Jordy chuckles, savagely biting into his quesadilla again.

I roll my eyes. "Shut up," I groan. "I'm serious. I want them to hurt like I did. I want them to feel my wrath from beyond the damn grave."

I want them to suffer at my hands like I suffered at theirs. They mortally wounded me. Left me to die with little regard for me. We were best friends and lovers.

I loved them with all my heart and they squeezed that from me when they slit my throat.

Looking up from my knees as they dig into the floor of my home, fat tears slip from my lashes and drip down my cheeks. I can't help the panic flooding my veins, begging for me to run away from this situation. No. They wouldn't do this, right? They wouldn't stand above me with black masks covering their faces, holding me down as their father rants and raves with a knife in his hand before me.

I only get a glimpse of their eyes, shining with an emotion I can't quite place. The same eyes I've gazed into since I moved here, and they became my best friends. Blue. Green. Brown. They look at me like an ant beneath their shoes as I beg for my mercy. As I beg for the lives of my mother, sister, and myself.

But it's useless.

They spare us no mercy. They spit words that rip me in two. And it's them. My best friends. The people I thought I could count on the most.

As I lay dying on the ground, I think of all the good times we had together—all the fun we had, the love we shared, and the laughs that filled our treehouse.

How could you fake that? How could you slit the throat of the girl you held the night before and professed your love to?

"You could play the long game. I won't tell Jonathan if you accidentally cut one of their dicks off," Jordy chortles, swallowing the rest of his quesadilla and reaching for another.

In theory, that all sounds wonderful. I could slowly attack them, one puzzle piece at a time, and bring them to their knees.

But I'm on a real mission. There's something more happening in this town, beyond them and their stupid gang.

"Maybe," I say, shaking my head. "Let me tell you about this stupid town."

And I do. I tell Jordy everything that happened last night and everything I found, making me think there's a deeper reason I've been sent back here.

Jordy chews slowly, digesting my words. "That's weird as fuck. You ask your little techy criminal to look into that chick's disappearance? Or our database?"

I roll my eyes. "No. He's working on something else for me right now. Besides, he's not a criminal." Speaking of, I need to send that tracker off in the mail so he can tell who is stalking me. My guess? That damn psycho. But damn, the sex, though. It was out of this world.

Jordy blinks. "You're going to investigate it, aren't you? Just can't help yourself. Always got to throw your everything into the damn ring."

"You know me so well," I snort.

Truth is, I can't stop myself from investigating everything I see. Maybe it's connected. Maybe not. Or perhaps there's more weird shit happening in this town. Or maybe I'm trying to distract myself from what I'm about to do. It's not every day a dead person can confront their past head-on. But that's my mission.

"All right. You ready?" Jordy asks, wiping his hands. "I'm supposed to work my magic and transform you. Like your own personal fairy godmother." He grins, jumping to his feet and gathering a black duffel bag.

I sigh, staring at the future dead on.

Now is the time. I'm about to do the unthinkable.

Now is the time to cut my hair, lock my feelings away, and face my past while pretending to be someone completely different. If that's even possible.

I swallow hard, getting up and going to stand in front of the bathroom mirror with Jordy on my tail. He doesn't say a word, opting to stay silent. For once.

A woman stares back at me with deadness in her eyes. There's no light, love, or any normal sort of emotion. Not anymore. Just the husk of a girl who once had dreams to live her life to the fullest under no man's rules.

I lived by my own set of rules. Until it was all taken from me.

Slowly, I run my fingers through my long brown locks,

which reach the middle of my back. I've grown it out, only trimming the ends to keep it alive for the last five years.

They took my name. My face. My voice. My fucking life. But this? My hair? They didn't take this from me. It's been with me since that night. Like a companion hanging on to the bits of my past I couldn't–wouldn't—cut away. It's the constant reminder of how they used it against me in my time of need.

A reminder for so much more than that. It fuels the revenge coursing through my veins. It's the reminder that I survived. All of me.

I swallow hard when my fingers hit the bald spot near my left temple. Where the fire ravaged through our home and seared my flesh, taking some spots of my hair with it.

My hair is more than hair. It's the reminder of my survival. That I came out on the other side a new person.

I cry out, begging with all my might for them to stop yanking my head back by my hair.

"Your time has come, Little Viotto. You're paying for your crimes," Franco says.

"No!" I shout, crying harder when Huxley's grip in my hair tightens, making it impossible to move away from the blade pressing against my throat and slowly carving its way across my flesh. I'm forced to stare into the eyes of my boyfriends. My best friends. As their father ends my life.

And they help him.

Jordy doesn't say a word when I pick up the large scissors lying on the bathroom sink. He doesn't make a peep when I suck in a breath and snip the first pieces off, watching as they fall and scatter on the ground at my feet.

He doesn't console me or hold my shoulder when the tears slip from between my lashes, dripping down my cheeks. He doesn't make fun of me when sobs wrack my body and my weakness comes to the damn surface.

No. His lips don't move an inch, because Jordy knows it all.

He's heard the night terrors. The cries for my mother and sister. The frustration. Everything.

Jordy simply watches with tears brimming in his eyes as I cut piece after piece of hair.

"You do the back?" I question softly, not bothering to look at him as he takes the scissors from me with a nod.

"Anything for you, Liv," he whispers, lifting the long strands left at the back of my head. "You're brave for this. You know? I wouldn't be able to step foot back in my hometown after..." He shakes his head, not wanting to relive his own tragedy.

That's the thing about the two of us. Hell, about everyone who comes to Veritas. We're like wounded strays with no names and families to rely on. Veritas becomes that for us. Our partners become our everything.

"How can I pull this off, Jordy?" I whisper, squeezing my eyes shut as he continues to cut my hair.

Doubt seeps in from every corner, infecting me like a sickness eager to take me down.

"Like you always do, Liv. You're the most badass bitch I know," he says softly, setting the large scissors down and grabbing a small pair, snipping again. His fingers work through my shorter strands, styling them into a shaggy style. The hair still covers the tops of my ears, but the air brushing against my neck has shivers working down my spine.

It's so strange not to feel the tension on my scalp or the strands at my back. It's all gone. Everything is gone now.

"What if I'm not strong enough?" All the vulnerabilities living inside me come to the surface.

What if I'm not strong enough? Smart enough? Fast enough? What if they discover it's me and want to finish the job they started? What if... What if...

Jordy snorts. "Not strong enough? Sometimes I wish I could smack you and get away with it." I glare at him through the mirror now, noting the tears on his cheeks. It's sobering and humbling to have my best friend sobbing alongside me. Especially Jordy. He's all laughs and jokes, but for him, it covers up the traumas of his childhood. Banishing them to the darkest recesses of his mind.

But not right now.

We're living this together.

"You're stronger than anyone I know. But don't tell anyone I said that. Or this…" he trails off, wiping the tears off his cheeks, and sets the scissors down. "Liv, you can do anything. You've taken down cults and serial killers. What's three idiots? You can poison their coffee or bash their skulls in their sleep. Which I'll help with, by the way. Because what are friends for? We can even chop them into little pieces and deliver them straight to Franco's doorstep." He gives me a watery grin. "You have a heart of fucking iron, Liv. You're strong, capable, and I fucking believe in you."

I swallow his words like razor blades scraping against my throat. "Okay," I croak.

"Pfft. Okay, she says. That's it? I pour my heart out for you, and you just say okay? Bitch, look in that mirror…" He softly grips my chin and forces me to stare at the new woman before me. "Tell yourself you're capable every time you see this person in the mirror. Tell them you're strong, independent, and a damn good person, too."

"I'm capable," I whisper to my new reflection staring back at me.

"More than capable. Do it again until you fucking believe it, okay?" He bends down, grabbing my hair from the ground and holding it in the air. "They took a lot of shit from you, but this? This is nothing. You're Olivia fucking Viotto. Former Mafia princess turned government agent. You're a badass in my book. You don't need a name or hair or what fucking ever. All you need is what lives in here." He points to his chest, poking it three times before he lets the hair fall to the ground. "Now, we good here? Need any more motivational speeches?" He grins at that when I turn and bury my face in his chest. I soak in the love Jordy has for me. Because in two point five seconds, we'll be right back into the brother-sister role we've carved out for ourselves.

"I don't think I could survive without you," I mutter, pulling my face from his chest and wiping away the tears.

"Don't I know it," he quips, shaking his head. "Now, no more of these tears, all right? It's time to try on some new clothes, put on your contacts, and kick some ass!" he whoops, harshly slapping my ass before he walks out of the bathroom, leaving me there to stew in my own shit.

I lick my lips, turning to view myself in the mirror again.

"I can do this."

"Hell yeah you can!" Jordy shouts from the other room, as the sound of the fridge opening and slamming shut has my eyes rolling.

We just ate.

I huff a laugh, shaking my head.

"I'm Olivia Viotto. Former Mafia princess turned agent of the law. I can fucking do this." I give myself a hard nod, before turning around and jumping into the hot shower.

OLIVIA

ONCE THE HEAT OF THE SHOWER SUBSIDES, I STAND DIRECTLY IN front of the mirror, wiping away the moisture built up on the glass. My tongue threatens to leap down my throat the moment I lay my eyes on the person staring back at me.

Short, shaggy brown hair hangs past the tips of my ears in the front, but it's slightly longer in the back, with its tips touching my neck. Green-colored contacts change my eye color. Thick, black-rimmed glasses rest over my eyes to record my every move and interaction. No makeup covering my scars or blemishes.

Not me.

My reflection stares back at me, yet it doesn't *feel* like me. I'm different. Yet the same. It's not really me. There's a stranger in my place—a man with glasses and green eyes.

Not Olivia.

Oliver.

My newest identity.

My fingers cling to the counter in the bathroom, curling over the edges and digging into the flesh of my palm, leaving indents. My eyes squeeze shut as the pain takes over, drawing my focus to the physical pain. Not the mental pain festering inside, trying to claw its way out.

Everything I successfully locked away into a black box in my mind comes back with a vengeance to haunt me.

Their faces. Names. Voices.

Our memories. The good. The bad. All the ugly parts of us scream from the depths of my mind, reminding me of who they are. Their claws reach out, attempting to pull me back to the moments we shared. The happy. The sad. The fucking devastating. Leading to the betrayal swimming before my eyes as a fire erupts and eats away at my existence.

I'm dead. Barely alive. Barely functioning.

Barely fucking breathing.

I suck in a breath, reminding myself that my lungs need the oxygen to survive. Blinking past the persistent memories flashing across my eyes, I stare at myself in the mirror. I force my gaze upon the person I'm about to become for however long this case takes to crack open.

Stop thinking about them. Stop thinking about what happened. Move forward. Take them down when the time is right.

Because that's what I'll do. I'll stick to my job. To a fucking T. I won't deviate, but I will bring them down. One by one. To their knees until Veritas drags them away and throws away the key.

They're criminals and deserve the prison that awaits them.

"Liv," Jordy's voice swims through the emotions piling high inside me and swirling like a storm ready to strike.

It's happening. It's real. I'm doing this.

I got this.

I'm okay.

Totally fucking okay.

I tilt my head, and the longer strands swoop over my temples and ears, tickling them, but not going over my shoulders like they normally do. Shaggy with uneven layers from a home done haircut, but yet, it suits me.

My gaze shifts to the long strands still lying on the ground unswept and mocking me.

We did it. We cut my hair. We made me into someone I'm not. All for the case.

My fingers run through the shorter strands, attempting to ground myself. Attempting to tell myself that my hair doesn't matter. It doesn't matter that I hadn't cut it in five years. Not since the night of their betrayal and the fire.

The long strands of my dark brown hair were my safety blanket. Hiding the physical trauma of that dreadful night. Concealing the betrayal I'd been subjected to by the ones I thought I could trust the most. Huxley. JJ. Mack. It hid the shame that festered behind my eyes. Never showing the world the stupid girl who fell for pretty words and ultimately fell and died at their hands. The long slash across my throat signifies the brutal end to our relationship, doled out by their blood-stained hands. The wounds may be healed. But the memories will forever be etched in the back of my mind, coming back at the worst possible time to haunt me.

Healing isn't walking away from the problem at hand and pretending it never existed. It's facing it head-on. And maybe apprehending the very people who killed you without a second thought.

Cutting my hair feels like I've jumped into the deep end of the pool, unable to swim to the surface, and I'm slowly sinking further into the darkness.

"Holy fuck," Jordy says, poking the side of my face and bringing me back to reality. "You're really going to pull this off. It's too bad for your tits they—umph!" He groans, stumbling back.

Sexist bastard.

A frown etches across his lips as he rubs at his chest. The very chest I just punched with my full strength.

"You're very mean," he pouts playfully. "That'll leave a bruise."

Good. That's what I was aiming for.

I level him with my best glare. "Leave my tits out of this," I grumble, returning my attention to the person staring back at me in the mirror.

It's unreal to see myself this way. Usually, it's wigs and false teeth. Maybe a little makeup to blend in. But this disguise is an entirely new playing field.

An entirely new person without trying hard.

Swallowing the lump forming in my throat, I square my shoulders. An eerie sense of confidence bursts through me. I've got this. This entire situation isn't about me. This is about taking them down. Taking Franco to Hell, where he belongs.

Finally, getting the much-needed revenge I've wanted to enact for years.

"You might actually pull this off, Liv. Like seriously," Jordy whistles, putting an arm over my shoulders. Leaning close, he whispers, "You fucking got this. You're a brave fucking warrior. We've been to Hell and back. Now's your chance to kick some ass." He squeezes me tight and kisses my temple affectionately.

And then promptly ruins the moment by opening his damn mouth.

"You know, I could shave some of my—umph!" He gasps, backing away from me and rubbing his stomach while wincing. "Yeah, you're gonna kick ass. Those dudes don't know what's going to hit them. Seriously! You're violent." He shakes his head with fake disappointment, but I see the truth shining in his sparkling eyes. He's proud of me. Knowing how hard I've fought to overcome the screaming nightmares and my past constantly chasing me.

He's the one who had to pick up my pieces. Over and over again. It's a wonder why we've never dated or seen each other in that light.

We're family, regardless.

"Violence is my middle name," I quip, sucking in a breath at the sight of my reflection again and tightening the towel around my body.

My stomach turns the more I prepare myself for the next few months of my future.

I'll have to face them. My ex-best friends. My murderers. I'll have to pretend that being around them doesn't upset me. In fact, I've been instructed to be their friend however I can. I'll have to follow them everywhere, but it won't be like before. When I was a child, the trust between us was strong. Now? I'll have to do it out of obligation and duty, so I can uncover as many of their misdeeds as possible.

My end goal?

Get into their frat. Get into their gang, which loosely ties into the college... Somehow. Find out what Franco is up to and why he's suddenly funding a college.

All in a day's work, I guess.

"Okay, I think I'm ready." It's a lie.

I'm slightly numb. Slightly freaking out. Slightly ready to puke my damn guts out.

You'll be fine. You'll be okay.

But will I?

"Fat chance," Jordy quips, rolling his eyes and seeing straight through my deceitful words. "You're so not ready for this. Besides, you can't go out in that towel. Come on, Livy Poo. I've got the hook up for you." He sings every word, darting to the side when I lift my hand to smack him in the back of the head.

Asshole.

"I told you not to call me that," I grumble, reluctantly following him out of the bathroom in a towel and stopping in the small living room where several piles of male clothes lie on the couch and floor, along with several pieces of clothing that look like sports bras and tight tank tops. An assortment of flashy tennis shoes sits neatly in a row. No doubt Jordy's doing with his love of name-brand shoes and fashion.

"Yeah, well. You tell me a lot of shit. It all goes in one ear and out the other." Jordy laughs again when I shoot him a look. He waves a hand. "All right, you ready for this, Olivia?" He mocks the way he says my name, slowing it down until I'm rolling my eyes. "Or should I say, Oliver?" He raises a brow when I flip him off.

If there's one thing about Jordy I love, it's his sense of humor. Ten seconds ago, we were crying our eyes out in the bathroom. And now, we're barely suppressing our smiles. He has this air about him that lifts the dark clouds hanging over my head, making sunshine appear.

"Oliver," I mutter, shaking my head. "So, I'm guessing these are my clothes."

"Yup! Jonathan asked me to bring you some clothes. So, I went shopping on his dime." He lifts a shoulder.

"Jesus, what did you buy? The entire store?" I start rifling through the piles of t-shirts, long sleeve shirts, nice button downs, baggy jeans, boxers, briefs, and everything I could possibly need.

"You know what? You're unappreciative of my fashion choices." He sniffs haughtily, lifting his nose in the air. "But yeah, I went to a men's clothing store and bought your size in everything." He grins. "It was fun."

"You and I have a different definition of fun," I grumble, standing tall. As a teenager, I loved clothes. Colors. Hell, even fashion trends. Nothing made me happier than dragging Hux, JJ, or Mack into a shopping mall and buying new outfits. Now, though? I loathe it. I'd rather buy something online and have it shipped to me. "But thank you, Jordy. I can only imagine what Jonathan would have bought me to wear." I wrinkle my nose.

"Probably something hideous. Pfft." Jordy promptly rolls his eyes with a huff. "Now, try on all these and we'll see if they fit you."

I wrinkle my nose. "For real? You want me to try on all the clothes?" *What a nightmare.*

"How else are you supposed to know how they fit? Besides, we have to try these, too. Can't have your girls peeking out from under your clothes and giving away your identity, now can we?" He raises a brow while holding up a piece of clothing that resembles a sports bra and a tight tank top. "No more titties for you. We have to hide those luscious pillows away with these binders, which are awesome as fuck, by the way." They are. He's not lying. It gives individuals a chance to live their lives the way they see it in their minds.

I lick my lips. "Fuck. I hadn't thought about that. And stop referring to my tits as luscious pillows!" I toss a hand out, earning a grin.

"But where is the lie?" He chuckles when I throw a fancy shoe at him, and he ducks. "Missed me!" he taunts, laughing when I huff. "Now, drop the towel, Livy. And show me the goods." He wiggles his brows, but I know he doesn't mean it. The number of times we've seen each other naked is... Well, it's a lot. Too much, actually. If I have to see Jordy's dick again, I might go blind.

"Okay, fine. Give me some underwear..."

"Boxers, Liv. Jesus. You'd think you'd know the terminology by now," he jokes, tossing two packages of boxers and briefs at me, and I catch them. "You're lucky you have me to teach you my manly ways."

"First off, Ew. Your manly ways? I'll pass. Secondly, I only had a sister and a mother growing up," I scoff. I don't mention the absent father who never taught me a damn thing except what darkness feels and looks like.

"Well, then you're in the right place," Jordy says with a chuckle, taking a seat on the couch with a sigh. He spreads out while sitting back with an expectant look. "Now, clothing montage. Choppity chop!" He claps his hands a few times, earning a glare.

"I'll choppity chop you," I growl, whipping my towel off and throwing it at his face.

"That's more like it! I like spicy Liv," he chuckles, leaning his head back and staring up at the ceiling. "Just let me know when you're decent."

I shake my head, holding out the black binder between my fingers. This is it. A transformation into someone new. My fingers brush against the tight fabric and over the stitching. I swallow hard as I stretch the material, noting how it almost fights me to stay tight and compress.

Good.

Without over thinking, I pull it over my head, fight to get it over my breasts, and suck in a breath when I look down. My breasts are flat, held into the tight material that takes my breath away. It's compact against my ribs, making it hard to pull in oxygen. But I do. The more I pull in, the more comfortable I get. I know it'll be an adjustment.

I feel like Mulan, preparing for war. Shedding my identity and becoming someone else to fight the good fight. Except, she did a better job than I'm going to do. She was a true warrior. Me? I'm just a girl, numbly becoming someone else for the sake of my case and bringing down the bad guys.

For the next hour, I try on a ridiculous amount of clothes. Jordy critiques everything, showing me how to walk, talk, and even gesture like a man. It's… something and a lot to learn. Essentially, I have to turn Olivia off and give Oliver free rein.

Talk about a difficult task. How am I supposed to erase twenty-two years of habits in a single day? The answer? I can't.

"I'm a text away, Liv," Jordy suddenly says, grabbing my upper arm, turning serious. "Okay? If bad things happen, if you want me to help you bury those bastards' bodies, I'm there.

Understood?" He squeezes my arm slightly until I nod. "I won't tell Jonathan anything, either. Those guys? Nooo, they disappeared!" He cracks a watery smile, displaying the raw emotions filtering past his goofy facade.

"I love you too, Asshole," I softly say until he lets me go with one nod.

We have a few hours before we have to check out of the hotel and make our way to Greenwood University so I can start my case.

"All right. I got your clothes there." He points to two large duffel bags that are tightly packed with my newly acquired wardrobe. "And some, you know, extras in there." He winks at me, pointing to another duffle bagged shoved full, looking as if it came straight from our shared Veritas room.

I frown, staring at it hard until realization slams into me. "You didn't..." I accuse. Horror crashes over me, locking up every muscle in my body.

I can tell by the grin on his damn face that he rifled through everything on my side of the room and packed everything he could think of.

Including my damn vibrators.

"Jonathan said to pack anything you might find useful. And I think orgasms are very useful. Good for anxiety and depression and..." he trails off when he notices my heat-filled cheeks and frown. "What? You don't think I know when you diddle the devil's button? Your vibes aren't as quiet as you think they are," he scoffs, rolling his eyes. "Neither are your moans," he grumbles, shivering in disgust.

I toss my hands in the air. "The devil's button? For fuck's sake. I don't listen to you when you slather your fucking snake. Ugh!" I pinch the bridge of my nose, huffing several times. Although, I'm embarrassed as hell that he's heard me reach climax, it's not a bad idea to have those around. "Thanks for the toys." I cringe. "I think." I shake my head. I need a damn good distraction before we take off. "I need to read more about this damn case before I go anywhere." And I'd rather not discuss my vibrators anymore or think about Jordy's dirty paws all over my things.

"Well, when you find them in your bag, you'll be very pleased with me. Just remember my name when you play." I glare at him. "Fine! You need to study your case more, and I'll study mine. Which is boring, if you ask me." He plops back onto the couch, pulling out a wad of papers, and flattens them on his lap. "Ugh. Art thief. How did they do it? No one knows," he trails off, muttering about his case and whining. "Nobody cares. Nobody knows their name or what they look like. How am I supposed to find a damn ghost that surveillance cameras can't even pick up? It's bullshit." He pouts more, studying his own case, which doesn't seem to have a lot of information for him to go on.

I sigh, reaching for the envelope Jonathan left me, filled with everything I'll need to know, and start studying my backstory, name, and everything in between, over and over again until it's memorized.

After what seems like hours, the words on the page melt together as my mind wanders to the psycho who attached a damn tracker to me. Mal. Malic. Whoever he is, there's something about him that feels so familiar to me, but I can't put my finger on it. Maybe it's his association with Wilder and whatever he's into. Shivers roll down my spine as phantom fingers roll over my cheeks and down my neck.

God. I must be fucked up to want another round with him.

I shake my head. For fuck's sake, Liv. He put a tracker on you. For what? Stalking? Trafficking?

I don't know.

All I know is, I should steer clear of him. Which won't be a problem now. He has no idea that I didn't leave town. Or that I'm Oliver now. I barely resemble the girl he met at the bar.

I hope.

Looking around, I take stock of the hotel room I'm about to leave behind. I came here as Olivia Viotto–Agent Seven with Veritas. Now, I'm leaving as Oliver Davenport in my baggy clothes, bound chest, and new identity.

"All right, let's roll out, Liv. Time to meet your roommates." I stiffen at Jordy's words.

My face drops immediately. "Wait! Roommates? I can't have roommates!" I don't remember reading that in the briefing. In fact, I know it wasn't there in words.

That means only one thing.

Jordy, the little shit, knew this entire time and decided now was the perfect time to drop that little bomb.

Asshole!

The knowing grin Jordy gives me has ice rolling through my veins. "Welp. We have a lot to discuss. In the car. Check out is in like five minutes. I mean, we could stay and make Daddy Jonathan pay for another night." He grins, stopping short at the door to look over his shoulder at me, grinning more. If that's possible. "Or you could move into your dorm. The quicker you take those douchebags down. The quicker you can come back home to our lovely room in the bunker."

Home.

What is home exactly?

Home is a safe space. Somewhere you can crawl into when you're sad, stressed, happy, crying, or any sort of emotion in between. The four walls of your home witness every aspect of you. The tears. The laughs. The freak outs.

And it protects you from the harsh outside elements of the world.

A home is foreign concept to me. A place I never had with my parents. The only home I ever knew was with the three boys who I gave myself to. Home to me was never four walls. It was human beings who would have given the shirts off their backs for me.

The only house I've ever had was here in Greenwood. A small three-bedroom ranch on Franco's property. Given to us when we had nowhere else to go and only had him as an ally. It was the place the Viottos sent us when my father attempted to oust his brothers from their leadership positions.

"Make the deal with Franco and bring him into an alliance with the family, and you can work your way back to Viotto status," Uncle Gabriel *spits, sneering at his brother, my father, as we kneel before the four Viotto brothers.*

Each one looks more disgusted than the next. Uncle Remiel shakes his head, his long, dark hair swaying with the motion.

"You need to prove to us that you can be useful," Remiel's *voice dips low as he twiddles his thumb, earning a glare from* Gabriel, *who begs for control.*

"More than useful, Rem!" he shouts, tossing a hand. *"He tried to take us out and take what's ours..."*

"He should be put to death then," Uncle Michael *scoffs. "If he is such a big threat to us, then why allow the man and his family to continue breathing? We've already let one brother slip between our fingers after leaving us for the fucking military and law. Jonathan shouldn't be breathing and neither should Raph."* He raises a brow when Mama gasps but refuses to lift her eyes to the men standing above us in the basement of a church in Briar Cove. It was the main hub of the Viotto family before they spread out, taking pieces of California to control.

"Because he can be useful," Uncle Samael curses. "Despite his fuck ups, Raph has proven he has determination..."

"Yeah, for himself," Michael scoffs again, shaking his head. "I have too much shit to do to be concerned with our little brother. Either kill him or send him to make this deal on our behalf and trust he won't take things for himself. Again."

"I'll do it," my father says slowly, getting to his feet with a grunt. He rubs at his cheek where a bruise forms from the rage his brothers rained down on him.

"There are no other second chances within the family. If you were anyone else, we would have put you the fuck down," Gabriel hisses, glaring at his brothers.

"I understand. The foolishness won't happen again." My father shakes his head slowly, looking at his four brothers in front of him with pleading eyes. A gesture he doesn't offer very often. Especially not to me or my mother.

I hold my breath when Michael reaches into his pocket, lifting his lip into a sneer. "See that it doesn't. The second you step a toe out of fucking line and betray us again, I'll put you down myself." With that, Uncle Michael walks up the stairs of the basement and is out of sight. No doubt retreating to his own territory.

"We're oddly putting our trust in you, Raph," Remiel mutters, lighting a cigarette and blowing out the smoke. "Think of Espie and Olivia."

My father briefly stares at our bowed heads. I swallow hard, quickly looking at the floor and counting the stones beneath my knees. We were instructed to not look up. No matter what.

"Yes. Them." The dismay in my father's voice nearly saws me into my soul and tears it in half. It's more than dismay. It's disgust. Hatred. He hates that he has to bring us along to wherever we're going. I feel it in my bones.

"Go on then. Franco is expecting you. You'll have a home on his property. Be a good soldier. Make the fucking connections *and align us with the most powerful man in Southern Califor-nia," Gabriel grunts, tossing out a hand.*

"And don't fucking fail us, baby brother," Remiel grunts, shaking his head. "We don't need any more fucking disappoint-ments from you."

The only place growing up I knew as home was here in this town. Then, it was taken from me. Just like the place before that when my father was exiled from Briar Cove and our family turned their backs on him for all the bullshit he did.

"You're sitting way too straight," Jordy snorts, slapping my thigh as we race through a red light at top speed, taking me out of my spiraling thoughts. "Firmer handshakes. Spread your legs more. Gotta accommodate your gigantic cock, Oli." I smack him on the chest for his stupid comment. "Umph fuck! I'm just trying to help, okay?" I glare at him, and he rubs his chest. "You'll have to learn how to lower your voice a little. You know what? Just pretend the world owes you something," he laughs at that, blabbering on as he continues driving like a goddamn maniac.

Talk about blending in and being a civilian. *Not.* I grunt, tossing his hand off me as I slide in my seat. The stinging burn makes my muscles tense as he laughs hysterically at my expense.

Bastard.

"Would you pay attention to the road and not me." I toss a hand, gesturing to the traffic in front of us, but he scoffs at me.

"Seriously, you're being too proper," he tsks, making a sharp turn near the entrance of the large campus that's morphed from a small-scale university to something massive. A place someone–AKA Franco–has put a lot of money into. The question still stands–why? Is it because more gangs are migrating here to learn? Form alliances? Fuck, my brain hurts thinking about it.

Coming close to campus a few nights ago in the dark of night didn't do this place justice. My jaw falls open at the sight of campus as we make our way down a long drive, leading to a large parking lot at the heart of it all.

"I got a map here somewhere," Jordy grunts, parking our borrowed SUV and searching around. "Fuck, here it is." He unfolds the large piece of paper, laying it over the steering wheel as he whistles, continuing to speak about what each building is. The truth is, he doesn't have to explain anything to me. I've snuck onto campus many times before with the guys before our friendship went up in flames.

Mack tosses an arm over my shoulders and pulls me close. People mill around the campus with cups in their hands, woohooing as they make their way to the first party of the year. The remnants of the August heat encapsulated us as we stand on the sidewalk outside the administrative building of campus.

"This is the heart of it all," Mack whistles in awe.

If there's anyone excited about higher education–it's him. He can't wait to start his career as a doctor, helping people and saving lives. It's all he's ever wanted to do since he was a kid.

"It won't be long until we're all here together." JJ stands beside me with his hands in his jeans pockets and a sense of wonder crossing his features. His dark eyes dart around, taking in the multitude of people celebrating their new lives with their degrees in hand and jobs on the horizon.

"One step closer to our new life," Hux says from behind us, leaning his head back, and staring at the stars illuminating the dark sky.

"Our new future," Mack agrees, squeezing my shoulder and gently kissing the top of my head.

Sometimes we sneak on campus since we live so close. It's always on nights we need a break from–well–our situation.

Life with Franco and his gang has become increasingly difficult, especially for the boys. Since high school graduation is a little more than a year away, he's increased their job load within the gang. Sending them out on different runs all over the state of California and even into the surrounding areas. They're picking up guns, drugs, and whatever else Franco asks of them.

"We've got a run this Wednesday," JJ mutters, looking at his phone with a frown. "To Nevada."

"Nevada?" I grumble as my shoulders slump.

I'm never allowed on their runs. In fact, my duties have dwindled into basically nothing. My father is away more, tending to the kid he decided to take under his wing, which is fine. I'd rather him not be present to torture us, but there's something in my gut that says something is wrong. Off.

"Fuck Nevada," Mack says with a grin, looking down at me with a sparkle in his blue eyes. "Let's party the night away, okay? We'll celebrate their graduation and then, we'll plan the future."

But the future never came, not after that night. We drank, danced, and had the time of our lives until we stumbled back to their mansion, tripping over our feet and laughing.

It was one of the last times we spent with each other.

My heart breaks as I continually stare at the large brick building sitting two hundred yards in front of us—the administrative building—the heart of campus. It's an old and weathered brick building touched by years of use. Green vines climb up the side of it, and a massive grassy courtyard stretches out in front of it, like the lawn of a palace.

Jordy looks up from the map in awe, sitting silently for one golden minute. But his silence never lasts too long.

"Jesus, Livy. This place is wild!" He whoops with excitement. "Remind me, I need to come to a party or two. Hell, I can become roommate number five. Fuck my assignment. I need a damn vacation, anyway." He babbles on and on, filling the vehicle with his words.

I glare in his direction, peering at him through the glasses perched on my nose. My jaw tightens, and my teeth clench. It would be a terrible idea to punch him square in the nose for being a nuisance. Right? I mean, it would definitely make him shut his trap for one second and stop that awful nickname from leaving his tongue.

Worth it? Possibly.

Jordy wrinkles his nose, staring at my hardened face. "What? Don't give me that look. You need to loosen up, Liv. Live a little and don't look so constipated all the time. It's very unbecoming of you," he quips, earning a smack on the shoulder. "Fine. Keep your face like that and see if I care." He rolls his eyes as he folds the map up and tosses it at me with a huff. "You need to spread your legs." I side-eye him, and he smirks. "Not in the sexy way. Take up the whole seat and slouch for God's sake," he gripes, pushing me down into the passenger's seat and forcing me to slouch.

God. He babbles way too damn much. Someone needs to shut him up. So, I volunteer as the person to do it, seeing as it's just me and him.

"Stop," I groan, pushing him away with a huff. "I'm fine!"

"Yeah, you think you're fine until they find you out because you're not man-spreading everywhere," he snorts, side-eyeing me as he slumps back in his seat.

My heart beats out of my chest as I lean forward. People swarm the vast campus, unloading heavy moving boxes from their cars and pulling suitcases behind them. They chatter with one another, hugging after being away for so many months. They're smiling, ecstatic to be back after so long.

"Seriously. When I go to sit down, I just spread my legs and take up as much space as I can," Jordy yaps endlessly, attempting to make me just like him.

I snort, dragging my gaze from the student body wandering the parking lot, and bring myself back to the conversation. It's something Jordy has been trying to pound into my skull since last night.

Do this. Do that. It'll make you more believable. It'll help your disguise.

"Typical fucking you," I quip, earning a wink from him.

"You ready for this? Damn." He leans forward, his mouth hanging open and practically drooling. "I wish I could go to real college. You're the lucky one. All I got was a degree behind the screen." His eyes light up as people walk by.

More specifically, a woman with a short skirt floating in the wind and no panties on. Damn. Go her. I wish I had her confidence to pull that off. She looks stunning and…. I tilt my head when she grins in our direction, connecting her gaze with mine. My cheeks heat when she giggles and quickly turns to a friend beside her, whispering something behind her hand. But her eyes find mine again.

"Damn, I think she likes you," Jordy mutters, slumping in his seat. "You'll give me the hook up, right?" He wiggles his brows. "Unless you want her, of course." He puts his hands up in defeat, continually grinning at me.

"Ugh. I tried to get Jonathan to let you take my place here, but he said no," I practically pout, peeling my gaze away from the people milling around campus.

I need to focus on this conversation before we step out of the vehicle and I'm forced to face my new reality as Oliver.

"Only you can do this, Liv. I wouldn't have a clue how to navigate through those douchebag's gangs and initiations and shit. That's a *you* territory." He grins, looking at a girl who bends over to get something from the back of her vehicle. Fucking perv. "You know, I'm supposed to leave here and go straight to my new case, but damn, staying is tempting." He wiggles his damn brows. "You should be looking, too." He slaps my shoulder. "Be a little suspect if you don't check out some more ass. You already have one chick who can't keep her eyes off you." He grins, waving at the girl through the windshield.

"Would you stop!" I hiss, pulling his hand down. My cheeks heat again when the girl giggles, but finally moves on past our vehicle, only turning to look at us once over her shoulder. "Maybe Oliver isn't into that," I huff, trying to calm my nerves. "Maybe he's not into anyone." I quirk a brow, attempting to take my eyes off the massive crowd of people.

But I can't.

They could show up at any moment and be unpacking their cars and moving into the dorms. Fuck. I need to reread my instructions and the information Jonathan left for me.

"Eh, it's a possibility." Jordy shrugs. Not taking his eyes off the woman bent over and picking up boxes. He grins more, shaking his head. "I'm so damn jealous. I want this!"

"So, you said I'd have roommates?" I ask, pushing my glasses up my nose with a huff.

I've really got to get used to wearing glasses again for this mission. Not to mention, I'll have to charge these discreetly every night while I'm sleeping so they're ready to record all my activities the next day. It's weird to think that someone in the agency gets to see my movements.

"Oh, right. Yeah. Roommates. Three, I think. Here, it's all in here," he says, shoving a new manila envelope into my lap. "I'd read it before we get up there. It'll probably be chaos." I glare at him. He did this on purpose to see the look on my face. It would have been nice to have gotten it before now. Like with my regular packet of briefings. But nooooooo. Jordy is a dick.

Chaos? This was already chaos. In fact, my entire life has been nothing but pure chaos. Why should this be any different? Especially with Jordy involved.

I flip through the pages quickly, examining the layout of my dorm room. Yup. Three roommates. All male. And only two bedrooms. And one tiny bathroom to share between the four of us. Wonderful.

"Ugh," I groan, rubbing my forehead. "How am I supposed to function if I have someone literally sleeping in my room with me?" AKA, how am I supposed to be able to relax and let my guard down? Or my tits out. These bindings are uncomfortable around my breasts. It's made to last me a day at most. Not through the night and twenty-four-seven. I'm not large chested by any means, but damn. The ladies got to breathe, and they aren't able to breathe right now.

"Just take extra-long showers, Liv. They won't suspect a thing. It's what we guys do to play with ourselves or whatever without interruptions." Jordy continues to grin, watching women and men walk by with interest. "You ready to move in?" Only then does he look at me, eyeing me up and down.

"I'm going to just gloss over the fact you admitted you tame your snake in the shower." He grins at me and shrugs. "Can we just… chill for a second," I say, putting a hand up and letting my head fall against the headrest with a sigh.

I need a minute to collect myself. A minute to process what the hell is happening. A minute to fully immerse myself in my new role.

Oliver.

"I don't mind chilling. The scenery is chef's kiss," he groans, falling back into the seat with a sigh, looking over at me with a critical eye. "Tell me what's going through your wicked mind, Liv?"

Everything. That's what.

The weight of this case and what's to come claw at me. Relentless. Sharp. Tearing through me and dragging me into the darkness of what-ifs.

And my mind?

It won't stop spiraling into the deep abyss. Flashing with the memories of their smiles, now twisted into something cruel.

Something malevolent. No longer the boys I grew up with and loved, but monsters walking among us.

"Everything," I fully admit.

He may give me shit and talk a big game, but Jordy has a piece of me. Like I have a piece of him. Platonically, of course.

"Wanna elaborate?"

I shake my head. No. I don't want to elaborate. My thoughts are too chaotic right now to truly answer. A darkness is seeping into me and dragging me down, kicking and screaming. Like the first time we entered this town and I knew this was the gateway to something new. Whether it was bad or good, I didn't know.

Now, I do. And it's happening all over again. The same bad omen resurfaces, letting me know I won't make it out of this mission unscathed.

"Eh, suit yourself. When you do want to tell me more, just ring-a-ling-a-ding me."

I whip my gaze to him, and he grins. "You're an idiot." I can't help the laugh that escapes me.

This is why he's my best friend. No one else in the world could pull me from the edge of a cliff like he can.

"Meh. An idiot you seem to love." He shrugs.

I scoff, avoiding his probing eyes. I opt for the swaying trees in the summer breeze, moving through Greenwood. Everything is shiny and beautiful here. Flowers planted. Mature trees. Green vines growing up the side of the buildings.

It's picturesque.

Silence engulfs the vehicle as more people come and go. Moving vehicles, large vans, small cars, and any sort of transportation pull through, unloading students and their belongings. Parents cry over their babies and then send them on their way.

"One day, My Liv. You will go to college and make your mama proud." She grins at me from across the small, round dining room table. *"Live the life you were meant to live."*

Sadness takes her over, and I know exactly what she's talking about.

"I will." I nod in agreement, biting into her famous dish. Something her mama made for her, and she makes for me.

That was always my plan. Go to college. Get an education and move far away from the mafia life. But my father always had other plans. Arranged marriage, for one. An alliance to keep me under control and a way to get back into his brother's good graces by marrying me off and solidifying everything with Franco and his brothers. It was a win-win for him. Killing two birds with one stone. If I married who my father told me to marry, I would be on the inside with Franco. And by being in with Franco, the Viotto brothers could align with him and make a deal for land, properties, and beyond.

I was the key to my father's future kingdom. Well, until the inevitable happened and it all fell apart.

A part of me thinks my father had a massive back up plan and that's why he hasn't shown his face in five years.

I guess that's another mystery for me to unravel at a later date when I've taken care of everything on campus.

Despite my plans going off the rails, I made it out of the life. But paid for it with my death. But this? Being in Veritas, an organization hellbent on taking down the bad guys, is where I was needed all along. It's my duty. My life. I wouldn't trade it for the world.

Even if it means being here. In my new-found hellscape.

The sun slowly moves in the sky as the parking lot empties, and more people come through. The air conditioning blows over my flesh, cooling it from the summer heat sizzling on the outside. If I could, I'd stay inside this SUV forever. I'd hide away from the world and pretend this wasn't happening to me.

How will I ever survive the ticking time bomb counting down in the back of my brain? Seeing them is inevitable. I know it will come. But if I hide away, can I avoid it forever? I don't know if my heart can break all over again just by seeing their faces. It's already held together loosely by duct tape and sheer determination.

What will be the final straw?

My eyes scan the large quad spread out before us. Lush greens. Colorful flowers. Tall trees. And people everywhere. Mostly students enjoying the sunshine on blankets with snacks and drinks, conversing with their friends after settling into their dorms. Several students toss a football around. Others throw a bright blue frisbee, laughing when it lands in the lap of a girl who shrieks.

My gaze continues to scan the horizon, stopping on crowds of people expectantly with my heart in my throat. Every look is another step in their direction. My skin feels overly tight and itching with anticipation.

I know it's about to happen before my eyes zero in on them. Like a sixth sense. The hairs on my arms stand on end. Oxygen halts in my lungs. Three familiar—yet so different—men walk through the middle of the quad. The sun seems to shine directly on them—a guiding light in the darkness of my mind.

They've changed so much. Gotten taller. Darker. More dangerous looking.

White hot rage boils through my veins at the mere sight of them. Walking around so normally. This is the life they've been able to lead. Living it to the fullest on the Greenwood U campus. I bet they fulfilled every promise they whispered in my ear. Except it was for themselves instead of me.

"We'll run away together. After college," Hux whispers directly in my ear. *"This will be our domain."*

"We'll get set for life." Mack grins, staring out at the campus with a beer in his hand. *"We'll get an education on Daddy's dime and then…"* he mockingly holds out the word daddy.

"We'll bolt," JJ offers softly from beside me. His big golden brown eyes taking in the crowds of college students.

"Promise?" I ask, grinning.

"2-2-4, Trouble," Huxley mumbles, kissing my temple affectionately.

"Hux! Oh my God!" A female voice rings out drunkenly, slurring. "You're here!"

I wrinkle my nose, stiffening under the weight of his arm over my shoulders. I try to pull away, but he doesn't allow me to. In fact, JJ and Mack move closer, encircling me protectively.

"Amanda." Huxley's voice comes out rigid and uninviting.

Amanda. Their biggest fan. A politician's daughter oozing privilege and entitlement. Oh, and she hates me. So, that's a plus.

She grins, tossing her blonde locks over her shoulder. "I'm so glad to see you guys made it!" She doesn't bother acknowledging my existence. It's fine, though. Because I'd rather vomit lava than say hello to her.

Shivers work through me at the memory. It's been happening so much lately. Those tiny slices of our history resurfacing out of nowhere.

Only this time, it's because of them. They're so close for the first time in five years. Physically near. My body feels it. Reacts at the sight of them. My soul reaches for them; despite the damage they've done to it. They darkened it. Betrayed it. Yet, it betrays me, seeking old comforts.

But I won't let it.

There's too much rage living within me to ever consider them again. I'm here on a mission to bring them down.

I can't peel my eyes away. It's like a train wreck at full speed, crashing into me with every damn emotion.

My fingers curl into fists. Jordy shifts beside me, following my gaze. Redness tints his cheeks, and his eyes narrow dangerously tight.

"That's them?" he says through a rushed breath, filled with a rage I haven't heard from him before. He's mostly butterflies and unicorns. Using his humor to deflect from the pesky emotions bubbling up inside him.

But right now? There's murder in his tone and promise in his eyes.

" Yup," I breathe, unable to say anything else.

It's them.

Huxley smiles at JJ, who tucks his hands into his jeans pockets with a familiar, shy smile. He was always so reserved, hiding everything from the outside world. Not me, though. I broke through his trauma. He was mine. My broken boy. And I, his broken girl.

JJ's dark eyes lift slightly as he shakes his shaggy brown hair out of his eyes. Long ago, he wore black-rimmed glasses, but they're nowhere in sight. Maybe he finally graduated to contacts.

Or…maybe I shouldn't care.

I shake my head. That's a thing of the past. I am dead in their eyes. No one. And they shouldn't elicit so many weird feelings that burst inside me. It's like my soul remembers the good times we had. The promises that were made. The small touches. The laughs. The everything we were to each other.

But my mind remembers almost every detail of their deception.

It's hard to process a betrayal when the ones responsible were held on a pedestal for so long. They were my protectors in the storms, hiding me from my father's rage and my mother's incompetence—until that image shattered like a statue crumbling to the ground and disappearing forever.

Mack frowns. A frown he never wore before. It ages him. Making him into a darkened figure filled with hate. Mack was always happy-go-lucky despite his circumstances. He felt relief when the state took him away from his mother, and he found himself in the Franco household. From there, he learned to become valuable to his new foster dad and became a permanent fixture by Hux's side. His bright blue eyes shined brighter. His smile grew wider. Happiness had found him once and for all.

"I'm serious about my promise," Jordy growls, pulling up the front of his shirt and revealing a handgun resting in his pants. "I have my long-range in the back. They'll never know what hit them." Rage fills his light eyes to the brim, darkening them with his promise. "I can drive two miles from here and still hit my mark."

I know he's not joking. Jordy is the best shot we've got. Well, besides me, of course. He's taken down people from further away, which shouldn't be possible. He's an asset. But don't ever tell him that, it'll go straight to his big head and he'll never let me live it down.

I quickly grab his arm as he reaches back with the intention of doing as he says. I squeeze him until he stops and blinks up at me through a red haze.

"Not here." I shake my head. "They don't deserve a quick exit." It deserves to be slow and agonizing, like what happened to me.

Karma will get them. That's for sure.

Jordy mulls my words over before slumping in his seat when he realizes I'm right. His gaze never leaves the men conversing with the group of girls. So full of life. Laughing. Breathing.

Do they ever think about me? And what they did to me? Or do they go to bed each night with a clear conscience, laughing at my naive expense?

I watch with bated breath as the girls walk away from them with smiles on their faces. Once out of sight, the three men stand shoulder to shoulder, crossing their arms over their muscular chests and eyeing the campus like Gods lording over their subjects.

Everyone who passed by waves at them. Men. Women. Even the parents seem to know them.

Huxley's eyes scan the parking lot with a flat expression.

Taking everything in like he was taught to do. A perfect soldier for Franco. He stands tall. Shoulders pulled back and ready for anything. The longer strands of his brown hair blow in the slight breeze, drifting across his forehead, while the sides are shorter, nearly shaved. From here, I can't see the gleam in his moss-green eyes. The same gleam I came to know well as a teenager whenever he was plotting something dangerous or fun.

There's a harder edge to Hux. Like Franco successfully molded Hux into the man he always wanted him to be. A leader. A fixture of his gang.

I hold my breath when he scans our SUV intently, taking it in and reading our license plate. Heat bursts up my neck and onto my cheeks until he moves on to the next vehicle full of people.

It's a good thing this is a rental, under false identities.

Once I regain my breath, I can't help but trace the multitude of tattoos etched onto his flesh. As a teenager, they fascinated me. He loved the pain of the tattoo machine on his skin. Ached for it.

"Did it hurt?" I whisper, running my finger over the colorful daisy resting on his bicep.

Hux smirks, lazily running his index finger up my thigh as we rest on the floor of the treehouse, watching as the sun sets in the distance and bathing the world in a hue of pink and orange, tainted by the storm clouds hovering above them and snuffing out the light. A cool breeze comes through the windows, spreading goosebumps down my flesh as the rain begins to fall, pelting the roof of our treehouse.

"They always hurt."

"Then why get them?" I whisper, staring up into his moss-green eyes.

"Because the pain is worth the beauty," he whispers before capturing my lips with his in a slow kiss and embrace as thunder rumbles around us, and I cling to him tightly. "We'll weather any

storm, Trouble," he says, gripping me tight and forcing my gaze to his.

Even when I want to cower away from the lightning spiking across the sky.

Fuck.

I squeeze my eyes shut, hoping to break the spell of watching them. I need to get my wits about me and fucking pay attention for our mission. Not fall victim to the past that's lingering beneath the shadows of my brain, striking me down. I need to keep my head above water. I can't keep falling into memories headfirst and remembering who they were. They showed me who they truly were under the masks they wore that night when they set me on fire and ended my existence.

"I really want to strangle those fuckers," Jordy grunts, pushing a hand through his hair. "I'm going to go rogue one of these days, Liv. Find out where they're staying and just fucking obliterate them." He shakes his head, bringing me back to the car and away from the three murderers waltzing around campus.

I lick my lips, watching as they walk away, weaving between the buildings. Presumably to move into the frat they occupy on campus. As for information on them, that's as far as I know.

That'll be a major focal point of my job. Getting close to them again and securing information.

What a joy.

"Let me do my job," I say. "Let me bring them to justice."

Justice is a fickle word. My justice or Veritas'? Which do they deserve? Prison time? Or punishment for what they did?

It's a toss-up.

"Fine," Jordy grumbles, slamming a hand into the steering wheel. "I'll give you that. Your face is the last thing they should see when you finally take them down and throw them in prison forever. Or better yet, in an unmarked grave. I'll have the popcorn ready."

He's right.

OLIVIA

"Okay, now I'm not so envious," Jordy chortles, hiding his laughs behind his palm. Fucker. "Uncle could have at least put you up in an apartment or something. God, you have to share a bathroom." He gives me the side-eye, smirking when I huff. "And there's only one." In this part, he sing-songs, mocking my entire existence. I discreetly flip him off.

Uncle. It's our code word for Jonathan when we're surrounded by civilians. No one will ever know that Jordy and I aren't true cousins. In our hearts, I guess we are. Family where it counts.

My nose wrinkles. The room is small. Well, smaller than I thought it would be. I guess I expected more than this. It's about the size of a damn jail cell. Okay, maybe a little bigger than that. Only slightly, though. It just feels like a jail cell. A punishment I didn't ask for.

After seeing my three exes out in the courtyard, my adrenaline hasn't stopped spiking. It's like, that at every turn, I expect them to be there and ready to hurt me again.

They won't. I'm dead in their eyes.

This will be home for the next few months. Or less, if I can help it. The faster I bring those idiots to their knees and eliminate

Franco's empire, the quicker I can go back to the bunker with my vibrators in peace.

My eyes gaze around the room, adjusting to the new glasses perched on my nose.

"Make sure you take off your glasses before you get into the shower," Jordy quips, shivering. "That way, no one has to see all that." He points to my body with a fake layer of disgust.

Asshole.

"You sure you don't want to see the goods?" I quip back, pushing at his shoulder.

"As if. I got my fill today." He winks before dodging another hit to his shoulder and laughs. "But you know it's not me who looks at the footage. That's all on IT, and they're hornballs who would give their left nut to get a glimpse of..." He looks me up and down, pursing his lips.

"Duly noted. I won't take my glasses into the bathroom with me." I shiver in disgust at the thought of our IT department getting a glimpse of my goods. Fuckers.

Two twin-sized beds occupy the space, located on opposite sides of each other against the walls. They are accompanied by two desks, chairs, and two sets of dressers—one for me and one for my roommate. One small storage closet rests behind me for everything else.

Male fucking roommate. Ugh. I want to whine about it. I've already lived with Jordy before. And it's a goddamn nightmare. Case in point, touching my damn vibrators. Am I thankful they're in my possession? Yes. But when the hell am I going to be able to use them? In the damn closet? The bathroom that I share?

I need to invest in silent vibrators, because at this rate, I won't get another orgasm unless I dress as Olivia and march myself back to that bar in hopes of finding Mal.

Wait. No. God, brain, why? We don't want that psycho! He put a tracker on you and wanted to live in your closet. God only knows what he really wanted to do. Take my skin? Probably. But damn, getting down and dirty with him was so needed.

Internally, I shake my head. No way in hell will I ever let that happen again.

Maybe.

Okay, fine. If he and I met in a bar again, I'd let him fuck me in the bathroom and then buy me nachos or something. Fuck. I really need to stop chasing dangerous men. It's a part of my DNA or something. Case in point–my ex-boyfriends.

My gaze slips across the hall, where voices ring out, talking lowly to one another. Two more men move around the other dorm room in our suite, across the hall from us. We are only separated by a small living space with a couch, TV, and a small kitchenette. It's almost like apartment living, but not quite. And my worst nightmare: There's only one bathroom between the four of us, located off the living space.

One bathroom. This is a goddamn tragedy. How will I hide myself if I have to share?

I'm going to kill Jonathan, after all.

I shake my head. "This is where I die," I grumble sarcastically to Jordy, who continues to gape at my newest living situation. I thought living with him and his bad habits and horrible aim was bad. Seriously, how hard is it for a sharp-shooter to aim his dick into the large porcelain bowl? Now, I have three strangers to contend with. Three strangers with dicks.

Yay for me.

"That's impossible," chimes in a male voice filled with joy as he skips into the room. His dark eyes take us in as his fingers twirl the small hoop lip ring pulling at the edge of his lip, and he physically lights up at the sight of us.

The grin that stretches across his face gives me a sense of reassurance. If there's one thing I know how to do, it's read people. There's always a tell in their expressions or hidden in their eyes. Some people know how to mask it well, but others not so much.

This guy? He seems harmless. For now, at least.

Everyone's a suspect in my eyes.

"What's impossible?" I ask before I think in my own voice, earning a head tilt from him. Fuck. I have to get used to speaking in a lower octave than my normal voice. Easier said than done.

Thankfully, he doesn't react to my slip-up, but Jordy elbows me, hard. *Way to stay inconspicuous, douchecanoe.*

"Didn't you read the living arrangements rules?" my new roommate says, holding out his hand. "I'm Simon. Si. Whatever you want to call me. I live in that room." He gestures to the identical room across from ours on the other side of the shared living room space.

"I'm Oliv—err—Oliver," I quickly correct myself and clear my throat, making sure my voice deepens this time. I take his hand firmly, shaking like Jordy reminded me to do before we got out of the SUV.

Jordy frowns. "Jordy," he says slowly, shaking Simon's hand. "I'm just the cousin. What's with the living rules?" He cocks his head like he doesn't know either.

Simon grimaces. "We have to live on campus this year. Either in the dorms, or we can rush the frats. But no off-campus living is allowed." He raises his brows. "Word on the street is because Greenwood is getting dangerous. It wasn't like this last year. I lived in an off-campus apartment last year. Now, pfft. We're all crammed into these dorms together." He rolls his eyes toward the ceiling.

"That's new," Jordy murmurs, so low only I can hear him.

I swallow hard, catching his gaze as Simon continues to talk about the rules. If Jordy didn't know the new rules about our dangerous campus, then did Jonathan have any idea, either?

If what Jonathan said was true, then Franco and his gang

have had their fingers dipped into academia. AKA this college. So, what makes it more dangerous this year?

"Interesting," Jordy says a little louder this time, rubbing his chin. "How are the frats? I'd love to visit my dear old cousin here and have some fun. Meet some ladies and gents. I'm not picky." Jordy grins mischievously, wiggling his brows.

Great. Jordy plans to make the drive and visit. He'll no doubt crash here at some point and probably try to christen my bed with his disgusting dick.

Ugh.

"Parties are fucking epic." Simon grins more. "I can definitely help show you around." His cheeks flush.

I blink several times as they continue their discussion, flirting relentlessly with each other until Simon gets called by a male voice, yelling for him from inside his room. I only get a peek at the man with shaggy blond hair and multiple sets of collared shirts before he disappears from view again.

"We'll talk later," Simon says, nodding his head at me and taking a few steps before stopping. "You're a transfer, right? A scholarship student?" I nod, curious how he knows. "Great. You and me? We're going to be great friends. And you..." He looks Jordy up and down with a suggestive look before sauntering off.

"Ohhh, I like him," Jordy whistles, watching him walk away. And I do mean watching him. His muscular ass, thighs, and calves. He can't take his eyes off the man.

That's the thing about Jordy. He doesn't care what sex you are. If he likes you, he likes you. He'll bang you, regardless. End of story.

I shiver. "Quit eye fucking my new roommate and help me..." I wave at my new dorm room.

"No can do, Oli." Ah, the new nickname has officially stuck and won't leave any time soon. Even after this mission is done, he'll call me Oli until I take my last breath, because it's a thousand times better than Livy. "I'll be making frequent visits.

Expect me soon." He grins, tossing my bag on my new bed near the second-story window overlooking the graveyard.

My graveyard.

How fucking poetic.

Now, every time I sit on my bed and look out the window, I'll see the reminder of where I could have been if I hadn't been miraculously saved. A window to the dead, buried deep in the dirt with nothing but a gravestone above them as remembrance.

I swallow hard, mechanically unpacking my clothes and setting them into the provided dresser. My gaze barely strays from the graveyard where my bones are supposed to be. But they're not. Someone else's are, though.

A cover to conceal my life. And it's worked for this long. No one questioned our closed casket services. Not even Franco, who pretended to show compassion to the community about our demise.

A tear slips down my aching cheeks as I look on from behind a tall oak tree swaying in the slight breeze. A dark veil covers my face and protects my burns from further damage. I can't believe this is happening.

"We really should get going, Olivia," Jonathan murmurs, standing at my back. "Our doctors are ready to examine you further." The moment he touches my shoulder, I flinch away, looking back at him in disbelief. "It's just me," he whispers, peering through my veil to look me in the eyes. I nod in response, returning my focus to the funeral being held directly at the cemetery. Three unremarkable caskets rest above their holes, ready to descend into the dirt and never see the light of day again.

"Espie, Olivia, and Sophia Viotto," Franco's voice rings out to the small crowd hovering around him. He stands tall in a tailored suit, more fitting for the casinos than here. His dark eyes scan the crowd, never straying to where we're hidden. "They were like family."

"Family my ass," I hiss through clenched teeth. "He killed

me! Them!" My fingers curl into fists, ready to punch that asshole where the sun doesn't shine.

But I'm too weak. Too hurt from the betrayal that is still fresh in my mind. And on my skin. I'm lucky Jonathan let me come here in the first place. I've only been out of the hospital for five hours.

"Deep breaths, Liv," Jonathan murmurs.

"He's a liar," I grunt, turning to face him as the funeral continues and Franco spouts his worthless speech. "We were never his family." Not ever.

His adoptive sons may have been something like family to me less than a week ago, but not now. Not ever again.

"He is a liar," Jonathan grits out, looking pissed on my behalf. "A lying cheat who abandons people when they are no longer purposeful to him." I stare up at him with furrowed brows as he loses himself in his words while glaring holes through Franco's head like Franco personally affronted him. "One day, our organization will come down on him and his empire. It's what he deserves." He shakes his head like he's clearing his thoughts. "But right now is not the time. It'll take years of patience and planning."

I swallow all the pain I have felt since I was rescued from my death by Jonathan when he pulled me from the flames. Turning on my heels, I force myself to commit this entire scene to memory.

Hux. JJ. Mack. Franco. They're all standing around, mourning the people they put into the ground with their devious actions.

They're unforgivable.

My lashes brush my cheeks several times when I finally shake myself out of the memory. Quickly, I wipe away the rogue tears glistening on my cheeks before Jordy can spot them as he shuffles around behind me, helping me unpack my bedding and pillows. Not that he'd call me out. He'd hug me within an inch of my life and then make fun of me for it. But if I'm not careful, I'll break character, and that can't happen in these circumstances. It's too risky to let anyone know who I am. Let alone what organization has come to investigate their campus and the people on it.

Jordy plops on my freshly made bed with a sigh, watching Simon from his spot with *that* look in his eyes. The–*I want to mount him*–look. I shiver, nearly puking at the thought. Gross. Picturing Jordy doing the deed is not on my to-do list. In fact, I think I need some brain bleach to remove that imagery. Forever.

"Don't ruin things with my damn roommate and make him hate me," I grit out, shoving his shoulder.

"Pish posh." Jordy waves a hand at me without looking up at me. "Why would anyone hate you because of me?" His head tilts as an easy smile crosses his lips. "I'm innocent."

I snort, pulling out my new phone and checking the time. I shake my head... "Innocent my ass. Don't you have your own thing to do? Like far away from here?"

"Eager to live the bachelor lifestyle?" he teases, getting to his feet. "Eh. I could hang out for the night. Maybe we can hit up a party or..." He sighs when his phone sounds in his pocket, blaring a siren ringtone, and his head drops back.

"It's Uncle, isn't it?" I give him a knowing smirk. Jonathan knows exactly what Jordy is like. Always dragging his feet and prolonging the inevitable. "I can't believe you assigned him the siren ringtone."

"Fucker is obsessed," he moans with frustration. "Fine. I'm leaving. You know the rules." His eyebrows shoot up, and he points a finger in my direction.

The rules of assignment. Check-in weekly, if not daily. Send briefs of findings through our secure network. Notify immediately if something has gone wrong. Leave for safety, if necessary.

It's all in a day's work.

"Of course I do."

Jordy grunts, throwing his arms around me and holding me tightly. "Call if you need me. Even if you don't. I'll miss you, Oli."

Dramatic asshole.

"Yeah, yeah. I'll miss you too," I say into his neck. "Now, go." I pull back, clearing my throat.

"Always eager to get rid of me." He rolls his eyes and pats my head before turning on his heels and exiting my room.

Of course, the horny bastard doesn't leave my dorm like he's supposed to. Nope. He stops by Simon's area across the hall just as Simon's roommate exits with a frown, hurrying out the door until it slams behind him.

I plop down onto my bed again, watching as they get closer and closer. I can't make out their conversation, but Simon blushes twice until Jordy steps back with a cocky smirk—no doubt planning something naughty for the future.

Eventually, Jordy leaves with a shit-eating grin and waving his phone as his last goodbye. Letting me know he swindled Simon's number from him. Poor Simon. Jordy's a *use them and lose them* kind of guy. He's always had regular hookups within the Veritas bunker, but that's the only time he keeps them around.

For now, I put everything I own away. Including my damn vibrators. Bastard. He really packed all three of them without blinking an eye. Ugh. Discreetly, I shove them into the back of my underwear drawer. Or should I say, boxer shorts drawer? And make sure they're buried deep. If anyone finds them, then I'm fucking screwed.

Why do you have vibes, Oliver?

I plead the fifth!

I shake my head as the weird scenario plays through my mind and dig deeper into my duffel bag. Who knows what Jordy decided to toss in there? He already packed away my orgasm givers. Why not a spare hand or body part?

So it shouldn't surprise me that when I reach the bottom of my bag, my fingers glide over smooth wood that forms the shape of a particular knife in a protective sleeve I've had stashed in my nightstand at the bunker.

"Jordy," I hiss to myself, shifting the large hunting knife into view and sighing. Attached to the end of the handle is a friendly handwritten note, written by the devil himself.

'Just in case you need to murder them.'

Right.

Just in case.

Just in case I need to put a damn knife through their hearts. He's so thoughtful, isn't he?

I blow out a breath, peeking over my shoulder. It's silent in the dorm right now, and I can't be sure who else is lurking around. So, I have to be careful about having a weapon on campus. Even if it's for my safety, no one can find it or I'm toast and the mission is up in flames.

Jordy may be a brat, but I know he has good intentions. It could be dangerous for me if anyone finds out I'm not Oliver. Especially if they find out I'm an undercover agent attempting to infiltrate their precious gangs.

With that in mind, I shove the knife under my mattress and settle it so it looks undisturbed. Hopefully, no one will look there. I'm sure their first guess would be the damn dresser where they would find a different kind of stabby thing. Whatever. With that taken care of, I claim my desk, setting my Veritas-sanctioned laptop into a drawer. If anyone found it, they'd think it was a typical laptop. There's nothing suspicious about it. Only if they opened it, accessed it through my multiple layers of passwords, and happened to know how to open our secure portal, would they be suspicious of me.

Of course, my laptop would immediately send me an alert

via my phone in a–*burn after reading*–type of message the moment it was opened by an unfamiliar face.

As I'm resting on my bed, lost in thought, someone else, presumably my new roommate, walks in with one box in his arms and a scowl on his handsome face. His large frame looms over me as his squared-jaw tics in annoyance at my presence. Angrily, he shoves his box on his bed and turns to me, squaring his shoulders.

His light eyes eat away at me, taking me in. His lips curl in disgust. "Stay away from my shit."

With that, he leaves as quickly as he came. Wonderful. He'll be a peach to room with.

"Yeah, well! Same to you!" I mumble sarcastically to his back as he retreats out of the dorm with another slam of the door.

Cool. Guess my new roommate is a real fucking peach.

AKA, a real jackass.

This will be a wonderful year.

HUXLEY

Something is coming. Something strange. It's in the air. A scent that floats on the breeze, tickling my senses. Like the scent of sweet rainwater flowing from the angry clouds twisting above us.

More rain? It's fucking odd for this time of year. Even in general. Thunderstorms aren't unheard of in our region, but they're far and few between. But lately? They've been occurring more often than not.

That means a storm is coming. In one way or another.

But what type of storm will it be? Rain? Hail?

I check over my shoulder, peering at the faces behind me, expecting to see a familiar one in the crowd. But it's only the other students, peeking through their eyelashes, aching to catch a glimpse of the kings of campus.

Us.

A title we've carved out for ourselves from the moment we stepped foot on campus our freshman year. The year Greenwood University became ours and the rules changed. For better or worse? I haven't figured it out yet.

"Things will be different this year," Franco says from the corner of his office overlooking the casino.

A crisp black suit molds to his frame, highlighting his muscles underneath. Neon lights flash through the window, painting his face in pinks and greens as the sounds of happy gamblers echo through the room. He turns on his polished heels, grinning victoriously.

My stomach churns. Something isn't right. College is our escape from it all. Him. This life. He insisted we get our degrees to further our family business, and so we are. But that grin on his chiseled face? It blares warning sirens in my mind.

"Yeah, they will! We're off to college," Mack agrees with a grin, excitement thrumming through him.

He's been ready to leave the nest for over a year and get Franco off our backs.

"About that." Franco points a finger at Mack, grinning more.

Yeah. There's something up his damn sleeve. Wonderful.

"We're still enrolled, right?" Mack asks cautiously, side-eyeing me like I might know something.

All the excitement and hope drains from him quickly. Mack was the most thrilled out of the three of us to get his degree, taking a step away from the life he was given. He's always wanted to do better for himself and put distance between himself and his mother's addictions.

I discreetly shake my head at Mack. Franco barely keeps me in the loop as it is. I have no idea where he's going with this.

"Two months ago, I made a sizable donation to Greenwood University. You're looking at one of the newest board members." He holds out his hands like a ta-da moment, like this is some sort of magic trick he's been hiding from us.

"Cool," Mack retorts with less enthusiasm.

"What's your angle?" I ask, cocking my head, knowing the bastard has something up his sleeve. A long time ago, Franco instilled his 'ask no questions, do as I say' policy. It was

hammered into our skulls the moment we started training under him and working for his cause.

But I've never been the kind of guy to follow the rules. Every step of the way—much to his annoyance—I question everything he does. Watch his every move, trying to figure out what's coming next. I want reasons and answers for his calculated steps. Sometimes I get a frown or a pop to the jaw. Other times, he gives me vague answers that satisfy my need to know.

Franco nods. "Don't you trust me?"

Not at all, but I don't say that out loud for him to hear.

Nothing he's ever done has proven we can trust him. He's put us through the ringer to become his heirs-in-waiting. Me more than JJ and Mack. They're more like my second-in-commands. Well, in Franco's eyes, anyway. They're my brothers. My best friends. We barely keep secrets from each other.

Franco raised me from the moment I was born. His wife brought me home swaddled in a hospital blanket, crying about how I had been abandoned and needed them to raise me. Her, more than him. When I was two, she died unexpectedly. I don't remember the specifics, and Franco never gives up the answers, but I know it was tragic. It sent Franco into a spiral, and he threw himself into his businesses, trying to expand, build, and grow.

The only sign that Mikayla Franco was ever alive is the pictures lining the walls of his office. She dreamed of filling her home with children's laughter but was unable to produce herself. So, to fulfill her wishes, Franco became a foster father, raising me, JJ, and Mack when we had no other place to go. Or them, more so. My origins are shady at best. Never knew who my real parents were or how I came to be.

"Greenwood University is the future," Franco says, shutting down my rampant thoughts. "I've taken the liberty of reaching out to other crime families, gangs, and criminals eager for a higher education. We'll be the premier university for master-

minds in the making. We'll offer courses for their benefit. And ours."

"Criminals?" Mack asks, twisting his expression. JJ, on the other hand, sits between us, studying Franco with a blank expression.

"You're wanting to create alliances?" JJ surmises, rubbing at his chin.

"Among other things," Franco says, not elaborating further. "Alliances. More opportunities. It'll be good for our economy and businesses. More money in our pockets. The return will be plentiful, and you boys will be the key to making this work."

"You want us to work with the other gangs coming?" JJ asks, tilting his head. "You want to create something bigger."

"Smart boy." He offers JJ a prideful grin. "Bigger and better than ever, boys. Imagine having feelers all over the globe. Allies who bring more money to our pockets." He raises his brows.

And more people under his thumb. He's not wanting allies. He wants playthings to manipulate and conquer. This is all a part of his chess game. He's strategically setting up pawns and kings until he can swoop in for the kill.

I can see it now. Our future of college freedom is gone. We'll be working and organizing shit under the other gang's noses. Spying on them, no doubt. If Franco has his fingers in the college board, then everyone else is already ten steps behind.

Including us.

"And what's the plan?" I ask, leaning back on the couch, feigning intrigue despite the lead filling my stomach with dread.

"Frat row has been dismantled, and those chapters have been sent packing. All five houses on Greenwood Ave have been assigned to the crime families who accepted our invitations. They get a free education for life, degrees, and a plethora of initiates to choose from in the student body. In return, I get money and alliances." The smirk lighting up his face as he reveals his master plan has goosebumps crawling up

my flesh. "This is a new future for Greenwood University. And us..."

And what a goddamn future he brought to Greenwood. Whatever his initial plan was for this place, it kicked off our freshman year. Exploded, more like it. The student body expanded. New classrooms, dorms, apartments, and libraries were built, expanding the campus to the edges of the properties, resulting in more land being bought and more shit being built.

Greenwood University boomed into a prestigious higher learning facility overnight. Everyone wants a piece of this place. It's the Harvard of our area. No one competes with us. We have the best sports team, filled with eager students ready for a win. The best in academics, earning multitudes of awards.

Greenwood University is the place to be. Too bad every person on the board of G.U. has a say in who enters this place and who doesn't. And their leader? Fucking Franco. So, you bet your ass he only picks the best criminals to bring here and offer them housing. Oh, and let's not forget the elites, as well. Governors. Mayors. Government officials. Movie stars. Models. You name it, he's allowing their children entry for a damn price. So, mix that in with the scholarship students that he hand-picks, too—it's a recipe for disaster. Not only have scholarship students been losing their lives or fleeing after a month's time here, but bodies have been piling up over the summer.

He's created the perfect scenario for himself. The perfect allies and soldiers can be recruited after they are vetted by us. His little sheep.

Fuck. I grind my teeth. We've never had issues with anyone on campus, except for a few run-ins here and there with other gangs, trying to show off. They never win, though. Neither do Malic and Wilder—our biggest fucking adversaries on campus. It's like their main purpose in life is to fuck with us and what we have. For whatever reason, it's like their mysterious boss came up with a checklist and put us at the top for them to knock around. It's been four years of this shit.

If it were up to us, we'd isolate ourselves from the masses. However, with Franco having eyes and ears on campus, we must play these parts perfectly.

"They found another body," JJ murmurs, putting his phone into his pocket. "Closer to the casino this time."

"Missing organs?" I ask, looking around the crowd again, making sure no one is paying attention to us. Not even Mack notices us huddling closer together.

"The whole nine yards. You don't think she…" He swallows a lump in his throat.

I shake my head. "Fuck, I hope not."

"Should we mention the body to Franco?" JJ's gaze shifts to me.

"He doesn't seem too concerned, but I'll shoot him a text."

Quickly, I pull out my phone and do just that. Not that Franco will care. If it's not harming his business, then he doesn't need to care. It's just another murder in his eyes. But there's something fishy about it all. Especially with the body of a student who showed up near the beginning of the summer.

"He should care. This is his damn territory. Doesn't he get suspicious of all the other families and gangs?" It's the same questions we've been asking each other since the bodies started appearing. Why isn't he more concerned? Does he not see it as the threat it is? Someone is stepping into our territory, taking our citizens, and butchering them for their organs. Each and every one that pops up is missing kidneys, hearts, livers, skin, and everything in between. It's fucking alarming.

"You would think," I huff, getting nothing in return from Franco. Typical of him. Why should he care that bodies are piling up in his fucking city? Unless he's the one responsible.

I lock eyes with JJ, who raises his brows like he's on the same wavelength as me.

"This year is going to be lit," Mack quips with excitement, oblivious to the important conversation happening around him. He flashes us his signature smirk. The same one that has been his mask for years, covering up the hurt bubbling inside him.

"Something like that," I mutter in response, earning a look from him. But I ignore it.

My eyes glide from left to right, taking in the multitude of familiar and new faces walking through campus. Some look terrified. Others are confident and ready for campus life.

"Fucking freshman," Mack grunts, shoving past a tall, scared looking kid who gapes at Mack. Probably hoping for an apology that won't come.

I shrug at the kid whose brows furrow. His lips pop open to retort, but we walk faster than he can speak. No matter, he can take it up with Mack at the Coliseum, if he sees fit. Although I'd advise him not to. Mack's a damn rage machine in the ring against opponents, taking them down with three or four punches.

"Don't be such a dick," JJ huffs softly, shaking his head.

"Eh. It's the little freshies that piss me off. Why're they always in my way?" Mack speaks the rest of his sentence loudly, parting the sea of people down the middle so we can pass through. Even parents pull their kids out of the way.

Normal people would offer the concerned parentals a placating tight smile or a shrug, but I don't offer either. I keep my eyes forward. Despite the nagging feeling pulling at my gut.

Something is wrong.

"How about a party tonight at the frat house? A real welcome to your new hell?" Mack grins, rubbing his hands together like an evil mastermind of some sort.

"Your new hell," JJ grunts, shaking his head.

"Sure. I'm sure our members would love that." They would, too. We currently have five frat brothers pledged to our cause.

Our house.

Our gang.

"Even the pledges," Mack chortles with a grin that could put the Grinch to shame.

"They won't be pledges for very much longer," JJ reminds him with a huff.

Soon, the people who pledged themselves, played our games, and took on jobs over the summer to prove themselves will be full members of our way of life. AKA joining Franco's ever-growing gang.

"We'll get new ones. New initiates. Just like we did last year. Another cemetery party and then the real games can begin. Should we make them stand naked in a field and pretend to be a scarecrow again?" Mack walks backwards, staring at us with hope in his cruel eyes.

"We'll devise new games this year. We need to test their strengths and discover their weaknesses. You know they're pledging to…" JJ wrinkles his nose, shifting his gaze toward our home on the hill, above the graveyard beside the college that has expanded to its fence line. "All that." He says it like a bad taste explodes on his tongue, twisting his expression.

"I do love our planning sessions," Mack says, wiggling his brows. "I got a whole list written down of fun activities to test them." AKA Mack has some sadistic shit written down that we'll all have to vote on.

Why my father left the three of us in charge of recruiting college-aged kids, I'll never know. Maybe it was to give us a purpose while we get our degrees, so we don't wander off, change our names, and start a new life. Or maybe he has trust in us to live for our cause and continue the gang when he's long gone. Either way, we're forced to stay and live this life without a choice.

The crowd's chatter fades as we leave campus behind, heading toward Syndicate Strip—the old frat row. Five grand, pristine houses stand in a row, representing a haven for mafia members and gangs that attend here. A place where they carve out their turf, study at Greenwood, and make connections that run deeper than any degree they could ever get their hands on.

These are our prospective kingdoms while we wait to rule.

I tune Mack out as he goes on about the initiation games, we make our new pledges participate in every year to join our faction. The Franco Syndicate. A gang organization. The rulers of Southern California. And now? Way beyond.

Franco sips his whiskey, staring at us the entire time. "We'll be bigger than the Viotto bastards," he grunts, slamming his glass down. "California will be ours. All of it. Every state in the fucking vicinity will be ours and then?" He smirks again, leaning against his desk with a dreamy expression floating across his features. "The world is our damn oyster."

"You want to take from the Viotto's?" I ask cautiously.

The Viotto's are a crime family. The fucking mafia. Raised to take pieces of California for themselves and rule them as their kingdoms. They have their slices, and Franco has his–Greenwood, California. A place they want, but have never got their greedy fingers on. Oh, they've tried, inciting war on Franco. But never succeeded.

In one last failed attempt at getting a slice of our pie, they sent Raphael Viotto. A disgraced member of their family, to assist Franco as a second-in-command. Franco wasn't dumb. He knew the deal had stipulations and a built-in spy. But he let Raph stay on our property. Assist in deals with other mob and mafia families. Raph Viotto was involved with everything Franco did, even coming to their own damn alliance.

Franco paces in front of his desk, going on and on about how the planet will be his, and there's nothing anyone can do to stop him.

Except us. Me, maybe. One day soon, Franco will be on his knees for the crimes he's perpetuated against others, including the three of us whom he called his children.

"We'll eliminate anyone who gets in our way," Franco huffs,

shakily running his hands through his dark hair. "Even those
fucking Viotto snakes," *he hisses with malice.*

"Howdy fuckers. Long time no see," Jaxon says, bumping
straight into me with the lazy grin he always wears. Nothing
bothers that fucker. He's pure fucking chaos. And also a part of
the mob–a set of families invited to Greenwood by my father.

His grin grows when he sees the tension lining my face.
Nothing pleases him more than riling me up and challenging me
to a fight in the ring.

"Sup, assholes," Mack says with genuine joy lighting up his
face.

"Ready for our last year here? Can you believe it? The last
time we stand here on a first fucking day," Jaxon says, turning to
look over his shoulder at the people milling around campus
across the street.

"Can't come soon enough," I huff, aching to go home and
surround myself with music and nothing else. My bedroom is my
damn sanctuary. The only spot I can be myself and relax.

"You're telling me. Levi and I were just talking about life
after this shit hole," he quips, slapping his brother on the chest.
In return, Levi shoves him off without saying anything.

"This is our shit hole," I quip, crossing my arms when Jaxon
smirks, eager to retort, but doesn't get the chance.

"Eager to rule your piece of your kingdom?" Mack asks,
wiggling his brows.

If there's one ally we've gained through the past four years,
it's these two, despite them being our supposed enemies or whatever Franco claims. We've done our best to keep up the illusion
of spying on the others brought here by him.

Jaxon rolls his eyes toward the sky. "Oh yes, so eager to run
the club and games and shit. I can't wait to leave the weather
here and go back to the cold winters and more duties."

Levi glares at his brother before slapping him on the shoulder
and nodding to the side.

"Anyway. Duty calls. We have to set up the house and welcome our new little pledges into the family business. They'll be so pleased to see what we have in store for them." He grins so brightly, I know it's going to be bloody.

"No deaths," JJ says, narrowing his eyes.

"In all the years you've known me, have I ever murdered someone?" JJ's eyes narrow at Jaxon, who huffs. "Okay, on campus? What do you fellas take me for? A killer? You guys are so insulting." He puts a hand over his heart, shaking his head as Levi pulls him away. I don't think that one likes us very much. Or anyone really.

With that, the Rizuto brothers march away down the sidewalk and walk up the stairs to their home on campus.

"Let's check in at the frat house," I say, nodding toward the large home looming a few steps away.

"Gotta check on our little pledges! You think they set up the margarita machine yet? That's always a hit." Mack wiggles his brows again with a laugh.

"You seriously sent them a list of shit to do already?" JJ huffs as we walk beside each other.

"Um. Of course I did! What fun is it to have little pledges at our disposal if I can't order them to set up the damn margarita machine?" He scoffs at JJ, giving him a dirty look. "It's like you don't even know me."

We continue our walk, and just as we're passing by our lovely neighbors, a familiar voice rings out tauntingly.

"Well, well, look what the cat dragged in!" Malic sing-songs from the porch, while sporting his familiar grin.

He stands tall near the railing of their wrap-around porch, lording over us. His massive muscles bulge as he crosses his arms. Malic is huge, but I could take him any day of the week. Maybe a punch to the gut would shut him up for once.

His partner in crime, Wilder, gives him an exasperated look, running his hand over his shaved head. It's eerie to see Wilder and Mack in the same vicinity. Not only do they want to murder each other on sight, but the similarities between the two are uncanny. You'd never guess they weren't full brothers. Same eyes. Same hair color. Same build. They'd be twins if Wilder hadn't decided to shave his head.

"Looks like shit to me," Mack hisses, cracking his knuckles, ready for a damn fight.

Sometimes I wonder how the two of them managed to get a home here on Syndicate Strip. No one knows exactly who their boss is. All we know is they're from Greenwood. We grew up with them. And now, they're working for some guy here? Franco hasn't said much on that front. Only that we need to keep our eyes on them and try to figure out the identity of their boss. But he says that about everyone who lives on the strip.

"Shit, huh?" Wilder quips, standing to lean against the railing with that familiar cigarette resting between his lips.

"Yeah, shit, asshole." Mack squares up, eager to get his fingers around Wilder's throat and take his brother's life.

"So brotherly," Malic jokes, cocking his head. "But this is a fight I'd love to feast my eyes on. Which brother will win? The loose cannon or the one with a stick up his ass?"

Wilder whips his gaze to Malic. "I better be the loose cannon."

Malic only grins in response, giving me time to reel Mack in.

"Cool it," I grit out, putting a hand on Mack's chest before he marches up the stairs and punches them both. He's prone to losing control of the anger clinging to him. "He's not worth it out here." I eye the crowds meandering through campus across the road from the strip. There's not a lot of traffic on this side of campus, but there are still witnesses around.

The last thing we need is someone calling the cops because a gang-brawl has spilled out onto the lawns. Franco is never pleased when we get ourselves into trouble. Even though the law is well on our side of things.

"Save it for the fight," JJ mutters under his breath so only Mack can hear him.

"Whatever. We got shit to do. Fuck you guys," Mack says, tossing them the bird before marching up the stairs to the front door of our house and stomping inside.

"Nice to see you guys again," I say sarcastically with a little wave. "So great to have you both as neighbors. Speaking of, are you ever going to beef up your numbers?" I grin when Malic stiffens at my comment.

For some reason, Malic and Wilder have never taken on pledges or filled their frat house with interested members. It's odd to me that they haven't been recruiting like we have. Isn't that the point of school now? Beef up the numbers in your gang?

"We don't answer to you," Malic replies stiffly, cocking his head until his body relaxes. "Something is coming, though, huh? I've seen it." His gaze turns toward the clouds moving overhead and casting shadows above us. "Something big. Familiar..." he hums.

"What the fuck are you talking about?" I grunt, narrowing my eyes.

"Seriously, Mal?" Wilder grumbles.

"Don't listen to me," Malic sings again, before turning on his heels and walking into the house, leaving me more confused than ever.

Wilder shrugs and follows him inside without another word or look back.

"Let's check in at the frat house and then go home," JJ sighs, nodding his head toward our house in the distance.

Our true home. The house on the hill we grew up in. The house that holds the precious memories from our youth. Memories of her. All the good times we had. Even the devastation of losing the one person we thought we'd run away with. That's our home. This frat house is merely the place we hang out at and show our faces so we can continue to fulfil our duties as the Franco Syndicate heirs.

I nod in response.

The moment I step into the large frat house, I'm greeted by the familiar dog that lopes up to me with his tongue hanging out. I grin, running my fingers through his golden fur. There's something so soothing about having our old dog around, following us everywhere.

"Waffles," I say, patting his head with a grin. "How's it going, boy?" He leans into my hand as I pet behind his ears. He doesn't make a noise or acknowledge my words when I pet him. "And how the hell did you get here, hmm?" I hum. "Last I saw, you were at home lying on the couch."

Waffles doesn't shy away from the questions; he simply begs for more pets and doesn't look the least bit ashamed that he escaped from our mansion on the hill. Again. Our elusive dog is constantly going missing for hours at a time and showing up later like he wasn't into something he shouldn't have been. No doubt begging for scraps at the local diners or keeping watch around campus.

"It's been decided," Mack says, coming down the hall with a grin. "We're throwing a welcome back to hell party."

"Tonight?" I question, raising a brow.

"We'll get a jump on all the newbies on campus. Everyone loves our parties. Duh." He shrugs, patting Waffles' head. "Hear that, boy? We're going to have people here tonight. You'll have to be on your best behavior."

"Best behavior?" Brutus, one of our recruits, asks gruffly, taking a step back when Waffles growls at him. "He doesn't even like us." He gestures to the other recruits standing beside him.

All six of them.

"He doesn't like anyone," JJ says, patting Waffles' head and quieting him down. "Good boy."

No matter how many people initiate into our gang, Waffles

hasn't liked any of them. Constantly growling at every person who gets close to him. Including Brutus, who has been with us for the past year. His family comes from Chicago. A prominent mafia family with ties in Miami and Boston. Franco was eager to have him on the team, so, here he is. He's a dickwad most of the time, but whatever.

Come this time next year, we'll be long gone and out of this life. No matter what it takes.

OLIVIA

"Don't worry about Dane," Simon laughs over the noise of the crowd congregating in the basement of our dorm while referring to my wonderful new roommate. "He won't be around very often. His girlfriend is in a sorority, and he hangs there like a puppy with a bone." He rolls his eyes, sipping the punch. "Pathetic if you ask me." He snorts. "He was my roomie last year. Same with Wade. We shared an apartment off campus. God, I miss apartment living. Ugh." He waves a hand. "You'll unfortunately run into more 'Danes' around campus. They all have a stick up their asses about scholarship students." He rolls his lips into his mouth and shakes his head. "Heaven forbid someone is smarter than them or faster than them and earned their place here."

I make a mental note of why other students seem to hate scholarship students. Is it because they got a full ride for academics? Fuck, I have so much research to look into. Not to mention, I'm supposed to be a scholarship student, too. This will no doubt leave a giant target on my back.

"So, scholarship students? Why would anyone hate them? Isn't that a part of going to college and saving money?" My gaze volleys around the room.

Men stand in every nook and cranny of the room, cramming

into what Simon called the common space. It has couches, a TV, a ping pong table, a pool table, a refrigerator, and a microwave in the kitchenette. It's a space for us to spread out in and relax while hanging out.

Simon snorts. "You would think. Listen, you're in the elite club now, Oli. Greenwood is for the best of the best. That guy over there?" He points to a man with a scowl, leaning back into the couch. "His dad's the Governor."

I blink. "Of California?"

"Yup! Oh, and that guy," he points to another on the opposite side of the room, "his daddy is a senator, and his mommy, too. You're in the land of the rich and famous with parents who're in all sorts of high places. That guy?" He points to another man, leaning against the wall. There's an aura about him. Something dark and dangerous. "His parents are in the mob."

I startle, looking the guy over. There's nothing about him that seems familiar. Thank God. Not that my father was memorable in the community. He was a damn menace in the Viotto Crime Family. The majority of the mob, mafia, or gang leaders have connections with one another so they can conduct business and live in peace. Pfft. Peace. There's no such thing between the families running empires. Only war.

"The mob?" I ask, swallowing hard.

"They all come from money," he says, waving a hand at everyone in the room. "Except for the scholarship students." He raises a sharp brow. "Normally, all the scholarship students are housed in the dorm we're in. Just them. Poor things, having to look out the window and see the dismal graveyard." He rolls his eyes. "But since we're all required to live on campus now, it's gotten a little messed up. So, we get the lovely view, too."

Half of me thinks I need to go through the information Jonathan left for me. This can't be a coincidence that I'm here as things are getting fucky in Greenwood.

"So it's a mix of scholarship students and regular students in our dorms now?" I ask as the RAs in front of the room clear their throats and begin speaking.

"Yup!"

"Good to know," I mumble, trying not to draw attention to our informative conversation. "And your roommate? I didn't get a chance to say hello." I need to find out as much information on everyone I'm going to be living with as I can. What's the phrase? Better the devil you know than the devil you don't.

Simon smirks. "I can teach you everything you need to know about this place, man. Including the people. That guy over there in the layered collared shirts?" Ah, yeah. I recognized him immediately from the brief glimpse I got of him when he left in a hurry.

Blond shaggy hair. Bright pink, purple, and green collared polo shirts. A heavenly tan anyone would be envious of and a smile to brighten the room.

"Yup. I see him," I say, clearing my throat.

"That's Wade. He bunks with me. He's the Dean, Amber Whittmore's son." He rolls his eyes dramatically.

"Snitch?" I surmise.

Simon side-eyes me. "Not from my experience. He's a nice dude. The kind to give you the shirt off his back, but he stays to himself. Volunteers a lot on campus and with the puppies and kitties at the shelter. It's nauseating." He shrugs, returning his attention to the RAs at the front of the common room, standing tall in front of the crowd.

"So, you've been here all four years?" I ask.

"Yup!" Simon hums, swallowing the rest of his red punch. "All four years."

"You like it here? It seems…" I shrug, trying to fish for answers.

He nods. "It's good enough. Not exactly where I wanted to go, but whatever. I had no choice. I'm just waiting for gradua-tion. Then my dad expects me to report to the corporate world as his CEO-in-training." He dramatically sighs. "So, I'm living it up this year until I have to become an adult." He wrinkles his nose. "How about you? Transferring your senior year? Scandalous."

I snort, clearing my throat. "I decided to move closer to my family. Plus, I got the scholarship. I couldn't pass that up." There. Short and sweet. If I leave it at that, he won't pry.

Simon's lips pop open like he wants to say something else, but the RA currently speaking at the front of the discussion clears their throat louder than before, gaining all of our attention. With a stern look, he looks around the room at the group of men and me.

"There are important rules to go over! If I could have everyone's attention!" He shouts for good measure, his voice echoing through the room. "Some of you are familiar with what to expect, but we do have several transfers and people returning to dorm life. Rule number one: This is a male dormitory. Not Co-Ed. If you want to bring visitors of the female variety," he chuckles when several men whoop in the crowd, including Simon.

"Don't look so surprised, Oli," he murmurs, bumping his shoulder into mine. "I love variety."

"Wasn't even questioning it. No judgment from me."

Simon's shoulders relax, and he nods at my approval. "You're cool people then," he mutters over the sound of the RA's voice continuing to go over the rules.

"Your guests must sign themselves in and out and be out by 11 P.M." He raises a brow, looking through the crowd. "11 P.M. also happens to be the new curfew put into effect by the school." Several groans ring through the air. "I know, I know! But we can't have you out on the streets after 11. You must be on campus. New security guards have been hired to enforce the rules. Not to mention the extra police presence. And the dorm curfew is 11. If you aren't inside, you're locked out!" The RA holds up his hands in surrender, not looking pleased to have to give out these rules. Let alone have to enforce them on his fellow classmates.

"Don't worry," Simon mumbles. "It won't stop us. There are ways in and out of the building without getting detected. You'll never be locked out."

"Good to know. You'll show me?" My heart rate kicks up at the prospect of being trapped in this building. What happens if I'm studying late? Or a party commences?

"Oh, a rebel. I like that. Of course. We're besties now, right?" He wiggles his brows.

"Of course."

"Quiet hour starts at nine. No loud music. Ya know what? Just respect each other, okay? We're here to learn and shit. Just have a good year. If you need me for anything, here's a flyer with my number on it. Also, there's a dorm mixer next Friday evening where we can all get acquainted. You're dismissed! Happy move-in day!" He sighs when everyone starts filing out, taking fliers, and heading back to their rooms.

And we do the same, following the flow of the crowd up the basement stairs.

"Ohhhh," Simon sings, staring down at his phone. "Let's cut out of the mixer next Friday and go straight to Fight Night."

I blink several times, staring at an app filled with campus events that aren't on the regular calendar.

"Who is throwing it? And what is that?"

"Oh! The SlamApp. You need it immediately. Not only is there juicy gossip to read, but there's events. Like this..." he trails off, pointing to an event next Friday. "If you want to feast your eyes on the campus elite going at it with their fists in each other's faces, this will be the place to be." He fans himself several times, turning a pink hue.

"The Coliseum?" My heart squeezes in my chest, but I don't show the emotions threatening to spill out of me. Ever since I stepped foot back into Greenwood, my walls are shattering, piece by piece, and displaying the feelings I've trapped for so long.

Simon and I march up the stairs to the second floor side by side as he continues to tell me everything I need to know. From what I can tell, there are only three stories and about fifteen suites on each floor. Who needs a tour guide when you have a Simon? Which is fine. I need to understand as much as possible before I have to pledge into an all-male frat with my three ex-best friends.

I need a damn vacation.

"I can't wait to show you around. The Coliseum is some ancient relic in Greenwood that the boys of campus christened as their secret spot for fights. There's even a bar there. A few dancers. It's a paradise," Simon gushes as we unlock our front door and step into our darkened dorm space. Silence rests around us as I eye the darkened shadows of our room. There's no movement from my shared bedroom or Simon's.

Good. Dane can stay as far away as he'd like. Forever.

"An old relic?" I wonder aloud, knowing exactly where and what it is.

"Oh, my sweet, sweet, naive new roomie. Prepare yourself for Friday. It's quite the spectacle. Big guys in the ring with their shirts off and sweat on their chests," he swoons, putting the back of his on his forehead before we part ways, going into our own living quarters.

I immediately shut the door, despite it not having a lock. It's the semblance of privacy that finally has my shoulders sagging and my mind reeling with the night's events.

Today was a fucking day. Coming here. Seeing them. Having to pretend I'm someone I'm not. It's a heavy weight on my shoulders. It's a challenge I never wanted to give myself.

But here I am, working for the man who saved me, trying to bring down the pricks that ruined me. All in a day's work.

Dane's lone box he left behind taunts me from the other side of the room as I plop down onto my mattress. It remains unpacked and unmoved on his empty mattress, void of sheets and life.

Maybe this won't be so bad, after all. If I had to room with someone who was here all the time, then I wouldn't be able to rid myself of my disguise. It's risky, though. There are no locks on my door. My only reprieve is the bathroom, but I can't constantly lock myself in there when I need to unbind.

Speaking of. This damn bind hurts. My tits are screaming for air. Maybe I'll try the tank top version tomorrow and see if it's looser. Whatever. That's tomorrow's problem and I'm too tired to pull off my shirt and binder. For now, I'll suffer and get used to it. I groan, falling back onto my small twin-sized bed with a huff, and pull out my phone, attempting to distract myself from well...everything.

SlamApp. An unofficial place for news, gossip, and unsanctioned events for Greenwood U, Greenwood, California. Must have a college-approved email to log in. Anonymous features are available.

I lick my lips, downloading the app, inputting my new college email and taking the welcome tour of whatever the app has to offer. The first thing that pops up is the same message Simon showed me in our meeting.

Fight. Friday night. Coliseum. Come and call out your opponent on the day, or click here—Jackson Wilder. (Photos from previous fight nights *available here.* Buy at the bar, bring your own booze, rides, and designated drivers. We're not responsible for your blood loss or anything else.)

My heart stalls, sputtering to a stop. Heat rushes to my face, then just as quickly drains, leaving my fingers ice-cold wrapped around my phone.

Wilder? Jackson Wilder? He's here? At this campus?

I shake my head. There's no way. It has to be a different person. A different Jackson Wilder. Right? That's a pretty common name. It has to be. Because if he's here, then that psycho who likes trackers is here. My traitorous body heats. Nope. Nu-huh. I'm living in delusional land all by myself.

They aren't here.

They can't be.

Or it proves that I'm the unluckiest girl on the damn planet.

Deep breaths, Liv. It's not like he'll recognize you. You're in disguise now, with annoying glasses, colored contacts, and strapped down boobs.

Sitting back on my bed, I get back to work scoping out the SlamApp. With my breath in my throat, I click on the photos and swipe through them. Static fills my ears at the images of the men I knew before, standing in the middle of the ring with blood dripping from their lips and ears. Vicious expressions blanket their faces, making me shiver.

What was the catalyst for their fall into the darkness? Me? Having Franco as a father? Their violence-filled lifestyle? Honestly, the possibilities are endless. But looking at their darkened eyes and bloodied flesh, they've come to the point of no return. Surfacing as the men their foster father always wanted.

Brutal soldiers.

Hux AKA Huxley Crewes preens at the camera with a half-cocked smirk and his arm above his head. Tattoos cascade down his chest, arms, and abdomen. They're everywhere. Marking him in colorful designs. Portraits. Small star shapes. Flowers. Animals. Most have been etched on him since we were teenagers. But some are new.

My eyes squeeze shut at the numbers etched on his chest, surrounded by daisies–my favorite flowers. A tattoo that wasn't there before. Something new. Something damning that has my stomach turning and knots forming over my aching heart.

2-2-4.

"Today. Tomorrow. Forever," I murmur aloud through a choked, rage-filled sob.

The number is everywhere when it comes to him. My grave-stone. His chest. It's like it meant something to him, but it didn't. There's no way it could have after everything was said and done. Not after they fucking killed me.

2-2-4 was once a number we said, on repeat. A promise. It was us against the damn world. Today. Tomorrow. Forever and always.

But now it means jack shit. It's just a number followed by 225. No meaning behind it. No love or pretty words to invoke any sort of feelings.

Or it shouldn't.

It shouldn't have knives plunging through my chest and tears on my lashes. But it does. And I can't let it anymore. I grieved this already. For five long years, I've thrown myself into work and recovery, getting over their betrayal.

Or so I thought.

Being back in Greenwood feels like I've taken a thousand steps backward, and I'm right where I was the day I watched my funeral.

In the fucking ashes of my life.

"You're alive. You're taking them down. You're free," I murmur to myself and clear my head from all the static, filling it relentlessly. "But now, you have a job to start."

With that sentiment, I shake myself out of the morbid feel-ings and focus on Mack standing beside him in the picture. He's a job. Not an old friend who hurt me and betrayed me. A job. A person who needs to go down for their crimes and be punished.

Macklyn Owens. AKA Mack. Doesn't have as many tattoos lining his flesh, but they're still there. On his arms. Hands. Shoulders. And slightly on his chest. Not as personal as Huxley's. No meaningful numbers or objects special to what we had stand out.

In the background of the photos stands JJ. AKA–Jasper Jeremiah Jones. With his hands in his pockets and his eyes focused on the winners in the circle. He takes it all in with his large, expressive eyes. Always the observer. Never the provoker. Peace was always the mantra he lived by, never wanting to ruffle feathers. But he was quick to stand up for what was right—taking injustices seriously. Well, back then, anyway. I'm sure Franco has sunk his claws deep into JJ by now, hoping he and the other two will step up once college concludes.

Swiping through several more photos, I take in the scenery of the building. And then it hits me. Pictures of the venue.

"Dude, I found this place, isn't it cool as fuck?" Mack grins, bouncing on his toes. "I call it The Coliseum. *You know, like that place in Rome, but with a different spelling. Look at all the stones." He points to the crumbling concrete littering the thick forest floor.*

Hux blinks, his jaw opening wide.

JJ's brows furrow as his neck cranes back, staring at the massive structure.

"What is this place?" I murmur, moving forward in awe.

"I bet it's only visible from the sea," JJ says thoughtfully, peering around the edge of the rounded structure and viewing the massive ocean below the cliff.

"Who do you think built this?" I swallow hard, following JJ to view the massive waves slamming into the rocks below. If I took ten more steps, I'd slip off the edge of the cliff and fall in.

"I'm surprised it hasn't fallen over." Hux rubs his chin, staring it down. "It doesn't look safe."

"This was in Captain Greenwood's log!" Mack excitedly exclaims, pulling up an article on his phone. "See? It's a sign his treasure is somewhere near here." He clears his throat, scrolling. "Through the sea and rocks, a structure hides within the vines and above the caves. X marks the spot." He grins, showing us the new piece of information. "The treasure has to be here!"

Hux nods. "It could be. But don't you think someone has been here already?"

Mack frowns, shoving his phone away. "They could have been," he shrugs, casting his eyes toward the dirt. "Doesn't matter, I'm going inside anyway." He turns on his heels and darts inside the massive structure with a huff.

"You pissed in his Cheerios," JJ murmurs.

"Someone needs to," Hux scoffs angrily. "There's no treasure. Someone found that gold a long time ago." His eyes roll toward the blue sky, gracing us with a beautiful day to explore the woods near our home.

"Rude," I quip, slapping him on the shoulder. "Now, let's go exploring."

We explored the space for multiple weeks, taking in the crumbling rock seats, hidden passageways, and dirt floors, never giving up on finding the treasure we were seeking. Something was planted here many moons ago when Captain John Greenwood, a pirate on the high seas, stumbled here after an accident, fleeing from the authorities.

His treasure has never been found, but this town was named after him. Casinos were erected in his honor. Similar to the eatery and bars. All for him and the memory he left behind after discovering this land.

And now, his memory is being used to help kids pummel each other on Friday nights for shits and giggles. Probably bets, too.

It's just another aspect of our childhood used for their fun and games, tarnishing what we once had there.

I sigh, drowning in the memories of our youth. An ache forms in my chest. The remnants of what we once had flooding behind my eyes like a movie on repeat. If I could step out of my mind and body and truly become Oliver, I would. No more memories. No more rushes of emotions I've buried.

I flick through several more photographs, taking in the

scenery and people in front of the lens. More fights. More carnage. More blood. Bloodied fists and missing teeth. All documented on the web for the people on campus to glimpse.

And then, there was him.

My delusional bubble pops into a million pieces at the sight of the bloodied Viking, standing tall with a grin on his face. His arm is above his head, raised in victory for all to see. People cheer around the make-shift ring. Their joy is written on their faces. Mouths open. Hands whooping in excitement.

All for him.

The motherfucker who fucked me in the bathroom and put a tracker in my pocket.

Great. Just wonderful. Everyone I want to avoid is here on campus.

Maniac—Undefeated champion! Who will take him on next? The caption reads as he stares into the camera with a wild gaze.

That's it. I've had too much time to look at half-naked men fighting until they're unrecognizable. I'll have to see it in person at some point to document it for my findings, but right now, I need something else.

Beyond the message board promoting unsanctioned events throughout campus. Like parties. Parties. And oh, more parties with multiple comments under each party announcement like a social media site made for Greenwood University only.

Next Saturday Night–Graveyard. Party. BYOB. Snacks. Selves.

Anonymous1: *This is it, isn't it! Omg Amanda!*

Amanda Devalle: *It is! This is the party of the century every year.*

Next Friday Night–After Fight. Party. @ Malic and Wilder's. Alcohol provided. Snacks included. Just bring you. Interest in joining us for the long term included.

Anonymous: *Wait. You're opening enrollment for your house?*

Anonymous3: I heard they haven't done that in four years!
Anonymous4: Because they killed a guy!
Anonymous5: Liars! He wasn't killed. He ran away...

The bickering goes on between each anonymous member for pages and pages. But I make notes to investigate the supposed guy who was killed. And why hasn't the frat opened any spots for incoming freshmen in four years? That means it closes with whoever is at the top.

Ugh.

Frats are weird. But this town is weirder.

I scroll through more posts, finding a confession page. A gossip page. Suspicious activity around campus page. Each having detailed posts about what's happening around campus and who is with who.

Anonymous: Amanda Devalle *is officially engaged! Did you see the rock he gave her?*

Anonymous 2: Wow. They've been together for over a year, and he's just now giving her a ring? Such a shame...

I sigh, taking in all the information about these people I don't know. It'd be easier if I had grown up with them, too. But people apparently come from all over to fill the college to capacity.

Eventually, my eyes grow heavy from staring at my phone for way too long. And just as I'm about to close the SlamApp, an anonymous post pops up on the screen.

AnonymousUser: A snake slithers through the forest in borrowed skin. Walk carefully when the sun and moon shine.

Whatever the fuck that means. But I take another note as I reach under my shirt, eager to free myself from the uncomfortable bindings on my chest and start to lift my shirt. I can't wait to take a full breath without feeling like an elephant is on my chest. Just two more seconds to freedom and then I can change into my sweatpants and go to sleep.

If only that were in the plans for me tonight when my bedroom door bursts open, bouncing off the drywall.

I rear back, instinctively reaching for the knife nestled between my mattress and box spring, but stop dead when Simon bounces into my room with his phone lighting up his grinning face.

"Oli!" Simon shouts with glee, launching himself onto my bed.

Doesn't he know what a personal bubble is? Or knocking, for that matter. Maybe I need to invest in a chain lock of some sort. Yeah, that's a good idea. I'll call Jordy and tell him there's a party and then force him to help me.

Cool. Good to know my roommates will burst into my room without warning, and there's nothing I can do about it. Well, except for discussing boundaries with him. It's on the tip of my tongue to beg him to knock as I carefully remove my hand from beneath my shirt. It's a good thing I wasn't topless yet. That would be an awkward conversation on the first night of knowing each other. *'Oh, hey, by the way, I don't really have balls.'*

Lesson number one million–never get too comfortable in your surroundings when you're undercover. Jonathan's voice rings in my head as I give Simon a tight smile, hiding the exhaustion pulling at my limbs.

I need to shut my eyes for like two seconds. Is that too much to ask?

"Simon," I say, breathlessly.

"Look." Simon holds up his phone with a grin, displaying the SlamApp. "This just popped up. Party on Syndicate Strip."

My nose wrinkles. "Syndicate Strip? Isn't that a place in Vegas?"

Simon snorts. "Could be. But it's what we call the frat houses here. Or, not so frats." He leans in slowly. "Remember how I told you some kid was a part of the mob? Well, there's more of them, and they throw the best fucking parties on the planet. Just don't get sucked into their initiations, unless you want to join. They live in the old frat houses. Besides, these guys have a margarita machine and a dog. Although you shouldn't touch him, he hates everyone but them." Simon wrinkles his nose, rambling more about the frat and how we should go to the party.

I blink several times. "Right. A margarita machine. I don't know, Si. I'm tired and..." Attempting to come up with any excuse possible not to be dragged to this. The last thing I want to do is run into Hux, JJ, or Mack again. I'm too fried from seeing them earlier. I don't know if my brain can handle a party filled with rowdy college kids ready to stay up all night.

"Oh, come on, Oli! Please! It'll be so much fun to experience this with you." He bats his eyelashes and puffs out his bottom lip. "Besides, it'll give you a glimpse at the gangs of Greenwood in all their glory. You should see how they try to outdo each other. It's like a competition and them begging you to join their ranks or whatever. I'm neutral, though. I just like the parties." He bats his eyelashes a few more times as I weigh my options.

I could tell him I want to go to bed and say forget the party, but what kind of agent would I be? It's prime time for spying and recon. I can watch everyone in their natural habitat before classes start and before the fight next week.

I lick my lips, watching as the hopeful expression on Simon's face grows. I'm so going to regret the next words that come out of my mouth.

"Fine. Take me to the party," I chuckle when he jumps from the bed and throws his fist in the air in victory.

"You won't regret this, Oli! I swear!"

Yeah, he says that now, but I'm not convinced. I'm either going to be extremely happy getting a glimpse at how the gangs work as frats on campus, or I'm going to regret ever stepping foot into close quarters with them.

I've yet to decide which one.

OLIVIA

I REGRET THIS DECISION.

Immediately.

Why did I allow Simon--someone I barely fucking know—to convince me to come to this party? No is a one-word sentence, after all. I should have said—no, Simon, I'm going to freaking bed. My tits hurt. My feet hurt. And I just want to pretend this entire adventure isn't happening. I need some Liv-time, far away from Oliver.

But I couldn't. This is all a part of the job. I'm Oliver Davenport—party animal extraordinaire, ready to go out at a moment's notice so I can spy on my peers and befriend my ex-best friends.

Good times.

Damn. I really need a drink. Something to drown out the tension bubbling in my gut and threatening to spew out my mouth.

From the moment we walked through the door of the frat house, my senses were assaulted by the stench of horny, drunk people. Jordy would fit in perfectly with this crowd. Me, on the other hand? I'll have to suffer through this for the sake of my case.

With barely a foot in the door, we bumped into fifty people loudly chatting, dancing, and drinking their lives away. The entire first floor of the large, Victorian-style mansion was over-filled with rowdy college students.

"Welcome to Greenwood U!" Simon shouts above the music, throwing his fist in the air. He bobs to the loud music I don't recognize and grins. "Follow me!" He waves me on, and I follow without hesitation.

Where else would I go? Certainly not in the corner where two people have their tongues down each other's throats and their hands exploring everywhere.

Nope. That's their corner now and not my business.

People. God. They're everywhere. Touching each other. Laughing loudly over the music and drowning it out. Girls cheer "woohoo!" so loud, I think my eardrums might have blown out.

Yeah, this was not a good idea. Just give me a walker and call me grandma, because I'd rather be knitting a sweater than standing here in this frat house. All I wanted was my warm blankets and a good night's sleep. Instead, I get this loud and out-of-control party with my new roommate. Who seems to have disappeared into the crowd and never returned.

I sigh from the corner of the room I've been awkwardly standing in since Simon left me with a promise of grabbing us drinks. I check my phone. It's been over fifteen minutes since he left me here. Did he get kidnapped? Lured away with the promise of booze and locked in a basement?

Fuck. My brain conjures nothing but terrible scenarios. All of which I've seen on the job. I'm sure he's fine. Maybe he met up with some friends, and now is the perfect time for me to run away and never look back.

But, ugh. Girl code. Or Bro code in this case.

I can't leave him behind at a damn party where anything could happen. Drugs in his drink? Kidnapping? A fire? Even if he's not a girl. He's still my party buddy, and I can't abandon him when he might need me.

Damn you, conscience. Why do you have to be so persistent?

I sigh, leaning against the wall in the far corner of the living room. Or what resembles a living room. There's ratty furniture pushed to the edges of the room with patchwork and stains. A large TV hangs on the wall above the brick fireplace, displaying a movie I don't recognize. Lots of guns, explosions, and early 1920s gangsters run across the screen.

My eyes scan the multitude of flushed faces, catching up with their friends. Maybe I should look on the bright side. I'm here. Alive. And this gives me a glimpse of the people who attend GU.

Buck up, Liv. You got this. Totally got this.

"Margarita?" Simon sing-songs, slurring his words as he dances with one in each hand.

Now he's speaking my language.

Simon slowly swings his hips. A grin stretches across his lips, reaching his glazed-over eyes. Holy shit. There's no way in hell he could be this intoxicated already. Right? We've barely had anything to drink. Or I haven't. He was gone for a suspiciously long time, which was okay for the job I'm on. The more I can observe and report, the better off I'll be. But from my vantage point, it's just a bunch of rich college kids drinking the night away.

Nothing nefarious.

Yet.

"Thanks," I say over the noise, grabbing the margarita from him eagerly.

I shiver at the cold glass and slowly bring the concoction up to my lips. As a rebellious teenager, I sipped margaritas while the guys drank beers or mixed drinks. We always took them to the treehouse and sipped our booze while the world passed around us. The treehouse, in the middle of the woods between our houses, was our home away from home. A way to escape the mobster lifestyle our parents led.

In true Mack fashion, he always made these types of drinks

for me. Using Franco's stash, of course. No matter how often he got into trouble for it, which was a lot. Franco even resorted to locking up his favorite alcohol in a cabinet. But Mack still managed to get some, despite the consequences.

Just for me.

I hum into my glass, squeezing my eyes shut as the familiar taste hits my tongue, igniting something deep within me. It's like a taste of home. A memory mixed into the liquid for my brain to conjure and relive over and over again. Like the night when I was sixteen and we were bored on summer break, hanging out in the treehouse.

"It's good, right?" Mack asks, grinning as he watches me sip his latest concoction with hope in his eyes.

This isn't the first or last time he attempts to find me something I'll like. We've gone through the list of mixed drinks, beers, and other assortments. Nothing tastes right.

But this? This delicious cold drink? It's perfect.

My eyes widen at the flavor as it hits my tongue. "Yes," I breathe, eager to take another sip. "What is it?"

Mack grins more, looking smug. "It's called a margarita. We now have a mixer in the kitchen. They had some left over from a party or some shit. It looked like something you might like." He blushes, quickly looking away.

Right. The party at Franco's. We all ducked out the moment the grown-ups decided to go into the basement of his mansion. We know what that means. They're going to talk mob business and probably do freaky stuff I don't want to think about.

"It's so fucking good," I whisper, putting a hand on his arm. "Mack, seriously! You finally found it." I grin when he perks up, smiling so wide I can't dispute the happiness flowing through me.

"Finally," Hux laughs, taking a swig of the beer he stole from the party. "I never thought we'd find you something you actually enjoyed, Trouble."

He's not wrong. I hate beer. I usually hate mixed drinks of any sort. So, to finally have something that tastes semi-good and will get me drunk? Yes, please!

I stick my tongue out at him and finish the rest of my margarita quickly, begging for more.

"Anything for you, Livy," Mack chortles, climbing out of the treehouse through the trapdoor in the floor, clinging to my margarita glass. "I'll be back."

Fifteen minutes later, he came back with a small cooler full of beer and an entire pitcher of margarita mix, claiming he took the rest of it before anyone could drink my new favorite. We drank the night away, laughing and scheming on what we'd do the next day after we worked at the casino.

And nothing ever changed. I still hate the taste of beer on my tongue, no matter how many times I've had to fake liking it for my roles. Me and beer? Yeah, we aren't ever happening. I prefer the 'girly' drinks, as Hux used to call them. Something sweet and flavorful that makes me happy. Or when I'm in a mood–straight bourbon or whiskey on the rocks to take the edge off.

The music from the party brings me back to the present, and my eyes widen at the chaos ensuing in front of me. A fight breaks out between two massive dudes. Blood spills. Noses crunch. And I cringe.

"Isaac! Isaac!" Half the crowd chants.

"Chance! Chance!" The other half chants louder and with more excitement in their tones.

More punches land. More blood spills onto the hardwood floors. Ouch. They'll be feeling this fight for days.

"No fucking fighting in the house!" a gruff, familiar voice shouts over the music and marches into the room red-faced. He huffs several times, emerging through the circle of people that formed around the two fighters.

I'm in a time warp. Or that's what it feels like watching someone I used to know with fury written on his face try to break the two up. No one else steps in to help when he grabs the fighters by the fronts of their shirts and pushes them away from each other with a grunt. They stumble over their feet, nearly falling on their asses, but stabilize. Blood seeps from each of their noses and lips. Isaac or Chance–I'm not positive on who–snarls at the other again, promising a world of hurt if he comes after him again.

"The only fights allowed are at the Coliseum." He crosses his muscular arms over his chest. "Not in my goddamn house."

It's odd having a deep-rooted memory of someone stuck in your mind for so many years and then finally seeing them in the flesh. I can't peel my eyes away from him as he scolds the massive dudes, growling at one another like they can't wait to get back to pummeling each other's faces in.

"Having fun yet?" Simon asks with a goofy grin, downing his margarita in one gulp. The immediate regret of his decision happens when he squeezes his eyes closed and his lips pop open. "Brain freeze," he wheezes, holding a hand to his forehead. "But so worth it," he sighs, peeling his eyes open.

I smile at his antics, attempting to shake off the tension building in my muscles from the memories pouring through my mind. Mack. He's here in front of me. Stoically standing in the middle of the room. He's familiar. Yet, not. Same facial features. Minus the now permanent scowl etched onto his face. I guess that's what being a murderer does to you.

"Yeah," I offer Simon a grin, toasting my margarita to him. "It's a blast." I lie through my damn teeth. But Simon doesn't need to know this is like tying me to a damn chair and water-boarding me for four hours until I break. Been there, done that. Didn't let any information spill.

So, I fake it til I make it. That's the motto, right? Pretend that I love standing in the house of my former friends who killed me and left me for dead. Yup. Good times.

"See! I told you, roomie! Stick with me and we'll have an

entire year of this!" He grins, hoisting his drink in the air. "To us and to this damn party."

"Here, here," I agree with a smile, trying not to let my sour mood take over my expression. At one point in my life, I was told my face shows every emotion I feel. Well, thanks to dear old Dad, he beat that trait out of me.

Now, I'm a stoic statue, smiling through the worst pain of my life.

"There will be a fight Friday. Sign up to fight each other then," Mack grunts, pointing toward the door. "Now, get the fuck out until after that." The men don't question him as they shoulder check people through the crowd and march out the front door.

"Ten bucks says those two throw punches on the lawn," Simon chuckles, leaning his head back against the wall. His glazed eyes take in the crowds of the party, sighing when he spots someone, but quickly looks away.

"Does that happen a lot?" I ask, discreetly watching Mack from beneath my lashes.

"All the time," Simon chortles.

A hurricane of emotions flutters through me, like a tidal wave slamming on the shores after high winds. Seeing Mack so close up has me wanting to retreat to the hills. Is my disguise good enough to conceal my identity from him?

I hold my breath when Mack scans the crowd, moving his gaze right over me, onto Simon, and finally, he looks away when JJ enters the room.

My stomach swoops, bottoming out. I thought seeing them from far away was bad enough. Now, they are a mere ten steps away, taking up space in this fucking house and infecting the air around them.

I swallow the lump in my throat as I watch the two of them discuss something. It's so strange to see the objects of my hatred living and breathing. But yet, staring at them, I don't feel hate.

It's rage. Betrayal. Heartache. Every emotion in between.

It all boils inside me. To the point I don't want to be here anymore. I want to give the job to someone else and let them figure out how to get close to them.

How can Jonathan expect me to lift my chin and take this like a damn man? I can't.

I rub over my aching chest, a mix between the binder digging into my ribs and the heartache continually festering inside me.

"Macklyn!" a very familiar feminine voice rings out, marching through the crowd with a grin splitting her lips. I physically cringe at the sight of her, refusing to fall into the nightmare she made my life in high school.

Newsflash—it was fucking hell.

Amanda is still the same Barbie doll she was in high school, looking perfectly perfect in every way. Her long blonde hair sways with every step until she's standing in front of them with a saccharine smile.

Ugh. I think I'm going to vomit. I thought it was bad enough being in the boys' presence. But her? She physically repulses me on so many levels.

"JJ," she practically purrs, running a manicured nail down his chest.

Well, until JJ scowls and tosses her hand off him. I lowkey want to clap my hands and cheer him on for sending her the look. You know, the 'if you touch me again, I'll cut your fingers off' look. He does it so well, which isn't like JJ at all. He was always so quiet and reserved, taking in the world one sound at a time. Obviously, that changed five years ago and even now.

"That's Amanda and her squad," Simon whispers with a look of disgust, and I agree. Amanda isn't just some random girl wandering the halls of Hux's fraternity home. She was once the bane of my existence. "They're obsessed with the kings of G.U." Well, I see that hasn't changed since high school. Ugh. "They stalk them everywhere, hoping for a bone or something. One of them might be in an arranged kind of deal with one of them. I don't knowwww," he trails off, looking down at his glass with a soft whine and leaving me reeling from the new information. Arranged marriage? That sounds awfully familiar. Especially in the world of the mob. "Damn, I need another margarita." He grabs my wrist and pulls me forward through the crowd. Not giving me the chance to say no.

"You will marry him whether you fucking like it or not." My father drunkenly sways before me as I rest on my mattress. His spittle flies with every furious word he growls.

I know I should keep my mouth shut. But how's that phrase go? People don't remember the good girls who follow the rules. They remember the rebels who stick up for themselves. And I'm determined to be that. Someone has to set a good example for my sister Sophia, and it won't be either of my parents. Mom's a doormat, too afraid to stand up to him. And Dad's an abusive prick.

"He's like fifty," I huff, crossing my arms over my chest.

Mistake number one.

I don't see the backhand coming, but I sure feel it the moment it connects with my cheek, and I land on my side. But who am I kidding? I should expect that kind of treatment by now. He treats me like the dog who shit on his shoe, and the golden boy gets taken everywhere like a king.

I resent that little fucker. Not that I want my dad's attention. I don't. But it would be nice to know what it's like to have a good father who participates in my life. Instead, I'm just the daughter he never wanted. Same with Sophia, my sister. We're girls. Useless to him.

How barbaric is that?

"Doesn't fucking matter. He wants you. You will want him. Now be an obedient bitch and prepare yourself. The wedding is set for after you graduate college. Be glad he's even giving you an education." He leans in over me, hovering above my face with a snarl. "Don't make me completely get rid of you before

then. Be fucking good and obey the rules." He spits on me before turning on his heel and marching out of my room. My door slams, and the lock on the outside clicks into place.

I sigh, turning toward my barred windows. It's only three in the afternoon. That lock won't come off until morning. No food. No drinks. Just me and my imagination, considering my father took everything of value away from me. It's a good thing I snuck a cellphone–thank you, JJ–into my room and left it in case of emergencies.

The joke was on him, though. Not only did I take care of that before he could ever marry me off to some fifty-year-old creep eager to bed me, but I died before the wedding could come to fruition. Obviously, the bastard didn't care enough because he fled like the pussy he was and started a new life. Or, hopefully, Raphael Viotto rolled over and died of alcohol poisoning like he deserved. Actually, that's too easy a death. I hope Franco caught him and burned him alive like we had to endure.

Two more girls show up behind Amanda with smirks on their lips and drinks in their hands. I don't recognize them. They aren't the same squad she had in high school. These must be her upgraded besties, far away from Chrissy and Stacy. Hurray for me. At least this time, I'm not someone they can stomp all over. I've grown a backbone. Oh, and I'm not a chick in their eyes. So, that's a perk.

As I watch the three girls circle around JJ and Mack like sharks drooling and begging for a bite, I take notice of all the girls in the room. They stare at the guys with moons in their eyes. Like they're the answer to world hunger. Or their hunger, more like it. JJ and Mack are their tickets to… Well, I'm not sure what they think. Sure, they have connections to the mob and the mafia, but that gives you nothing but death and destruction. They must be thinking about all the Hollywood movies they've seen about rich mobsters and expensive cars.

Sorry, ladies. That's not a real perk here.

"Margaritas!" Simon sings when he pulls me into the empty kitchen and beelines toward the margarita machine on the counter.

It looks so similar to the one Mack constantly used back in the day; I'm convinced he took it for this house. But why? Wouldn't he want to throw that memory away and never look at it again? I know I do. A mental image of me throwing the margarita machine out the window and watching it die a sad death comes to mind. But what am I saying? That's blasphemy. It gives delicious drinks. No matter who the dickbag owner is.

Simon quickly fills our glasses again to the brim, sloshing the red, iced liquid around. Mmmmm. Strawberry. Like an orgasm in my mouth, temporarily relieving me of the pain in my chest from being here.

"Cheers to you, roomie," Simon slurs, clinking his glass against mine.

"Cheers," I say with a tight smile. "How many of these have you had?" I eye him suspiciously. He had one with me, and he's already slurring his words and wavering on his feet. Not to mention, the glossy eyes and crooked smile.

Simon is toasted.

Simon groans, downing his drink completely again and smacking his lips. "Only three. Why?" He says clearly this time, smiling when I examine his face. "Don't worry, Oli. I'm a light-weight, but I can handle my booze." His grin widens when a song comes on over the speakers, and he instantly perks up. Setting his glass down, he bounces on his toes. "My favorite song!"

And just like that, Simon proves how well he can handle his three margaritas.

Before I can say anything or grab him, he's gone like the damn wind, throwing himself into the crowd and finding a girl to dance with. I tilt my head when their mouths connect and fuck… should I stop him? That's a pretty quick, hi, hello, how are you?

Let's kiss. God. He's like an overgrown toddler I'm afraid to leave alone in the kitchen with potential dangers. Except the dangers here are the alcohol he's been drinking and the girl he's grinding with on the dance floor.

Whatever. I'll keep my eyes on him so he doesn't end up getting naked or streaking or... What do college kids do these days? I sigh, drinking the rest of my margarita, begging for the alcohol to do its thing. If I could reach Simon's level of awesomeness, I'd be in a better plane of existence. Being in the guys' domain has my skin crawling with anxiety, like ants dancing across my damn skin.

My need to run and hide has me cowering in the kitchen when I should be snooping or observing the crowds. From here, I can keep my eyes on Simon as he practically has sex with that chick on the dance floor, looking happier than ever.

Yup. He's good.

I cringe. He's not the only one getting frisky on the dance floor. They're all doing it now. Standing on the blood of the two guys who almost murdered each other ten minutes ago. Now, it's a damn orgy. Where's Mack to stop that? Oh yeah, nowhere in sight. Probably having his own orgy or whatever somewhere else.

Ew. That's the last thing I want to think about.

Murmured voices drag me out of my thoughts. This has been happening a lot lately—getting stuck in my thoughts and not paying attention to whatever is happening around me. I think it's a symptom of being back here and doubting every step I take.

Three girls—the ones Simon pointed out earlier—sashay into the kitchen with their chins raised. Oh, someone alert the press, Amanda is in the building! I roll my eyes toward the ceiling and take a step back, hiding myself from view. The last thing I need is Amanda zeroing in on me, standing here and spying.

"Did you see Wilder sitting on the porch when we came in?"

the redhead asks with a giggle, biting her lip. "I can't believe they're neighbors and haven't bombed the house next door."

Oh, so she wants Wilder the neighbor, too. How bold. She was just all over JJ and Mack, practically offering herself to them. And now, she wants to pounce on the poor neighbor Wilder? Ugh. College. It's such a horny time for them. Wait... I stiffen.

Wait a damn minute.

Wilder? As in Jackson Wilder? Malic's Wilder? His keeper? The very man who interrupted our bathroom fuck by knocking on the door? That man?

Fuck.

This day just keeps getting better and better. One perk is that the trio of Charlie's Angels don't pay one bit of attention to me as I hide in the corner of the kitchen nursing my margarita. I'm invisible as I can be. Just a lonely boy in the kitchen, drinking his girly drink. Well, at least I hope that's what they think. I push my stupid glasses up my nose and make sure to face them. Whatever they say in this kitchen will definitely be used against them later when I rewatch this and take notes before sending it to headquarters.

"Oh my God, yes," the brunette girl whispers excitedly. "He didn't have a shirt on! Did you see his muscles and tattoos?" Well, no, I did not. Is that what he's packing under all his clothes? I wonder if he's similar to Malic in that regard. I shift, rubbing my thighs together. Get yourself under control, Olivia. You're spying, not fantasizing about the two of them. Together. With you.

Shit.

They're criminals, I whine to myself. Bad boys. Bad for your health. Psychopaths! Don't you dare envision yourself squished between them as they pound into both your willing holes because they would definitely be very willing in a Malic and Wilder sandwich. Whoa! Hold the damn phone. What am I doing?

Thinking? Man, I really want to smack myself for these thoughts. Am I ovulating? Is that what's happening? Because that can be my body's only excuse for wetting my boxers, which is mighty uncomfortable. And this wild fantasy? Yeah, I'm blaming my ovaries and the release of my eggs—stupid ovulation horniness. I guess me and my vibes are going to get along swimmingly soon. If I can find a private time to use them, that is.

"He's forbidden, Sabrina." Amanda scowls haughtily. "You know that. We can't mess around with them. They're the enemy." She waves a hand toward the house next to this one.

Sabrina instantly deflates and nods obediently. "I know."

Amanda rolls her eyes and opens the fridge. "Ugh. Why don't they have Smirnoff or White Claw? Or anything good? All they have is cheap beer and cheese sticks," she whines, stomping her foot when they throw the door closed. "I'll have to have Hux stock more drinks catered to me, since we'll be here more often." She tosses her blonde hair over her shoulder and promptly displays the massive ring on her finger.

An engagement ring.

OLIVIA

So, I guess it's true. Amanda and Huxley are engaged. But did he pick her? Or was it an arranged type of deal? He moved on so quickly from me. But I guess that's to be expected, isn't it? Why wouldn't he, when he threw me away so easily?

Oh, well. Jokes on them. I'm alive and all. That won't be a very successful wedding.

I smirk to myself, covering it with my drink. I love low-key sabotaging events that haven't even happened yet. *Surprise, bitch. Thought you saw the last of me.*

"Oh, Amanda!" the redhead squeals. "It finally happened!" Oh, so this is a new development? Very interesting. I'll add Amanda to my list of suspicious things happening around here. And if she just happens to fall down a well or something, well–it wasn't me.

"Trinity," Amanda giggles, holding out her left hand, displaying a rather large diamond. "He has to cater to me now. I'm his fiancée. It happened this morning!"

Yeah, from past experiences with Hux, the word fiancée doesn't mean shit to him. Prepare to die a fiery death before he even walks down the aisle, Amanda.

"I'll buy you a better one later." Hux's eyes shimmer in the moonlight leaking in from the small window of our treehouse. I

nearly choke when he pulls out a small golden band shaped like a ring and takes my left hand. "This is my promise to you. Forever and always, Trouble," he whispers, kissing my knuckles and then the ring. "Say you'll be my wife. Say you won't let Gary take you."

Ugh. Gary. The fifty-year-old fuck my father swears I'm going to marry when I graduate from college. I don't know how I'm going to sneak away and never set eyes on that bastard. Maybe I can convince him to give me to Hux in the end.

But this gives me hope. So much damn hope for the first time in months as the world has slowly been falling apart around me.

"Hux," I whisper, holding my hand up above my head and staring at the ring on my finger in awe. It shines in the moonlight, sending my heart into a frenzy, beating chaotically against my bruised ribs.

"I know it's not a diamond or anything. But I want to show you that I mean it. One day, Olivia Viotto, you'll be my wife." He traces the ring on my finger with a slight smile pulling at his lips. "I found it at the Coliseum. It's a treasure, just like you. You're my future. My treasure. My troublemaker." I grin at the nicknames he spews.

"You're the one who is trouble," I quip, kissing his stubbly cheek with a hum.

"Always your trouble. Promise you'll take care of me when I'm ninety and barely able to move?" He waggles his eyebrows.

"Always and forever. And my answer is yes. I'll be your wife. But you better hurry, Gary is eager to..." I don't get the words out of my mouth before his lips are smothering mine, and his tongue plays and twists with my own.

Some treasure I was. In under a month after he gave me the ring, took my virginity, and professed his love to me, he murdered me.

My fingers tighten into fists as the three girls move on from the kitchen, giggling to themselves. He moved on, alright. To the girl he was repulsed by in high school that made my life a living hell. I shake off the memory that's hanging in the back of my mind and begging to come forward to torture me more. No thank you, brain. I don't need to think about all the times that bitch cornered me and swore she'd take my men from me. Well, mission accomplished, Amanda. You really got what you wished for.

I hate these memories. I hate remembering how they made me feel. How good it was between the three of us before it all went to hell. Sometimes, when alcohol runs through my veins and I'm drowning in my misery, I wonder how it led to this? My destruction? Why they suddenly turned their backs on me and ended me?

Nope. Nope. This is exactly why I should stay away from alcohol. It brings me nothing but heartache and tears and massive hangovers. Sure, it's my crutch in the best of times when I need to unwind and get my head on straight. But I know it doesn't do me any favors. It opens sealed doors that have no business being forced open again. Oh, and makes me bone people I shouldn't. *Here's looking at you, Malic.*

With reluctance, I set my half-empty glass of strawberry margarita on the counter. Fuck. I want to drink it all, but it'll only make me think of them more. I'd probably do something stupid like walk to the treehouse and maybe burn it down.

Actually, that's not a bad idea. I'll add that to my 'destroy the boys' list, for later.

I have to get out of here. First, I have to collect Simon and possibly his new gal-pal. Hopefully, he's quiet when he gets down.

With that in my head, I make my way out of the kitchen and into a tight hallway, leading toward the front door. I could be an asshole and leave now, but I like my roommate. And no man gets left behind. Especially a drunk man who happens to be a super lightweight, unable to handle his booze. Or keep his tongue to himself.

The narrow hallway separating the kitchen from the foyer is clear of anyone. Even in the small bathroom and empty room down the hall. Surprisingly. When we came here, the place was packed, but now it seems to have cleared out a bit. Much to my damn relief. With so many bodies in here, it was like a sauna. And getting overly heated with this binder on is a recipe for disaster. And uncomfortable, too. God, I'm so sweaty beneath these clothes. I can't wait to shower.

Once I'm awkwardly standing in the front foyer, trying and failing to take in several deep breaths. I linger by the stairs, contemplating jumping over the chain blocking anyone from going upstairs. Sure, the sign hanging there says do not enter, but when has that ever stopped me before? What would they do? Kill me? Been there. Done that. They can try. I'm nosy enough to risk everything and claim I was looking for the bathroom.

Just as I'm about to climb over the rope, loud footsteps hurriedly coming toward me stop me in my tracks. Drats. There goes that idea. Maybe another time. I'm sure this won't be the last party Oliver Davenport is forced to show face at. Two guys with flushed faces murmur secrets beneath their breaths as they march into the foyer and nearly mow me down.

"Party next door!" one guy hisses to me with wide, glassy eyes. "I heard they got strippers and body shots. It's epic!" He pumps a fist in victory.

I wrinkle my nose. How classy. A frat with a stripper and body shots. But whatever floats their boat, and good for the strippers for being so confident.

I had to be an undercover stripper once. It was... awkward. And my dance moves? Pathetic. The club owner called us in because their girls were going missing, and the cops were doing fuck-all about it. He had to beg me not to get on stage again. Thanks, asshole.

I know I'm not coordinated. Thankfully, that job only lasted a month, and I got the hang of being at the club and serving drinks in my skimpy outfits. Thankfully, we caught the bastard who was taking girls and selling them on the black market. God, why does the black market have to be a thing? Why do we need to sell girls, guys, and body parts, anyway? Can't everyone just be morally good?

"You think Mal and Wilder will take any pledges this year?" his friend asks, darting his eyes behind him and catching me lurking. "Rumor is they are. We should totally fucking do it!"

"One can only hope, bro. Getting in their organization would be epic as fuck. No one knows who their boss is. But they're badass. I heard Malic killed a guy this summer for looking at him funny."

"Bro! All the more reason." They high-five like some dude-bros and walk out the front door, making a mad dash next door.

Killed a guy? Yeah, that's reassuring. Note to self, never get into bed with Malic again. If that bastard finds out who you are and who you work for, you're screwed. That should be enough to calm down the ovulation activities.

But it's not. Ugh.

This place just keeps getting better and better. The mystery deepens, and I have a feeling that by the time I'm done at GU, I'll have grey hair and need a massage. Or need to be laid again to loosen me up.

But not with Malic. Nope. Not him. Or Wilder. I need a bar, a stranger, a bathroom, and… No, we're not letting history repeat itself. Even if it was a good time. Psychopath. Tracker. And so on.

More people pile out of the party, while stumbling over their feet to get to the party next door. Those strippers must be a sight to see, because this party is dwindling into almost nothing. I'm half tempted to follow them over there just to see the sights. Soon, the air isn't as heavy with bodies, and I can take a full breath. Well, kind of. I really need to drag Simon out of here so my tits can breathe for the night. I rub my temple, fighting off the headache already forming. How am I going to get Simon out of here?

I peek into the half-full room and groan. He's still having dance-sex with the girl on the dancefloor. Only now, there's another girl with her and him, sharing a hot and heavy three-way kiss. *Huh. Never tried that before.* He's clearly having the best night ever, and I'd hate to drag him away, but I'm no longer having fun. I pout to myself, feeling the slight effects of my margarita. Mentally, I cheer the alcohol on, aching to feel its effects more. Maybe I should go back and down another glass.

Yeah, sounds like a plan.

Leaving Simon to his amazing three-way—Go Simon!—I take a step back into the foyer with the intention of going into the kitchen. But the sight before me has me stumbling back a step, nearly losing my balance. Golden fur streaks by, heading down the hall toward the kitchen. His claws click against the worn wooden floors, echoing as he moves. My chest tightens at the sight of him.

The golden fur. The big, furry ears. The familiar black nose with dark whiskers.

Waffles.

"I found him!" Hux proclaims through a crack in his voice, holding up a blond fluff of fur who squirms and whines. Hux's cheeks heat when Mack grins, eager to rip into him about the newest development—a squeaky crack in his voice. "Shut up," Hux grunts, deliberately lowering his voice so it doesn't squeak. Something it's been doing lately. Along with his growth spurt, making him nearly six feet tall at thirteen.

"A puppy?" JJ asks, petting the squirming furball.

"Yeah! I found him running around in the cemetery." Hux shakes his head, sadness pulling down his features.

That can only mean one thing.

I frown. "Someone dumped him?"

Hux stiffens, looking down at the little guy with a frown. "Yeah, I think so."

"It wouldn't be the first time someone dumped an animal at the cemetery," JJ offers sadly.

"We need cameras at that damn entrance so no one can do that again." Mack leans in and chuckles lowly when the dog licks his face.

"Are we keeping him?" There's hope simmering in my chest when the dog licks Mack again, waggles his little tail, and squirms out of Hux's grip.

"I..." Hux stutters slightly, staring down at the puppy in question, running playful circles around us.

This wouldn't be the first animal we've found wandering around the property. People see big woods, a cemetery, and think it's the perfect place to leave their unwanted animals. Normally, we give them to the animal shelter for quick adoptions.

But this puppy feels different.

"We can totally hide him from Franco," Mack says, plopping on the forest floor below our treehouse. The puppy jumps into his lap and licks his face over and over again. "Oh, yeah. This dog is ours. See? He already loves me!" Mack proclaims with a laugh.

"Waffles," I say, sitting next to Mack and reaching a hand over.

"You want waffles?" JJ asks seriously, hovering above with concern in his eyes. "Have you not eaten? We can go to the diner for breakfast. They serve it all day." He checks me again, taking in the size of my cheeks and chapped lips.

"No!" I laugh, running my fingers through the puppy's fluffy fur. "He reminds me of waffles."

"I like Waffles. Waffles John Owens Jones Crewes Viotto." Mack lifts his chin with pride.

"So...you gave him all our last names and John? Who the

hell is John?" Hux huffs. "And why is my last name fifth and almost last?"

"What do you think you should be? First?" JJ cocks a brow at Hux who shrugs in response, sitting next to me as Waffles crawls all over us.

"Our little secret?" I ask, petting Waffles behind the ears as he attacks my face with kisses.

"Yeah." They all agree at once.

Waffles wasn't a secret for long. Franco found out almost immediately after finding Waffles curled up in Mack's bed, despite the promise to leave him outside. He forced us to live up to our responsibility and take Waffles to the vet for shots and registration and clean up his messes. It was the one time Franco gave fatherly advice instead of barking orders. Or hurting us. Instead, he let us keep Waffles as long as we trained him.

"Waffles," I whisper faintly before I can stop the words from falling from my lips. It's hard not to call out to him. One of my old pals. My furry companion. The dog who looked after me when my life was at its lowest point. Or what I thought was my lowest.

The lock clicks into place on the outside of my bedroom door, sealing my fate for the night. I sigh, sitting on my bed, and stare at the clock. There's nothing else of substance left in here to entertain me.

No computer. No TV. No lamps.

It's a prison.

"You're lucky you get a mattress to sleep on!" My father barked at me before he shut the door in my face sans dinner.

Yeah. Lucky friggin me. I get a mattress. I guess it beats the damn basement he was once obsessed with throwing me in. At least in my bedroom, I can sneak out the window without detection and call the boys from my secret cell phone. Even with the bars on my windows. They've become useless to keep me in.

Somehow, JJ maneuvered the bars in a way that my father will never find out they've been tampered with.

"Yo, Buttercup!" Mack hisses through a whisper, tapping on the bars over my windows. "I'm here to bust you out!"

"Come out," JJ whispers with excitement, lightly tapping on the bar.

A loud bark rings out through the night air, pulling me to the window with a grin. Waffles wags his tail, yipping at the two standing outside my one-story window.

"Waffles, man! You can't be so loud. We're busting our girl out. Not trying to get caught." Mack glares at Waffles, who slightly whimpers and sits on his furry butt while pouting.

"You hurt his feelings," JJ mutters, patting Waffles on the head. "Be a good boy." Waffles raises his nose and nudges JJ's arm like he understands the command.

I grin. "Please hurry. He just left like twenty minutes ago."

Mack scoffs, "Yeah, I know. Had that kid with him, too." He rolls his eyes. "Got in his loud ass car. That's how we knew it was safe to come and get you. Probably driving away and plotting his takeover or some shit." Facts. My dad hasn't been around a lot. At first, I thought it was jobs Franco was sending him on, but now I'm not so sure. Not to mention the companion he brings with him. A kid I met once, the night he was rescued from a terrible situation. Now, my dad keeps the kid around him, but never here. Oh, no. He has a special place where he hides him, and then they do business together. Probably in an upscale apartment or some shit.

I frown. "Yeah. He's been with him a lot lately. I'm starting to think he's up to something. You don't think?"

Mack shrugs. "Hopefully nothing serious. Maybe it's something for Franco or whatever. Let's roll. We're going to the Coliseum to dig for more treasure." He grins at that, earning a soft bark from Waffles. "Boyyyy!" he whines, tossing his hands like a father chastising his son. "You're not a good jailbreak buddy.

Next time, I'm bringing Hux to the window, and you'll be the lookout out there." He gives Waffles a sharp look again while waving toward the forest.

That's how it's always done. One of them waits in the woods, looking to make sure no one else is around. Usually JJ will walk toward the front of my house and keep an eye on my dad, but today was different. And Waffles? Well, he's always right here beside Mack, barking up a storm and alerting the damn world that I'm leaving. Surprisingly, though. We've never been caught.

My lips quiver. The memories are a gut punch. Uninvited and consuming. How dare they run through my mind without my damn permission. It's like every glimpse of this world they've built in Greenwood has memories dislodging in my mind.

I don't want to think about the past. Their smiles and laughs. I want to think about the future. AKA when I get to leave Greenwood again. Only this time, I'll be on top while they're squirming in a Veritas prison begging for freedom.

Our dog. Waffles. He was our baby. Family, even. When I left town, I tore out everything the boys had done for me and threw them in the trash. Including Waffles. But he never betrayed me. He was always there, looking out for me. Except that night. They must have locked him away so he wouldn't follow them to my house and have to watch while they decimated me.

I suck in a breath when Waffles stops mid step. His ears raise. His head tilts.

Goosebumps break out on my flesh when I jerk back, practically falling into an unoccupied room. Tears form in my eyes as I lean my head against the wall.

I can't face my dog. What if he doesn't recognize me? What if he does? I am completely different. Especially in this disguise. But I don't want him to recognize me. I don't want him to know that I'm me. It'll hurt too damn much to face that reality.

An ache forms in my chest as more memories pour through

my mind like a damn movie. The same memories I hid deep inside my mind, practically erased.

They kept our dog.

But threw me away like trash.

I can't be here anymore. I can't walk in a figurative graveyard of the ghosts who haunt me relentlessly. Including Waffles. He never turned his back on me. Not intentionally. But the other three? I can't continue to stand in their weird frat house with my heart in my throat and pretend I'm okay.

So, I find Simon on the ratty couch, pouting about the girl who ditched him for the other girl. Who happened to be her girl-friend. Simon is crestfallen when I drag his drunk ass out the front door and past the raging party happening next door. It's the same type of thing. Loud music. Partiers screaming woohoo on the inside.

As we pass by on the sidewalk in front of their house, the hairs on my arms stand on end when Malic leans over the railing of his porch and grins at me knowingly.

"Wanna party?" he asks, raising a glass.

"Too much partying!" Simon grunts, covering his mouth with his fingers. "Oh, snickerdoodles," he gags out before bending over and tossing his cookies on their lawn. And oh boy, that's a lot of red margarita vomit.

How poetic.

"We're all partied out, thanks," I say, making sure to lower my voice. He's psycho enough he might recognize the cadence of my voice, and I can't have that. He'd probably follow me home and live in my closet.

"That's a shame. Tell Simon to feel better." Malic tosses back his drink and continues to watch us until Wilder comes out on the porch with an unlit cigarette between his lips. They exchange heated words with Malic gesturing all over the place, but I'm unable to hear them over the sound of Simon's heaves.

And damn.

I rub Simon's back as he continuously vomits on their lawn, and I eye Wilder under the rays of the moonlight. He's shirtless, and just as I suspected, he has tattoos on almost every surface of his body. Fuck.

"I'm good now," Simon slurs, leaning into me when he stands tall. "Goodnight, boys!" he shouts, waving to Malic and Wilder like they're lifelong friends.

I raise a brow when Malic waves back, but Wilder doesn't bother. His eyes sear into me, though, like he's attempting to figure me out. Just like he always did when we were kids. Except back then, he hated my damn guts. Just like he hated his brother's.

We couldn't get out of there fast enough and back into our dorm, where I tucked Simon into his bed and made sure he fell asleep on his side. Little snores pour out from between his lips as I leave a plastic bowl, Tylenol, and a glass of water at his bedside. At least if he vomits in his current position, it should hit the bowl, and I'll hear everything he does. His roommate is MIA, and so is mine, leaving Simon in my care. I sigh when I step through his open bedroom door, opting to leave it open so I can hear if he needs me.

Once the quiet of my room sinks into my skin, my brain won't stop turning over the night's events. Them. The dog. Hux's apparent fiancée.

For the first time in a long time, I sink into my fluffy pillow, pull the comforter over my head, and cry.

I sob for the ghosts of my past. The memories. How they ruined everything. Stole my life from me. And for what?

This? This life they're living now?

OLIVIA

His lips press against mine. Possessive. Heavy. Eager and needy. Like I'm something he can't wait to have over and over again. Well, the feeling is mutual, Hux. I've been hot and ready for a long time now.

"Olivia," Hux rasps, pushing a hand under my shirt as the bark of the tree roughly pushes into my back. His mouth runs down my jaw, nipping and biting and leaving his marks all over my flesh.

As if to say–she's ours.

And I am.

"Huxley," I groan when his fingers squeeze around my breast, and I cry out when he pinches my nipple, hardening it to a painful point. He tugs several times, making my pussy clench and ache for them to fill me already.

"You are hogging our girl," Mack grunts, stepping up to my other side. "But damn does she look happy and so fucking hot," he groans the last part, biting his fist.

Lazily I grin at him as Hux continues to work me over. Lust rests in Mack's hazy eyes as he takes us in, and he adjusts himself.

"Flushed face. Swollen lips. Glossed-over eyes," JJ says with pursed lips. "She's definitely happy." And so very horny.

The guys and I have done everything under the sun, except the deed. The P in the V. The getting down under the sheets. And I'm so ready to break that barrier. I'm ready. They're ready. All you have to do is look at the boners poking through their jeans at the sight of me moaning against the tree to know they want me. And I want them.

"But an orgasm could make her happier," Mack quips. "Ain't that right, Buttercup?" He leans in, taking my lips with his while Hux continues to work me over and sucking my skin between his teeth.

"Yes!" I practically shout into Mack's mouth with a moan as his fingers find my breast, and he groans with pleasure.

"We should go to the treehouse," JJ interrupts breathlessly. "We should..."

"I'm ready," I say, nibbling my bottom lip as they hover around me. *A normal girl would be intimidated to have three men around her, eager to pleasure her. But I'm not. I've been ready for over a year and counting down the days until this happened.*

"You're sure?" Hux asks, stroking my chin.

"Of course she's sure, look at that look on her face." Mack grins, squeezing my boob again. "God, your tits are amazing. I can't wait to suck them into my mouth," he groans.

"Treehouse," JJ interrupts again with a huff. "You know Franco uses these woods sometimes. Last thing we need is one of his soldiers or bosses marching through here and seeing her like this."

"He's right. We're the only ones who should ever see you like this." Hux nods, reluctantly untangling himself from me.

"Now, how about those orgasms?" Mack wiggles his brows when we make our way up the small ladder and enter through the hatch in the floor.

"I'm down for orgasms." I grin, nearly squealing when Mack launches himself at me and we land on the floor.

"Then prepare yourself, Buttercup," he murmurs, hovering above my face. "I'm going to bury my face in your pussy for the next thirty minutes and then...." His eyes soften at the implications.

"You'll fuck me?"

"No," Hux says from beside me, forcing my eyes to him. "We're going to show you what it's going to be like for the rest of our lives, Trouble. You. Me. Mack. JJ. It's us against the world. And this?" He motions between us as Mack slowly undoes the buttons of my jeans and pulls them and my panties down. "This is forever." He grins, running the tip of his finger over the golden ring on my ring finger.

Our little secret—his eyes say.

"Forever." I moan the second Mack connects with my clit, and he throws my legs over his shoulders roughly as he dives straight into my pussy with his tongue, wiggling it around. His fingers dig into my thighs, sending thrilling shivers up my spine as my back arches off the ground.

A glorious orgasm bursts through me as I cry out, feeling their hands on every inch of my body and...

I wake with a start, sweat dripping from almost every surface of my body as a real orgasm breaks through dreamland and my pussy contracts around nothing as my fingers work over my clit.

Wonderful. A sex dream on my first night at college. Nothing beats images of your ex-boyfriends turned murderers going down on you and giving you a real orgasm during our first time together. Honestly. I'm blaming my lack of vibrator time last night and ovulation. Even though my periods have always been off, weird, and out of sync. I know it's coming for sure, and my body is warning me.

I blow out a breath, wiping my hand over my eyes and collecting the moisture cascading down my cheeks. Attempting to settle my raging heart rate and the ringing in my ears. My breaths continue to heave. The remnants of an orgasm flows through my veins, dripping my brain in heavy doses of dopamine and oxytocin, leaving me to float on a cloud. Despite how torturous it is to know that it was them in dreamland giving me all the pleasure.

I obviously didn't drink enough margaritas to drown out the lingering memories. At least this wasn't a nightmare. I could have screamed the entire dorm room down with my shrill cries. I stiffen in my sleepy state. Shit. What if I moaned?

"You moan in your sleep," a gruff voice accuses me. "Like a fucking girl."

I scream at the sound of an unfamiliar voice and quickly cover myself up from the intrusion. Like a girl? Shit! It's because I am a girl! My surroundings come into focus. Forget the sex dream that woke me up mid fucking orgasm and my fingers down my pants.

My roommate is sitting on his bed, watching me with a curious gaze filled with disgust. Fucking stalker! I need to ask for a room reassignment or something. Maybe they'll feel pity on me and give me a better roommate so I can orgasm in my sleep in private and not have some asshole roommate stare at me like I'm a show.

"What the fuck?" I hiss, staring at my murdery-looking roommate, lounging on his bed.

His nose wrinkles, looking me over. "I said, you moan like a girl in your sleep. Your scream was really high-pitched, too. You sure your balls have dropped yet?" He sneers at me, sitting up and shaking his head.

I rear back. My balls? It's on the tip of my tongue to ask him what he's referring to. There ain't no balls down there, buddy. But at the sight of his scowl and beady, judgmental eyes, I remember where and who I am.

Oh, and who he is.

My asshole roommate Dane.

I blink several times at his bare chest sprinkled with dark hairs and the boxer shorts cling tightly to his very hard dick.

Oh my God.

It's goddamn morning wood. Or I turned him on with my girly moans. No! Not that. Ugh.

I squeeze my eyes shut and clear my throat. "Yes, asshole," I grit out in my lowest voice, scratchy from my apparent sleep-screams. "My balls have dropped and are fine. Thanks for asking, though." See? I'm good at this undercover shit.

"Right," he scoffs, walking to his dresser and gathering a pair of jeans and slipping them on. How does he do that without bending it? "The rule still stands. Don't touch my shit. You scholarship kids have sticky fucking fingers."

"Just because I got here on my academic talents and don't have to pay a dime, doesn't mean I'm going to steal your shit," I snap, sitting up without a thought and glaring at him. "You stay out of my shit too, asshole. I don't know you. You could be a rich little thief whose Daddy gets him out of jail." My chest heaves, and his eyes stray to it briefly before meeting my eye again.

Fuck.

I pull my comforter over my chest and up to my chin. Yeah. Not suspicious at all. Good thing I have a solid B cup for boobs and they aren't as noticeable under my baggy t-shirt.

Dane raises a brow as he pulls a shirt over his head with the GU blood drive advertised on it. "Whatever you say, Roomie. Let's just agree to stay out of each other's way. Yeah?" He proceeds to put his socks and shoes on and stands a solid six feet, looming over me with a frown.

"I'm fine with that. But no reason to be a dick all the time," I practically hiss between clenched teeth, watching him closely as he grabs his wallet and keys from his desk.

He shrugs with a grunt, throwing our bedroom door open and waltzing out of the dorm suite. The front door slams, rattling the entire place with his exit. I stare after him with a huff. Fucking prick. Why did I have to have a roommate again?

Ugh.

I swallow hard and check my phone. It's only seven in the damn morning. Where is that prick heading off to so early? And why did he come back? I was really hoping to have this room to myself. But that's my naivety talking. I always have to be on my toes. No matter what.

To ease my mind, I scroll through the SlamApp again, trying to catch anything suspicious happening. But it's mostly the same gossip, new events popping up, pictures from the party we attended, and something about an annual blood drive coming to Greenwood in a few weeks.

Staying in bed for the extra ten minutes calms the nerves left over from my damn sex dream and orgasm. Just as I'm about to put my phone down, an email pops up in my notifications, letting me know I have an advisory meeting this morning to discuss classes and goals. It's mandatory. Also, I had no idea it was planned. But I have three hours until I meet with her, giving me plenty of time to get ready and go over my case instructions again for clarity.

With that in mind, I slowly sit up in bed again, making sure my chest is covered with my baggy shirt. After a night filled with orgasmic memories I'd rather not relive, I need a hot shower and a fresh pair of clothes. My only hope is that my new roommates won't interrupt me or try to barge in. From my experience, they don't particularly care if you're in the shower and have to piss. Or maybe that's just Jordy and his rudeness. Whatever. I have to stay vigilant and in character.

I'm thankful this isn't a dorm that has only one large bathroom the entire floor shares. Small miracles, I guess. I could have it a lot worse. I would have to shower and use the bathroom with other men in the stall next to me. Now that's a goddamn nightmare.

Silence encompasses our dorm suite as I make my way to the bathroom with an armful of fresh clothes, boxers, my contacts, glasses, binder, and soaps. It's a simple bathroom with the necessities—probably smaller than it should be—with a small pedestal sink, one toilet, and a shower hidden behind a white shower curtain.

Before I climb into the shower, I double-check the lock on the door and climb under the hot water with a sigh, running my fingers through my hair. I swallow hard when I get to the short ends of my shaggy cut. After so many years of keeping my length, it's all gone.

I squeeze my eyes shut and blow out a breath. In and out. Over and over. The heat of the shower curls around my flesh, anchoring me in the moment.

Don't lose yourself to the memories. Hold yourself here in the present. Here, they can't hurt you again. They may be physically close–a breath away. You're safe. You're in control. You're...

My eyes fly open when the doorknob jiggles again and again. Someone pounds a fist into the wood, echoing through the tiny space.

"I'm showering!" I shout above the sound of the water.

I hold my breath when the jiggling stops. I swear I hear a voice on the other side of the door, but can't make it out. Apparently, though, whoever it is doesn't get the damn memo I'm in here. The bathroom door flies open and hits the drywall with a thud. He mutters under his breath, something I can't quite make out again. Feet shuffle, thudding hard against the floor, like he's staggering in here disoriented and drunk.

Fuck.

My heart thunders in my ears, barely cutting off the sound of the toilet lids raising and smashing into the back of the toilet without care.

Ice flows through my veins. Oxygen stalls in my lungs. The sound of water hitting water and the smell of urine fill the room.

Good God. What did that man eat? Asparagus? I think he needs his damn bladder checked out.

I put a hand over my mouth and nose to stop the gag in the back of my throat. The last thing I need to do is wretch in the shower and have whoever is pissing their life away, peeking inside and finding a naked woman. Instead of their roommate, Oliver. Instinctively, I take a step back from the white shower curtain concealing me. Or not so concealing me. My breath shudders when his shadow moves, swaying left and right. Fuck. I shift backwards, praying to whoever is above that he can't see my shadow through the curtain like I can see him. I'm not shapely, but if he looked hard enough, he'd see the outline of my breasts. Or the shape of my muscular ass.

I hold my breath until the last drop of his nasty urine hits the toilet, and he flushes it.

"Sorry, bro!" he grumbles, hitting the shower curtain with his hand, knocking it into the steam of the shower. "Had to go."

It was locked, you asshole! Is what I want to say. I grit my teeth and uncover my mouth, moving my hands to hide my breasts.

"No worries," I say in a low voice, trying to sound okay with it. Even though I want to nut punch whoever it is.

From the sound of it, it's not Simon. Dane is gone. So, it has to be Wade. The collared shirt guy who Simon says is nice. Yeah, so nice, Si. He just burst in while I was showering. Is there no privacy here?

I count down the number of staggered footsteps until the door slams shut again. Everything goes quiet except for my breath frantically escaping through my nose. My eyes roll toward the ceiling, and I shake the nerves skittering through my body.

Peeking through the crack in the curtain, I make note of the empty bathroom. Great. I thought I'd at least have privacy here with it being the only lockable door in the suite. But I was wrong. Very, very wrong.

After getting dressed in the bathroom with my back to the door so nobody else could barge in, I come back to my room and fish out my laptop. Plopping down into my provided computer chair, I log into our secure network and reread my case instructions. Everything will be there on the portal for me to view. Even the papers Jonathan handed me before coming and what I studied in the hotel room.

I can never be too careful.

> OLI
>
> Jordy! One of those fuckers just walked in on me in the shower! I didn't know I'd be rooming with another version of you...

I snort, setting my phone on my desk. Just as my phone dings with a message.

> CARTER
>
> I got your fucking tracker.

I cock my head. Right. I sent it in the mail to him before I left the hotel, so he could look it over and tell me if he found anything.

> OLI
>
> And?
>
> Wait! How did you get this phone number? You creeping?

There's nothing that gives me more pleasure than busting Carter Cunningham's chops. He's so grumpy and pissed off at the world. Sometimes I wonder how Kaycee and the other guys

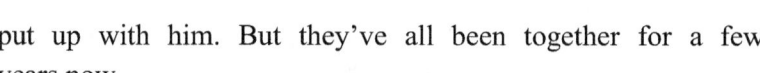

put up with him. But they've all been together for a few years now.

That's beside the point, though.

The moment I stepped foot on Greenwood U turf; my personal phone was taken from me. And in its place a Veritas issued phone fit with AntiEyes–a program that deletes every shred of evidence on the phone into a secure cloud blocked by red tape.

CARTER

Don't ask stupid questions.

OLI

It's not a stupid question, but I'll leave it alone. You sound like you're having a terrible day.

CARTER

Fuck off. Do you want to know about this mysterious tracker or not?

OLI

Duh.

CARTER

Say pretty fucking please...

I stifle a laugh at his idiocy. Sometimes talking to him is like having a brother. He's always up for helping me with technical things when I can't unravel them myself. I don't have the bandwidth to understand what he does. Hell, I can barely operate our private portal. Logging in for me is a miracle in itself. And email? Don't get me fucking started on navigating that.

OLI

Please?

CARTER

It's registered to Malic Monroe. Some fucker from Greenwood. He has the app on his phone. Want me to hack it? Watch his movements? I'm fucking bored.

OLI

Aren't you running a company? How are you bored? And no. Who knows if he's got tech on his side.

CARTER

You're no fucking fun. *middle finger emoji*

He doesn't have tech on his fucking side. He's a goddamn idiot.

OLI

And how do you know? Did you...

I shake my head with realization. It's because he's already tapped into Malic's phone. It must be a slow day in his home office.

CARTER

Because I could hack into his phone without mirroring the damn thing and snoop. You there to watch him? Because you fucking need to. He's got someone in his phone named fucking Boss. How goddamn obvious.

OLI

Boss? Any messages? Calls?

CARTER

Oh, now you want me to fucking help you look through this asshole's phone?

OLI

STFU and give me the answers, Cunningham!

CARTER

Fucking no. Not on this device. Maybe you
can find out if he has another one?

OLI

He's technically not a part of my job...

CARTER

Then how the fuck did he... No wait. You
didn't... Don't even fucking tell me the details.
puke emoji

I roll my eyes toward the ceiling. Give me strength, Lord. I need it to deal with this moron.

OLI

Please don't make me say it, okay? It was a
bar. And...

I'm back in this godforsaken place and needed to numb my pain.

CARTER

NOPE. Fucking Nope. I don't want the dirty
fucking details of your bar hookup who just
happened to put a tracker on you.

OLI

Then don't ask stupid questions.

CARTER

Just keep a fucking eye on him... FUCK. I will
too. If anything pops up... I guess I'll fucking
tell you. Now, leave me the fuck alone.

OLI

Asshole. You texted me first. But thanks.

I don't get a response after that. Typical. He's so moody, but he's helped me with the Malic situation. I wonder who this boss person is and why he has him on his phone at all. Even more suspicious is there are no messages or calls from the person supposedly in charge of him. How are they getting around that?

I get another ping.

> **JORDY**
>
> They didn't see any tits did they? It would be a shame if we had to trade places. I'm bored. This thief is good. But ugh. So boringggg!

Must be a common theme today. Boredom. But not for me. I've had way too much excitement already. I need a goddamn drink.

> **OLI**
>
> NO. If you keep talking about my tits, I'm going to think you're obsessed.

> **JORDY**
>
> With yours? Ew. Hard pass. With that chick in the parking lot who bent over with no panties on? Yes. Yes, please.

I roll my eyes again, huffing when I set my phone down. Thankfully, Jordy isn't the world's biggest texter, so our conversation is brief and to the point. I'll have to be more careful using the bathroom when everyone is here. I'll have to figure out their schedules and shower when they're gone. For me, classes aren't that important to pass, but I'll have to watch the students and professors. Get a feel for the people of Greenwood and see what it's all about.

But for now, it's time for my meeting with my new advisor in one of the administrative wings.

OLIVIA

THE SMELL OF OLD PAPER AND COFFEE HAS MY NOSE WRINKLING the moment I sit across from my newest academic advisor. Dr. Temperance Moreau. Her glasses perch on the tip of her nose as she riffles through page after page in a file marked with my new name.

Oliver Davenport.

Her teased and curled blonde hair sways every time she licks the tip of her finger while sorting through the copious amounts of papers in a stack. Odd. Why would they have so many on me? What the hell did Jonathan send to her?

"Okay, Oliver." Her nasally voice rings through the small office as her dark eyes dart to me. "It looks like you're here on scholarship." Her eyes narrow, looking me up and down. "You understand you must keep a 3.8 grade point average to stay here on scholarship, correct?"

There's judgment in her gaze as she does another sweep of my body, refusing to look me in the eyes. I keep my eyes forward, my Veritas issued glasses trained on her facial expression and how her lips tighten with disgust. It's something I'll have access to later and can watch for signs of deceit or trickery.

"I'm well aware." I wasn't. I have no idea what the fuck

scholarship I was on. I've already been through online classes and graduated with ease—between missions, of course. So, actually going into a classroom and having to keep a good GPA puts a wrench in my—watching everyone during class and coasting through the education part of this mission.

Fuck.

And I can't come out and say, *"Well, I'm not here to learn. I'm here to shake your institution up and get rid of the gangs and crimes and whatever else is happening within these walls."*

The *whatever else* is the important part. I know there's something fishy about this school. Between the rules the RAs laid out and now the looks Dr. Moreau is giving me, has my mind spinning in every direction. Fuck. I need a partner on this case. How am I supposed to do all of this alone? The campus is huge, covering so many acres of land and tons of students.

How can I pinpoint the funny business happening when it's happening everywhere around me? The frats. The institution. The streets. Businesses.

Where the hell do I even start?

My mind spirals as Dr. Moreau speaks. It's probably important what she's saying, but I can't seem to focus until she clears her throat, unimpressed with my lack of concentration.

She raises a haughty brow, her bracelet jingling with every move she makes as she slams my file shut. Obviously unimpressed with that, too.

"You understand that your performance will need to be high to maintain the grades and workload at Greenwood U. We have a very rigorous program." Her lips form a straight, tight line like she doesn't quite believe I'm up to snuff. I wonder if she has a bias for scholarship students, too. It would make sense if all the other students hated them. They learn from their leaders. "Now, it says here that you were a Criminal Justice major at your previous institution." She lifts a dyed blonde brow, waiting for me to acknowledge her.

"Yes," I say, clearing my throat.

"And you're hoping to continue that major here?" I nod again wordlessly. "Good, good," she hums to herself, sliding over a sheet of paper. "Here's a tentative list of classes for you to look over. It looks like you're very close to completing your hours and classes. Your other university speaks highly of you."

I offer her a tight smile, looking over the classes she has down. They're all the classes I've taken online and should be easy to fly through. Maybe that's why Jonathan gave her the transcripts. He knew I'd appreciate having easy classes.

"They look good for the fall semester," I say, handing the paper back, feeling confident in my class options.

This will give me the time and energy to look into the people around me without suspicion. I'll know the material—probably better than the teachers—and ace each class with ease.

At least, I fucking hope so. If this place is as rigid as Dr. Moreau is making it out to be, maybe the material will be harder than my online courses.

I blow out a breath, my shoulders slightly slumping from the relief. Jonathan has had me in questionable positions before. Cases I didn't think I'd make it through without getting killed. Like my previous one right before this job. I almost didn't make it out alive, scrimping by the skin of my damn teeth.

But this one? It can't be too bad, right? It's simple. Straightforward as they come.

Famous last words.

She grins, opening her laptop and pounding out a few words while humming to herself. "Well, good. This will be your schedule for the Fall semester, then. I'll have it emailed to you promptly with class times and a list of your professors. Four classes. 12 credit hours. And then the same next semester." She taps a few more times and sighs, sitting back in her seat. "Your teachers will update me weekly on your performance, and if you're slipping up and falling behind, we will have another discussion. Tutors are available through the library, if you need them." She raises her brow, emphasizing her point.

"Weekly?" The words slip out before I can think about it.

So, they're going to be keeping an eye on me. At all times. Interesting.

"Yes. We take ourselves very seriously here. If you haven't noticed, we produce top-ranking students. Senators. Presidents. Even movie stars." She holds up three fingers, cockily smirking. "And scholarship students have to prove themselves to us. You're here because we want you to be here. So, prove your worth."

That's a good pitch, lady. Prove my worth? This place is fucking weird. I feel like I'm about to enter some sort of challenge to show the leaders of this place I can be an asset. It makes me wonder if that's what's happening.

"And I thank you for the opportunity." I try to sound as polite as I can, but I'm feeling rebellious. My skin itches with the way she looks at me like prey she wants to devour.

Note to self—keep an eye on her, too. In fact, watch everyone working on this campus. They're fishier than fucking frying fish.

"Oh, and Oliver. Here's a flyer for the upcoming blood drive. All scholarship students are heavily encouraged to participate." She slides over a flyer featuring the upcoming blood drive. "If you read there, we're in competition with another university. Whoever gives the most, wins a prize and bragging rights."

I eye her as she grins proudly at the thought of giving blood. It's something I've never done before. But it seems to be important to her and the school.

"Um, thanks. I'm not sure…"

"Please consider. If you do happen to donate, your professors are considering it as an assignment and giving A's to everyone who participates." She cocks her head. "And you could use a few A's to start off the year well."

"Uh, sure," I trail off, shoving the blood drive pamphlet into my back pocket, and pick up my schedule again.

"Well, off you go, Oliver. Enjoy Greenwood. And if you ever need anything, please make an appointment through our online portal." She grins, sending an uneasy wave of nausea through me. "Oh, and please send in my next appointment. She should be right outside."

After bidding Dr. Moreau goodbye and getting shooed away, I step out of her stuffy office into the main hallway of the administrative building. It's quiet out here. Refreshing. No students meandering the halls on this desolate Monday morning. It's nothing like I thought it would be. I always dreamed of coming here as a kid. It was something I thought I could achieve with the guys. We dreamed of partying, joining clubs, frats, sororities, and everything under the sun to be normal. But normal? Pfft. What the hell is that? We were dreamers. Kids raised in the damn mafia and mob. Brought up to murder those who did us wrong and work under the bosses. Well, me anyway. The boys were the future rulers of Greenwood.

Then, we were escaping the inevitable that was bound to happen. Hux was bound by his duty to his foster dad to take up a high-ranking position within the gang. Close to the top, it would be impossible for him to walk away if he changed his mind. And JJ and Mack at his side, fulfilling their duty to Franco. A thank you for taking them in and training them within the gang.

And then there was me. The daughter of a disgraced mafia member. I was a stain in Franco's eyes. A stain he couldn't do anything about. Well, until he did.

As I drag myself out of my thoughts, I ground myself in the present. The marbled floors are thick with grey veins, swirling whites and gold, reflecting the chandelier that rests above the imposing double doors. The crest of the school, hanging proudly below the motto—Morior Invictus | Death before defeat.

Everything about this place screams money and privilege with its arched ceilings, accented gold light fixtures, and dark-stained wooden walls.

A sadness hits me out of nowhere. A feeling I've been too accustomed to lately. It's overwhelming and encompasses my whole body. A buzzing realization that I was meant to be here. But as Olivia. If I had lived past my seventeenth year and graduated from Greenwood High, I would have walked these halls with Hux, JJ, and Mack.

We would have made it. We would have become the people we wanted to be. Who we were destined to become outside the roles our family ties dictated we would be.

Our own people.

But we didn't. I didn't.

They've lived the dream we mapped out, living on campus and going to classes. But not me. I'm no longer a part of the equation.

Do they ever miss me? Wish I were here?

Fuck.

I knew coming here and going undercover would be a bad idea. Everything about this screams stupid. Whenever I'm up close and personal with them, I'm going to lose it. I know I will. I was safe at the party. Hell, even in the parking lot. They were far away and I could view from a distance. Whether it was a hundred feet or ten, I was still unnoticed. But face to face? Looking into their traitorous eyes and having to pretend that it doesn't affect me. These tears will come when I least expect them to.

Greenwood cut me open once, and I know it's going to carve me open completely this time, leaving nothing but a crevice of darkness behind.

As I gather myself one last time, I take a few steps into the hallway, stopping dead at the sight of the girl from the party sitting on the bench outside Dr. Moreau's office, staring down at her phone. Ugh. Amanda. Long blonde hair. Flawless, tanned skin. Dressed in name-brand clothes with an expensive purse.

She's a fucking cloud of suck, staining the room with the

darkness that seems to live deep inside her that gets pleasure from terrorizing everyone.

Including the past me.

"Your boyfriends aren't here to protect you this time," Amanda sneers, *punching me straight in the gut as her two friends hold my arms back in the middle of the women's bathroom. Several girls come in and promptly leave after witnessing the violence with wide eyes and squeaks. A few brave ones roll their eyes and do their business before leaving.*

"They don't have to protect me," I wheeze, *spitting at her feet.*

I gave up struggling against her friend's—Chrissy and Stacy's—hold five minutes ago. Better to conserve my energy for something else. Like plotting her death.

"Why, because you're going to run off and tell them what I did?" She grins, *rolling her eyes like a bitchy, plastic mean girl.* *"You're so predictable and a rat."* Chrissy and Stacy stiffen *when Amanda pulls out a switchblade and waves it in my face several times. The sunshine leaking in through the windows casts a light on the shiny, sharp metal, making my stomach drop to my feet.*

Amanda is untouchable. The daughter of a prominent politician in bed with Franco. No matter what happens, Amanda won't get in trouble for the crimes she commits. Even against me.

I snort, raising my chin. *"I won't have to tell them a damn thing."* *It's true. I'm sure by the time I leave this bathroom, Hux, JJ, and Mack will be waiting for me. There have been too many witnesses who have been in and out. They'll hear it through the grapevine eventually and come running. Not that I want them to fight my battles for me, but it's nice to have back up. Especially when my attacker is wielding a sharp knife and threatening to stab me.*

"Yes, you will, you rat. You'll squeal the moment you leave here. I should just put an end to your miserable life." She grins,

running the blade down my arm until my flesh parts like butter. It pools there, slowly dripping onto the ugly green tile. "But I won't. Not now." With that, she shrugs, putting her knife into her pocket with a demented grin. "Come on, girls, we're going to miss lunch. Have a good day, loser." I blink several times when the girls slowly let me go and follow their leader out of the bathroom.

"Fuck," I grumble, marching to the sink and washing the blood off my arm.

Psychotic bitch. I don't understand why she targets me the way she does. Doesn't she have anything better to do with her life than make mine miserable? Everyone at Greenwood High gives me a wide berth thanks to my three best friends and their association with the cruelest man in town. Nathaniel Franco could take her down with the flick of his wrist. If he wanted to, that is. She's nearly invincible because of her father and his association with people in high places all over town, coveting high profile officials in his pocket. All the while working with Franco.

My trembling fingers work up the edge of the long scar on my arm. Carved by a jealous high school girl who couldn't handle the fact that my guys wanted nothing to do with her. No matter how many times her rich daddy tried to intervene and secure her prized golden goose. Franco never considered it. Not back then, anyway. Seems Amanda's daddy worked his way onto Franco's good side.

So, this is where the mean girls go when they've graduated high school. They don't leave town to seek better opportunities. They stay here, go to college, and probably make everyone's lives miserable until they move on to a townhouse in the heart of the city, never leaving unless they're on vacation.

I blink several times, coming to the realization I've been staring at my former bully with a twisted expression. Unfortunately, it doesn't go unnoticed by her like it did at the party last night. She stares back with a vicious expression that would turn a lesser man's stomach into knots. Good thing I'm not a man.

Her nose scrunches up when she stands from the bench, tossing her bright blonde locks over her shoulder and putting her phone in her purse. "You've got a staring problem, asshole." She says it so easily like a melody on the damn breeze. Or a record scratching.

I clear my throat, lowering my arms to my sides. "Not really." I shrug, turning on my heels and giving her my back with the intention of getting the hell out of dodge.

To her, I'm a man standing in the hallway staring at her weirdly. But to me, I'm still that helpless little girl subjected to her bullying tactics and refusing to tell my best friends about it. I didn't need them interfering. It made me look weaker than I was. Besides, they only made the bullying worse. Even if they knew what was happening. That day, they were waiting for me outside the bathroom with grim expressions. They didn't force me to tell them who it was. Because they knew. They always did. So color me surprised to find out that she and Hux are engaged. What does it matter, anyway? They killed me. She bullied me. They're a match made in hell.

"No, I think you do," she sneers, her heels pounding against the beautiful marble floors and getting closer to me. Her tiny fingers dig into my shoulder, stopping my retreat until I'm turning and facing her. Well, looking down at her. Being a girl who is over five-foot-ten has its advantages sometimes. Like now, when I'm pretending to be a man. Or staring down the girl who made my life miserable.

Damn, she's stronger than she looks.

I glare down at her, raising a brow. "I don't." I shrug with indifference. If there's one thing I've learned over the years, it's not to give in to your bullies and simply leave them with indifference. It pisses them off.

Her nose scrunches further. "You do! You were staring at me!" she hisses, poking me in the chest aggressively.

Yeah, I was trying to figure out what I was looking at. It's what I want to say, but I bite my tongue. Nothing good would come out of me mouthing off to her. It would only put a target on my back, and I don't need one of those. In fact, I need to get into her good graces. But if she keeps poking me with her fingers, I might snap.

Without thinking, I grab her fingers and hold them mid-air. I don't twist them or squeeze with all my might, but I do make a silent threat with my steady grip. "I didn't give you permission to touch me." My gaze flicks between her fingers and her open jaw. "I don't have an issue with you. It's you who is making this an issue." My voice drops so low, it's so unlike myself. "Now, don't fucking touch me again." I level her with my best glare, leaning in close so she gets the message.

"Let go of me!" She shouts loudly enough that her voice echoes off the damn walls. Her left hand, shiny with a pretty engagement ring, pulls at my fingers to release her. "Let go of me, you pervert!" She shrieks again with urgency, her breaths frantically heaving in her chest.

I'd believe her panic if there wasn't an evil shadow lurking in the backs of her eyes whenever her gaze flicks over me.

"She said to let the fuck go of her."

Everything inside me freezes. Ice flows through my veins at the sound of his deep voice reverberating from behind me. A voice that hasn't graced my presence in five years. A voice that haunts me every fucking day. Fuck. My fingers lose their grip, and Amanda stumbles backward, whining about her wrist and the pain it's bringing her. Yeah, fucking right.

But nothing compares to the vise around my heart, relentlessly squeezing it. I knew coming face to face with one of them so closely was going to be a challenge. Seeing them from a distance in the car was off-putting. Being in the same vicinity as them at the house party was earth-shattering. Even when I saw his lookalike so many years ago, sitting in the restaurant in East Point, California. Right before I enrolled in their prep school as Espie, the new student. I froze in the stranger's presence then. It was like looking at the man I had fallen in love with. Tattoos on every inch of him. The same moss-green eyes reflecting back at me. I couldn't take my eyes off him. Not until I realized it couldn't have been him. Not in this lifetime. Not in East Point.

It was at that point in my life when I wished upon a star, begging the universe to never bring me face to face with Huxley Crewes again.

Boy, did that star let me down.

Now, Huxley Crewes stands before me, coddling Amanda Devalle in his massive arms. His jaw twitches when he looks from her wrist to me. I swear the moment his moss-green eyes flick up and down my body, the hairs on the back of my neck stand on end. My chest tightens being so close to him, yet so far away.

And rage boils inside me.

Who can completely forget about the boys who murdered me? I couldn't. Not fully.

Now, I have to face them all again. My demons. My murderers. Talk with them. Pretend I'm not dying on the inside every time I look at them or see their eyes.

"I don't know what's wrong with him!" she wails, tears flowing down her reddened cheeks. "I just asked him what his problem was with me because he was staring like a perv!" she accuses, throwing her arms all around.

I swallow the thick lump lining my throat. "I was leaving and she approached me," I say, standing tall. Yup. Time to seal those pesky emotions bursting at the seams inside me.

Don't show him your fear. He's like a bloodhound, sniffing it out. Don't show him your weaknesses, or you'll never get close enough to send him and his friends to prison.

So, as much as I want to say that bitch started it. I play it cool. I fold my hands in front of me with my schedule still squeezed in my fingers and rock on my heels. I can almost hear Jordy's voice in my head telling me to puff out my chest and seem more alpha in the face of danger. Sure, Jordy. Easier said than done.

"No," she wails again, snotting all over Hux. "He approached me. He asked me if I was down to fuck and being a perv."

I cock my head at her lies, making sure my glasses record the entire event for later. So, this is how Amanda continues to play her games. Spouting lies to get her way. Kicking and screaming like a toddler to make her point. Back then, Hux didn't spare her the time of day. None of them did. No matter how badly she wanted them. They ignored her antics. Now, though, it seems like she has him wrapped around her little finger.

Great.

What other surprises do they have in store for me? So many changes in so little time.

"Go into your meeting, Mandy," he says, squeezing her shoulder affectionately. "I'll have a little talk with the perv." His deep voice rattles through my fucking bones. Just like they used to. Only this time, I'm unaffected. Everything I felt for him at one point in my life has been replaced with hatred and rage.

I'm trying not to run back to my room, fetch my knife, and kill him on the spot for revenge. Unfortunately. That's not a possibility I can even entertain. I can't let any of these emotions cloud my judgment or make me act stupidly.

I'm Oliver now. I don't know Huxley. Fact. Maybe I never did. But I need him right now for my mission. All of them. Alive and intact. Which is quite unfortunate, if you ask me. I'd rather bury my problems alive and leave town. But that would be considered a bad work ethic. Bummer.

My fingers curl around the edge of my schedule. If I'm about to get pummeled in the hallway, I know how to defend myself against him. I can take out a grown man with two fingers to the side of the neck and make him piss himself before he can even blink. Just ask Jordy. Poor guy.

Amanda sniffles, nodding. "Thanks, Bunny," she whispers, getting on her tippy toes to kiss his scruffy cheek.

From here, I can see the day-old reddish stubble lining his jaw, cheek, and over his lips. I also bear witness to the small twinge of disgust the moment her lips land on his flesh. His chest heaves when she pulls away with a grin, darting her gaze to me. As if to say, have fun being a dead man, loser. She lifts her fingers and waves before turning on her heels and marching into Dr. Moreau's office.

"Look, man," I start to say when his gaze whips to mine and fury takes over his expression. Before I know what's happening, his chest is flat against mine, and my back meets the hard wall behind me.

Well, that's really fucking forward of him. Do not go back to your dorm, grab your knife, and shove it up his pee hole. No matter how much he deserves it.

You need him. You need him. Ugh.

"Don't fucking 'look man' me," he snarls in a low voice, getting in my face. "You stay the fuck away from her. Don't look at her. In fact, you should go pack your fucking bags and get the fuck off my campus." He waves a hand, pointing out the door. "It would be better if you fucking leave." He looks me up and down now with a snarl, snatching my schedule from my hand. Taking a step back, he scoffs, ripping the paper in two. "Oliver Davenport, huh? Scholarship student." He nods a few times, sneering at me. "That explains it." He tears my schedule into little pieces, tossing them on the ground and spitting on the pile. "Should have fucking known it would be a weak ass scholarship student pulling that shit. Pack your bag, shitstain. No one wants you here."

Shitstain? What the absolute fuck is wrong with him? His

words do nothing to calm the raging storm brewing inside me. If it's a fight he wants, then it's a fight he's going to get. I won't play around and let the people at this school think that just because I got a full ride, they can push me around.

"How about this, you pompous, rich asshole," I growl back, shoving him in the chest and knocking him away from me. He stumbles over his feet, looking at me with wide eyes, like he didn't expect me to do anything but whimper and beg for mercy. No more. I had enough bullies when I went to Greenwood High. This high school bullshit ends now. "Keep her away from me. I didn't do shit. She can lie to your face all she wants, but I won't fucking allow it. Now, it's time to get off your high and mighty horse and get the hell out of my face," I sneer at him, poking him in the chest and letting him feel my wrath.

It's the only time I'll let the fire unfurling inside me spread through my body like lava, free to unleash the anguish that's been bottled and buried for so long.

Fuck you, Huxley Crewes.

Before I know what's happening, I realize I've backed Hux up against the wall, and fury lives on his face. But his hands remain in the air, suspended there with his palms facing me. Almost as if he's refusing to put his hands on me again. He can spout off all the words he wants, but it seems he won't be laying a hand on me. Which is fine. But also, I'd like to see him try.

"If this is your campus, maybe you should fucking check the cameras, huh?" I gesture to the cameras hiding in the corners of the hallway, capturing every move we make. I take a step back, dusting off my chest with pursed lips. "And I won't be leaving. I kind of like it here." I don't. It's a lie. I'd pack my bags in a heartbeat, but I can't.

Hux blinks several times, his eyes dilating slightly until he shakes his head. "I don't trust you, scholarship student." He looks me up and down again, stepping off the wall. "I'll be watching you." Those are his parting words as he walks out the double doors, slamming them shut behind him with a growl.

"Yeah. Well, the feeling is mutual," I mutter so only I can hear the words spoken and not the cameras. If there's one thing I know about the three of them, Hux is heading off to JJ, who can expertly hack into anything he can get his fingers on. Especially cameras.

JJ

My favorite time of day is the hours between 1 am and 3 am. With the moon above, the stars sparkling in the sky, and the quiet. I relish in the silence—the nothingness after existing in a world always on the louder side of things.

Every corner of Greenwood seems to dim beneath the bright neon lights. Even the casino goers stumble back to their beds with empty dreams and pockets to keep them company.

The world seems to cease. It's quiet. Desolate. Dead for at least a few hours. But Greenwood is never truly dead. The underbelly is always alive, crawling through the shadows, and ready to emerge at a moment's notice.

There's something about the silence that soothes the itch in my flesh that seems too tight. It takes the anxiety from my mind and tosses it out—the stress, the emotions, the past. Everything ceases the moment I step into the moonlight and surrender myself to the night. It's familiar even—something I can fall into with open arms, diving headfirst with my eyes closed.

Especially when today's world is too loud and chaotic, over-whelming my senses and begging me to retreat to a quieter environment, like my bedroom. My sanctuary away from all the bullshit I call my life.

Like now.

Campus is alive. Packed with people lining the sidewalks, cafes, and even the library. Nowhere is safe from their incessant chatter and scuffing shoes. Even the breeze carries their conversations to every corner of the property, haunting me with the very thing that makes my teeth sit on edge.

Noise.

It's in every molecule in the air. Making my teeth grind and an uneasiness crawl through me.

It's been a long, quiet summer without my peers. I retract that. Quiet was not included in our summer adventures. The homefront was loud and chaotic. The empty campus was our sanctuary. Quiet and empty, devoid of noisy humans. Leaving only Hux, Mack, and I here, running jobs for Franco throughout Greenwood like one of the dutiful foster sons we are. Sitting in on meetings at the casino, running contraband from city to city, participating in car races, and leading raids.

The quiet was soothing, but I knew it would end when everyone returned to their college life at one of California's most prestigious institutions.

Louder than fucking ever.

Fuck. I pinch the bridge of my nose, wishing I could hide behind my screen and never emerge into the real world. But I can't. We have business to attend to. Shit to do. And with classes starting on Wednesday, there's no time to slack off and hide in the silence. I need to face the noise head-on, even if I'd rather not.

Silence is my comfort. A soundless environment I found peace in when I was eight and the world suddenly stopped turning and making noise.

I sigh with relief when my hearing aids naturally adjust the volume, blocking out the voices and muffling their existence. The pressure on my skin eases, and I no longer feel tight and scratchy with the urge to run back to our home.

I promised Hux I'd help him today. Well, until Amanda

texted and whined she needed him, throwing a wrench into our plans. Per her fucking usual.

So, that leaves me, watching my peers from the shadows as I rest against the weathered brick of the administrative building, waiting for Hux to deal with Amanda's—well, I'm not quite sure. There's always something with her. She never leaves him be. Always up his ass to do this and that for her. And now, after being forced to put a ring on her finger, per Franco's request, it'll only get worse. For all of us.

Unless I find a loophole in their grand scheme to marry Hux and Amanda for alliance purposes. And if anyone can do it, it's me.

Adjusting my posture, I lean against the weathered brick with the muffled noises of everything happening around me softly in my ears. Relief hits me out of nowhere, and I close my eyes, unfurling my muscles. When I peek an eye open, a few girls I recognize walk by, but they don't notice me here watching them from the shadows.

I may be unable to hear their conversation as they pass by, none the wiser of my presence. But I can read their lips. Every word spoken. Every sigh passing between them. In my world, it comes in handy to be able to read people. Their expressions. Their lips. Their body language.

My specialty.

I cringe, turning sharply on my heels with wide eyes when the double doors of the admin building burst open, smacking into the brick with a loud thud and revealing my scowling best friend. His shoulders reach his ears, bunching with every step he takes down the small set of stairs leading to the sidewalk. Other people notice his sudden outburst with slack jaws and whispers. Yes. That's the infamous Huxley Crewes. The King of Greenwood U that everyone drools over when he makes an appearance.

"Hux?" I question loudly, not garnering his attention.

He continues to march away from me, pounding his feet into

the grass and kicking up dirt in his wake. Every person he passes gives him a wide berth now, no longer staring with admiration. Instead, it's fear wafting from their pores. Smart. He's likely to start swinging if someone gives him lip or the wrong sideways glance.

Always with the violence.

"Huxley." My voice dips low, attempting to catch his attention as I jog after him. "What did she do this time?" I gasp for breath, putting a hand on my racing heart.

Running is not my forte; if I had it my way, I'd stay behind my computer screen to accomplish what I needed. Hell, I'd even go to virtual classes just to avoid the noisy world and everything it has to offer.

Too bad that's not in the cards for me.

"I run Greenwood U now, boys," Franco says with a grin, pacing in front of us as we sit in the suite overlooking his casino floor. Something in my stomach drops when he stops, looking between the three of us with something odd sparkling in his eyes. "So, you'll be good to show the student body who their kings are."

"Kings?" Hux asks, tilting his head.

Franco's grin widens. "You're the Kings of Greenwood U now."

"And you run it now?" Mack asks, smacking the gum in his mouth loudly. Well, until Franco sends him a glare, he stops with a huff.

Franco shrugs, not exactly confirming a change in command. "This is where you boys come in. The future is in your hands. Our organization. This town." He licks his lips. "Greenwood has potential, and we're going to exploit it for all its worth."

Whatever that meant. That day, we were given instructions on how we should run our clubhouse. Hold initiations. Find more members. Introduce them to our life and expand our business around the United States.

"Not here," Hux grunts, slowing his steps to a normal pace. "Let's go home." He nods toward the back of campus where our house sits on the hill overlooking the entire damn world.

Well, that wasn't our original destination.

"You don't want to..." I trail off when the fury in his eyes connects with mine, and my lips snap shut.

Okay, then. We're not doing that right now. Not that I don't blame him. That's an entirely different type of shit show he's involved us in. Albeit necessary for the good of campus, but very fucking messy.

"No." He doesn't have to elaborate anymore.

I blink several times, looking around the bustling campus. There are many things we can't discuss in the open with ears, cameras, and everything else around. Contrary to what people like to believe about us, we're just pawns in a ruthless game with no clear winners.

Well, except for Franco. He sits at the top of the food chain here in Greenwood. The puppetmaster behind so many things people can't comprehend.

I simply nod, following down the winding sidewalks toward the back of campus.

My least favorite spot.

A heaviness presses hard on my chest. Oxygen becomes thick and difficult to drag in between my lips. I almost stumble over my feet.

My heart aches when we skirt around the cemetery, following the iron fence that lays out the perimeter of the dead. They're in there rotting beneath the world, and we're out here. Alive and barely breathing. Some passed naturally. Others passed suddenly without rhyme or reason.

And some passed too soon at the hands of someone else.

My gaze scans the multitude of headstones bursting from the freshly mowed grass. Instantly, I spot the one that always has my attention.

She's in there. *Our* girl. Resting in a wooden casket, filled with silk lining and what remains of her. Olivia. Like she has been for the last five years. Killed way too young and taken from her destiny.

From us.

So cruelly ended without a proper goodbye.

We all had dreams of leaving this place. Together. For always. The four of us as a unit.

Our dreams never included staying here. Not in the family business. Not fulfilling our duties that were so graciously bestowed upon us. We were going to run. Leave to the other part of the country with new identities.

But we never made it.

Hux, Mack, and I are all cogs in Franco's well-oiled machine. Come this time next year, we'll officially step up to our destined roles given to us by him. For now, we're watching over the college and recruiting people under the guise of our fraternity house.

I stand with my garbage bag at my side, filled with the only things that belong to me. The world remains quiet, engulfing me in the nothingness I've become accustomed to. And has been since the moment our tires squealed and our car crashed. That one incident ruined my entire life, taking out my parents and my sister.

That was years ago.

I've been to two foster homes on the opposite sides of California. Two separate and different families, unable to handle me and my lack of hearing. He's too much trouble, one foster mom said with a sneer, breaking my little heart into pieces. She didn't think I could understand her as she talked on the phone with my caseworker. But I could read every word on her lips. I may be deaf, but I'm not inadequate.

So, here I am. Third time is the charm, right? My caseworker stands beside me, gently squeezing my shoulder and staring down at me with hope in her eyes.

"You'll love it here, Jasper," she says slowly for me to comprehend and read her lips.

I nod, letting her know I understand.

Then, a man walks in. He looks larger than life. Striding in with a fancy suit, matching the fancy house. I can't understand what the two of them are saying as they face away from me. But I'm sure she's warning him about me. I'm a lot of trouble. I'm a lot of work.

I'm not.

I'm just a sad ten-year-old boy, begging for stability after my family was taken from me. I just want them back. I want to go home. I hate being the new me.

My eyes flick up when two boys who look my age approach me. The taller one with brown hair holds out a notebook with words written on a page.

Hey, I'm Hux, and this is my friend Mack. I heard you can't hear.

I lick my lips and nod, waving in greeting.

Hux nods again, writing something in the notebook.

Jasper, right?

I nod again and gesture for the notebook.

My mommy calls me JJ.

And that was the first moment I met Hux and Mack. They immediately took me under their wing and showed me what true brotherhood could look like. Franco did his best as a foster dad, even getting me seen by a professional and getting me hearing aids. We all learned sign language together and formed a real bond that continues today. I still ache to hold my mother's hand one last time or tell my sister I love her. Those feelings will always be there.

My family now is the two boys who helped dig me out of the depression I had fallen into. Another thing that's never truly gone. Especially when I look out at the graveyard and spot her name from a distance.

With one last lingering look, I take in Olivia's final resting spot, making a mental note to order another charm for whenever I visit her again. I can only hope her spirit looks down and smiles at the many gifts I've left her in the past as a reminder that I'll never forget her.

"Spitfire!" I whisper, knocking on the bars over her windows excitedly. "Happy birthday!" I say again, noting the movement coming from inside her bedroom.

She grins, looking at me through the thick metal bars. "Yes, happy birthday to me," she quips sarcastically, twirling a finger in the air. She leans her chin on her hand and sighs. "How's the outside world today, JJ?"

I grin, puffing out my chest. "I've come to break you out."

Her brows raise. "Break me out? But he'll know if you mess with them." She blinks several times when I dig out tools.

"He's gone, right?"

"Well, yeah. He always leaves around this time…" she trails off when I nod, getting to work and loosening the bolts on the bottom part of the bars.

"Good. I'm breaking you out, and then I have a present for you."

She instantly perks up, looking wide-eyed. "A… A present?" she hums. "You didn't have to get me anything…I…." she trails off when I pop the bottom sets of bolts off the bars and gently lift the solid piece up with a grin.

"You're free now. Come and get your present."

There's fear in her eyes when she looks over her stiff shoulders and nibbles her bottom lip. She's been getting locked in her room for months now, and the bars were a new feature. Raphael is keeping her locked up tight, trying to keep her away from everyone around her so he can continue to manipulate and isolate her.

I couldn't take it anymore. Not seeing her after school or hanging out on the weekends was killing my heart. So, I devised a plan, keeping it to myself, to break her out permanently without her dad getting wind of it.

Liv doesn't question it again as she climbs out the window with an umph and wraps her arms around me.

"JJ," she whispers on the verge of tears. "Thank you for getting me out of there." She doesn't say it feels like a prison to her, but I know it does.

"You look beautiful today," I whisper, wrapping my arms around her and squeezing her tight. "Now, you want your present?" She nods eagerly when I dig into my pocket and pull out a small jewelry box wrapped in birthday paper.

She grins as she opens it, tearing into the paper and letting it drop. "Oh, JJ..." she trails off, holding up the small silver bracelet with one charm hanging from it.

"It's a lighthouse, Spitfire," I say, running my finger over the small charm. "I'll get you more charms to go on it. But this felt.... right. You're the light of my life." My cheeks instantly heat when she gently kisses my cheek and pulls away quickly.

It's a punch to the chest every time we walk past this graveyard. I can never forget Olivia. The feelings she invoked inside me. Or the way she laughed and talked about her favorite things. Walking beside her final resting place every day is a constant reminder that I let her down. I let her get swallowed by flames and let her slip between my fingertips.

"Spitfire," I mumble, taking her hand in mine. Her supple skin softens as her head leans on my shoulder.

"JJ," she mumbles as softly as she can, scooting closer to me in the tree house overlooking the forest surrounding us. The faint sound of the waves crashing against the cliffs in the distance infiltrates my ears.

This. Right here. Everything to do with Olivia calms the storms inside me. She's the lighthouse on the rocks, bringing me back from the brink of losing myself. If I didn't have her, I'd drown in the endless ocean.

"JJ, what's going on?" she asks sweetly, tightly clinging to me.

How can I explain what's going on? It's all inside my head. Like a bad feeling sinking in my guts. Something is coming, but I can't put my finger on it.

"I'm not sure, Spitfire," I sigh, snuggling closer to her.

I find peace in the silence of the night when no one is around. No one, but her. My Spitfire. The girl who took me by the hand, learned ASL with me, and helped me adjust to a world without my parents in it. The girl who soothed the angry boy who lived in silence and showed him that life was worth living again.

Her big brown eyes gaze up at me when she tilts her head. Her lips a breath away from pressing into mine.

"Whatever it is, I'll be here, okay?" She smiles at that, tugging at the edges of her lips.

"Always and forever, Spitfire."

But it wasn't always and forever. The feeling I had came true. In the form of taking her away from me. One second she was there, grinning at me. And the next? I was standing above her casket, attempting to be strong for everyone else around me, when I was anything but.

When Olivia died, she took pieces of me that I could never get back. She took the only noise I could stand to listen to. With her at my side, the world wasn't as fucking dismal as it is now.

Without Olivia, the world is too noisy. Too dull. Too fucking grey to ever exist in. Sometimes I wonder why I'm still here, and the love of my life is buried in the graveyard I'm forced to walk by. Why I still have oxygen to breathe, and she only has dirt, darkness, and a pit of nothingness.

Much like my soul.

The world used to shine with her by my side. She quieted the demons and terrors that kept me up at night.

And now...

I shake my head, following behind Hux up the steep hill. The warm breeze blows the slight sweet smells of the white English Daisies planted outside our home. As the heat barrels down, the flowers slowly wilt, curling their petals for relief, and soon, they'll close up completely like they had never even bloomed.

Sometimes, I wonder if Hux thinks of her, too, when we stroll by the graveyard or walk by the flowers he planted in her honor. Does her smile warm his frosted heart? Does the memory of our time together bring out the softer side of him that once existed? I know Mack does. He can't help himself, even though he would never tell us.

Olivia wasn't only my safe space. She was all of ours.

Ours. Together. Forever and always.

224.

JJ

HUX'S SHOULDERS BUNCH WITH EVERY STEP HE TAKES TOWARD the mansion. The level of rage coursing through him hasn't cooled off since we left the administrative building, and he hasn't uttered a word since we started our trek through campus. I know once we're in the safety of our home, he'll explode and open up. But for now, I eat up the silence between us until we're striding up the walkway toward our home. It towers above us. The gargoyles perched along the roofline of our gothic-style home look down on us with varying degrees of facial expressions. Some snarl, showing their sharp teeth, and some leer with hollow eyes, sending shivers down my spine.

They're a fascinating creation meant to ward off the evils of the world. Only here, they add to the unease I feel every time I'm in their presence. Like they're watching me. Spies from another dimension.

"So," I hold out the word as he slams through the double doors of our home, marching through the foyer, and straight into the open-concept kitchen. The refrigerator door slams open, clinking the condiments around, as he searches for a frosty beer hidden on the second shelf. He slams it shut, cracks the top of the beer, gulping down several mouthfuls of the liquid until it's gone, and throws it into the recycling without saying a word. His dark gaze doesn't stray to me as I stand there, waiting for him to answer. "Hux?" I question again slowly, like I'm speaking to a wounded animal backed into a corner.

Hux leans his hands on the granite-countertop island, spreading his fingers out and heaving in breaths. It's been many years since I've seen this type of reaction from Hux.

"I need out of that," he grunts, finally lifting his head. His red-rimmed gaze meets mine, and I nearly stumble back at the emotions screaming at me through his eyes. Something I haven't seen in a very long time. But I hold my ground. For Hux. "I can't do that with her." He shakes his head, groaning with frustration.

Frustration, I completely understand. Before I can open my mouth to ask more questions, the front door slams open, revealing Mack's sweat-soaked bare chest, damp blond hair, and tiny running shorts, followed by a panting Waffles trailing after him in search of his water bowl.

Poor old dog. I'm surprised he's able to keep up with Mack's intense pace every day.

"You really don't leave anything to the imagination, do you?" I quip about his outfit, earning a snarl and a middle finger.

I wasn't the only one who wilted away the moment we learned about Olivia's death. We all did. Hux uses violence to sate his pain. Mack runs himself to death and makes reckless decisions. He also uses violence to sate whatever demon lives in him. And me? Well, I hide myself from the world. What's the point of existing in a world where the sun doesn't shine anymore?

We're a miserable mess.

"Fuck off," Mack grunts, bursting into the kitchen and pulling out a water bottle from the fridge and a container of grapes. He sets them on the counter and stares down at Waffles melting into the floor. "Need some water, Old Man?" he questions playfully, picking up his water bowl and filling it. But not before adding a few ice cubes—Waffles' favorite.

Waffles groans when he picks himself off the floor and lopes to his fresh water, taking several long licks.

"You good?" I ask, looking Mack up and down until he levels me with a glare that could puncture through my skull. "I'll take that as a no."

"It's always a fucking no," Mack grits out, shoving the stool back and plopping down with a huff.

"Welcome to the fucking club." Hux shakes his head, looking slightly lighter. He blows out a breath when Waffles trots up to him with renewed energy, spilling water from the end of his tongue. Hux doesn't hesitate to reach down and rub his head a few times. No doubt calming the raging storm inside him. Waffles is the only living thing that could approach Hux when he's too angry to form words and live to tell about it.

Waffles takes his pets and slowly looks around the room. I swear, some days he's looking for Liv, despite her passing away five years ago. It's like he expects her to walk through the door and hug him like she used to.

"Waffles!" she squeals, marching through the front door and grinning when he comes running with a woof. "Good to see you, boy," she murmurs, dropping to her knees and wrapping her arms around his body.

"Sometimes I think she loves the dog more than us," Mack quips, walking into the living room and wiping the sweat from his face after a leisurely jog around town. He never pushes himself too hard, just enough to exercise for the Water Polo season.

Olivia's glare blasts through us, and she huffs, kissing Waffles' head. "You're funny," she says sarcastically. "Of course I love the dog, but not as much as you three." Her cheeks heat when the words fall from her lips, but she doesn't backpedal.

"We love you too, Buttercup. Now, come on. Let's eat some dinner while Daddy Franco is out policing the casino."

"So, what did Amanda do this time?" Besides annoying him to the point of insanity. Obviously.

"We could murder her," Mack pipes in, shoving a grape into his mouth. Hux side-eyes him with a frown. "What? You act like it hasn't happened before."

"Yeah? And what would Franco say?" Hux raises a brow.

"He'd say. Oh, well. I'll find a new alliance for my business," Mack says nonchalantly, like the alliance between Amanda and Huxley hasn't been carefully planned and executed by Franco and Mr. Devalle. There's too much money and too much time invested in the two of them to not bring their businesses together.

"More like he'd have our heads. You know that's his ticket into the big times," I mumble, sitting beside Mack. My nose wrinkles. "You need a shower."

Mack scoffs, forcefully shoving another grape into his mouth. "That's the smell of fitness victory," he rumbles, curling his arm and showing off his thick muscles. "Besides, I'm getting ready for Friday and the season."

"It can't come soon enough," Hux grits out. "I'm going to beat that motherfucker's ass." Something haunting lights up in his dark eyes, flashing quickly.

"You're really going to take on that giant motherfucker?" Mack asks through several grapes in his mouth before swallowing them almost whole.

Hux levels Mack with a glare. "Why wouldn't I? He challenged me. I'm not going to back down. Besides, he needs his fucking face rearranged." For many reasons that Hux won't be willing to discuss. "Would you not take on your fucking brother?"

Mack stiffens, swallowing his mouthful of grapes. "I'd never back down from that fucking fight." Hux throws his hands in the air as to say—see, motherfucker?

Speaking of Malic… I nod, putting my elbows on the countertop. "You heard from her?" Every motion in the house stops, and I swear a pin could be heard dropping.

They all know the *her* I'm referring to. Meredith. It's where we were going before Amanda called. We'll keep trying to find any sign of her, but we're losing hope. It's been over a week since anyone has spoken to her or seen her face. We're hoping she's lying low somewhere, keeping out of sight. Even her brother is getting concerned, and he doesn't seem to have any sort of feelings.

But we can only hold out hope for so long before, internally, we know something awful happened.

"No." Hux's jaw flexes at the mention of her. I know he's blaming himself for whatever happened. If something bad happened. It was their plan together. Her idea. Hux will carry this on his shoulders for eternity if we don't find her alive.

"We'll find her." I try to sound reassuring, but even I'm feeling doubts about my claims. Will we find her? Alive? Dead? She's not a part of this world. Or the other. She was out, living her dreams, but suspected something, and instead of going to her brother, she came to us for help because she was too afraid Malic was in on whatever was happening.

"It's the Shades," she says, shaking her head. "It has to be them. It has to be…"

"Is that why you came to us instead of your brother?" Hux asks suspiciously. For all we know, this could be some weird ploy to infiltrate us. It wouldn't be the first time someone came into our organization, attempting to relay information back to their bosses. Only to get caught.

"Yes," she says with a firm nod. "My brother is too closely associated with them. Always has been."

"What if it's us?" I ask, leaning back in the small booth of the deserted restaurant.

Her eyes widen slightly, and a pallor takes over her face as if she hadn't thought about that.

"It's not, for fuck's sake," Mack grumbles, biting into his burger like an animal. *"Franco doesn't allow that shit under his nose. Organ sales? Pu-fucking-lease. That's Shades bullshit right there. Right up your brother's alley and mine, too. Wanna make a club for the world's shittiest brothers?"* He offers her a food-filled smile, and she frowns.

"I love my brother. You don't know how much guilt I felt when CPS tore us apart, and I was sent to my dad's house. A blessing for me, but he was stuck with her." She shakes her head. *"What he went through is not to be made lightly of."*

Mack chews his food. "Whatever," he scoffs.

"Back to this. So, you overheard a doctor, and he was going to sell a kidney?"

Right then, Meredith sighs, pulling out her phone and playing us a video. "My friend and I were right there on the opposite side. They couldn't see us, but we could hear them, and I got this. There are multiple highly accomplished doctors in that recording, operating on a man who was supposed to get a simple appendectomy." I swallow the bile in my throat, watching them operate on the man and taking all his organs without a second thought. Before they closed him up and took him off all the machines, his heart was the last thing to go.

"We have to get to the bottom of this. That man was a father. A family doctor, too." Meredith shakes her head, turning pale. She knows she can't go to the police. Not with this matter. Her friend already tried and went missing from opening her mouth.

And that's how our alliance formed. In a dingy restaurant with poor lighting and good burgers.

Mack doesn't say a word as he eats, but I know what's going through his mind. It's something he thinks every time someone gets close to us. It's our fault. We're the poison in the world. And maybe a part of him is right. Maybe we are the ones who bring death and destruction to everything we touch.

We're broken.

Mack pulls out his phone, clicks a few times, and sets it on the counter with trembling fingers. "Someone fucked with her grave."

Ah. That explains the unhinged rage when he entered the house. My heart may break every time I walk by Olivia's grave, but Mack relishes visiting with her. After every run or when he's feeling down, Olivia is his person, even in death. He'll sit there with a rock in his hand and Waffles at his side as he divulges the day's events to her ghost.

I blink a few times, zooming in on the headstone with a frown. "Who?" My mouth gapes open at the damage. It's completely torn apart, hit with something hard, and broken through the numbers engraved on her headstone.

"If I fucking knew, you think I'd be sitting here sucking on some goddamn grapes? I'd be tearing their throat out and making a fucking example of them," Mack grits out, aggressively biting into another grape, spraying its juice onto the countertop. "No one fucks with that." Not even Franco. He's respected our grieving through the years, helping us come to terms with the fact that she's gone.

But never forgotten.

Hux's fingers flex over the edge of the countertop again, turning white from the force. Red takes over his cheeks, and veins burst from his neck and forehead. "Fuck!" he shouts, picking up a glass and flinging it across the room until it shatters into pieces on the ground. "Fuck! God damn it!" he explodes, clutching his hair and pacing in front of us until he stops, turning his deadly gaze to me. "There are cameras in the fucking area, right, JJ?"

Of course there are. He knows that. We had them installed so we could keep an eye on the people passing through and dumping their animals. Especially after Waffles came about.

We've saved quite a few animals since then because of the cameras hanging on the trees.

"Yeah." There's a burning lump resting in my throat when I nod in agreement. "I'll take a look at it and see if I can find anything." And when I do, that asshole will be in a world of fucking hurt. I'll make sure they never see the light of day again.

"Macklyn." Hux stands tall, his fingers flexing at his sides with the need to hit and bleed to relieve whatever had him worked up in the first place.

"Huxley." Mack doesn't bother meeting Hux's eyes when he shoves more food in his mouth and downs several gulps of water. How he doesn't choke, I'll never know. "Let me finish my recovery. Some of us run five miles every goddamn day." He rolls his eyes, swallowing his grapes and taking more in.

"Fine," Hux spits, heaving a breath.

"So, what has you so worked up?" I ask, trying to diffuse the situation. If I don't get him talking, he'll take it out on the two of us instead of working it out in the gym beneath us.

Hux has been a ball of tension for years now. I hardly recognize him from the man I knew five years before. Of course, Olivia's death affected us all in different ways. Losing someone so important to us imploded our entire universe. Fundamentally changing the molecules inside our bodies.

We lost our entire fucking universe that night, and we've never recovered from it.

"Besides Amanda," Mack says, cracking his neck a few times.

"Besides her." Hux curls his fingers over the edge of the countertop, squeezing tight until his knuckles turn white. "I need to see surveillance footage outside the fucking advisor's office, too."

Mack's face twists. "Why?"

"Because," Hux breathes out, attempting to relieve some

tension. "I think I found a new fucking recruit for this year." His teeth grind, and he blows out a breath, clearly thinking about whatever happened again. "I don't fucking trust them, either." I raise a brow. His gut instincts are hardly ever wrong.

"Keep your friends close, but your enemies closer," Mack mocks, pushing the container of grapes away with a huff. "Weird, you want to add some stranger to the roster, though. It's usually those fuckers who put their names into the jar at our interest party. You've never handpicked someone." He stares Hux down suspiciously, and I don't blame him. Hux never takes this part of our job seriously.

We're supposed to recruit people to our frat, which gives them an open door to Franco's organization. AKA the mob and our connections in return for their loyalty. And the interested party? One night each year, we hold a graveyard party. How morbid, if you ask me. But if you're brave enough to eat pizza where the dead lie, then you're brave enough to join our fraternity.

"How can you be so sure? And why should we trust him here?" I ask, tilting my head and examining his expression. It's shuttering. Almost closed off for interpretation. Weird. That usually means he's hiding something from me.

"That's why I want to watch the fucking video. So, shall we?" A perfect evasive maneuver from the expert known as Huxley Crewes.

"You heard the man," Mack says, slapping me on the arm. "Get the goods and let's see the newest potential so I can judge." He grins, but it no longer lights up the room like it used to. Long gone is the carefree Macklyn. In his place is a robot, smiling and laughing like his former self, without the same happiness behind it. The same nothingness we all feel day in and day out of our rotten existences because our sun set a long time ago, and now nothing is the same.

I nod, running up the stairs toward my room, and grab my laptop. Once I return, tension holds thick in the air as Huxley moves beside me with anticipation bleeding from his limbs when I take a seat.

"What makes this guy special?" I've never seen him this worked up about a potential recruit to our cause. Sure, we've had some good members come into our house and prove themselves throughout the four years we've been here. But nothing like this.

Hux eyes me. "You'll fucking see." He gestures for me to bring up the surveillance footage, and I do. Clicking through, I bring up the time we were there and start the video. My brows furrow. "Him? He's so..."

"Lanky and fucking soft looking," Mack snorts. "He'd never survive the trials of initiation. Can you imagine that tiny mother-fucker on the obstacle course? Or in paintball? Please." We all lean in when Amanda pokes a hysterical finger into his chest, and he grabs it without pause. He doesn't seem to hurt her but restrains her from touching him. I roll my eyes. "Let me guess, she made up another story to try to get you to beat his ass." If there's one thing about Amanda, she likes to create chaos for Hux. If she's not the center of his attention, she makes it her mission to be. That's all she craves from him—attention.

I watch with deep fascination as Hux backs the dude into the wall with a vicious snarl. All for the cameras, of course. He has to protect Amanda even when she isn't watching. Per the rules of their engagement. Even if it fucking kills him on the inside. Most men back down from the vicious stare of Hux. But not this guy. He doesn't cower an inch. Instead, he raises his chin, staring directly into the eyes of the beast without fear. Standing slightly shorter than Hux's six-foot frame, he should be terrified. He should be anything but calm and collected. And... Holy shit. My lips part.

"Jesus," Mack says, slack-jawed. "You let that tiny fucker push you against the wall?" He shakes his head. "Why didn't you just hit the bastard? Not like Franco would fucking care. We rule this goddamn place, dude. You can beat whoever you fucking want without consequence."

"What, like you do?" I grumble, earning another glare and scoff.

Mack has a bad habit of throwing punches, or getting other people to do it for him, like hired hands. He's reckless. Violence lives in his veins, feeding him whatever it is that he's been lacking since Olivia left us. I guess that's why we created the fights at the Coliseum so Hux and Mack could punch away their frustrations without repercussions. Not that there are any for us. With Franco practically owning the administration and college, we're invincible. At least, that's what Mack thinks.

"New. Recruit." Hux emphasizes with force. "Besides, I can't fucking go around hitting everyone I want to. That's what the Coliseum is for. Franco may have the administrators and the Dean in his fucking pocket." And bed. But we don't dare talk about that. "The kid could have pressed charges. Or some bull-shit. The last thing I fucking need is Franco on my ass." More than it already is--are the words he's not adding. "There's something about this asshole, okay? We just need to keep an eye on him."

Hux is Franco's golden child. He holds him on a pedestal despite not being blood-related. In fact, none of us are blood related. We're foster brothers, raised in the same home by the same sadistic man who brought us up in his likeness. If he couldn't have his own children, he chose us carefully to continue his legacy—just the three of us, though. He saw something inside us.

Especially Hux.

"Then the new asshole obviously doesn't know how shit works around campus." Mack grins. "We're the fucking kings. Now, prove it to the little fucker. I could probably snap him like a goddamn twig." He snaps his fingers for dramatic effect. "We have a reputation to uphold. Those other little fuckers on the strip think they can swoop in and become us. Pfft. They got a shitstorm coming for them."

Hux rolls his eyes toward the ceiling with a huff. "Don't fuck with him, Mack. Or anyone, for that matter. I swear to fucking God." Hux's gaze narrows on Mack, who loves tormenting people around campus with cruel practical jokes.

"You're a buzzkill," Mack fake pouts, crushing his empty water bottle. "Now, let's go beat the shit out of each other." He grins again like he wasn't complaining about jogging five miles and having practices soon.

"Just the goddamn bag," Hux grumbles. "If you want to participate in the fights in a few days, then you have to fucking chill." He points a finger at Mack, who recklessly shrugs.

"Whatever you say, Huxley." Mack grins, shoulder-checking him as he passes by, heading toward the basement with pep in his step. Obviously, the thought of throwing a few punches has Olivia's headstone out of his mind. For now.

We'll punish whoever dared to put their hands on what was ours. She may be dead, but we'll protect her memory until our last breaths. Then, we'll join her in eternity and cement our love for one another.

"He's getting goddamn worse by the second," Hux says in a low voice. "He's going to..." He shakes his head, running his fingers through his hair.

"Fuck someone up? Kill someone?" I suggest replaying the video. I watch with fascination again at the man on screen, pushing Hux around easily. It's almost as if Hux let him corner him. But why? Hux isn't the type to back down from a fight. Sure, he doesn't throw punches like Mack tends to do, but he'll show the other person who is boss.

"Amanda needs to fucking go," he says in a low voice, fingering the necklace beneath his shirt with a sigh. "We need to find out who the fuck did that to Liv's grave." He swallows hard, averting his eyes. "And we need to find a way to get out of this shit hole town before the wedding in May. We need a lot of fucking shit to go right for us."

"I'm working on it." I side-eye him. "There has to be a loop-hole somewhere. And I'll try to find the graveyard feed."

"If I have to marry her, I'm going to end up throwing her out a window before we walk down the aisle." He stands, pushing the stool with a loud squeak behind him with an agitated huff. "Now, I'm going to vent my goddamn frustrations and try not to kill my best friend." He takes a few steps before coming to a stop and looking over his shoulder. "His name is Oliver Davenport. Transfer student. Scholarship student." He raises a brow. "You know what we need to do." He cocks his head until I nod.

"Of course." Keep our eyes on him at all times.

Because if there's one thing about scholarship students, they tend to disappear. Either by quitting mid-year or disappearing into the ether. It's something we haven't quite figured out yet. It's been happening for two years now. One by one, they get picked off until graduation happens, and there are only ten of them left.

But why this one? Why is he so insistent that this scholarship student gets our attention and access into our clubhouse? If he were here, he'd be a little safer. But that's it.

Hux walks away, down the stairs with heavy steps, and heads into the gym. I can tell the moment he starts pounding his fists into the bag, because his loud thunks echo through the house, followed by Mack's hooting and hollering. They may butt heads more than they get along, but they have a bond for life. We're all practically brothers.

Oliver Davenport.

I cock my head when I break into his digital records, meticu-lously going through his past credentials.

"Online college," I mutter to myself, googling the name of the school. "Northridge University Online." I cock my head when one official website pops up. To the naked eye, it looks legitimate. But to the trained eye, it's a facade. Everything about it is fake. Starting with the stock photos representing the students to the address listed at the bottom, which leads me to an empty warehouse somewhere in East Point Bluff, California.

What else can I find out about Oliver Davenport?

No social media presence. That makes him even more suspicious. False social security number, matching to a Derek Vaughn who passed away in the 1980s, in Fresno. In addition to the false college site, I also found falsified high school records. Apparently, his only living relative is an uncle named Jonathan Davenport, residing right here in Greenwood, California.

I look toward the stairs where Hux and Mack continually grunt and punch, beating their frustrations out. I could march down there and tell them everything I've found. But what's the fun in that? Besides, I need to do my own investigating on the subject. I brush my hand through Waffles' fur as he comes to lie beside me with a groan, eager to sleep off the five miles Mack ran.

What are the odds that a new scholarship student shows up in their senior year with false records and a vague background? Slim to fucking none. This Oliver guy could be dangerous for us all, but throwing Hux and Mack into the mix is a deadly combination. So, I'll keep my eye on him, watching his every move until I can decide what he really came here for.

Because it's certainly not for an education.

With that in mind, I pull up the surveillance feed from the cemetery, going over the footage. An SUV carrying two occupants pulls through the small gravel roads, traveling slowly until they come to a stop near Olivia's grave.

Two figures climb out of the vehicle, obscured by the darkness surrounding them. I zoom in, trying to make out their features, but I come up empty-handed. Their license plate is blurry. Nothing I can't undo, though. Unfortunately, it'll take some time to deconstruct the video footage and make it a little clearer.

Fuck.

At least one thing came out of today. A new target to set my sights on and slowly unravel the mystery surrounding them.

OLIVIA

Someone hacked into the school's portal, accessing student information. *My* information. Someone–a stranger–tried to look into my false identity, my previous college experience, grades, address, and Jonathan's association with me.

Oliver.

Fuck.

As soon as I got back to my dorm on Monday, my phone sounded with an alert to the intrusion. I shudder at the thought. Were they able to unravel my true identity? I fucking hope not. Jonathan said he had it all taken care of. That I shouldn't worry about anything happening to my undercover alter ego.

But here I am worrying about my alter ego.

Good thing I have a tech genius on my side, who so rudely promised he'd help me track the IP address of the unknown spy.

It all happened on Monday after my encounter with Hux. Although 'encounter' seems to be too small a word for that. War is more like it. The start of it, at least. Something deep in my gut tells me that won't be the last time I have an explosive reunion with him. And possibly the others. It's only a matter of time, anyway.

Get close to them. Watch the college. Infiltrate their frat.

That's my mission. The entire reason I'm here. So starting

fights with them isn't smart, but being on their radar is. Gaining their trust and proving myself to them is all I have to do. And I've already gone and pissed off Hux.

And now, someone is looking into my information.

JORDY

Have a good first day, squirt. I'm still here... bored as hell. Where is my thief? HEY. Is there a party this weekend? A fight? You know you want to invite your best bud Jordy.

OLI

Best bud, huh? I dunno. Maybe.

JORDY

Thatta girl... I mean boy... I mean... Oli...

OLI

Smooth, dick. You're lucky these go poof after fifteen minutes.

I snort, putting my phone away and lifting my head, letting the sun shine down on my bare face. The one advantage to this undercover disguise is not having to wear make-up. Or high heels. Or small dresses. Or a damn wig. Being a woman is exhausting sometimes.

This one is all me. Just short hair, baggy clothes, and my bound chest. So far, so good. No one has questioned the slight scarring on my face, which has faded slowly through the years. It took time to heal after being burned.

But the one wound that will never fade is the long scar across my throat. It'll forever be there as a reminder to my past.

With a heavy sigh, I weave through the clumps of people making their way toward the cafes and dining hall, animatedly chatting with their friends, and hysterically laughing. Nothing is that funny at nine in the morning. How're they so peppy and perky this morning? I'm half awake. Like a damn zombie waltzing through campus looking for a brain to gnaw on. Even though I'm armed with two cups of coffee in my system, my eyes are heavy and I'm ready to hibernate for a week. Scratch that–a month. Why isn't that an option, again?

Maybe I should have been born a bear.

I stifle the yawn begging to be released, and I finally make my way toward Bryer Hall. The criminal justice section of Greenwood U. Almost every class I'm taking this semester resides here. Apparently, they have a little bit of everything for everything. Including a law degree and a medical degree. You don't even have to leave campus to go through all the years of schooling you need to complete your education, which wasn't available when I lived in town. Greenwood U has certainly grown since I last stepped foot on Franco's territory. Maybe that's his doing. A way to entice people to come here for college and stay longer. A piece to add to my notes when I submit them to Veritas tonight.

Butterflies bloom in my belly the moment I step up to the large building, and I stop dead, staring at the name scrawled above the double doors leading into the building where I'm supposed to take my first class.

Livy Hall.

"You're my dream girl, Livy. My Buttercup," Mack says with a grin, taking my hand. "Now, jump into my arms."

And so, I do. I jump into his arms with a squeak, trying to be as quiet as I can so my father doesn't hear us. I nestle my face into his neck, taking in his clean scent.

"Thank you, Mack," I murmur, gently kissing his cheek.

"Anything for you, Livy. I still can't believe he put bars on your windows. Too bad he can't keep me out. I always find a way." I feel the shake of his head from where I'm snuggled tightly in, and his hands tighten around me. "Now, let's go sit under the stars."

No. That can't be right. The map said this was named Bryer Hall. Not Livy. Not this...

Why is it this?

A bronze plaque sits in the weathered brick, and my breath catches in my throat.

To a loving friend who never let the world dim her shine. You will be missed. Until we meet again on the other side. 2-2-4

I'm going to be sick. That's all there is to it. Every fucking turn I make; there's something here to remind me of who I was and who stabbed me in the back–or throat, more like it. They're everywhere. Every damn step of the way.

How can I escape my past when the reminders are planted on every molecule of this town?

I squeeze my eyes shut, holding back the bile burning the back of my throat. More memories run through my mind as I blink up at the name. It isn't until someone shoulder checks me passing by, and briefly apologizes, that I realize I've lost myself again. To the memories of the past. To them. It's something I vowed to myself that I wouldn't do. Couldn't do–surrender myself to all the photographs and movies in my mind that consist of them.

It's so hard not to fall into the good times. Even the slightly bad times. We had fights. Barely spoke. But we always came back together again.

Until that night they did the unthinkable.

So, no. I can't keep thinking about those happy times when they saved me from my dad's relentless fists and controlling ways. I only think about the fire that slowly crept across the carpet, coming straight for my bloodied body until I passed out and gave in to the darkness.

Because if my best friends could so easily dispose of me in one swipe, was it worth living to see another day?

Too bad I didn't have a choice. By some miracle, I woke up in the hospital after an intense surgery to heal my slash mark and care for my burns.

I shouldn't be alive. Be here. Or anywhere.

But I am. And I have a mission to complete before I can hightail it out of this godforsaken town and continue on with the new life I've carved out for myself.

Hopefully, this time with my life, heart, and soul intact.

I push my shoulders back and lift my chin. Like I've always done, I push those pesky feelings and emotions to the back of my subconscious, tie them in heavy chains, and toss them into the deepest, darkest part of my mind so they can't resurface ever again.

Now, time for class.

"You're Oliver, aren't you?" I peer up from my spot in the back row of the medium-sized classroom with furrowed brows.

My lips pop open to retort–*No, I'm Olivia. Who is Oliver?* But then I remember, before I utter a word–I am Oliver. Oliver Davenport. Male student at Greenwood University.

Maybe I do need more than two cups of coffee this morning. Ugh.

I've lost count of how many times I've dressed up as someone else and slapped a new name on a false birth certificate. All to play a role. To spy on the enemy. Those went smoothly. This? I'm having a hard time remembering my cover name, let alone watching the entirety of campus for suspicious activity.

"Uh, yeah. You're Wade, right?" I ask, clearing my throat as I stare intently at my elusive roommate.

Wade. The Dean's son. And Simon's roommate I have yet to meet, other than talking through the curtain during our brief shower encounter. He's been away from the dorm almost twenty-four-seven. Doing God knows what. There he stands with a double-collared pink shirt, styled blond, shaggy hair, and tanned skin like he's been out in the California sun for days on end. He smiles at me, and it reaches his sparkling blue eyes. Simon says Wade is a good guy. Someone who devotes his time to charities and animal shelters. Nothing raises red flags about him. His record is as clean. To the naked eye, Wade is normal.

"Ah, we haven't met yet. Sorry, man. I'm Wade. I bunk with Simon." He grins easily, holding out his hand for me to take. "I've been really bogged down with last-minute summer volunteer work at the shelter. It's something I help my family with."

"Good to meet you, man," I say, shaking his hand with a firm grip. Okay, maybe too firm. Wade winces, slowly pulling his hand away from mine, and sits in the chair beside me, discreetly rubbing his fingers.

Shit. I can hear Jordy laughing in my head now. If he were here, he'd never let me live this down. I already had to text him to see if guys wear sweatpants to class and if my outfit seems convincing enough. All he sent me was the laughing emojis. *Really helpful, asshole.* So, I went with a loose pair of jeans and a baggy shirt. Pretending to be a man is a lot harder than I thought it would be. I adjust my posture, sinking down into my seat and spreading my legs wider than normal. Man-spreading, as Jordy would call it. I rest my face on my palm as I lean on the arm of the rolling chair I'm in.

Wade settles beside me, putting his laptop beside mine on the long, built-in wooden table, taking up the entire third tier of the classroom. It's strange to be in an actual college classroom. For so long, I studied through a screen by myself, getting the degrees I had always dreamed about.

Growing up in a criminal family definitely had its downsides. I wasn't expected to go to college. In fact, my father wanted to marry me off to the highest bidder. Gary won that bid, I guess. I wonder where that old fuck is now? Hopefully, in a grave after he was murdered. Fucker. Although, at one point, I heard my father and Franco in talks for my hand in marriage to Hux.

Someway, somehow, my father fucked everything up. At least, I think he did. Sometimes I'm not sure why my entire family was wiped off the map. Why I died. Was there a real reason behind the attack? I'm sure in their eyes there was. But for me? There were no answers to my questions as I begged for my family's lives. Only betrayals, with zero remorse and death.

"So, it's your senior year, right?" Wade asks, looking at me expectantly as I lose myself to my endless thoughts of the past.

"Yup," I say, running a hand through my shaggy locks–something I'm not sure I'll get used to.

I haven't had short hair since I was seven and took the scissors to my locks. Man, my mama freaked out, cursing me up and down the hallway. And then, when she calmed down, Mama took me to the hairdresser she used and fixed it into a cute bob. From then on, I swore I wouldn't do that to myself again.

Sorry, Mama. I broke my promise.

It's been an adjustment in the shower too, using less shampoo. Not to mention the men's *Head and Shoulders* Jordy left me and insisted I use it on everything. I mean, come on. They make men's body wash. Why am I using this 3-in-1 shampoo/conditioner/body wash on every bit of my body?

Ugh.

I can't wait for this case to be over so I can leave and forget I ever came back here. But that would be too easy, wouldn't it?

"Me too," Wade says, filling the silence as more students walk through the classroom doors and take their seats, talking with their friends, and laughing loudly.

"You been here all four years?" I eye him as he nods, his shaggy blond hair falling into his eyes.

"Oh, yeah. I'm sure you've heard by now that my mom is the Dean." His eyes roll toward the ceiling, and he huffs.

"It may have been brought up in conversation." I shrug.

"I'm not a snitch, if that's what you're thinking," he says, leaning into me slightly. "Your secrets are safe with me, I swear to fuck." His hands go up in surrender.

"Uh, thanks, dude. I appreciate it. Your secrets are safe with me, too." I nod in confirmation as the teacher walks in from a doorway near his podium at the front of the classroom, fiddling with a stack of papers.

"So, are you going to the Coliseum this weekend? I'm assuming Si is dragging you along." He smirks, popping a dimple in his left cheek.

"Uh, maybe."

"If Si is going, he won't give you much of a choice," Wade chuckles. "You're all he can talk about these last few days. He's been insistent I introduce myself, but I haven't had time," he sighs, running a hand through his hair.

"So, you volunteer at a shelter?" I inquire, attempting to get a read on the guy. Everyone seems to like him around here, including Simon. Students pass by, saying hello to Wade with grins and blushes.

Wade's eyes light up, pride shining back at me. "Oh, yeah. The animal shelter a few blocks from here. My aunt owns the place, and I stop by to help bathe the dogs and cats before they see the vet. It's really rewarding to get them healthy and adopt them out." His chest puffs out with pride. "I really love the job. I try to go there throughout the week during the school year, but it's hard sometimes. If you ever want to join, I'd be happy to introduce you." He grins more, leaning over my way, ready to say more.

"Well, well, well," a familiar voice taunts with a haunting voice that's been slithering through my nightmares and kicking up my heart rate.

"I'll always love you, Livy," he whispers in my ear, pulling me closer to the warmth of his body. "Forever and always, Buttercup."

"Forever and always," I murmur sleepily on the treehouse

floor as the moon shines brightly and the stars illuminate the dead of night.

This is where I find my peace.

Or did.

"Fuck," Wade grunts, pulling back with a frown and flicking his eyes to the new figure standing in front of our table. "Mack."

My heart skips a beat at the sound of Mack's voice. His presence. The fucking aura emanating off him. The hairs on my arms stand on end when I finally lift my chin and stare into the iciness of his eyes. Being this close to the man who decimated my being makes me want to run in the opposite direction. My fingers twitch at my sides as he looks me up and down.

"You're that fucker." Mack points a menacing finger at me as a demented grin twists his lips.

I tilt my head, unable to utter a word in his presence, which doesn't do me any good. I'm supposed to get on their good side, join their frat, and be their bestie. But after provoking Hux on Monday, I don't think they like Oliver very much. Too bad, so sad. Those fuckers are going to have to put up with me whether they like it or not.

"Mack," Wade warns in a low voice.

"What? I'm just saying hello to our newest scholarship student. How's my college working out for ya, huh?" Mack's grin widens when I purse my lips and shrug. Concrete sits on my damn tongue as it sticks to the roof of my mouth, drying out every second he stares at me with those beady eyes and examining me. "I wanted to drop by and give you a little lesson on who rules this fucking school." He leans further in, and my breath catches at the scent of his cologne. The same cologne he's always worn. The same scent I gave him for Christmas when I was thirteen and couldn't afford anything but that. It was from the Dollar Tree. Cheap. But it smelled so good, I couldn't pass it up. Besides, I only had three dollars in my pocket. "I am the fucking king. Along with my two brothers, JJ and Hux. You remember him, right?" His face turns deadly, hardening with every word he says. "So, I suggest you stay in line and stop poking the fucking bears. We can make your life fucking hell." He raises his brow for good measure.

Yeah, whatever you say, dickbag. It's what I want to say. But I have to play it smart. I'm not Olivia Viotto. She was wronged. Murdered. Buried without tears.

I'm not her right now. I can't be.

I'm Oliver Davenport. A man on a mission. I have to remain calm and take whatever they throw at me with a smile. All for the mission. All for the greater good of Greenwood.

I can do that, right?

Thick walls erect in my mind, cutting off the past. I toss them away. I can't think with my heart. Or the betrayals that led me here.

I can only think with Oliver's brain.

"Whatever you say," I finally spit out through clenched teeth.

Yup. I'm smooth. I can tell by the way his facial features darken and his soulless eyes glaze over that he didn't like my response very much. His lips pop open, and he leans in again, getting closer to me.

How mad would he be if I broke his nose? Probably rage-filled. Would it be worth it? Oh, yeah. I'd love to see this douchenozzle bleed. I curl my fingers into fists, ready to beat him down and show Greenwood U that I'm not some pushover. But I don't get the chance.

"Sit the fuck down!" My head snaps to the left at the same time Mack's does as the voice carries throughout the room.

My heart nearly drops. Wilder. I knew he went to GU. As does Malic. I saw the proof after the party while they sat on their porch watching us. But him in one of my classes? That surprises me. If all these gangsters are coming to GU for an education, I assumed they were merely handed a degree without stepping foot into a classroom. Well, I guess I was wrong on that front.

Mack straightens, frowning at the new voice interjecting in our disagreement. Perfect timing, if you ask me. I'd rather Mack get out of my face and sit down before I do something stupid like kick him in the balls. Then, I'd really have a problem on my hands. But hey, this is good for my assignment, I guess.

"Or what?" Mack asks cockily, loosening his shoulders as if he were preparing for a brawl. "What are you going to do about it, huh?"

I swallow hard when Wilder stands from his seat, glaring holes through Mack's head. Oh, Wilder. Mack's slightly older brother by eleven months. His short, blond hair almost makes him look bald as he crosses his thick arms over his chest. His chest, displaying copious amounts of muscle lining his body with loads of colorful tattoos. *Wait,* I shake my head. You're Oliver now. You can't be checking out dudes! You're indifferent to both sexes. Not interested. Because the last thing I need is someone flirting with me and wanting in my pants. They'd get a huge—or not huge–surprise when they don't find a penis between my legs. But ugh, he's so beautiful. And under the fluorescent lights of the classroom, I have a way better view than last night after the party.

Just great! This is amazing. I let my vagina lead me into this situation. I mean, okay, the booze helped, too. And fucking Malic wasn't all bad. It was amazing. I swear, five years of stress fell off my shoulders the moment we both came with a cry of relief. But God, the complications it led to. Like this! What if Wilder takes one look at me and recognizes me? I'm fucked. Cover blown! I'm sure Malic would lock me in his closet and interrogate me about why I'm here dressed like this.

I sink further down in my seat, attempting to shield my face. That night at the bar, I had make-up on with long hair and was dressed in tight-fitting clothes. I don't think he'll recognize me. None of them should. But I still can't take the chance. If only I hadn't gone to that bar and let him do bad

things to me in the bathroom, this would all have been avoidable.

"I'm going to make you do it," Wilder says with an eerie calm.

Everyone in the classroom lowers their voices. Wade mutters under his breath about them being idiots. It seems we're all holding our breaths as they square off, but don't move an inch to punch each other. What a great first day that would be.

"Is that fucking right?" Mack asks with a humorless laugh. "If you're so cocky, we should take it to the fights."

Wilder huffs. "The day you get into the ring with me, little brother, is the day the world stops fucking turning. You prepared for that?"

"I could take you," Mack grits out, slamming his fist onto the table.

"Fine then. You. Me. Friday night in the ring." Wilder raises a brow when Mack deflates a little, like he doesn't want to fight Wilder.

"If that's what you want."

"It so fucking is." The largest grin I've ever seen spreads across Wilder's face, and he nods.

"Gentleman!" a voice rings out from the center of the classroom. "Is there a problem here?"

I almost snort. Is there a problem here? Of course there is. They were getting ready to square off and throw down right here and now, and he wonders if there's something going on. Pfft.

"No, Sir," Mack says, never taking his eyes off Wilder. "My brother and I were just working something out."

"Yup," Wilder chimes in with a shrug and retakes his seat.

"Then, shall we get started?" the professor asks in a low tone.

Mack turns to me, narrowing his eyes. "We'll discuss this more later." *We most definitely will not.* He saunters off, taking a seat next to a larger man with bulky muscles. Every now and again, I feel their eyes looking through me, but I don't pay them any mind.

"Stay clear of him and his buddies. Even that one," Wade murmurs lowly, nodding toward Wilder under the sound of the professor introducing himself and what we should expect in this class.

"They dangerous?" I ask, finally unsticking my tongue to the roof of my mouth.

Wade turns an ashy grey, confirming to me what I suspected all along. "Just be careful, okay? Scholarship students tend to go missing around them." He shakes his head, backing away, just as I have more questions to ask.

"What do you mean by that?" I hiss, leaning in his direction.

Wade's eyes dart between the professor and me before he clears his throat. "It's a rumor. I guess. Not really, though. My mom had to deal with all this shit. But last year, ten scholarship students just poof! Disappeared. I mean, some of them dropped out and ran back home, but there was something that spooked them. I'm not saying it's those three for sure. Or even Wilder and his buddy. But something fishy is going on between those two houses. They're like the Montagues and Capulets from Romeo and Juliet. Minus the love interest." He shudders. "They hate each other. Besides, there's also the dead body that showed up at the end of last year."

So, a dead body showed up a few months ago. Is that why I'm truly here? To figure out who murdered the student? I stiffen. Am I in any danger? I am a scholarship student on paper.

Fuck. This just keeps getting more and more complicated by the second. Wade is insinuating that the gangs had something to do with the body. But do they? Or is there a new big bad in town? So many questions.

"Dead body?" I question, trying not to draw attention to our discussion.

Wade discreetly nods. "Yeah, man. It was a scholarship

student. It's why we all have a curfew now. Scared the campus shitless. Never found out who did it. But the guy showed up with his heart, lungs, liver, and kidneys missing."

I blink several times. Vital organs missing? What was this, a supernatural academy? Are vampires and werewolves walking among us? I shake my head. No. This is something.

"And no one ever figured out why or who did it?" I mumble.

"Nope." Wade scrunches his nose. "So, just be vigilant. You're new here and a prime target for assholes like that." He gestures to Mack, a few rows ahead of us, leaning over to talk to his friend.

I catch myself watching Mack intently. Was it him? Does Franco have them doing more dangerous operations than before? Are they spiraling into a situation they never wanted to be a part of?

Probably.

A long time ago, they told me they wanted out. They were doing what they had to do to survive under his roof, including college. Then, they were done. We were going to run away to a better life.

But are they doing more than that now? Are they murdering people for Franco?

I shake my head when the professor dismisses us with a hand wave twenty minutes early. I shouldn't care what they're up to now. Not really. I should focus on the case at hand. But I've always been way too nosy for my own good.

Getting up from my seat after the majority of the class has left, I dig out my phone and open up my text messages and message the only person I can think of for help.

OLI

Can you do me a favor? I'll owe you.

CARTER

> All you fucking do is take, take, take... And you always fucking owe me. I swear to fucking God you're always begging me for some sort of help...

I can practically hear the growl in his voice through text messages. I peer around the empty classroom, relaxing in the silence. Even the professor left with a huff, not noticing my presence.

OLI

> Can you track this IP address and tell me where it's originating from? Also... can you dig up information on the murder that happened at Greenwood University in May of last year? The missing organs case?

For several beats, I don't hear anything back from him. But I continue slowly making my way out of the classroom, attempting to get an answer out of Carter before I hit the quad.

CARTER

> Missing fucking organs? Wtf have you gotten yourself into? You know what? Fuck it. I don't want to fucking know. I'll look into it. Now, stop fucking texting me.

I roll my eyes at his message. Typical Carter. But whatever. The quicker I can get the information, the better off I'll be with this mission. Maybe I can find out who murdered the poor kid last year and solve it once and for all.

But for now, I'm heading back to my dorm to prepare for my second class in two hours.

Or I would be. As soon as I step into the hall, I'm met with a familiar face leaning against the wall near the double doors with an unlit cigarette between his lips.

Jackson Wilder.

WILDER

My teeth clench at the sight of my so-called brother and Brutus hanging outside the double doors, cracking their knuckles and cackling like dickheads.

"Fucking high school bullies," I grumble under my breath to no one in particular. "Grow the fuck up."

That's impossible for them. Especially Mack. He's perpetually twelve-years-old with no sign that he'll mature any time soon.

Someone needs to knock both of them on their asses to teach them a lesson. Punch a tooth loose. Break their bones. Which seems impossible with how massive Brutus has become over the summer. Obviously, those shit heads have been training him for Franco.

He'll make a great enforcer for their cause one day. I can see it now, having to take him out whenever our plans come to fruition. They're grooming him for the future.

Fuck.

The future. It's full of possibilities and unknowns. I hate not knowing what to expect or who I need to protect.

Mack has always lived a cushy life. The youngest. The favorite. I was the responsible one. The one forced to pick up the slack around the house when he went to play with his friends.

And I let him. Why should he have to be responsible like me? I had it covered for the both of us.

At least one of us had a real childhood.

And then the little bastard betrayed me. His brother. The one who put food on the table and clothes on his back.

"Why the fuck is social services talking to Mom?" I hiss, *slamming through our bedroom door and shutting it behind me.*

My heart pounds rapidly at the implications. Do I want a better home with a parent who is present? Yes. But Mack needs me to take care of him. I'm his older brother. The provider of this family.

Mack momentarily stops packing a duffel bag and squares his shoulders. Almost with pride in his eyes.

"They're taking me."

My breath nearly leaves my lungs. "T-taking us?"

"Not us. Me." He goes back to packing like his words weren't an ice pick to the heart. So cold and calculating.

"J-just you?" I breathe, furrowing my brows. "B-but what about me?"

"Yeah. Me." He shrugs nonchalantly like I don't matter. Like I didn't sacrifice everything to give us a good life. I might be young and stupid, but I know how to survive.

Always survive.

"Why you?" I growl, balling my fists.

It doesn't make sense. There are two neglected kids in this mold-infested house. Hello! I'm here, too. I deserve better than a mom who wants to smoke her money away and forgets to get food for us. I'm the one in line at the food bank and using our assistance to get food at the grocery store. Not her. All she feeds us are insults and cigarette burns.

"I dunno, man. I was with Hux and telling Franco about this." He waves a hand at the room with several holes in the wall from our fights.

Our mattresses rest on the floors, and clothes barely hang in the closet. The scent of cigarettes and body odor hangs like a black cloud throughout our home. It's not much. There's never peace here. But it's a roof over our head—protection from the weather.

And the one perk we had—we had each other.

Now? I'll be on my own, unless they take me, too. My mom wouldn't survive a day without someone cooking for her. Since her last boyfriend took off, taking all her savings with him, she hasn't been able to function.

Mack doesn't pause once to think about what he's done or who this affects. He never does. His impulses get the better of him.

"So, you're leaving me here to take care of her?" I swallow every emotion bubbling inside me. My fingers ball into fists. It wouldn't be the first time we've gotten into a full-on brawl.

And it won't be the last.

Mack's brows crease. "You could always come with me. He's got plenty of room. It's a mansion, man! With so much food, they could feed an army. No more scrambling until the first of the month. Mom doesn't need us."

That's a lie. Mom always needs us. Even though it should be the opposite, we should rely on her to raise us like when we were little kids. She was healthy then. Happy, even.

Until one day she wasn't. She got a new boyfriend who knocked her around, and then he introduced her to drugs. Those were the days Mack and I hid in our room with the doors locked until they went to bed. He was in my arms, crying while I consoled him.

I was his parent, despite only being eleven months older than him.

That day I watched my only companion walk out the front door with social services, leaving me behind to care for our mother as she descended further and further into drug and alcohol addictions.

And the kicker? I still care for her even when she doesn't remember my name or what day it is. Even when she looks in the mirror and doesn't remember the woman staring back at her, as Dementia eats away at her brain, stealing everything she once knew.

I still overextend myself to make her life better.

"It's Dementia," Dr. Hudson says, tightening his lips.

"Dementia?" I whisper in horror, looking at my mom as she blinks rapidly at the doctor. I don't tell him about the drugs she's consumed over the years. Or how she's started drinking herself to death.

My ears ring. "Is that why she's having trouble remembering?" I ask, scrunching my brows. "Is that why she's been so confused?"

She's been forgetting her car keys. Asking me if I wanted dinner repeatedly. I thought it was the drugs. But Ronnie left her high and dry. She's been on a downward spiral, and I couldn't help her. Until she forgot to get dressed and walked out the door.

Now, we're here. The cops warned me she needed medical assistance.

"Unfortunately, yes. And it's only going to get worse." He offers me a slight smile. "It's a lot to take in. There are medications that can help. And we have resources for care."

Within a year of her diagnosis, she was in a care facility. I was working my ass off on jobs to save money, and now, everything I earn goes to her care, picking up the slack of what the state doesn't cover, which leaves very little in my bank account at the end of the day.

I pinch the bridge of my nose, keeping my eyes on my brother and his stupid friend.

They lean in like girls whispering secrets to each other. No doubt waiting for their newest victim to torture a little bit more. Considering I ended their fun before class started.

Oh, what a joy it is to have to see Mack twice a week, so early in the morning, in a confined space.

I guess that's why I'm loitering in the empty hall, leaning against the wall with an unlit cigarette between my lips and the hint of nicotine on my tongue—the poison I refuse to ever put in myself again.

I've seen what foreign substances in a body can do. Deteriorate it. Skin and bones. Crying for a fix. And the memory loss it brings. I once was addicted to the thing loosely hanging from my lips, aching to inhale the smoke and fill my lungs with the poison.

A buzz in my pocket pulls me into the present, and I sigh.

MALIC

> Heard baby bro is going to put his fists into the ring and finally face you. So unpussy like of him. *Devil emoji*

An emoji? My face twists when I read it again. That's new for him. And odd. But who am I kidding? Malic is weird as fuck sometimes. I'm used to it by now. We've been friends for over five years, meeting at a time when I needed someone the most.

WILDER

> And how do you know that?

The showdown literally happened forty minutes ago.

MALIC

> That's the thing about me. I know lots of things about lots of things.

WILDER

> How very specific of you...

MALIC

Also, it was on the SlamApp. *Giggle emoji*
Pictures and all!

WILDER

Of course it is…

Fucking SlamApp. Whatever asshole created that wanted chaos across this damn campus. Sure, it helps us get the word out on fights and who we want to call out. It's entertainment.

But nothing here is a true secret. Spies are everywhere, eager to enhance the bad blood between everyone and continue the feuds.

WILDER

Did you suddenly find the emojis?

MALIC

You could say a songbird told me all about
them… *Bird emoji* *Knife emoji* *Blood
emoji*

I tongue the end of my cigarette and sigh.

MALIC

You were asleep, Old Chap. I couldn't disturb
you when duty called. He was singing so loud
too. *Grinning emoji* *Hehe emoji*

You really missed out. *Shrug emoji*

WILDER

Wake me next time you run off to torture
someone…

Or you might get yourself killed.

MALIC

Yes, Keeper! *Salute emoji*

I lean against the wall with a sigh, tucking my cell phone into my pocket. My next step is putting a tracker under Malic's skin so he stops sneaking out and torturing people without me knowing.

I'm sure whoever he put in his chair deserved it. Hell, I'm sure Boss Man called him specifically to take care of the problem.

But I'm his fucking keeper. His conscience. The one who keeps him in line when he wants to lash out and can't contain his feelings. And he was let loose without my knowledge.

Fuck.

I run a hand over my near-bald head, deep in thought. I'll have to be more vigilant and keep an eye on him. Every step of the way. More than I already do. But I can only be in so many places at once. Like being here in class. Malic has his own shit to do, and I have mine.

Maybe I should put him on a damn leash. It's not like he's actually here to learn, unlike me. If I can get my college education and earn my degree, maybe I can make more money for my mom's care.

But Boss Man will always know where I am.

Fuck.

I never wanted this for my fucking life. It's the entire reason I stayed behind after Mack took off to work for Franco. The Mob brings nothing but bullshit to your doorstep.

But there was a time in my life when I had no choice but to find alternative ways to make money.

And then, I met Malic.

Meeting him in the alleyway between buildings as I beat my fist against the wall to feel the ache of my desperation was fate.

"You should come with me," he says, tilting his head as I shake out my hand, ignoring the blood pouring from my knuckles.

"*I don't even know who the fuck you are.*" My face twists into a disgusted expression when he steps closer, towering over me.

"*You may not know who I am now, but I know who you are. My boss wants a word. Seems you need a job, and well, he can facilitate.*" He grins wide at his words.

I didn't want to follow him out of the alleyway into a waiting Cadillac idling on the road. I didn't want to shake his boss' hand.

But I did.

Because the offer was too good not to consider.

"*Run jobs for me, kid. Watch over Malic. I'll pay you well. You two will be my seconds-in-command.*"

He must have seen the desperation in my eyes as I thought it over. It was either this or dance on stage to make some quick bucks.

So, I chose the gang life, giving myself over to the boss and helping Malic with whatever he needed.

The sun shines through the small windows on the double doors, leading out onto the quad, when Oliver catches my eye and pulls me from the sour memories infesting my mind.

His eyes catch mine when he puts his phone away, and something shudders through him as he pushes his glasses up his nose.

"Oliver, right?" I ask, eyeing him up and down with interest.

Every year, new scholarship students arrive with dreams in their eyes, eager to learn. And the majority of them drop out, leaving with haunted shadows dancing in their gazes.

This place is a fucking haunted. If I could escape, I would. But Malic and my mom need me here.

"Yeah. I'm Olivi-er," he stumbles over his name, turning red and rigid the moment it leaves his tongue.

Weird.

The hair on my neck stands on end. I offer him a tight smile, doing another once-over.

Oliver stands slightly shorter than me and is lanky as hell.

Probably doesn't have an ounce of muscle under his loose t-shirt. I can't imagine this pipsqueak climbing into the ring to fight anyone. Or God, Brutus. That big bastard destroys people like Oliver with one punch. Maybe I should warn him not to come near the Coliseum unless he wants his ass kicked by the two idiots standing outside. If someone wants to call you out for a fight, they can do it on the SlamApp. Or they can wait until the night of the fight, and if you happen to show up, you have no choice but to jump into the ring and take them on. There are social consequences if you turn them down--banned from parties, a pariah on campus, and isolation.

It's brutal as fuck.

There's something hiding behind his misty green eyes when he holds my gaze and lifts his chin, displaying the softness of his face and straight nose. His supple lips pinch together.

Maybe it's a tougher front he puts on being a smaller guy than Mack. Or maybe he's been through some shit. Judging by the scars lining his face and neck, Oliver has been to Hell and back.

I gently rub the burn scar on my right forearm. The pain of the cigarette burning through my flesh is fresh in my mind, despite the years between the incident and now. It was right after Mack left me to fend for myself, and Mom's new boyfriend got his hands on me. Half of me is thankful my brother got his dream at the mansion with the mob. But my other half? It resents the shit out of that asshole for turning his back on me. And thanks to Greenwood being close-knit, I've had to see his face walking the streets and running jobs.

It's fucking torture.

"You were brave as shit standing up to Mack like that." I gesture out the window, drawing Oliver's eyes to Mack and Brutus lying in wait. "But now, they want to beat your ass."

Oliver's jaw clenches when he peers out the window.

"He can try," he grits out, shaking his head.

"Brave or fucking stupid," I laugh, nodding toward the hall. "If you want to avoid the idiot, there's another door this way."

Oliver frowns but nods when we head down the hall.

"Why did you warn me?" he asks when I push out the back door, overlooking a patch of trees and empty sidewalks.

Not many students use the back entrance. It's shaded, away from the sunshine and open space. Everyone on campus is slightly on edge from the murders popping up and students dying.

Fuck. My heart aches thinking about Meredith and where she might be. We're no closer to finding Mal's sister than we were a week ago when she vanished.

"Because my brother is an idiot." I shrug, because I'm not entirely sure why I'm helping this stranger out.

Maybe it's because there's something familiar about him. Perhaps I didn't want to see him get beaten to a pulp. Whatever the reason, I find myself striding beside him as we walk along the back of the building. I tongue the end of my cigarette again, huffing before putting it behind my ear.

I will not fucking light that up. I will not give in to the temptation I feel every day. All the stress. The fucking betrayals nipping at my heels, cheering for me to give in.

I won't.

These unlit cigarettes are the representation of my fucking vices I've beat off with a bat to remain in control of everything. My life. My mind.

"Yeah, he fucking is," Oliver huffs with annoyance and a hint of knowing.

Good. He sees what I see when I look at Mack. A fucking dumbass.

"You're new here, right?" I already know the answer. I'm pretty sure I'd remember someone who looks like him wandering around campus. Men here attempt to be the biggest and baddest, knowing they're running with the future presidents, governors, movie stars, and mob leaders. They want to prove themselves to us.

But Oliver? Fuck. Something stirs inside me. Something foreign I can't put my finger on.

His gaze whips to mine, and his eyes narrow. "Uh, yeah. First year here." His eyes shift from me to the sidewalk in front of us. His shoulders tense.

"You ever been around? You seem familiar." There's something there. A touch of familiarity. Damn it. I can't put my finger on it.

"Unless you count my friend tossing his cookies in your front yard last night, then nope. Just arrived on move-in day. Never been in Greenwood before."

I purse my lips when he keeps his eyes forward. His shoulders bunch further toward his ears, and he tugs on his left earlobe.

Liar.

He's hiding something, which is intriguing. Yet, irritating. I want to know what he isn't telling me.

"Cool." I remember sitting on the porch as our party really kicked off. It didn't hurt that we brought extra entertainment to entice the crowd from the idiots next door. Worked like a damn charm. "Your friend good?"

"Yeah," he chuckles softly. "How about you? You from here?" he asks, finally gazing at me.

"Lived here my whole miserable life," I chuckle when we finally round the building and come out on the other side of the quad.

Across the way, Mack and Brutus continue staking out the front entrance.

"You think they're going to wait there all day?" Oliver asks, cocking his head while watching the two idiots.

"Until they get hungry," I quip, shrugging. "Or if something better comes their way." Like a fight. "You know, if their shitty party didn't convince you to pledge to them, we're always looking to add to our ranks."

The way Malic had his sights set on Oliver the night of our party has my interest piqued. And the fact that there are lies etched on Oliver's tongue.

Oliver is something. Enemy? New recruit? I'm sure Boss Man would be over-fucking-joyed to let us expand our family. Finally.

Oliver's brows raise, and he nods jerkily. "Uh, yeah. Thanks. Not sure I'm pledging." He shrugs nervously.

"Give me your phone. If you reconsider, you can text." Oliver hesitates for a brief moment before digging out his phone and handing it to me. I quickly type my number in and then text myself so I have his. "You ever get into the fighting ring?" I hand him his phone back, brushing my finger against his dainty hands. I swear, a jolt spears through me, but I shake it off.

Jesus. Guys don't have dainty hands. But his are small and his fingers are long. And his skin...

I shake my head when he clears his throat, and his cheeks flame red.

"Sometimes. Fought my cousin a lot." He almost smiles at that, but holds back.

I snort. "If you ever want to work out or get in the ring to really throw down, come to the gym on 5th Street. Shades Gym."

Oliver nods a few times, taking a step back. "Uh, thanks," he says softly again, losing the gruffness of his voice before walking away quickly.

I eye Mack one last time before walking home with my hands in my pockets.

The moment I walk through the front door, the scent of steaks grilling fills my nose.

"Mal?" I call out, walking into the kitchen, and raise my brows.

There stands a tried-and-true psychopath. A man I witnessed

ram a tire iron through the throat of a traitor, wearing a blue apron that says 'Kiss the Cook'.

"Old Chap!" He claps slightly, putting a plate on the counter. "You're home. I hope you're hungry."

"Starving," I say wearily, sitting at the kitchen island. "What's with all this?" First the damn emojis. Now steak? Mal's behavior is erratic at best on his good days and downright terrifying on bad days.

Right now? He looks like someone has plucked the stress from his shoulders and relieved him.

This is almost like the night he lost his V card to the woman in the bathroom. For the next forty-eight hours, he was a goddamn joy.

"Good night and day!" he sing-songs, putting his plate beside mine and getting himself a beer and me a Coke.

"Care to elaborate?" I raise a brow when he cuts into his barely cooked steak and takes a bite.

He grins at me, cutting into another piece as the juices stain his plate red.

"Boss Man has finally given us the green light to recruit. Buck up, Old Chap. We've got people to woo."

"Woo?" I wrinkle my nose, cutting into my rare steak. "We don't woo people. We…"

"Seduce?" He gives me a bloody grin. "Intrigue? Kidnap?" His eyes light up at the word kidnap.

"No kidnapping. You know the rules. We have to play fair."

Mal pouts, finishing off his steak in a hurry. "But I don't like to play fair. I like to play dirty and rough." There's something in his grin that has my hackles rising. Like he knows something I don't know.

"Mal?" I question with a sigh.

"Don't worry, Old Chap." He claps my shoulder a few times before standing and taking his plate to the sink. "This year will change everything." He wiggles his brows and then disappears, leaving me alone with my thoughts.

Change everything? I want to think he means we can build our ranks and finally take Franco down. It's our boss's desire, anyway. But the way Mal smiled and wiggled his brows has me questioning him.

Fuck.

OLIVIA

IT'S BEEN TWO DAYS SINCE I'VE HEARD ANYTHING FROM CARTER. Two long days of classes, dorm life, and getting used to being Oliver.

Oliver Davenport.

It's weird to say the name aloud. I'm a fraud. Undercover. Deceiving everyone around me.

But the more I'm in this skin, the easier it gets to convince myself and the world I'm a man named Oliver. In the silence of my dorm room, I slightly relax under the thick covers of my bed, hiding myself from my roommates. It's the only sliver of space I can unwind and become Olivia again.

Thankfully, Dane hasn't slept over again. Instead, he spends all his time with a tall brunette–usually attached to her lips. They're all over campus together, giggling. Hell, I think I saw him actually smile once. Thank God. You know, the last thing I ever want to see is Dane's gross morning wood again. Do dicks just pop up to remind you they're there every morning? Ugh.

It works for me, though.

He's the ideal roommate because he's never here. He can't discover my secret if he's not here to witness it. It gives me slight relief. If I don't have time to unwind and relax in my own skin, I might go stir crazy.

But I still have to be careful. Dane could barge through the door at any given time. Like Simon does without thought. Thankfully, I've been fully clothed both times.

What I wouldn't do for a lock on the door.

"I can't believe Mack and Wilder are actually fighting!" Simon laughs. "You know they've never done this before, right? This fight is going to be epic! Have you seen the SlamApp?" He shoves it in my face as we walk through campus in the dead of night.

"Let me see that," Jordy quips, plucking it from Simon's grip.

Oh, yeah. Jordy came for a visit.

"But I'm bored, Liv. Please let me come hang out with you." AKA he wants to fuck my roommate. He doesn't have the decency to give me earplugs, either. Asshole.

"So, they're brothers?" Jordy asks, raising a brow as he looks through the SlamApp. It's been buzzing with the news of these two fighters for days now. Someone even recorded their bickering on Wednesday and posted it the moment class let out.

Speaking of, since I met Wilder after class, we've texted a few times. Nothing serious. But it's nice to keep tabs on him. He's not too bad, either. He's invited me to his gym to spar or work out, which eventually, I'll take him up on the offer.

"Yup! And they've never fought before." Simon snatches his phone back with a saucy smile.

"So, these fights. They happen often?" Jordy asks.

"Only once or twice a month. They're the highlight of this establishment. But very hush, hush," Simon says, putting a finger to his lips.

"I don't call announcing it on an app hush, hush," I quip with a snort.

Simon snorts. "Well, call it whatever you like. The school doesn't break it up. In fact, I think they profit off it."

"So, the app isn't made by the school?" Jordy asks, cocking his head.

Simon shrugs. "Nope. It just showed up when I was a freshy and spread like wildfire. It's almost a rite of passage to get it when you come here. Really informative, too." He wiggles his brows a little, flipping through the pictures of the fighters and holding them up for Jordy to see.

"Very interesting," Jordy hums, side-eyeing me with a smirk.

"But there are rules to this fight night," Simon says, stopping abruptly in the middle of the sidewalk.

"Rules?" I ask. "You didn't mention any sort of rules when we got ready." No. Simon was too enthralled with Jordy when he suddenly showed up at our dorm room door and burst in with a grin. They've been enamored with one another since the moment they set eyes on each other. So, no rules were given.

Simon sighs. "I guess I should have warned you guys from the get-go. The rules are simple. No fighting unless you're in the ring." He cringes slightly, running a hand through his hair. "You can only fight once a night. And if you show up to the ring to watch, there's a possibility you can be called out to fight."

I blink several times. "Called out to fight? So anyone can…"

"Walk up to the organizers, say your name, and you have to fight? Oh, yup! Exactly. But you don't have to worry, it's so rare for that to happen." He waves a hand.

"Is there a punishment for if you refuse?" Jordy asks.

Simon cringes again, taking a step in toward our destination. "Oh, nothing too bad. Just the wall of shame. Shunning from your classmates for an entire month where they can throw tomatoes at you or whatever tickles their pickles. And um, no parties allowed."

"Cool. So public enemy number one," I say, raising a brow.

"But don't worry, Oli!" he says, tossing an arm over my shoulders. "You haven't made enemies here. Wait, have you?" He stops dead and looks me in the eyes.

"No. Not yet." Unless you count Mack and his threat in class. Or when Mack and Brutus waited for me after class to taunt me more, but I don't divulge that information to Simon. The only person in our circle who knows is Jordy, who is holding back a laugh at my expense.

"Doesn't matter. If Oli gets called out, he can take anyone." Jordy shrugs, pushing us along until we're following a small crowd of students.

"Oh, you're a fighter?" Simon asks.

A fighter? I can take down a grown man with two fingers to his pulse point. But I don't say that. It was all in my training. Jordy knows it. I know it. Hell, Veritas knows it, too. I've just never had to use it on a job before. And hopefully, I never will.

"I've trained for a few years." I don't elaborate any more than that. No one needs to know what I'm truly capable of. Even Simon.

"Don't downplay it, bro," Jordy smirks, pushing my shoulder. "He can take down anyone without trying. Even the biggest motherfucker on campus."

I side-eye him. I'm supposed to keep a low profile while I'm at Greenwood. I need to observe, blend in, and get to know people.

"Shut up," I grumble, slightly blushing at his compliment.

I worked hard after what happened to regain my strength. I felt so weak. So fucking pressed down. I never wanted another man to overpower me again and end my life. So, I took it all back through hand-to-hand combat, MMA, and boxing. Jordy helped me out a lot, taking me to the ring and showing me how to air out my frustrations.

So, if I ever end up in a bad situation, I'll know how to handle myself. Well, if they stab or shoot me, then I might be fucked. But I've learned how to disarm someone, too. It's all in my training.

"That's good to know!" Simon claps excitedly. "Because you don't want to be on the wall of shame."

I snort, following him and Jordy the rest of the way to the Coliseum. Up the hill, on a paved path made through the woods, straight to the massive structure we found so long ago.

I crane my neck, looking up into the night sky at the large piece of building. It's changed since I was last here. It's been repaired. To an extent, anyway. It still gives the same vibes from the day we found it lost in the woods with the ocean only a hundred feet away.

"You coming?" Jordy asks, nodding his head toward the short line waiting to get in.

I nod in response. Something stirs in my gut. Possibly a warning. Or maybe it's the memories this conjures. How could they take something we found and turn it into something so violent and bloody?

"I'll get us some drinks!" Jordy shouts over the noise of the crowd and loud music, nodding toward the bar at the far end of the round dirt floor.

Fuck.

I take it all in. The familiar–yet–different surroundings. I'm almost frozen in the midst of my peers as they converge around the bar and the fighting ring.

Every object has the capability to hold memories. Good ones. Bad ones. Neutral ones. They're deeply embedded within them. Even walls. Or buildings. Or old T-shirts that still hold the remnants of their scent.

The Coliseum possesses the echoes of our past. It clings to every crack in the façade. Every leftover footprint in the dirt.

It once belonged to us.

Ghosts of our past remain suspended here. Our childhood playground. A place we escaped to, running far away from the troubles back in Greenwood.

Our parents. Our duties.

Our fucked-up lives.

These walls hold more than memories. They hold pieces of us in every damn corner. Like fingerprints left behind. Faint. But they're on every surface we touched and explored.

My eyes flick to the large bar stacked with booze, fairy lights, and bar stools. Several bartenders work behind the space, taking orders, and pouring beers from the tap.

The memories come alive, flashing like a gritty movie before my eyes.

In the spot where the bar sits is where JJ finally got the nerve to seal his lips over mine. It was tentative and quick. Shy, even. But he did it, and I reciprocated. Of course.

The crush I had on all my best friends was magnetic, pulling me in three different directions. They each held a piece of my heart in their palms, offering me many forms of love.

I never acted on impulses, though. Fearing I'd ruin everything we had. We were best friends. Doing everything together. We lived and breathed for one another.

I suck in a breath, grounding myself in the chatter of the crowd. People move in so many directions. Toward the bar. Toward the fighting ring sitting in the middle of the large space, with a crowd chanting before it.

It was once the spot where we all decided that our relationship was special. Something unorthodox in the eyes of everyone in town. But ours, nonetheless. I couldn't choose between the three of them. They didn't want me to. So, we came together as one.

My soulmates.

Or so it seemed at seventeen.

Too bad we fell apart as one, too.

They were mine and I was theirs. Temporarily. Our bliss lasted a short while. A moment in time that should have extended longer—possibly forever—but was cut short by the cruel end of a knife and a roaring fire.

I gently rub the reminder of my time with them. The faint scar across my throat and the burns etched onto my face. Some nights when I close my eyes, I can feel it all over again. My gasps for oxygen, begging my lungs to work. My incessant pleas cut off while they silently watch me dying on my knees, begging them to help me.

But they never did.

Every piece of this old building holds something special to me. Or maybe it shouldn't be so meaningful to me. They hurt me. Betrayed me. So, why must my mind go back to the simpler times?

It's hard not to look back with fondness on the boys who shaped my childhood and teenage years. The first loves of my life. Then, I remember the night they brutally ended me. Us. Our ending was so reckless. Filled with blood, tears, and death. I was the person they promised to hold close to their chests and keep away from the bad. They were the bad. The worst of the worst.

And I never saw it coming.

They've tainted this space with their filth. Their violence and cruelty. Overshadowing the love these walls once saw.

The echoes are just that. Echoes. Nothing more. Nothing special. At least, not anymore.

They can't mean anything to me. Not now. They're like the tainted echoes—nothing. A job. Men I have to watch and get close to so I can close this case and move on with my life once and for all.

After they betrayed me, I thought seeing them again would help me move on. Resolve the treachery swirling in my mind. Hell, maybe I could even forgive them for what they did to me.

Or at least, get them out of my head. Being here, though. It's doing nothing but stirring up old feelings, broken trust, and vengeance.

The roar of the crowd taking up every inch of the Coliseum miraculously pulls me from my swirling thoughts. Something that's been happening a lot since stepping foot in Greenwood. My mind continues to lose itself in what used to be. Instead of living in the now and taking in the people around me.

Blood stains the floors. Old footprints sit in the dirt, scuffed with all the foot traffic. People mingle in the boisterous crowds, throwing their hands in the air as two men viciously fight in the center of the ring, pounding their fists into each other's faces. Blood spurts. Grunts ring out. Cheers fill the space again, echoing off the tall stone walls.

I watch in amazement as Simon talks excitedly into my ear, pointing out the fighters, their names, and who they are to this campus. One is undefeated. The other is, too. So, whoever loses, has to lick their wounds under public scrutiny.

"If they lose," Simon whistles, shaking his head. "It's almost worse than turning down a fight."

"Jesus. You guys are ruthless here," Jordy comments, watching the fight with a sparkle in his eyes. I'm sure if someone called his name, he'd gladly fight. And with no rules, he could thoroughly mess someone up in one punch.

"What happens if they lose?" I wonder aloud as we slowly make our way toward the ring, as the vicious fight continues.

Simon side-eyes me. "Well, for starters—the shame of it all. Losing in front of these blood-thirsty animals?" he snorts. "These people crave superiority. If they lose, it's their reputation on the line. They can get called out more and tested against weaker opponents. Plus, you can bet on who you want to win. So, people get mighty upset when their fav loses and costs them money."

I wrinkle my nose, eyeing the chanting crowd. They go wild

when the smaller of the two knocks the bigger one back a few staggering steps. Blood spills from his nose, and he snarls viciously before charging his smaller opponent. The crowd gasps when the smaller opponent lands another punch, knocking the bigger guy to the ground with a loud thud.

"So, if the big guy loses…"

"Like he is right now," Jordy smirks.

"Yeah, that. His reputation is ruined?"

"Tainted, at best. If there's one thing you should know about Greenwood, it's that there's a weird hierarchy here. You have the kings of campus." He quickly gestures to Mack and Hux lounging at the table, watching the fight. But JJ is nowhere in sight. "And then you have the rest of us peons trying to swim through the chaos." Simon gets on his toes with a grin, shouting obscenities as the smaller opponent pummels his fists into the bigger one's face. Over and over again. He's on top of him, MMA style, knocking his brains out through his ears. More blood spurts onto the white mat, and every hit thuds.

"Stop!" yells a familiar voice through the speakers, and a person dressed in black and white stripes jumps into the ring, pulling the man off him. "I said back off!" Hux bellows through the speakers.

Everyone stops dead at the seriousness in his voice. Quieting until nothing can be heard but the slap of the referee's footsteps on the mat and the grunt of the smaller opponent being dragged off the bigger one.

"Oh, no," Simon murmurs. "Now, that? That's worse. He'll be punished for punching after the fight has been called." He whistles under his breath.

"Punished? I thought there were barely any rules here?" I grumble, watching the fighters closely as they're taken out of the ring. One unconscious. One barely walking without stumbling forward.

"Officially, there are none. Unofficially..." he trails off, raising his brows.

Of course. There are unofficial rules here that everyone must follow. An etiquette, I assume.

"That's what you get for crossing me, asshole!" the smaller opponent shouts, spitting blood onto the side as he wobbles down the small set of stairs leading to the ring. "Come after me or my family again..." He lets the threat hang in the air as he drags a finger across his throat. But it falls on deaf ears. The other guy is still out and being dragged off toward a set of double doors on a make-shift stretcher.

"What's the story there?" Jordy asks, handing each of us a drink with a grin. I frown at the sight of the beer bottles, and Jordy offers me a discreet shrug, shoving it into my awaiting hand. Fuck. I hate beer so much. But it's all these places seem to have. "Seems brutal." He cocks his head, watching the unconscious guy get carted off from the ring and taken through a door. Hopefully, to get checked out.

"Oh, don't worry about him. A whole team of medical students is back there, eager to put their hands on real patients." Simon grins, sipping his beer.

"Medical students? Jesus. What is this college?" Jordy quips, knocking back his beer and chugging it until it's almost empty. "I'm going to need about fifty more of these."

I snort. "You're a lightweight. How about just one more?" I tease, knocking his shoulder.

"Speak for yourself, Liiverrrrr," he holds out my name, chuckling. "You should see this guy. He can barely hold down three drinks. If you don't watch him, he'll end up in the bathroom with some chick."

My cheeks heat at his words. Asshole. "Fucker," I grunt, punching him straight in the chest with all my might. He stumbles back, cackling at me and shaking his head. "I had a good time."

Speak of the devil himself. Shit. Shivers roll through me at the memory of our time together. Seems like a lifetime ago. But only a week has gone by since I was Olivia and he railed me in the bar bathroom.

Discreetly, I watch him saunter through the crowd—well, him and his shadow—Wilder. A single cigarette rests between his lips. They don't greet anyone as they come to stand by the bar.

"Oh, Oli. You've got game, then," Simon chuckles, sipping his beer.

I shrug. A few men jump into the ring with black and white shirts, quickly cleaning it and dusting it off. I keep my eyes peeled, hoping my glasses record the events here.

"So, what happens now?" I eye the shifting crowd, moving closer to the ring, while some weave their way out, heading toward the bar. A few men head to a small table in the corner of the room, forming a line.

A desert forms in my mouth when Hux and Mack sit behind the table, talking to the men in front of them. I swallow a drink of my beer, grimacing at the bitter taste I hate. But it's all they have and I'm trying to quench my thirst after seeing the two of them together. Their presence is overpowering, nearly knocking me back a few steps. One-on-one, I can take them in small doses without wanting to punch their noses. But together? The memories invade me more, taking me back to when we were all best friends playing in this very room.

"It depends on if they have more fights scheduled," Simon says, pulling me out of my thoughts. "But it looks like they're taking challenges right now. You know, where you have to fight if you're called out." He shakes his head.

"Have you ever been called out?" Jordy asks, downing the rest of his drink.

"No, thank the skies fucking above," Simon huffs, eyeing the ceiling with relief. "I'd probably be on the wall of shame and shamed out of parties. I'd run like my ass was on fire. Simon? Simon who?" he chortles, sipping his beer again. "The last place you ever want to be is in that ring."

I shiver at the thought. Getting called into the ring wouldn't be the worst-case scenario, but it wouldn't be good for me. Most of the men who get into the ring have removed their shirts and jeans, opting to fight in loose gym shorts and nothing else.

Jordy and Simon flirt uncontrollably with one another. I don't think I'll be the one hooking up with a guy in the damn bathroom. With the way Jordy is batting his eyelashes and moving in closer to Simon—I'm going to need earplugs tonight. Shit. I don't think I have any. I'll have to go to the store and...

"Oliver Davenport!"

Ringing forms in my ears, like I'm deep underwater. I can barely hear the crowd's murmurs as they look around with excitement, waiting for Oliver to step forward and claim his fight. Their eyes peer around with anticipation.

Every muscle in my body coils tight. *Run away. Go now! They'll never know you were here.*

"What the fuck," Simon gasps, looking at me slack-jawed.

"Oliver," Jordy hisses, shaking my shoulders and getting my attention. Looking deep into my eyes, he gestures toward the ring. "You've been summoned."

I rear back slightly. "No, wait. I..." Can't fucking fight these people. My throat closes as my heart spikes in my chest, beating a frantic tune to the panic swirling in my mind.

"You can say no," Simon whispers. "I won't hold it against you. We can hang out in the dorm, eat chocolates, and emerge in a month. Just no party tomorrow... or next weekend. Or..." he huffs, slumping his shoulders.

"I..." I swallow hard when they call my name again.

"Please come to the back table!" Hux shouts impatiently while I internally freak out that I have to get in front of all these people and fight.

OLIVIA

"You got this," Jordy grunts, shoving me forward and wrapping an arm around my shoulders to help march me toward the gallows. At least, that's what it feels like. He peeks over his shoulder as Simon obliviously follows us through the crowd. "I swear to God, Liv. Who did you piss off already?" he grits out angrily.

Oh, you know. Mack, Hux, and that fucker Brutus. The fucking kings of campus, apparently. This is just great.

I keep that to myself, though. The last thing I need is getting an earful from Jordy on how I should be lying low and making friends with them. Not enemies. Thanks, Dad. I don't need that lecture when I'm internally freaking the fuck out.

"No one!" I hiss, shaking my head innocently. "This has disaster written all over it. What if they expect me to take off my shirt and..." My hands fall on my wrapped chest. I can't fight like this. I can't take off my shirt.

My skin prickles, heating under the glare of the jeering crowd, getting louder by the second. A few laughs ring out mockingly. The air thickens around me. It's too heavy. Tearing straight through my disguise and seeing me for who I am— Olivia.

I could refuse this fight. Sit it out and take the shame of saying no. But where does that get me? Nowhere. I'm already on Hux's radar. I'm sure he and Mack would find a way to make my life even more miserable. Fuck. I have to prove myself to them. Make it seem like I'm a good candidate for their club.

There's no backing out.

No weakness. No hesitation.

I roll my shoulders back, sinking into the feeling of my newly found confidence. Fake it til you make it, is what I always say.

"You obviously have made waves somehow." No shit, Sherlock. Thanks for that observation–is what I want to say, but I bite my tongue. "But maybe this is an opportunity for you to make yourself better known. It's a part of your job, right?" I hate him. He's always making sense. I guess that's why he's technically my in-the-field partner. Usually, we aren't alone on cases. Someone is always nearby investigating something else. Or we work the job together.

My shoulders slump. "Ugh. I guess." It's a necessity that I make myself known to Hux, Mack, and JJ to infiltrate their organization. Maybe this will bring me closer to being their friend instead of hating me for whatever I did to them on Monday. I guess it was the poking Hux in the chest for being a dickweed to me. Or maybe it's for grabbing his girlfriend's wrist in the hallway so she wouldn't poke me anymore. Nothing provokes me more than some asshole poking me in the chest to get a rise out of me. Well, mission accomplished. You'll get a rise out of me.

"You have to check in at the table." Simon's long face and pale features have my stomach churning. "But you got this! I believe in you." He doesn't. I can tell by the sadness in his eyes that he thinks I'm going to die a swift death from a fist.

It could happen. I'm not that cocky. But I've been training for five years now to regain my strength and learn how to defend myself. Fighting with Jordy and the other guys at the Veritas bunker.

"I'll be okay," I say, squeezing his shoulder and turning toward the table to face Hux and Mack head-on.

Mack smirks, tossing his shaggy blond locks out his eyes. There's something there in his gaze. A cockiness I can't place.

"Well, well, well. It's you again, Oliver fucking Davenport." He folds his arms over his chest. "You here to back off from the fight? Run away like a little bitch who…"

"Fucking, Mack," Hux growls, almost pushing him out of the way and looking deep into my eyes. It's weird, sending shivers down my spine. "You…'"

"Oh, I'll fight," I interrupt, leaning forward and placing my palms on the fold-out table, glaring into each of their eyes.

Hux blinks several times, shutting his mouth tight. I don't know what he was going to say, but whatever it was–it's too late.

It's almost too bad it's not Mack who is fighting. I'd love to show him a thing or two about my skills. Say goodbye to your balls, Macklyn Owens. They're going to eventually belong to me.

"You will?" Hux asks, rubbing his chin with a displeased frown. "That's unexpected. You sure you're up to it?" He frowns more, taking me in with an intense gaze like he's sizing me up to fight me himself. An uneasy feeling unfurls in my stomach when he shakes his head, ready to retort something else, but Mack cuts him off.

"I bet you won't last a fucking second," Mack snorts, shaking his head. An easy grin spreads across his lips. "But that's on you. Don't worry, we have trained medical professionals who will help you after the event."

"Who is he fighting?" Jordy asks, stepping up to the table and standing beside me with his chest puffed out. There's murder on his mind as he gets up close and personal with Mack and

Hux. No doubt, he'd stab them both in the heart right now. Instead, he throws an arm over my shoulders again and tucks me into his side protectively.

"Who the fuck are you?" Hux's teeth clench when his gaze connects with Jordy's, searing through the arm over my shoulders and then examining Jordy's features. "You don't belong here."

"Now, why is that any of your business, big guy?" Jordy asks, cocking his head with a knowing smirk. "I'm here to enjoy the fights. Oliver invited me." A challenging expression hardens Jordy's face, and he steps closer to the table and drops his arm from me. Reading the room, I grab Jordy's arm and discreetly shake my head.

"It's my business because this is my fight. My fucking kingdom and you're invading. Maybe I should kick both of you out and stop the fight right now." Hux raises his brows like he's gotten something over on us.

"Our fight," Mack huffs, getting to his feet. "Our fucking business." He glowers at Hux. "And they can't both leave. He's been called out." He tosses a hand in my direction.

"I'm Oliver's cousin." Jordy shrugs off my arm, stepping back.

"And I want to fight," I retort, sending Jordy the stank eye. Even if I'd rather swim with crocodiles and flail like a dying fish than be here in front of these two. I have to fight. This is mandatory. No matter who they're pitting me against. I can't be a fucking pariah. I'm supposed to become besties with my ex lovers.

How fun.

Fuck. This is escalating quickly. Jordy will be over that table in a matter of seconds, choking the life out of Hux and Mack at the same time and successfully killing them with little effort. They may run these fights and have experience throwing punches from their lifestyle, but Jordy is a trained assassin. I've seen him drop a guy by flicking his forehead. It's nothing new to him. He may not seem like it with his flirty ways, but he was serious about taking them out with his sniper rifle.

"Cousins?" Hux raises a brow, seeming to relax slightly. Only slightly, though. His jaw clenches again as he looks between the two of us and opens his mouth, but nothing comes out.

"Enough of this," Mack says. "You're fighting?"

I give a shaky nod. My confirmation. I may die at the hands of my unknown opponent, but I don't have a choice. If I don't fight, then I can't go to parties. And theirs is a necessary party to go to. It's the initiation interest party for their frat. And I have to be there. So, tonight has to happen. No matter if I face a guy who could kill me with one blow. I have my advantages. I'm scrappy as hell. I can kick out their legs and knock them out with one punch. My petite frame makes me faster.

"You're going to get yourself killed," Hux grits out, slumping in his seat with a look of defeat.

What the hell? Did he want me to run away scared? Why is he so damn concerned about my wellbeing?

"His fucking funeral, bro!" Mack quips, knocking Hux on the shoulder twice. "You're on in five minutes. There's a locker room over there. Take everything off and put on a pair of gym shorts. There's a selection back there. Pick your size. Then, when your name is called, you're on, asshole." He gives me a cocky grin. "Oh, also. Good luck."

"You'll fucking need it," Hux grumbles, running a hand down his face and shaking his head.

"I'm not taking my fucking clothes off," I say, taking a step back. "I'll wear the shorts, but the shirt stays."

"Are you forfeiting?" Mack asks with a smirk. "It's no shirt or no fight. The choice is yours." He looks me up and down.

"Are you afraid that we will see just how little muscle you have under those baggy clothes?"

"I'm not fucking afraid," I bite out, rolling my shoulders back.

"It's fucking fine," Hux grits out. "It'll only slow his ass down. Maybe he'll remember not to put his hands on other people outside of fight nights."

"Dude," Mack groans, glaring at Hux. "Fine. You wear the shirt, it's an immediate five points off."

"Fine," I say, shrugging.

"Just fucking get ready. You got ten minutes," Hux grunts, waving a hand for me to leave his sight.

I release a breath, finally pulling in oxygen for the first time in five minutes. That was close.

"Holy fucking shit," Simon whispers, following behind me and Jordy. "You're really going to fight. If it's something I said. If it's..." I stop dead, turning to put a hand on his shoulder. His mouth closes, but worry hangs in his gaze.

"Don't worry. I practically grew up with only boys. I can handle myself, okay?" I raise a brow, but it does nothing to ease the worry lines forming on his forehead.

"I don't think I can watch," he murmurs, shaking his head. "But I believe in you! You're better than me, Oli. I would have tucked my tail and run home." His lips form a tense line.

"Tomorrow we'll celebrate at a party." I grin, earning a snort from him.

"Fine. Just... don't die, okay? I kinda like having you as a roommate." Yeah, and having a hot *cousin* for him to ogle isn't too bad, either.

"If I die, you can have Jordy," I say with a snort, turning on my heels and heading through a pair of swinging doors that say locker room above me. I try not to think about the impending fight. How big will my opponent be? Will they obliterate me?

They might. I'm muscular and fit, but nothing compared to some of the guys on campus.

"He can have me either way," Jordy quips, stepping into the locker room beside me. "Damn. They have everything, don't they?" he whistles, looking up at the tall ceilings that weren't there before.

"There's no roof here." I lean back, staring up at the stars twinkling above Mack and me.

"One day, we'll fix it up." Mack grins, shoving his hand in mine and squeezing. "This is ours."

It was our space. Something we discovered together in our hunt for treasure and peace. Now, it's theirs. They've turned it into something profitable for them. Something I can't wrap my mind around.

"You can't die." Simon's words drag me out of the painful memory of this room. This place. Half of me wants to beg Jordy to take me back to base camp and drop me off. The other half wants to discover the many mysteries surrounding Greenwood University. The missing body parts. Where Meredith went off to? Also, what Franco is up to these days.

"I won't," I breathe, taking the filled space in. It once resembled a crumbling room, and now, they've built it into something extraordinary. It makes me wonder what the state of our tree-house is. The place we snuck off to in the middle of the night was close to our homes.

"Oli," Jordy clears his throat, nodding toward a table filled with stacks of gym shorts. "Small, right?" he smirks, picking up a worn pair of green shorts, sporting a GU on them. "They're nice and tight, too. Perfect for movement." He stretches the material a few times.

I lick my lips, looking back at Simon, who is lost in thought, looking around the locker room in awe. He's obviously never been called to fight, so he'd have no reason to be here. I use this to my advantage and step up to Jordy.

"Won't they be able to tell?" I whisper, gesturing to my crotch with a frown. If I had a package to show off, it'd be noticeably absent in that pair of shorts. "Won't they expect it to..." I flop my arm around a bit, earning a small snort.

"You'll move better in these..." Jordy shrugs, picking up a longer pair of shorts. "But these will hide that..." His eyes fall to my crotch, and he shivers. "You know they have di...."

"Shut up," I groan, yanking the gym shorts out of his hands. "I don't even want to hear it." Because I won't be here long enough to know. I need to get this done and over with so I can move on from whatever the hell this is.

"Wow, this place," Simon murmurs. "How do you think they found it?"

My heart pangs. With me, I want to say. As Olivia. Who I really am. But I don't know her anymore. That girl seems to be a million miles away. She's nonexistent. Snuffed out. Replaced by this version of her. A girl who rarely lets people into her heart to catch a glimpse of her soul. Including Jordy. I think he's the only one I've truly bonded with since I died.

"You have five minutes!" a voice yells as someone bursts into the locker room with a frown, pounding their feet into the dirt.

"That better not be who I think it is," Jordy murmurs, stepping behind me.

"And who do you think it is?" I'm in denial. If I'm back here selecting a pair of gym shorts to wear while fighting someone. Then surely he's not doing the same, right? Fucking Brutus. The asshole who was waiting to jump me after class. Or harass me. Kill me? I'm not sure. Wilder didn't know, but he got me out of dodge, and I'm forever thankful for that. The last thing I wanted to do was confront those two on my own again. Sure, I can take them, but I'd rather not. I scan Brutus in all his glory. Up close and personal. He's huge. Bigger than Malic at the bar. More muscular, too. I swear if he sat on me, he'd crush my organs into soup, and I'd die a slow death.

I might be fucked. Super fucked.

Listen, I'm a lean girl. I have muscles. Fighting isn't a problem. I just have to be faster than my opponent. Outsmart them. This guy? His arm reach alone could knock me into next week without having to take a step.

"You're going to die," Simon squeaks, stepping back until he's beside Jordy. *Thanks for the vote of confidence, Si.* "Oh, it was nice knowing you, roomie. You can still back out. We don't need parties or a social life. We can live on the fringes of society and have our faces on the wall of shame." He frowns now, watching the big man remove his shirt, showing off his eight-pack abs and bulked-up biceps. Jesus. He drops his jeans, letting them pool at his ankles until he kicks them off into the dirt.

I think his quads are bigger than my damn head. He's going to squish me like a watermelon between his thighs. Oh, God.

"I won't die," I say, holding onto the pair of gym shorts tightly.

If I say it enough, I'll manifest it, right? I've survived so much in my life; I can survive one measly fight against a mammoth who glares at me with hate in his eyes. Well, more than hate. Shit. I think he wants to eviscerate me. His massive shoulders roll back, nearly hitting his damn ears and then, he marches toward me with intent. Fuck. I can hear Jordy in my head. *Don't back down. Chin up. Show this big oaf you aren't afraid of him.*

So, faking it, I lift my chin and harden my eyes. I can do this. I can beat this big guy. He may have more muscle and height than I do, but I can outsmart him. Right? Fucking right.

"Oliver Davenport." The way he says my name sends chills down my spine. Like I've kicked his puppy and thrown it off a bridge.

I look him up and down. Poor guy has got one of those faces

that you never forget. Down to the scar on his right cheek, lip, and eyebrow. This guy has taken a beating before and lived to tell the tale.

"Do I know you?" I goad, sucking in a breath when he puts on the pair of gym shorts, snapping them around his waist loudly.

If there's one thing bullies hate, it's not getting recognized.

"We met in class." He shrugs. "But even if you don't know me now, we're going to get very well acquainted." He steps up to me, and I square my shoulders, readying myself for whatever is to come.

I will not let some gym rat intimidate me. Well, not anymore. So, okay. He may be six-foot-six, towering over me with muscles for days. But those muscles will do nothing for him in combat. He may be able to bench a thousand pounds and crush my face like a watermelon between his thighs, but they'll slow him down. He's too bulky and meaty for a one-on-one match.

"I look forward to it." I grin, letting all my anxiety go. It pulses through my body and slowly drops through my toes into the floor, leaving me with nothing but a blank void of emotions. Fear runs. Anxiety tucks tail.

Maybe this fight is what I needed after all. Something to numb my worries and take them away. For the time being, at least.

Brutus steps back with a cocky smirk. "When I wipe the mat with your face, you'll regret this." With that, he turns on his heels and marches out the door with an air of confidence.

"Tool," Jordy snorts.

"Let the fighting begin!!!!" Hux's voice shouts over the speakers again.

"Well, that's our cue, Si. Let's give Oli here some privacy to change."

"Right," Simon says in a daze. "Oli..." he trails off.

"Don't worry about me, okay? This will be fun." I try to

lighten the mood as Jordy puts an arm over Simon's shoulders, practically dragging him out of the locker room while whispering in his ear.

I sigh, listening to the chants of the crowd. My heart beats wildly. But I close my eyes and dive into the nothingness coursing through my veins.

I can do this.

With that in mind, I find a more private space and open an abandoned locker with a sigh. Clutching the metal until my knuckles turn white, I battle the anxiety reigniting inside me. Heat bristles at my back, working its way up my neck and onto my cheeks. A thousand eyes seem to peer at me from every angle.

But there are none.

The quietness of the locker room encapsulates me, lulling me into a false sense of security. I'm okay. This fight will be fine. Even if I lose and get pariah status. I can't run. Showing my fear to my peers will do nothing for me. Especially with my mission.

I shimmy my baggy jeans down my legs and kick off my shoes and socks, tossing them into the empty locker. A dirty, thin mirror sits on the inside of the locker, reflecting back at me. I run my fingers over my thighs, slowly dragging them up, until I'm peeling my binder and shirt to expose my ribs.

There it is. The one thing I've avoided looking at for years. The reminder. My memories aren't the only thing connecting me to my former best friends. I run the tip of my finger over the word—Always—etched onto my flesh between my ribs. Centered there in cursive.

It's a piece of them that will remain with me forever. Always. That's what I was to them.

Today. Tomorrow. Forever. Always.

A door slams somewhere in the locker room, knocking me from my stupor as it echoes throughout the room. Quickly, I cover myself back up and pull the long shorts on, readying myself for the fight that's about to come. I can't let my head be clouded by all these thoughts.

I have to clear myself again. Center myself so I don't get fucking killed by that behemoth.

This is it.

The time is here.

And now, I have to show everyone what I'm made of. I'm Oliver Davenport. Badass.

OLIVIA

THE MOMENT I EXIT THE LOCKER ROOM, I'M READY. MY CHIN IS raised. My mind is blank. And all I see is the biggest fucking man ever standing in the center of the ring. He raises his hands, waving them at the crowd with encouragement to chant his name.

"Brutus! Brutus! Brutus!"

Sounds right. He looks like the type of motherfucker to stab you in the back.

"Don't worry. I'll call your mommy when I put you out," my opponent grins wildly, standing at the center of the ring as I walk up the stairs.

"You a fan favorite?" I ask, nodding toward the rambunctious crowd, loosening my neck slightly as his tightens with his movements.

"I'm undefeated," he says with a grin. "And I plan to keep it that way. Be a good little bitch and go down in the first round." Oh, he sounds very confident. I should probably change that.

"Why? Cuz you can't pick on anybody your own size? Are you that insecure?" I chuckle, cracking my knuckles and jumping from foot to foot. Damn. My muscles are way too tight for this. I need more time to loosen them before he chews me up and spits me out.

I'm fully aware I'm taunting the bull. I'm like a damn red flag, waving in the wind for him to race after. That's okay. I want that. He needs to exude all his minimal energy before the fight commences.

Brutus's face tightens, and he exposes his teeth. "I'll show you insecure, asshole."

A referee steps into the middle of us with his arm in the air above his head, eyeing the tension between us.

"Once I back away and am out of the ring, the fight will begin. There are no rules, except—don't kill each other. You will be declared the winner if your opponent is knocked out or doesn't move for more than three seconds. I am the judge. If you harm me, then you're banned for life." He raises a brow at Brutus, like this might be something he's capable of. Might be right. Brutus looks a little unhinged. Okay, not a little. A lot. He smiles like he's got something over me. "No more than five blows to the head are permitted. We do not allow death in this ring." He takes a small step back and lowers his arm.

I grunt, knocking back when Brutus the fucking cheater slams his fist into my jaw and then my ribs. Pain rings through my brain, and the breath leaves my lungs as I gasp. But I have enough mind to duck when he sends his second fist flying, attempting to catch the same spots on the opposite side. He meets nothing but air as I dance away from him, shaking my head and trying to right myself.

"That was a low blow," I grunt at his back, making him turn on his heels and wildly punch at my face and body, never landing a blow. "You call yourself a fighter," I wheeze, rubbing at my ribs until I can stand up straight.

"This is a fight. There are no rules, remember?" he asks cockily, heaving several breaths as I sidestep every punch he throws at me.

That's right, big boy. Tire yourself trying to catch me. I may not have his strength, but I'm nimble on my feet.

"You gonna throw some punches or be a pussy?" he asks, cocking a brow when he takes a step back. He opens his arms wide. Way too cocky for his own damn good. He's asking for me to attack him.

"I could," I say with a shrug, ducking under another one of his assaults when he realizes I'm not falling into that trap.

He heaves a breath, snarling in my direction. "Fight me, pussy boy!" he grunts, nearly charging at me like the bull I accused him of being earlier. I swoop out of the way, pissing him off more until he's facing me. Red takes over his cheeks, and he cracks his bare knuckles several times. "You gonna keep running? This won't end well for you." He grins again, looking at me like I'm the prey he's been searching for all his life.

It's creepy.

I lift a shoulder, nonchalantly taking a step back as he takes two steps forward. He's so determined to take me out that he doesn't see the coordinated dance we're having. It's all part of my strategy. One Jordy knows all too well and keeps me on my toes. Only Jordy is much more lithe than this guy, who is practically stumbling over his large feet.

"Then come put me out of my misery," I jest, curling a finger in his direction.

"Gladly," he growls, bulldozing toward me at his highest speed.

I jump to the side just as he gets to me and kick the back of his knees out. He lands with a loud thud, expelling the air from his lungs. Before he can think about standing again, I punch him. Over and over again until he's collapsing on the ground and unmoving. But I don't stop. I grunt, smashing my fist into his face over and over again. Strong arms wrap around my waist, pulling me off the big man now out on the mat, drooling and mentally begging for his mommy. Whoever plucked me off Brutus sets me on my feet and stands beside me as I catch my breath. The entire room sways in my vision, but I right myself, lifting my chin.

I may be smaller than him, but I'm goddamn mighty.

The crowd blinks back at me when I finally look around until they explode, cheering my name. My arm immediately gets thrown in the air victoriously by the man who pulled me off. I expect to see one of the referees standing beside me, but it's not. It's Hux, looking down at me with pride shining in his eyes and confusion written on his expression.

"Well I'll be damned," he mutters, squeezing my wrist. "You really fucking did it. You beat the unbeatable," he grunts out gruffly in awe.

I don't say anything back. Too stunned by having his hands on my wrist. When I get my wits back, I yank my hand from his grip.

"Thanks for the confidence." I roll my eyes and take a step away.

Medics immediately jump into the ring with a stretcher, rolling Brutus onto his back and taking him away. The crowd continues to chant my name with excitement.

I cringe when something hits my face and blanch when I hold the lacy material in front of my face. Blinking several times, I take in the bra as heat billows onto my cheeks, and I drop it.

"Fuck," I grunt earning a chuckle from Hux. Everything in him seems to relax as he stands beside me.

"We're having a party," he says offhandedly, pulling my attention back to him.

"Oh, yeah. Another one at your frat?" I'm well aware. But I'd love to hear it straight from his mouth. It's the party of the century, according to Simon. It happens every year, and it's for anyone interested in drinking and losing themselves at the graveyard where they hold it. It's also the first step into showing interest in their frat.

"More of a clubhouse," he says, shrugging.

"And what does your clubhouse do?" I raise a brow, gently rubbing at the bruise forming on my aching jaw. Fucker. Those were the only hits I allowed him to get on me.

"A lot of shit." He shrugs.

So damn informative.

"Okay. What kind of shit specifically?" I want to know what this mysterious frat or clubhouse is responsible for. Criminal activity?

"Let's just say, if you're wanting to get ahead in life, you'll join us. From here, you can get any job you want. Any internship that interests you. Business investments. It's good for your future to have us at your back, and vice versa."

"Is this how you sell it to everyone?" I snark.

He shrugs, sending me a glare. "Come or don't. But I'm extending the invitation. We could use a guy like you in our frat."

A guy like me. I want to snort. If he only knew.

I pretend like I'm thinking about it and shrug. "Sure. Simon was going to drag me there, anyway."

Everything aches from the exertion of the fight. My jaw. My ribs. My fucking feet. It's been too long since I've jumped into the ring with someone. Spared and punched like my life depended on it. Tonight was a necessity, though. I couldn't say no to Brutus. Although, I'm betting now he wishes I did.

"Good," he grunts, taking a step back and collecting himself. "I expect you here for more fights."

"And why would I do that?" I raise a brow. He assumes I'll come back.

"Because the more you win, the more status you gain. You just knocked down the biggest fucking douche on campus." A slow grin spreads across his face. "He'll be after you, too."

"After me?" I glower, curling my fists.

"Yeah, so maybe it's best you join. We're the fucking kings, and no one will bother you."

I roll my eyes. Typical fucking Hux thinking. He's a king? Puh-lease.

"Only fellow douchebags call themselves the kings of campus," I quip.

He blinks several times before a chuckle erupts from him. It's low and rumbly, making my stomach swoop. But he's still on my shitlist. No matter how many cute smiles he throws my way.

"You'd better go back and get checked out. Medical is back there in an office waiting."

"I think their priority should be the asshole I knocked flat on his back." I take another step, determined to leave this conversation. I can't get too comfortable with them and let my guard down. No matter how many emotions it's stirring inside me. I don't want to laugh with him. I want to take him down. It's all about pretending that I'm not the girl he abandoned.

Hux doesn't say another word before climbing out of the ring first and making his way toward the table in the corner. Once he's seated, Mack frowns at him, saying something I can't quite read on his lips. Hux's furious glare burns through Mack, and he pounds a fist on the table. Mack shrugs, grinning maniacally at Hux until they're in a heated conversation.

"Dude," Jordy says, putting a hand over my shoulders as he leads me back into the locker room. "You good?" he breathes, leading me to the back of the place for privacy. He forcefully sets me on the bench with a huff.

"Define good," I groan, rubbing my jaw. I can tell there's going to be a bruise there.

Jordy sits me on a metal bench, bending to look me in the eyes. He examines me thoroughly, shaking his head. "You could have fucking died," he hisses with worry.

"Um, yeah. I could have died at any fucking time," I groan,

rubbing my temple. "I thought you had faith in me?" I raise a brow when his face slightly falls.

"I always have faith in you, Liv. But fuck. It was like watching my baby sister about to meet her end." His eyes widen, shaking his head. "Don't do that shit again." Like he could stop me from coming here on my own. I can take these motherfuckers. All at once. Well, maybe that's a little too cocky for me. But still. I'm a badass woman.

"I'm older than you." I roll my eyes and lean closer. "I didn't really have a choice. Even if he knocked me out. I had to..." I trail off, darting my eyes through the empty locker room. The only sounds come from the far end, which I assume are the medical students eagerly awaiting patients.

"Fuck," Jordy whispers, squeezing his eyes shut. "I know you had to. I know we get into some shit situations, but I think you should stay away from this place." He gives me a pointed look.

"And why is that?"

"Because they're blood thirsty motherfuckers, and you just punched out an undefeated champion who will want revenge." He raises a brow to emphasize his point.

I shrug. "I go wherever the job takes me," I mutter.

"Let me see the damage." Jordy stands tall, waving a hand for me to raise my shirt so he can see where the big oaf got a punch in. "How do your ribs feel?"

"Like shit," I grumble truthfully. Which doesn't fare well for me. They're already aching from his punch, maybe they're deeply bruised or worse, broken. That would make wearing my bindings more difficult.

"Only you would get into this bullshit," he mutters under his breath as I slowly rise from the metal bench. My eyes dart around again when I turn my back to the large open space and stand before Jordy.

"Si is hanging out at the bar. It's just you and me right now." His eyes dart in the same direction. "But who knows for how long. So... show me your tits." He smirks and then grunts when I throw a fist into his arm too quickly for him to step back or block. His smile broadens.

"Stop it," I cringe, lifting my shirt and peeling my binder up, grunting when it attempts to stick to my skin and pushes on my injury. "Fuck." I thank the skies for my binder, it does a damn good job of hiding my breasts, but it's so tight it's almost impossible to lift for him to examine my aching ribs.

"Oh, yeah," Jordy hisses, rearing back. "He got you fucking good. This is going to hurt like a motherfucker for a month or so." His eyes lift to mine, concern glistening through them. "Are you going to be okay? Oliver can have an emergency back home."

"I'll be fine," I grunt, shoving my bindings back into place and lowering my shirt before anyone gets a glimpse of what I'm hiding. "Maybe another drink or something?" Seriously, more drinks will help to dull the ache of that brute's punches. Besides, I need to come to terms with my new reality.

Brutus is going to murder me for knocking him out. Plain and simple. Maybe I should have Jordy plan my actual funeral. One better than my last. With flowers, more tears, and people who actually love me in attendance.

"Liv," he groans, shaking his head, but stops when he sees the serious expression crossing my face. "I can't talk you into returning to your dorm, can I?"

"What are you, my father?" I quip, squaring my shoulders and ignoring the twinge in my ribs. No, scratch that. All over my damn body. Is it possible to already feel like I've been hit by a train? I mean, I guess that's what Brutus is—a damn train. "It was just a little hit. I'll be fine." It hurts like a bitch, but I can tell by the way Jordy is looking at me protectively that he wants to argue, take me to my bed, and force me to rest. That's the thing about unblood brothers, they're really overprotective and compassionate when they aren't being pains in the asses.

My brows furrow when a noise like slamming lockers catches my attention. "That's our cue," I murmur, nodding toward the sound. "Cover me?" He nods, crossing his arms over his chest and turning on his heels. I know he wants to say more about me sticking around the fights. But I have more recon to do. Not to mention, Malic, Wilder, Hux, and Mack are all fighting each other—I can't miss that.

Quickly, I get dressed back into my baggy clothes. They've become an odd comfort this past week, hiding who I really am. They're my mask against Greenwood U's weirdness.

"Well, this was definitely more fun than attempting to find a thief who doesn't want to be found," Jordy murmurs, walking beside me as we slowly make our way through the maze of the locker room. It still astonishes me that they've developed an entire fighting venue here, fit with power and everything, considering it sits on a hill in the middle of the woods. I wonder if Franco helped to fund this venture for them and if he makes a profit from their earnings.

"Any leads on that?" I press. He's been very tight-lipped about his case. Only indicating he was after a thief who stole millions of dollars' worth of paintings from a museum without getting caught.

"Nope. I think they might be a ghost or something. There's Nada on the surveillance footage. I'm going to have to recruit some newbie agents to come and help me infiltrate whatever they have going on," he says in a low voice, trying to keep it from echoing throughout the room. "Anything on your end?" He eyes me.

I snort, looking around before stopping. "It's weird here, right? Like… the vibe…"

"I saw your notes," he says, leaning in. "About the murder and missing organs?" He whistles lowly.

"Yeah. I think that's the main thing I need to look at and see who the hell is involved. It's weird, right? But also, why isn't the school doing more? The police?" I raise a brow. "I'm still waiting for confirmation from Carter."

Jordy snorts. "That asshole."

We make our way through the locker room, coming to a halt near the doors when they burst open. Wilder and Malic force their way in with deadly expressions on their faces.

Fuck! I duck my head, staring at the floor, despite knowing I'm wearing my colored contacts and glasses. Something Jordy instantly notices. We aren't secret agents for nothing. And Jordy? That man has an eye for the details. Discreetly, I watch through my lashes as Wilder takes the unlit cigarette out of his mouth and puts it behind his ear.

Wilder brushes past me, only acknowledging me with a nod and grunts when he stops at the gym shorts table and grabs a pair. Agitation rolls off him, giving me major–fuck off–vibes. But Malic? I hold my breath when he stops and cocks his head. Fuck. Run! He's going to know exactly who you are and ruin your identity.

When I lift my eyes to meet his, an intensity I've never experienced before burns right through me.

"Tell me your secrets," he says in a low voice, leaning in to take his fill of my bewildered expression. I'm sure I'm a sight to see right now. Flushed with bruises forming all over my flesh.

"Secrets?" I almost squeak but catch myself before it happens.

A grin bursts across his lips, and his eyes light up. "Tell me how you knocked that asshole out? I'm very curious how someone so..." He purses his lips. Those intense blue eyes take me in from head to toe, like he's memorizing every detail. "Small, could accomplish something so big. Maybe I should call you out." He grins at that and then shakes his head. "Nah."

"Mal," Wilder grunts, causing Mal's eyes to dart toward him, and he frowns. "Leave Oliver alone," Wilder adds, gesturing to me with a huff.

"I take offense to that," I mutter, cringing when my arm brushes against the bruise on my ribs. I've been numb to pain before. Forced to ignore it when it lights up my nerves, but right now, I'm unable to hold back the hiss.

Malic's eyes light up at the sight of my cringe, and without warning, he pokes my ribs several times. "What the fuck?" I hiss, tossing his massive hands off me. No way will I admit that my nerves lit up under his touch.

He shrugs. "Pain is delightful, isn't it?"

Uh, no, psychopath. Pain is not delightful. It's fucking pain, and it hurts. Especially that.

"Not for me," I say through gritted teeth.

"Malic!" Wilder barks with impatience. "Quit poking the man, for fuck's sake." Wilder's look he sends my way is full of concern, and his gaze asks *'are you okay?'* I nod without saying words, and his shoulders sag with relief. "Malic…" he trails off impatiently.

"My keeper calls," he sing-songs. "Have a good night, Oliver Davenport." He tilts his head when my fake name leaves his tongue, and he hums. "Until next time." He grins, waltzing over to Wilder and immediately pulling off his shirt.

Fuck.

"We need to leave this locker room," I mutter, pulling Jordy along by the collar of his shirt and slamming through the doors to the packed house of people, waiting for the next fight to start.

Hux passes me with a determined look, followed by Mack on his tail, who abruptly stops beside me. "Did you like that?" he asks, stopping me in my tracks.

God. What is this?! Every psycho stopping me from enjoying a few drinks so I can numb my pain?

"What exactly?" I ask, releasing my grip from Jordy. He adjusts his collar with a frown, glowering at me for messing it up.

"The match?" Mack grins. "Set it up just for you. Although

you were supposed to go down." His eyes dart to the empty ring, and anger darts across his eyes. "You lost me a grand in a bet."

And whose fault is that? Certainly not mine. Asshole.

"Supposed to go down..." I trail off, and realization hits me.

Mack grins. "Fuck with us. We have our ways." He shrugs, shoulder checking me as he makes his way into the locker room.

I wonder if he knows his leader Hux was trying to recruit me to their cause? Probably not, judging by the victorious grin which I would gladly wipe off his stupid face with one punch before he disappears through the lock room doors.

"Prick," Jordy mumbles. "The offer still stands about the murdering, by the way. I'm getting sick and tired of that douchebag and his mouth. I could shove so many things inside of it to make him stop talking..." he trails off, snorting when I whack him on the chest.

"The imagery I didn't need, thanks." I roll my eyes and continue walking with or without Jordy on my tail. "Besides, you've only had the pleasure of meeting him once."

"Once is fucking enough, Liv," he grumbles, running a hand down his face. "Seems he has it out for you."

I shrug. "He might. But Hux seems to think I should join their frat."

Jordy cringes. "Be careful around them."

"You think I won't be?" I raise a brow as we weave through the crowds, spying Simon by the bar with three drinks waiting in front of him.

"They're..."

"Dead to me," I hiss. "They..." I lean in further so no one else can hear me. "Killed me, Jordy. They stood by and..." I run a finger over my throat for dramatic effect. "They're nothing to me but a fucking job. A means to an end. The quicker I get the fuck out of this town and can return to being Olivia, the fucking better." I raise a brow to emphasize my point.

Jordy nods a few times. "Okay. I believe you." He doesn't. I can tell by the tone of his voice that he thinks I'm about to spiral down the rabbit hole and they're the center.

But I'm not.

Those three can rot in fucking Hell for what they did to me. In fact, I'm going to make sure they do. One way or another, my old besties are going to wish they had actually murdered me, because I'm about to tie them to this murder if it's the last thing I do.

WILDER

"Why are you looking at the door like that?" It's odd to see him so frozen. Emotionless, even. Not that he shows what he's thinking very often. But Oliver? He ruffled Malic's feathers.

And no one ever does that.

Not me. Huxley. Macklyn. Or even that fuck JJ.

Malic only responds to our boss and his demands. He is extremely loyal like that. For good reason, I guess. The man basically pulled him from a cage and gave him purpose again. Instead of being stuck in a small hotel room, watching what he had to watch. I shudder at the thought of it all. My stomach tightens.

We all go through shit, I guess. Some more than others. What you do with that shit matters, though. Mal and I work for the big boss, recruiting new members to our cause. Slowly but surely, we're taking this city back from its evil overlord. Nathanial Franco. Who has overstayed his welcome by at least thirty years. I don't know who died and gave him the crown, but we're going to snatch it off his head and wear it ourselves.

"Mal," I say, snapping my fingers in front of his face.

Nope. Nothing. Not an ounce of recognition. Wonderful. I sigh. See? Mal doesn't respond to me, either. And I'm his goddamn keeper. At least that's what he says. I'm more the watchful eye that keeps him out of major situations. Like murder or assault charges. No biggie. Although, our boss could snap his fingers and free us from anything. I try not to let it escalate to that.

Malic won't take his darkening eyes off the double doors leading out of the locker room. I'd never tell those assholes that they built something pretty cool here. Especially in this fucking town. This fighting arena with booze and plenty of money coming in from our peers, fuels us to live another miserable day. It serves its purpose. This neutral place is where we go when we want to beat the shit out of other people, make some money, or maybe make some connections.

Malic's eyes narrow, and he purses his lips. Fuck. He's deep in thought about something. Which is never fucking good. It means he's plotting. It could be a death, a fight, or fucking someone.

It's frightening.

And I don't get scared easily.

Mal finally peels his eyes away from the door with a frown, shaking his head. "No reason," he finally states, answering my question from five minutes ago, while humming a song under his breath as he undresses, leaving him in only a pair of gym shorts. Ready for the fight ahead. Tonight, the status of our frat balances on the edge.

If we win—everyone will flock to us. If we lose—everyone will run to Hux and his crew of idiots like they always do.

Fuck. We have to win this.

I blink several times. Just like that, he's snapped out of whatever had him captive and moves around like his normal self.

I don't believe him for a fucking second. It's nothing? There's something there. And it all has to do with the new guy who knocked out fucking Brutus. Idiot. Now, that motherfucker is going to be gunning for the scrawny kid. Probably snap him in two when he least suspects it. Great. Another murder on campus. At least this time, we'll know who the culprit is.

The question still stands, though. Who is Oliver Davenport? Where the fuck did he come from? Transfers so late in one's college career don't usually happen. Especially here at Greenwood U. There's still that nagging feeling in the pit of my stomach from when we first met. He's cagey, at best. Avoiding eye contact and tensing his muscles. Underneath his loose clothes and soft skin, he's hiding something big.

Maybe that's why Mal was staring after him. The man's a human lie detector. Well, sometimes. He can sniff out a lie in a matter of seconds. Shit. I'm going to have to keep my eyes on him for a whole new reason so he doesn't squish Oliver before we can get some answers from him.

Malic freezes again. His eyes wandering back to the damn doors. Something sparks in his eyes, and my stomach drops. Fuck! I know that face. That's the face of determination and wanting. Shit. Is that desire?

He wants this bastard in our club.

"You want him in?" Just call me the Malic-whisperer. Sometimes I feel like I know him better than I know myself.

"In?" he hums again, rubbing at his chin. "Something like that. Seems we might need to recruit the kid?" A bone-chilling smile crosses his lips, sending goosebumps down my flesh. "Yeah. Yeah. That's what we need to do, Old Chap! Recruit that guy." The way he emphasizes guy has me rearing back.

Listen, I don't judge others' preferences. Unless they're a disgusting pedo, then off with their fucking heads and light them on fire. But Mal? He's never shown interest in anyone sexually. Not an ounce. Until that chick at the bar. And now, this guy? Did he suddenly awaken his dick and now it stands for everyone? I'm going to have to watch him closely, so he doesn't get himself into any trouble. Or his dick.

Ugh.

Sometimes being a keeper is harder than it sounds.

"Recruit?" I ask, fiddling with the cigarette behind my ear. "You want him in, then?" Honestly, it's something I already offered the guy.

"Keep an eye on him, Keeper. He'll be important in the future." He squares his shoulders, showing off his mass of muscles. The tattoos are etched on every inch of his flesh and flex under the glow of the fluorescent lights hanging above us.

Fuck.

"I'm not your keeper," I groan when Malic simply grins at me again.

"Don't deny your label, Wilder." He slaps my shoulder a few times, knocking me forward. "And get your head in the game. You've got a brother to decimate. A little blood to spill. Can you taste it? It's in the air!" He leans in, putting his forehead against mine with ragged breaths. "Victory is ours, Old Chap."

Mal steps back with that familiar grin plastered on his face. Whatever mood he was in before has slipped away and transformed him back into himself.

I crack my knuckles. I'm still in disbelief that my brother agreed to this. A fight? Really? He's not so much as looked at me since he was carted away into foster care and left me behind to pick up the pieces.

"Speaking of..." I trail off, dragging my phone out of my pocket. "Bobby texted. He's got something for us to look at." I quickly show Malic the text message, and his expression drops. It's been over a week since Meredith disappeared. No word. No sightings. I'm beginning to think the fucking worst about the situation. Not only for her, but Mal, too. He's circling the damn drain with his sanity creeping in and out. He can only distract himself for so long before he snaps.

"When?" His shoulders square, and all humor drops from his expression.

"Monday. Nine PM at the casino." I lift a brow; he knows

what's coming next: Bobby's payment. He doesn't do shit for free, and he knows exactly who we work for because he associates with the same man.

Mal cracks his neck a few times and then nods. "You think..." Mal isn't one to get emotional. He lashes out in anger, mostly. Punching things he shouldn't be punching. But that's why we're here: to alleviate the pain of losing his sister. The only blood relative he was able to track down.

"He'll have something for us. If he didn't have something, he wouldn't have texted and told us to come by. "

Mal nods a few times. "He better. She can't just...disappear."

"No, she can't. There has to be some sort of trace of her. Somewhere. Even if she ran away. Cameras are everywhere."

I firmly believe that. Cameras are on every corner in this town, detecting the activities of its citizens. If it's not Franco— the man who thinks he's in charge—or our boss, then it's the police attempting to catch us. Although, in the venture, I don't think they're very fucking helpful. She's an adult in her early thirties. She's allowed to leave town. Yeah? What about her apartment? Why is nothing missing? Even her purse, keys, and phone were left behind. She didn't just walk out of her apartment door and decide it was all too much. She was a nurse, for fuck's sake. She had a stable job. Unlike us. We're the ones who should want to disappear. Working under a man who remains in the damn shadows and depends on us and his other men to get shit done.

To keep Mal grounded, I tiptoe around him on the subject of Meredith. I don't want to confirm his worst fears by telling him mine. He's already too much in his head about it. Stalking the damn bar she was last seen at and trying to intimidate everyone in sight to give him the answers they don't have.

I'm losing faith we'll find Meredith alive.

Fuck.

My eyes swing to the double doors when Hux and Mack

come through. Mack looks absolutely pleased with himself, and I roll my eyes. Spoiled ass, little fucker. He's never known the struggle. Ever. Mom lost him when he was ten and I was eleven. But me? Oh, I had to stay. All because the little prick opened his mouth about our living conditions to Franco. And of course, wanting to look like a knight in shining armor, Franco had the state take care of it and transfer Mack's care to him. We both grew up under the same roof for many years, yet the state took him while I was left to rot with the woman who couldn't even make dinner without assistance. She's always too doped up to fucking care about us. Me, mostly. So, why do I continue to support her? Or care?

Because you're her oldest son. The only one who stayed around and cared. And despite the bad times we've had, she didn't use to be this way. She used to care before her boyfriend screwed her over.

I guess that's the price I pay. The role I was given in life. Taking care of everyone else but myself.

My phone buzzes in my hand, and I sigh.

EGG DONOR

Jackson! I need you. This is a 911!!

Why doesn't that surprise me? Sometimes I wonder how she's still mobile and able to get to her phone. They should have taken it from her by now.

I squeeze my eyes shut, counting to ten in my head. If I don't answer her, she'll continue to text and call nonstop until she gets what she wants. Probably food. Or company. Or she forgot where or who she was. Again.

WILDER

Mom. You okay?

I stare at the screen, ignoring the looks from Hux and Mack. I'm sure they're glaring at us like we're the damn enemies here.

But my mom never replies. Fuck. Not only will I have to stop by and check on her, but now it'll be in the back of my mind throughout our entire fight tonight. I can't leave, or Mack will think he's won and blacklist me from everything, including my only outlet.

"Well, well," Malic says, standing tall. "Our opponents for the evening."

"You got what you wanted," Hux says, lifting a shoulder.

"I did." The way Malic says those two words has my eyes snapping at him. He's insinuating something. What? I don't have a clue.

Ever since he fucked that chick in the bathroom, he's been acting stranger. Okay, stranger than usual. Not only did he lose his V card, something he never seemed to care about, but now he's become obsessed with finding her. I see it in the way he peeks at every corner and looks over his shoulder. Fuck. He even dragged me back to that bar. Sure, we were trying to find Mer again, but he was also looking for her. The oddly familiar girl that I feel like I should know. But I shouldn't, should I? There's no way.

"I got exactly what I wanted. But you wanted it, too. Didn't you?" He cocks his head, stepping up to Hux. Nose to nose. Chest to chest. He's ready to take him right here and now.

"Back off," Mack says, pushing the two apart forcefully.

"Hands off," I growl at him with gritted teeth. I can't wait to punch his fucking lights out and make him bleed for everything he's done to me in the past.

"Make me," he taunts, turning in my direction. "What're you afraid of? Huh?"

I run my tongue over my teeth, grab Mal's shoulder to pull him back, and step between him and the other two idiots. "I'm not afraid of shit. But I don't fight in the locker room. I fight on the mat. Or I could meet you in a back alley and show you what you should be afraid of, little brother." I cock a brow when his chest heaves. There's no fear in his eyes. Only tension in his muscles. Good. He's finally toughened up.

"Do you feel like a big man now?" Malic asks my brother with a laugh. "When you realize what you did later..." He shakes his head, using cryptic words again. Jesus. I'm going to have to check on him, too, tonight. Make sure he's in bed and not building a damn bomb to put under my brother's bed.

"Realize what?" Mack grits out. "That I'm about to show my brother up?" He's way too cocky for his own damn good.

"Just get dressed," I say, gesturing for them to get away from us.

"Can't wait," Hux murmurs, eyeing Malic up and down.

"Ditto!" Mal says giddily, stepping back and standing beside me. "Can't wait for the bloodshed." And I know he means that. He's been ready to beat their asses all his damn life. It's like he was born with a grudge against the three of them.

"Malic," I say in a low voice, bringing his gaze to mine. It's the only way I can tell what the fuck is going through his mind.

"Wilder," he quips back, cocking a brow.

"What's up with you?" I murmur.

He grins. "I'm a new man." With that, he yanks his gaze away from me and walks out the double doors, toward the ring. The crowd goes nuts at the sight of him. They fucking love his fights. The terror it brings the guys who call on him, thinking they can take him down. Malic is indestructible.

I rub my temple. I don't know what the hell he means by a new man. Was it him finally losing his V-card at the bar? Losing Meredith? Whatever it is, something has fundamentally changed Malic, and I can't tell if it's for the better. His obsessive tendencies have ramped up, making him hyper-focused and losing himself in his room for hours. Well, until we have a job to do.

EGG DONOR

I need you, Wilder! I'm so scared...

There's a fine line between loving someone and loathing them for what they did in the past. How am I supposed to hate someone for ruining their life when they can barely remember who the hell they are?

WILDER

Mom. What's scaring you?

I plop on the metal bench with a heavy heart. I run my fingers over my nearly bald head, reveling in the feel of the tiny hairs slowly growing back.

EGG DONOR

The man... he's back!!!

My head falls forward into my hands as I sigh. I'm twenty-two years old. I'm a senior in college. Next year, Mal and I will be on our own, with degrees and working for our boss. But I can't seem to shake this toxic relationship with my mother. She barely knows who I am some days. When I walk in, she swears I'm her first boyfriend—my father. And sometimes, she looks at me like I'm a stranger visiting her at the nursing home.

I shake my head when Mack and Hux walk through in their gym shorts with their chins raised.

"Looks like our fight is last," Mack says with a grin, coming to stand in front of me.

"Great," I mutter, putting my phone away. The only reassurance I have is the round-the-clock nurses stationed there. I quickly text her nurse and let her know what's happening. Because if I don't alert them, she'll call 911 and bring the cops to her room. I don't need that again.

Mack doesn't say anything else. Hell, he doesn't hang around to ask about mom. He walks with Hux out the double doors to watch the fight between him and my best friend. I should go, too. But sometimes, being the caretaker of everyone around me is the most exhausting job of them all.

OLIVIA

The crowd around me goes absolutely bananas when Huxley and Malic jump into the ring with murder in their eyes. I swear every muscle on their impressive bodies bulges with every move. Malic carries himself with more ease, though. Floating across the space with a grin, enticing the crowd to scream his name. Hux glares at Malic with an intensity that might set him on fire. He rests in the corner, watching Malic exude all his energy.

Smart tactic on Hux's part. If Malic were a normal human being, then he'd waste all that on hyping up the crowd instead of rearranging Hux's face. Too bad Malic seems to be an extra-terrestrial with pent-up energy stored somewhere deep inside him. Hell, he doesn't even break a sweat when he jumps up and down, thudding his feet into the mat.

I shake my head. "Idiot," I murmur, sipping my beer to stifle my remarks. If only this bar served margaritas or something else fruity, I'd be in heaven. Instead, I'm stuck with this to drown out my pain.

Jordy eyes me with amusement, knowing exactly what's going through my mind. But he doesn't say anything.

"Oh my God!" Simon howls happily, throwing his arm in the

air. His body sways slightly, and Jordy puts an arm around his waist to steady him.

"Careful there, Si," he mutters, pulling Si into his side protectively. "I'm cutting you off." Jordy looks sternly at Simon, causing the man to pout and stomp his foot.

Oh, yeah. Simon is absolutely wasted. It happened between the time of my fight and now. I guess we can't leave him to his own devices. He's not to be trusted around booze.

"This is just so exciting! Isn't it?" Simon shouts, tossing back his fifth and final beer of the night, emptying it. Jordy discreetly peels it from his hand and hands it back to the bartender, who nods in thanks. "They only fought once last year, and it was..." He whistles under his breath. "It was a sight to see! And Mack and Wilder? It's a night full of surprises!" he howls, throwing his head back. The rest of the crowd seems in sync with him as their voices carry through the Coliseum and cheer the two on.

Hux finally steps out of the corner of the ring, stretching his neck back and forth. The lights shine down on his body, highlighting the new ink he's procured throughout the years. I swallow hard, viewing the giant 224 located on his chest surrounded by white daisies. Up close and in person, it's massive. A dedication. But to whom? Certainly not to me. How could it be when he was directly responsible for my untimely death? Or not-so-death. Whatever.

His ink decorates almost every inch of his abdomen, chest, arms, and back. They're abstract. Mostly shapes, faces, and others I can't quite make out. My breath catches in the back of my throat. I expected it to be there. Maybe covered up. But it's not. It's small. Our first tattoo together.

"You're sure about this?" I ask, nervously biting my lip.

"What? That we want to dedicate our lives to you? Uh, duh," Mack says, kissing my temple and lingering. "We wouldn't have it any other way."

"It's our promise to you, Spitfire." The neon signs of the tattoo shop illuminate

JJ's face in pinks and blues as we stand outside the establishment.

"Okay," Hux says, coming out the front door. "He says he can get the four of us in together in about an hour. Seems they're having a slow day." Hux grins, holding out a piece of paper. "This is the font we chose." How he managed to get us an appointment when we're underage, I'll never know. They probably know who his father is.

I swallow hard, looking at the words printed in pretty cursive. Today. Tomorrow. Forever. Always.

"You're the always," JJ murmurs, circling the word several times with his finger as his eyes linger on my watery expression.

We're really doing this. Cementing ourselves to each other.

"I'm the today," Mack snorts, shaking his head.

"I'm the tomorrow," Hux says.

"I'm the forever," JJ says smugly.

"You all planned this out, didn't you?" I ask, looking between the three of them with wide eyes. There's no way they hadn't fought about this without agreeing beforehand who got what word on them.

"You know it's us against the world, Trouble," Hux says, taking my chin between his fingers. "This is a symbol of our dedication. We talked about it before we came or said anything to you."

"It won't hurt, will it?" I ask, blinking several times. I never dreamed of having a tattoo. Not with my father's watchful eye. But now? It's time to defy him in every sort of way. He trusts these guys because they're Franco's sons.

"Will it be worth it if there's no pain involved?" Hux asks, tilting his head. "That's what this world is, Trouble. Painful."

I understand immediately what he's saying. We all share pain in our lives. Some of us more than others. They understand what

I go through with my dad. The only reason I'm able to come out with them tonight is because my dad is occupied with his newest apprentice. Someone who takes precedence over me. Everyone is above me in his eyes.

"No pain. No gain," Mack says in agreement.

"And the placement?" JJ asks.

Hux stares into my eyes intently, grabbing me by the soul and pulling me into him. That's what they are. That's what this means. We're soul mates. The four of us together. Today. Tomorrow. Forever. Always.

"On the ribs," I mutter.

Malic marches toward Hux with determination. They stand there. Nose to nose, glaring into each other's eyes. Their muscles tense in unison, and it makes me wonder where all the hate between the two of them came from?

"Hey, Simon. Why do they hate each other so much?" I don't take my eyes off them as they mutter words to each other.

"Rivals," Simon says with a dreamy smile. "Rumor has it that Mr. Viking is in a rival gang or something. You know this town is full of criminals and their underworld. Hux's not-so-real-daddy, is the leader of the Franco Syndicate. And Malic? Mmm. His boss is a shadow. That's why we call them the Shades. No one knows who the boss man is. But he's a slimy fuck. They have a gym." Simon hiccups, shaking his head. "In the middle of town, where Malic and Wilder work. An all-dudes gym," he rolls his eyes.

"A gym," I surmise, nodding a few times and remembering the invitation from Wilder to spar and train there. "Interesting..." They have a gym that they help run for their shadowy boss? Weird. Normal gang leaders are out and proud about their criminal enterprise. So, why not this guy? Why does he hide in the shadows and use those two as the face of it all? Fuck. Just add that to the list of things I need to investigate while I'm here. I guess Jonathan was right. There's a shit ton of moving parts to this case that I need to immerse myself in.

"They have fighting lessons there. Maybe I should go and get all tangled up and thrown to the ground," he giggles, covering his lips with his fingers.

Jordy snorts, "Why get thrown around by strange men when you have me?" He winks, and Simon melts, putting his head on Jordy's shoulder.

"So romantic, Jordy," Simon hums. "Throw me around later. I like it rough and dirty."

I gag. "Uh, please. None of that. I don't need to know about what's going to happen later." I cover my mouth with my fingers, pretending to gag again. Having images of my newly appointed best friend tangled up with my not-so-brother, has me aching to vomit everywhere.

Where's the brain bleach when you need it?

"Next-next time, I'll try to be quiet. I'm a screamer," Simon says way louder than necessary with a giggle.

"Seriously, no more booze for you, big guy," Jordy chortles, pulling Simon closer to his body. "We'll make sure to get you home safe tonight."

The people around us don't notice our conversation once the fight starts. Hux and Malic stand tall, staring each other down without throwing the first punch.

"Come on! Hit him!" they all start to chant as they circle one another.

Malic grins at the crowd, taking his eyes off Hux for one split second, and meets my gaze for an uncomfortable amount of time, almost as if he's saying something with his eyes. But what? I have no idea. Before I can examine why he's looking at me, all hell breaks loose. They go at each other with vicious punches. Blood spurts from their noses and lips, and Hux's brow splits, running red down his face. Even then, the referee doesn't step in to stop anything as they continue to pound into each other. The crowd loses their shit. Jumping up and down and screaming at the violence before them.

It's so sad that a place that once meant a lot to the four of us has become this. Bloodshed. Violence.

I swallow back a few sips as a familiar twinge in my stomach causes my breath to leave my lungs. I put my hand there, slowly rubbing back and forth, hoping it's from the fight and not what I think it's from. Stress should reduce the risk of my period coming. Besides, it's so erratic that it's hard to track my cycle.

Fuck.

The pain comes on again. A little more intense than the last one, squeezing my uterus like it's trying to give birth. I squeeze my eyes shut, pleading it's just from the pain of Brutus and his vicious fists. Asshole. He's lucky he struck me before our time had started. Otherwise, he wouldn't have gotten a single blow in. I know next time, if I ever come back, that I won't be so damn lucky. Pain erupts in my jaw and my ribs. Again and again. It's like my body is suddenly letting me know it's revolting against the fight and everything else going on in my life right now.

Oh, God. I think I'm dying. It's all hitting me at once. My body rebels against me.

"I need to go to the bathroom." I toss a finger toward the bathrooms, hoping I can peek at the bruises forming under my binder and on my jaw, which feels like it's pulsating over my cheek.

Jordy blinks a few times, a smile encroaching on his lips. "Sure, man. Have a good piss in the men's bathroom."

Fuck.

My heart sinks.

The men's bathroom. I swallow hard. I've heard rumors of them being gross. Piss all over the floor and urinals. But I've never experienced it before. Not intentionally, at least. I've had those moments where I almost waltzed into the men's bathroom by accident. But this? I have to purposefully walk into the men's bathroom and do my business. Oh, God. My eyes flick to Jordy so fast, they nearly fall out of my head. My bladder screams at me now, begging me to relieve the pressure building. I can't wait. I have to go.

Maybe I should brave the woods outside. Piss on a tree and try not to get caught by all the drunk buffoons. They'd be in here, right? But how suspicious would that look? On the other hand, everyone thinks I have a dong, I could just water the bushes without going into the men's bathroom. Damn it.

"Right, the men's bathroom." I clear my throat, handing him my beer for safekeeping.

I can do this. Just like I put these baggy pants over the uncomfortable briefs this morning. They keep riding up and giving me wedgies, but I'm suffering through. So I can suffer through the men's bathroom without looking suspicious. Of course, if there's anyone in there, they'll see me having to pop a squat and ugh. I'm so fucked.

Jonathan, I hate you for this.

"I've got my eyes on this one." Jordy gestures to Simon, who *woohoos* a few more times, watching as the fight continues. "Hope it all comes out smooth!" Jordy chuckles at my pain when I flip him the bird and walk away with my heart in my throat.

I'm a guy. I have to go into the men's bathroom. I'm undercover. I can't destroy my disguise and slip into the girls' bathroom. It could be an oops. Like, sorry, ladies! I thought this was the guy's bathroom! I'd be labeled a creep, then. Shit. And my cover would be under more scrutiny than it already is. I suck in a breath when I'm standing outside the bathroom labeled for men.

My stomach turns. Either that's dirt on the damn sign, or someone shit and touched it. Why is this my life right now? I just need to pee.

I got this. Totally got this. Yup. That's what I tell myself over and over until I'm standing in the middle of the disgusting, piss-smelling men's bathroom. Only to see two men standing at the urinals with their dicks in their hands and a steady flow streaming from them. Holy dicks, they're peeing. Out in the open without anything shielding their junk from peeping eyes. Shit. My cheeks heat when one guy I don't recognize clears his throat and twists his expression like I'm the Peeping Tom. Shit! I am! I cover my eyes as he mutters something under his breath, but I don't stick around to hear what he says. I find the only stall available and hide inside, locking the door behind me.

That was close.

I lean against it for several breaths, hoping the other two scram before I have to sit down to pee. Fuck. Maybe I should invest in one of those tools for girls so they can stand up while they're doing their business. If they weren't suspicious of me getting startled by them at the urinals, they'll be suspicious when I sit down on the....

I wrinkle my nose. Does no one clean this place? The toilet rim looks like someone tried to paint it. With pee. And probably shit. I want to bang my head against the wall and leave. Maybe watering a few bushes outside isn't such a bad idea after all.

Nope.

Knowing my luck, I'll get caught out in the open with my vagina on display. Or get poison ivy in places that would be very uncomfortable. Reminds me of the time Mack got it on his dick. Idiot. We had to sneak to the doctor to get the medication to stop it from itching and spreading. I crack a smile at the memory. He evidently got it on his hands first, then his wang, and then his buttcheeks. He was thirteen and couldn't stop scratching. Thus, he spread it everywhere. Dumbass.

My shoulders slump with the realization of my predicament. Hover City, here I come. Because there's no way, I'm putting my bare buttcheeks on that seat.

Whatever.

As soon as footsteps bound out of the bathroom, I sit—hover, thank you very much—on the toilet and do my business as quickly as possible. It's only when I'm staring at my thighs that I notice the blood smeared there. It's not from the fight. Nope. That'd be too damn convenient. Wonderful. The world is against me right now.

My period has shown its ugly face. Is it too much to ask for a simple one? A period that isn't too painful or messy? Probably not. My periods take me down for at least five days of rolling around in bed and begging for death. Even birth control doesn't touch what my uterus reigns down. All my doctors have dismissed my concerns, tossing me birth control and painkillers like that'll solve the problems I'm having.

I roll my head back until I'm staring up at the equally disgusting ceiling. How am I going to navigate being a guy while I'm in my painful cycle and not get caught? I'll figure it out. I guess. I mean, I have to, right? Fuck me.

I put some toilet paper in my briefs, praying to the stars that they don't ride up again. But I know they will. I pull up my pants and turn to flush the toilet behind me. I peek through the crack of the door and sigh. No one seems to be in here. Thank God. I don't think I can handle seeing another dick right now.

I emerge from the stall, heading straight to the sink and washing my hands with soap. As my gaze meets mine in the mirror, I confirm the massive bruise decorating my jaw and encroaching on my cheek. Yay. A battle wound. I'll have to check the one under my bindings tomorrow, which I know will hurt like a bitch. Even now, as I move, it aches under the pressure of the binding on my ribs.

I move to dry my hands as the door swings open and stiffen when a familiar face comes into view in the dim lights. His curly, dark brown hair almost covers his eyes until he swoops it away and takes me in with those golden-brown assessing eyes. A pair of eyes I fell into so many times years before.

But not anymore.

JJ is a stranger to me. Maybe he always was.

"You fought pretty good out there, man." The low timbre of his voice sends goosebumps down my arms and back. It's been so long since I've heard the tone of his voice and how it used to soothe me when I was frightened by the storms.

I raise my hands instinctively to sign my words, but abruptly stop, dropping them back to my sides. That was once the way we communicated. Through ASL. I'm sure the guys still use it to keep their conversations private.

But I can't do that right now.

"Thanks," I rasp, clearing my throat, drying my hands again, and tossing the paper towel into the garbage can. I move to leave the bathroom, but JJ stands in my way, crossing his arms.

"Where'd you learn to fight like that?" There's a slight suspicion in his tone, like he doesn't believe I could pull it off again.

Believe me, I don't want to. This will be the last time they catch me at this fight. Well, as Oliver, anyway. I'm hoping that if I can sneak in here as Olivia—or Claire, as I like to use—I can watch people without interruption. Or getting called out to fight.

I shrug. "I grew up with three older brothers." It's a lie. I only had a sister. Well, until my father picked up a straggler and turned him into a son. "We wrestled a lot, and they taught me everything I know."

He doesn't believe me. I can see it in his eyes as they look me over again until he stops at my shoes and frowns. "Are you bleeding?"

I blink, looking down at my shoes. Yup. It's confirmed. The universe absolutely hates me. "Uh, yeah. Just a little. He got me good, yeah know?" I laugh it off, plucking the bloodied toilet paper from my shoe and tossing it into the trash. So much for the stupid toilet paper staying in place in my stupid briefs. Ugh. I'm toast. I physically feel my cheeks heat when he frowns, eyeing me more. It feels like he's undressing me with his stare and unraveling the Oliver mask I've put into place.

"We have med students here. Did you get it looked at?" He points toward the door from over his shoulder.

"Nah, I'm fine. It was just a little cut. Nothing serious."

He still doesn't believe me, but he shrugs. "Suit yourself," he says, rubbing at his chin where a tiny scar rests. It's the only spot any person could see that's the evidence of the car crash he was in when he was eight. Well, that and his hearing. Nestled in his ears are an upgraded version of the hearing aids he once had. Shiny and new. Probably helping him process words. I wonder if this loud environment has him turning the volume down like he used to before.

But then again. I don't care. I can't care.

They saw to it that I shouldn't anymore. My heart aches at the constant reminder. JJ may have a scar on his chin from the car wreck that took his parents and brought him to Greenwood in foster care. But I have one, too.

I brush past him with a huff, knocking my shoulder into his. There. That'll teach him to interrogate me in the middle of the disgusting bathroom. I know he's picking me apart, trying to figure me out. Too bad he won't be able to. Or I hope he won't be able to. What kind of shit would I get myself into if I had him up my ass discovering who I am?

I quickly return to Jordy and Simon, who is almost passed out on Jordy's shoulder.

"Smooth sailing?" Jordy asks with a cocky grin. I glare at him in return, and he shrugs. "Let's roll?" he asks, gesturing toward the door. My eyes flick to the empty fighting ring that sits empty. "It was a draw. There's a rematch in two weeks," Jordy says, answering my question.

"It'll be epic," Simon slurs. "T-to-totally epic."

"Yeah, Si. Epic," Jordy says, smoothing a hand through Simon's hair. "But let's get you to bed now. How about a gallon of water and ibuprofen?"

Simon groans in response, lifting his head. His eyes are red-rimmed and glazed over, but he still grins at me. "You're good people, Oli," he mutters, turning a slight shade of green.

"He's going to puke," I mutter with urgency, shoving Jordy until we're out the door and into the forest.

The poor trees witness Simon tossing his cookies into the plants and giving them the alcohol his body wouldn't process. Maybe I should keep Simon away from alcohol from now on. This seems to be a growing theme of him losing his dinner to the grass and trees. Poor guy.

"You're doing great, Simon," Jordy murmurs, rubbing his back as he heaves again and again. Finally, he comes up for air and wipes his mouth.

"You know... I'm-I'm not usually a drinker," Simon hiccups again. "But damn..." he slurs more, heaving a breath.

"Yup. Let's go home," I say, taking one of his arms over my shoulder as Jordy does the same on his side.

"You guys-guys are the best. Can I keep you both forever?" Simon slurs, stumbling over his feet as we practically carry him down the long wooded trail in the direction of our dorms.

"Always, big guy," Jordy quips with a genuine grin.

The trail crunches beneath our feet until we finally emerge onto the darkened campus. Everything around us is as quiet as a mouse. The moon shines high above us, and the stars twinkle down.

"It's just-just too bad we'll miss Mack and Wilder fighting, because you're taking me home," Simon grumbles, staggering a little. "It would have been epic, too."

"We'll check Slam tomorrow and see the pictures," I chuckle, squeezing his shoulder. Simon nods a few times as we weave through campus, attempting to stay in the shadows. "Didn't our RAs say there would be police on the grounds?" I mutter, looking at the empty spaces. If there are police here trying to keep people on campus, they're either doing it through camera work or they're really good at hiding.

Simon snorts, "Why would they actually do that when the administration is responsible for everything?"

I stiffen, snapping my gaze to Jordy, who frowns. "Oh, yeah? You know something about that, Si?" he asks carefully with a soft tone.

"Nah, just rumors," Simon slurs. "Rumors that the dean is the one doing it. Whatever *it* is." He shrugs.

We don't push him any further until we're standing at the back of our dorm building.

"Here," Simon stumbles away from us, going toward a window, and yanking it open. "Gotta climb through..." he slurs and stumbles forward, falling through the empty window.

"Simon!" I yelp, running forward and stopping suddenly. He's cackling on the ground of the room he landed in. There's a mattress beneath him as he laughs, holding his stomach.

"Well, that broke his fall," Jordy quips, shaking his head.

My stomach cramps again, and I sigh. "What car did you bring here?" I murmur.

"SUV," he murmurs back, cocking his head. "Why?"

"Because I need to use it."

"At three in the morning? What you got? A booty call at a bar? Please don't give me the details..." he trails off when my face twists.

"No. I need fucking tampons," I whisper-hiss.

He pales, holding up his hands. "I thought we had a brother-sister agreement to never talk about that. Oh, and your sex life. My sex life. But periods are at the top."

"You asked," I say, sending him a glare as he fishes keys out of his pocket.

"Here. Just don't... Nope. I'm not saying it. Have fun. Don't get caught. I'll take care of Simon." he looks through the window as Simon continues to laugh himself into a damn coma. "I gotta make sure he doesn't yack again. I kinda like the guy." He looks at Simon affectionately.

"That means you're going to visit more often, doesn't it?" I ask, getting to my feet from the crouching position.

"What? You act like you don't want to see me all the time." He grins. "Good luck."

And with that, he climbs through the window, helps Simon to his feet, and makes his way through the open door. Weird. I wonder what the story is with that. An empty dorm room for kids to climb in and out of.

Whatever the case, I need to get tampons ASAP.

OLIVIA

It's confirmed. The world is against me. The moment I reach the parking lot to commandeer Jordy's SUV, I see the security guards making their rounds. Hell, they even stop two classmates and reprimand them for being out, giving them a slip of paper. A ticket, I think. So much for using a vehicle to get me to the corner store. A walk is good for me, right?

Damn.

I need a strawberry margarita, ice cream, cookies, and a whole lot of pain medication. All in that order. And immediately. Why can't teleportation exist? Ugh.

I rub my temple when I enter the slightly busy convenience store, which is strange for the middle of the night. The bright fluorescent lights buzz above me. Several people move through the aisles with snacks in their hands. The lone worker resting behind the counter greets me with a tight smile as I enter.

Yeah, buddy. I don't blame you. It's way too late to be perky and welcoming.

Especially after the long walk here.

It took me ten minutes to get here when it could have taken seconds with Jordy's car. Mentally, I'm sending bad vibes toward the police officers for car-blocking me. Sure, they're there for our safety. But ugh. I just want to sleep and get this little trip over with. Listen, I get it. They want to keep everyone alive.

Thankfully, no one else was on the road. Not a driver. Walker. Nothing. Just me and the night sky getting acquainted once again. It was oddly silent and comforting to my psyche after being surrounded by people all night, bumping into me. Oh, and the asshole who fought me. Can't forget him. I wonder how old Brutus is holding up after going limp against me.

Speaking of, my jaw twinges with pain as I walk down the aisles, searching for everything I might need. With the long list of stuff in my head, I grabbed a small basket to hide it in. Hopefully, no one else from the fights has the same idea and comes here. Although it's pretty quiet and emptying out. A few rogue murmurs here and there float through the air, but they're aisles away.

A sharp cramp in my guts almost takes me out, zinging like lightning through me. Fuck. I hold a hand to the side of my stomach and grimace, eyeing the space around me. I'm not regular by any means. Even the birth control pills I take don't make me any more regular like they were supposed to. One month, it'll show and nearly kill me. And then not show up for another three months. It's chaotic at best. So, I knew this day would come. I didn't expect it to happen so soon. The only indication I ever get is the slight bloating of my stomach and the twinges of pain in my uterus.

I should have known it was on the horizon. But with all the craziness of this new job, I didn't even notice. Maybe I need to wear baggy pants and t-shirts more often. They're way more comfortable, and my bloat is less noticeable.

That's the only thing that will be unnoticeable. How the hell am I supposed to hide pads and tampons from my manly roommates? Not to mention, there are no locks on our doors, and I'll be curled up in the fetal position for at least two to five days trying to find relief. You know what? Add a heating pad to my list. I grab one from the shelf and toss it into my small basket, heading straight for the feminine products aisle. I keep my eyes peeled, but no one my age is out right now. Especially not here.

"Finally," I mutter, grabbing a box of super tampons and tossing them into my basket. As my eyes browse the other sizes, the hairs on my neck stand on end like someone is watching me. Before I can turn to look, my watcher speaks.

"You," a familiar, gruff voice says behind me, startling me until I turn around. I blink several times, watching Dane stand there with a scowl and several pints of Rocky Road ice cream under his arm.

"You," I automatically say back with a startled look. I'm sure I look like a deer caught in the damn headlights.

Get your shit together, Olivia. You're a man in the tampon aisle. Dane looks me up and down with a weird expression twisting his face. Great. He's thinking the same exact thing.

"The fuck are you looking at tampons for?"

That's rude as hell. I don't know why he hates me so damn much, but I need to figure it out. He thinks I'm a waste of space because of my scholarship student status. Now, he's going to think I'm an even bigger freak for buying tampons and pads. This whole remaining under-the-radar thing isn't working out, especially with my roommates.

Case in point—Dane.

"My girlfriend," I spit out quickly, attempting to put my basket behind my back and out of his sight. Too bad he follows the movement with even more suspicion.

I am a seasoned agent of Veritas. But you certainly wouldn't know that right now. I feel like a noob. This shouldn't be that hard. Easy peasy. But not lemon squeezy.

"Girlfriend," Dane laughs under his breath mockingly. "Really?"

Again. Rude as fuck. "Uh, yeah. She's in town for the weekend." I cock my head. "So, remain away." Please. Stay the hell out of our room until my period is done. Or I might bite his head off and hide his body in the nonexistent closet. Besides, the last thing I need is him and all his pissy glory ruining my weekend. Not to mention the party I have to drag myself to tomorrow while pretending my body isn't attempting to murder me from the inside out.

Ugh.

This mission blows.

"Well, now I want to come back and see this invisible girl-friend." He laughs more at my expense, browsing the tampons with pursed lips.

"What the fuck are you doing buying tampons?" I ask, raising a brow when he plucks a variety pack off the shelf confidently and places it under his arm.

"I have a real girlfriend," he says, gesturing to the Rocky Road ice cream and chocolates piled in his arms. "Who happens to need these. You on the other hand?" he laughs, throwing his head back and snorts.

Right. His girlfriend.

I shrug. "Well, looks like we're on the same page again." Do not blush. Do not let your face heat while he's staring you up and down. Don't embarrass yourself.

He snorts. "Whatever, Scholarship Boy. Have a good night with your hand." With that, the asshole struts away toward the cash register, laughing the entire way at my expense.

Is it against the law to smother your roommate while he's sleeping? Yes, yes it is. But it doesn't stop me from fantasizing about it. Besides, I could get away with it. I am the authority in this situation.

"Dick," I mutter, shaking my head. Turning back, I grab a small box of regulars, too. And then some thick pads for the worst of it. With my periods being so damn ridiculous, I have to make sure I have everything before it hits and I bleed through all the clothes I wear. Because I definitely will.

With my selection in hand, I make my way through the store. Although Dane's rude appearance in the tampon aisle made me want to punch him in the nose, he had the right idea. Ice cream. Cold. Chocolatey. It'll soothe all the hurt I'm about to endure over the next week.

My mind wanders as I cruise the aisles, picking up anything and everything I'll need to survive and throwing it into the basket. Hopefully, I'll still be able to make it to class. I don't know how I'll pull off the whole "I'm sick; leave me alone" schtick for long. Simon will get concerned and want to baby me, which sounds delightful.

I'll figure it out when the time comes. For now, I want to make the walk home, crawl into my bed, and never leave. A line has formed when I make it up front to the cash registers. Dane is at the front of it with his ice cream and tampons. He smirks at me when he picks up his bags and meanders out of the store with a laugh. Fucker. For the most part, it's mainly college students, from the look of their condom purchases. Mixed with a few bottles of wine, vodkas, and whiskeys. They're ready to have a good rest of the night.

Me too, guys. Me too.

I blow out a breath. This night has been so weird. First, I get called out for a fight. Thanks for that, Macklyn. Revenge will be so sweet when I finally get my hands on him. Not only for the fight, but the fuckery from five years ago. Every time I see one of them, it's a knife to the heart. The hurt is still there, like it happened yesterday. Looking into their eyes and knowing they looked down at me when I was at my lowest and most desperate, sends rage through my blood.

I'm a professional, though. And being that, I have to keep my wits about me. *I am the calm.* Will revenge come later? Oh, you betcha. I'll bring it so hard, they won't know what hit them. It'll be me—I'll hit them where it hurts. Until then, I'm being a good undercover agent because there's more to this case than meets the eye. This school is a hotbed of illegal activities. I just have to figure out where it's all coming from. Franco, probably. Or hell, maybe the mysterious other gang leader.

Whoever it is, I'll find them. And when I do, they'll wish they never fucked with me or anyone else.

I sigh, moving forward in line, smiling at the older woman who is working the register. When I return to my dorm, I still need to send in my weekly notes and attach the footage from my glasses. I can only imagine what they've caught.

Finally, I pay for my items, grab my two bags, head to the public restroom and put a tampon in, and then, finally, leave the store before I run into Dane again. Knowing him, he's probably lingering outside just waiting to pick on me again. Something odd happens when I step out the door. There's no Dane there, but all the lights have gone out in the parking lot. I'd suspect an outage, but nowhere else has lost electricity. Quickly, I inform the store of the outage so no one gets hurt and make my way back to my dorm.

The hairs on my neck stand on end as I walk down the sidewalk. It's eerie out here without the parking lot lights. At least there is still some lighting up the sidewalk. As I look over my shoulder, the lights flicker back on in the parking lot, illuminating the area.

"Hey, Oli!" I blink several times. How many people can I run into on my way to the store?

I stop short, turning as Wade runs toward me with a pint of ice cream. The lid is off, and a plastic spoon rests in the thick Rocky Road. Rub it in, why don't you? I can't have mine until I'm in the safety of my own bed. I mean, I could totally eat it now, but I have patience.

"Wade." I look him over as he jogs to stand beside me. "Why are you out so late?"

"Hey, man. You just came from the store? I had to stop and get something, too. The fights always leave me hungry. Besides,

I think your cousin is with Simon." He snorts when I wrinkle my nose.

Ah, he's avoiding our dorm, too. I'm surprised he didn't find an alternate place to stay. Although I haven't seen him hanging around other people on campus. Maybe he's a loner. Besides, when was he at the dang store? I would have seen him. Right?

"Yeah, he is." But I doubt they're hooking up. Not in the condition Simon was in. Jordy won't do that sort of thing with anyone who's been drinking as heavily as Simon had been. He may be a little shit, but he's a respectful guy in that regard. In others, though? He's an asshole. But I love him. Just don't let him know that.

"Good ass fight today, though. Dude. You rocked Brutus." He shakes his head, whistling under his breath. "Careful, though. Brutus is..."

"An asshole with a bone to pick?" I quip, shaking my head.

"Yeah. One of those." He shakes his head. "Let me know if he gives you issues." He gives me a look like he has some sort of connections. Shit. His mom is the dean of the university. The last thing I need is her sticking her nose in my business, though. No thanks. I can solve this on my own. I hope. If not, I'll have to call in reinforcements and create a special team. Again, no thanks. If Jonathan trusted me with this case, then I'm going to give it my all to prove myself. Hello, future promotion. It's on the horizon.

Silence engulfs both of us as we walk down the sidewalk together. It's kind of nice having someone beside me, rather than being alone, and not being alone while it's dark and eerie outside. Once again, no one else is roaming the streets. Maybe they're the smart ones by staying inside and not getting kidnapped. Or having all their internal organs plucked out of their bodies. I shudder at the thought.

As we get closer to the school, I expect more police officers out like there were thirty minutes ago when I tried to leave. I wonder where they all went off to?

"Didn't the RAs say there would be security guards out? How can we all get away with breaking curfew?" I peek over at him as he shoves a bite of chocolate ice cream into his mouth with a satisfied hum. He seems awfully giddy tonight, with an extra pep in his step.

"Yeah. My mom hired extras because of all the shit going on. They're around, but they know when the fights happen. And they know students will be out. Honestly, sticking to campus seems impossible, ya know?" He offers me a warm smile.

"Yeah," I say, trailing off when we finally return to campus.

"Just stick close, and we'll sneak in through the window. I'm guessing Si showed you?" Wade asks, gesturing for me to follow him.

"Yup," I agree, following close behind him and trying to keep my bags concealed. The last thing I need to do is have him suspicious of me, too.

"Good. They don't guard this window, and they don't put anyone in the room, either. For obvious reasons." Obvious for who? Certainly not me.

"Why is it an empty room?" I question softly.

Wade grunts, opens the large window, and hops down onto the mattress with ease. Extra points for holding tightly to his ice cream and not spilling an ounce. "Give me your bags, and then you can jump."

Fuck. Whatever. I give him my bags and jump down beside him on the cushy mattress. He doesn't give me funny looks or ask questions before he closes the window behind us, and we head up toward our dorm room.

"I told you all kinds of shit happens here, right?" he murmurs when we come to our door on the second floor. I nod in agreement when he pushes open our dorm door and closes it behind us. He shoves a massive bite of chocolate ice cream into his mouth and sighs. "Some kid was attacked in that dorm room two years ago." He shakes his head. "Don't know what happened after that. But Mom made sure no one else occupied that room."

Great. Another thing I need to ask Carter about.

"Weird," I say, wrinkling my nose. "Did he survive?"

"Oh, yeah. He survived, but he left after that. And so did his roommates. It must have spooked them all. I think the window is faulty, I guess that's why we can get in and out." He shrugs. "Don't know what happened to him or whatever." How fucking morbid. Wade turns and looks at his closed bedroom door with a sock on the damn doorknob and sighs. "Well, looks like I'm on the couch tonight." With that, he saunters to the couch and plops down with his ice cream, finishing it in five large bites.

Before I wave goodnight, I put my ice cream in the freezer. I'll eat it later. I need meds, bed, and nothing else.

"Night, then," I say, slowly going to my room. I could offer Wade Dane's bed since the asshole never stays here. But I don't. Tonight is not one of those nights where I need an audience. I'm already dying from the pain in my stomach, face, and every-where else.

Now is the time to sleep.

OLIVIA

"LIV. LIV. LIV. LIV..." JORDY'S ANNOYING VOICE DRIFTS through my dreams, stirring my conscious mind. "Oliviaaaaaa," he softly sings, poking me in the side repeatedly.

He really wants to lose a damn finger. I can either cut it or bite it off. His choice.

I groan, slapping Jordy away. Why is he waking me up, anyway? It's way too early to converse. Can't he leave me alone? I was out too late. Jordy doesn't usually greet the day until noon. Unless he's on a case, of course. Being awake means feeling the pain in my stomach, which has evolved into a full-blown, constant period cramp. My face aches. My ribs ache. I'm one big ache today. There's no way I'm emerging from the cocoon. I live here now. No one disturb me.

"Olivia," the voice hisses, lightly slapping my cheek two times, right over my damn bruise.

Motherfucker!

"You really want to die a painful death, don't you?" I whine, slapping at him again, but he catches my wrists with an annoying chuckle.

"Liv, I'm heading out before Simon can ask where I've gone. He conked out hard last night. He'll be... in some pain whenever he wakes up... from the alcohol, of course..." A warm kiss presses against my cheek. "You're doing good things here, Liv. Keep up the good work, alright? I'll see you in a few weeks. Simon invited me back. Maybe next time I'll bring you earplugs. Because I plan on bending him over..." LA LA LA, I do not want to hear the details of his future hook up with my roommate, who I have to look in the eyes for the next... however many months I'm here.

"You better bring me earplugs. The last thing I need to hear is… that," I gag out, peeking an eye open, and am greeted by the darkness surrounding Jordy's figure.

Great. The sun isn't even up. Even it's too tired to make an appearance yet. I probably got two hours of sleep. Maybe less. Good thing it's Saturday, and the only event we have is the raging party tonight at ten P.M. I have plenty of time to turn myself from the period goblin I'm about to become into a beautiful prince, hiding beneath my false skin.

It's a great day to be alive.

"Love you, too. By the way, your bestie Carter texted you." He grins, waving the bright phone in my face. I rear back, squeezing my eyes shut. But it does nothing. Now, there's a shining light trapped behind my eyelids, slowly blinding me. "Probably something important. You're lucky the texts don't disappear until you've opened them."

"Probably. It might be able to wait until after the sun comes up," I groan, but my heart pounds in my chest with anticipation. I've waited so long for him to send me everything I need.

"You going to survive?" he whispers, putting my phone on my pillow and releasing my wrists. "You know with..." He gestures to my stomach, no doubt frowning. If I hadn't been blinded by the damn phone, then maybe I'd be able to read his expression.

"I always do, don't I?"

Jordy snorts at my answer. "Uh, yeah. Sure. You call that surviving? I've had to console you more than once. I won't be here to do that. You know, I actually got a damn lead from the museum last night. Might have some footage of my thief after all."

"Keep me updated?"

"Ditto. Be careful here, Liv. There's something so off about this damn place. And the people?" He whistles softly, shaking his head.

"You mean them?"

"Besides them," he murmurs, stroking his chin. "Everyone on campus gives off weird vibes." That's the understatement of the damn century. Everyone walking the grounds of Greenwood University is a goddamn villain.

"Wade walked me home from the store last night and told me about the kid who got attacked in his dorm. He didn't know anything about it." Just another thing on my mysterious list of bullshit about this place. Can't this case do me a solid and solve itself? *A girl can dream.*

"Ask fucking Carter. He'll hack into the damn White House if he has to," Jordy snorts.

"Planned on it," I groan. "I'll check our database first and see if there's anything on it. Also, your keys are over there." I wave to my desk, and he picks them up.

"Good thinking. Love ya, Liv. Be careful. Call if you need me. And for the love of God, don't get yourself killed." With one more kiss on my head, Jordy heads out the door as quietly as he came in and leaves campus.

I'm sad to see him go. Having him here has really helped me come into my own as Oliver. Sometimes, you need someone familiar to help walk you through the trials and tribulations of your newest case. And Jordy, no matter how annoying, is my person through and through.

"Now that I'm awake," I mutter, looking at my phone.

CARTER

Your goddamn information. Make sure you save this shit before it disappears into the ether. Now, fuck off.

He's always so pleasant, but damn, did he deliver the goods like he said he would.

Miles Brummet, a student at Greenwood University in Greenwood, California, was found dead this morning, lying on the stairs of the administrative building. Police suspect major foul play and are looking into every possible lead, including bringing the FBI in to handle matters.

I scroll through more of the article, keeping everything brief and without descriptions. Until I get to the part about his missing organs. Everything was taken from him like a damn buffet for vampires. If they existed, that is.

Police indicate they have no leads at this time on the disappearance of his organs, but they will be interviewing several suspects in the coming days, trying to track down their whereabouts.

CARTER

I know you'll be fucking asking for the transcripts of the police interrogations, too. So, I did you a goddamn solid and took care of it. You're fucking needy... Although, you'll be fucking disappointed. They gave up on the investigation within a week... Fucking kid died and they gave him a few days. The FBI was never involved. Wasn't even called. Sounds like you got another shitty case full of murdery assholes. Have fun!

That's an understatement. Ugh. Why wouldn't the FBI get

involved with this? And no police investigation? The article must have lied to soothe the people of Greenwood. Strange, though, that Miles was the only one mentioned as being torn apart. Were there others? Probably. Like the kid who was attacked in his dorm room. I need the details on that to see if it's connected in any way possible. Probably is. There's no coincidence in investigations. It's all leads that take you to the killer.

Now, if only the killer would show their face.

CARTER

> Also, here's the address of the creeper looking you up. It originated from this address: 501 Greenwood Way. It looks like some ancient type of house, twenty minutes from your location.

Such a pleasure to work with, I swear.

I shake my head, rereading the address a million times to make sure the words say what I think they're saying. *501 Greenwood Way.* Pins prickle my skin. A coldness engulfs me as all the blood drains from my face. Oh, God... That's not just any address. Nope. It's a familiar place. I almost wish it were someone I didn't know. It would make my life easier. Instead, I get this. Another blast from the past. Nathanial Franco. The man who killed me. And now, his address has eyes on my every move. Great. This is fucking fantastic.

I throw off the covers and sit on the edge of the bed. There are so many things going through my head. But if Franco is the one looking into me, then I'm absolutely fucked. If he knows I'm back or alive or whatever, he'll skin me alive. Again! I could be ground beef by the time the sun comes up, and there's nothing I can do to prepare. Well, there is. Feeling around my mattress, I run my fingers along the wood handle of the knife Jordy so helpfully packed for me. The only thing he packed for me, besides my new clothes, that will come in handy.

OLI

> Do you by chance have the deed for that property? Can you see who currently owns it? Or who specifically looked into me?

CARTER

See? Needy...

OLI

> I am needy, asshole. That's the address of the dick who tried to kill me so...

CARTER

Fucking hell... Fine.

I tap my fingers, drumming them several times on my legs.

CARTER

Nathaniel Franco still owns the property. Looks like it's been the same person for at least thirty fucking years... Fuck. You going to survive this shit? Or should I call in reinforcements for your ass?

Even though my heart pounds out of my chest, threatening to beat across the room, I suck it all in.

OLI

> Thanks for your concern, fucker. But I'll be fine...

I'll be fine. My famous last words, right? Ugh. Now, I have to make sure I'm not getting tracked by Franco.

CARTER

Did you really fucking think I couldn't sabotage whoever was looking into you? If I can mirror bathroom fuck's phone with just a name, then I can track down the asshole looking into you... BTW, that guy's phone is as blank as blank can be. What's that asshole up to? Hmm?

OLI

Well? Have you?

Three dots appear in the chat, disappear, and reappear several times before he finally answers.

CARTER

Fucker's good... got good equipment, but he's no Carter Cunningham.

I can almost hear his evil chuckle from here. Also, how humble of him.

OLI

And?

The suspense is fucking killing me. I swear everyone around me talks in damn circles.

CARTER

A Jasper Jeremiah Jones... Ring any bells?

My heart drops into my stomach, and I groan. Of course. That's why JJ was all in my business. He's tracking me around, trying to figure out who I am. I almost forgot he was sort of a computer whiz and always had been. Gaming, mostly. As kids, he meddled in hacking, trying to get into anything he could as a beginner. I bet Franco has trained him to do his dirty work, and that's why he's gotten so good now.

OLI

Great...

CARTER

Take it you know the fucker that's responsible?

Know him? I abhor him. But I don't say that.

OLI

> You could say that. Looks like I need to be
> extra careful.

CARTER

> Fucking right. Not only does he watch fucking
> anime porn...

I throw my head back and groan at his words. That's a detail I didn't need to know about my former best friend. He can do whatever the hell he pleases, anime porn included, but that visual? Ugh.

CARTER

> But he's been looking into your school records
> obsessively. Fucking hell. He knows a lot
> about your fake persona... Not to mention how
> fucking easy and suspect your files are. Who's
> in charge of making that shit? Should have let
> me do it. Here... I'll fucking fix it.

OLI

> What the hell do you mean, easy to get into?

CARTER

> Like I fucking said. Easy to fucking spot that
> your shit is fake. Veritas let some hack do this
> shit... He's onto you. And if he's onto you...
> who else fucking will be? Sorry to burst your
> bubble, Agent fucking Princess, but you gotta
> be careful. Now, if you'll excuse me, I'm all out
> of fucks for today.

I toss my hands into the air with a huff. Agent fucking Princess? That's a new one. Especially coming from him. How bored is he that he's willing to do all this stuff for me? You know, if we had been on the phone, he would have hung up on me without saying goodbye. At least he's always here to hand over the information. I guess.

"Rude fucker," I grumble, rubbing over my aching stomach. It cramps harder, making my eyes squeeze shut.

I sigh, grab a water bottle, and gulp it down. My jaw aches with every move. My stomach hurts. Everything fucking hurts. I need a hot, uninterrupted shower and lots of sleep before I jump into anything. Is this a life-and-death situation? Uh, huh. But I need to take care of myself first and sort out my body before tonight.

With that in mind, I swallow my anti-inflammatories, grab some clean clothes and chest binder, and head to the bathroom. Everyone seems to be still passed out. Wade is snoring on the couch with an empty ice cream carton on the coffee table. I sigh, longingly staring at the small freezer where I put my ice cream before bed. Later. I'll eat it later. First, I need a hot shower to warm up my muscles, and then I'm going for a jog. That always seems to help the merciless cramps invading my uterus. Even if it's goddamn torture. Who willingly runs through the woods like their ass is on fire for exercise? Psychopaths, that's who. If I am running, then you should probably run, too. It means danger is afoot, and I'm getting the fuck out of dodge.

Ugh, I hate jogging.

Plus, I need to investigate Franco's former home and pray to the fucking stars he doesn't live there anymore. If JJ is doing his dirty work for him, he might know I'm here, and I'll have to be extra careful around campus to keep my life intact. Because, despite everything, I'd rather stay alive, thanks. Or, I'll have to leave, and I can't have that. I need to investigate what I came for.

Once I hobble to the bathroom, I put my clean clothes on the countertop and stare at my reflection. Ooof. Yup. I look rough as hell. Who is staring back at me? A stranger. That's who. Ugh. Right there on my jaw is a large bruise, turning black and blue. Brutus better count his days for his dirty tactics. Oliver fucking Davenport is ready for him again. Well, maybe. I'm sure he'll be gunning for me around campus and probably hoping to make my life miserable. News flash, buddy, I already live in Misery City —population one.

My fingers tremble as I trace the massive bruise around the edges, testing it. The pain sparks instantaneously the moment I press hard into the black and blue surface of my flesh, sending white-hot pain through my damn veins. It ignites something inside me. A war cry wanting to fall from my lips and display everything that I'm bottling inside.

But I don't.

My lips hold firmly together, hiding the cry in my throat and the tears misting my eyes.

I refuse to fall victim to the pain that was inflicted on me. Because of him. Mack. He set it up, wanting to bring Oliver Davenport down a notch.

This is my battle wound. My win. Proof that the boy who once loved me and then discarded me couldn't get rid of me again.

Sucker.

I sigh, slowly lifting my shirt over my head and cringing at the large bruise on my ribs. Thankfully, I didn't have to sleep in my binder last night. Even though I was paranoid Dane was going to come in to check on me and my nonexistent girlfriend. My comforter is thick enough to hide my body beneath it and not show off my curves.

My fingers graze over the bruise, looking like I got kicked in the side by a damn boot. Repeatedly. It expands over my ribs, looking gnarly and aching like a motherfucker with every move I make.

"Jesus," I hiss to myself, trying to remain quiet as I poke at the bruise and hold back my desperate yelp. Without a second thought, I start the shower to get it heated until the steam fills the room and continue to look at myself in the mirror.

It's odd to see the woman I've become. As a kid, I swore I was in Mafia hell. My dad promised to marry me off to the best match for our family. A family that could get us from beneath Franco's cruel thumb. Since Dad got exiled from the damn Viotto Crime Family for his crimes, he was forced to work with Franco and help him manage Greenwood in order to get back into his brother's—the other Viotto Crime members—-good graces. I've never truly known why they came together so well. Or why Franco let us live on his land in a small house fifteen feet from his mansion. Probably to keep an eye on my father. I guess that's how I got to know the guys so well. All we had to do was sneak through the woods to see each other whenever we wanted, even when my dad put bars on my window and locked me in our rickety old basement as punishment.

Then, I was free from it all. My dad disappeared into a black hole and apparently hasn't emerged yet. I'm sure he'll resurface like a damn cockroach in the middle of the night. Or maybe he died already. That would be the best Christmas present on the planet. Bye, Dad. Ya dick.

Reaching in, I check the temp of the water. Perfect. It's hellish hot and will boil my skin off. Just what I need. With that confirmation, I slide my boxers and pants off and toss them aside, being careful not to upset my bruises.

I stagger, trying not to jostle my injuries as I go to the side of the tub and pull back the curtain. Just as I'm about to lift my leg and step into the hell water I can't wait to enjoy, the bathroom door bursts open.

I'd love to say I was graceful and hopped into the shower, covering my bits before the intruder got a good look at my nonexistent package. But that would be a lie. Also, I'm not that graceful. Not by a long shot. With a peacock yell, I windmill my arms and fall backwards into the blaze of hot water, taking down the curtain, and probably my dignity. The back of my head slams into the sidewall of the shower. White spots dot my vision, and I swear the room spins.

I groan.

They gasp, stumbling back and thudding the bathroom door closed with them on the wrong side. Probably staring at me completely naked and discovering that I am not the Oliver they think I am. I don't even have the balls to look at them as I squeeze my eyes shut and wait for the inevitable.

There goes the damn case. Spoiled by me trying to get relief in the shower and one of my roommates not understanding privacy. Like, who the hell puts a broken lock on a door? I can't even use the restroom in peace!

Because there's no way with how I landed that one of my roommates isn't getting the best show of his life.

Fuck.

OLIVIA

One Mississippi...

Two Mississippi...

I mentally count the number of seconds ticking by with no one saying a word. The silence suffocates me. Well, more than the fucking water pelting my face. Can I pretend I just died? It would be of embarrassment. Or possibly drowning. I'm never living this down. Ever. Especially if Jordy finds out. Note to self: Never let him get wind of this. Fucking ever. He'll toss it in my face every chance he gets. And that's the last thing I need.

I'll force whoever is standing against the door to sign an NDA. You never saw a thing. Not my tits. Lady bits. Or my shaved legs. Speaking of, I don't think Jordy packed a razor for me.

Ugh.

Just let me die in the hot shower. This is my coffin now.

Three Mississippi...

Four Mississippi...

Fine. I guess it has to be me. Not to mention, I'm slowly drowning in the blazing hot water peeling my skin off. Normally, it feels refreshing. But right now, when I'm down, it feels miserable and ominous.

Peeling my eyes open, everything is blurry. Fuck. Have I lost my vision from the hit? I shake my head as the white ceiling swirls and then comes into focus. Holy fuck. False alarm. I'm all right, for the most part.

"Oli!"

Oh, good. It's Simon. In the same sentiment... Fuck, it's Simon. Now, he knows all my secrets. Every freckle, tit, and lady bit secrets. I'm so boned. And not in the good way, either.

I groan in response, running my hand down my face. At least my arms still work. My fingers wiggle. My toes wiggle. Yeah, I think I'm okay. My dignity, however? It's taken a minor hit. Okay, a major hit. Like in the back of my head, too. Ugh. It throbs with my heartbeat, threatening to dismantle my skull.

Maybe death is better than this.

"Are you okay?" he asks hysterically, inching closer to me.

Way too close. Fuck. He's hovering above me, staring down at my face. As he scans my body, his eyes grow wider and wider. His mouth falls open, and he takes a small step back.

"Can you shut off the water?" I groan, pointing to the temperature controller with a shaky finger.

"Right. Fuck. Yes," he squeaks, shutting off my hellfire water.

I take a deep breath, expecting questions. Or more looks. Or something other than his silence. But Simon shakes off his initial shock and runs to grab me a fresh towel from the rack—my hero.

"Are you hurt?" he asks, bending down and covering my chest and lady bits with the towel. "Oh, your bruise! That heathen!" he gasps, holding a hand to his chest like he's realizing little old me—Olivia—beat a grown man's ass. "I can't believe..." He shakes his head.

Yup. There it is. It's all dawning on him now. Every piece of me is this girl who got into the ring with a massive man on the order of my ex-best friend. Okay, he doesn't know that piece of the puzzle yet. But he might soon. Hopefully not, though. Fuck. I'm going to have to tell someone in Veritas what happened.

How am I going to explain this to him? The great Viola from *She's the Man* rings in my mind, and how she played it off about her brother. I could use the same excuse, except for a little creative tweak. *I'm here in my brother's place because he's an idiot and went backpacking through Europe— AKA sticking his dick in every skirt he saw.* What else can I say? *Oh, I'm here on a super secret mission to investigate my ex-best friends and their devious frat while trying to get into their good graces and join their gang so I can take down their father. Who, by the way, killed me about five years ago. Want to see my grave?*

Yeah, that'll go over really well.

Not.

"My body? No. My ego? Probably a little," I groan, holding the towel tightly to my body. It's not like he hasn't seen it all now.

"Oli..." he trails off. Here it comes. My body stiffens. "Do you want me to help you up?" His Adam's apple bobs when he holds out a hand for me to take.

I blow out a breath. So not what I expected.

"You're not going to ask?" I grunt when I take his hand, and he slowly brings me to the edge of the tub.

My entire body screams at me. Places I didn't even know existed pulse with my heart, whooshing in my ears. Fuck. I think I have a damn concussion. The world spins as I hold the towel tightly with one hand until he lets my hand go and sits beside me on the ruined shower curtain—no doubt soaking his soft sleep pants.

"Not really my business," he says softly with a reassuring smile. "You are who you are."

You know what? I take it back. Thank fuck it was Simon who walked in on me and not Wade. Or shit, Dane.

Sincerity reflects back at me in his eyes, shining bright and conveying his message. He's not talking out of his ass. He's being real about his statement. Maybe because he's faced backlash for who he is and loves, which he shouldn't, by the way. We're all human beings with different tastes, ideas, and hopes. Some people look in the mirror and don't see themselves looking back at them. So, they make those changes to feel how they feel on the inside. I can't pretend to know how that feels. The closest I can relate to that feeling is when I look in the mirror wearing my disguise, I know that's not who I am. The day I get to be Olivia again, I'll be happy. And that's what everyone should feel when they look deep into their eyes through the mirror.

Happiness. Comfort. The real version of themselves.

I blush a little, holding my aching head. "Thanks, Si," I murmur.

He grins. "I only judge people on their actions, and you, Oliver, are an outstanding person." He lightly shoulder-bumps me. "Speaking of, do you remember what happened last night? I have a very foggy memory of puking in the woods and stumbling home..." he trails off. "Did I fall through a window?" he murmurs, rubbing the back of his head suspiciously and wincing. "Yeah, I think I fell through a window. And Jordy..." Hurt tinges his tone when he looks down at his fingers, rubbing them together nervously.

Oh, right. He was absolutely wasted last night. Poor guy. If I were in his shoes, I wouldn't remember a damn thing, either.

"Jordy took care of you and made sure you hydrated and all that good stuff." I peek a look at him, and he nods thoughtfully.

"And he is...?" On a case, but I can't exactly say that. Fuck, I don't even know what Jordy told him.

"He was really sorry he had to go but was called back to work." Usually, Jordy doesn't mix with my cases. He's usually either on it with me and we're playing cousins or whatever. But this time around, my partner is in a different city, chasing someone else.

"Right," Simon says, nodding. "On-call railroad worker

stationed 30 minutes away. He said he might have to go back." Simon puffs out his bottom lip with a sigh.

"Exactly," I say. "It's nice he was so close. Too bad he had to leave. He said he'd visit soon when he got some time off work." Honestly, I'll miss his annoying ass. But at least I have Simon in on my secret now. It honestly feels like I added another ally to my short list of friends here. I know I can trust him.

I rub my temple when everything continues to ache, including my damn period pains.

"You sure you're going to be okay?" Simon asks softly. "You took a hell of a spill."

"I think I just need that hot shower, some bed, ice cream, and maybe a Buffy marathon." That solves everything. Especially this pesky period that snuck up on me. Thank you, stress, for giving me the gift that keeps on giving.

Simon immediately jumps to his feet. "You said Buffy? Oh, Oli." He claps his hands. "Do that," he waves toward the shower, "Then, meet me back in your room for a marathon."

I grin at him when he turns to leave. "Hey, Si. Thanks for..." I gesture to myself. It's nice, I don't have to explain or lie to him. I can't exactly say I'm investigating this school for a secret government agency, and they insisted I go undercover as a man.

For the next few hours, Simon climbs into my bed and watches *Buffy the Vampire Slayer* with me on my laptop. We eat junk food, order in McDonalds, and relax until it's time for the party to start. By then, my period symptoms have gone into hibernation. Thanks to the multitude of vitamins, Midol, and my trusted heating pad. I should be good for the next few hours of partying. Then, I can hibernate again.

"You're really feeling okay to go to the party?" Simon asks, waltzing into my room after changing into jeans and a nice button-down. His brown hair is tousled to perfection, looking every bit messy, yet, dignified.

I snort, tying my tennis shoe. "I should be asking you the same thing. You were wasted last night. How's the hangover?"

Simon grins. "What hangover? There's no hangover here. Only this guy, ready to take some shots." His brows wiggle playfully. "And you're going to be okay with all that..." He gestures to my body again. He doesn't cringe or turn pale like Jordy usually does. So, that's an improvement. Maybe Simon should become my number one bestie instead of Jordy. In fact, I pull out my phone and text that very thing to him.

> **JORDY**
>
> Really? I thought it was bros before hoes...
> Besties for the resties. Are you going back on
> your word now? Rude.
>
> Also, send me a pic of him... ;)

I snort, typing out a quick response. A big fat fuck no. He can come here and take all the pictures he wants. I'm not his middleman. So, I accompany the message with three middle finger emojis and then silence the damn thing. Once he gets going, he'll never shut up, and I need all the concentration I can get tonight. Besides, we both have important cases to focus on.

As Dexter says—*tonight is the night.*

Initiation interest night. Where I put my name in the jar and hope they pick me. And if they don't? Well, I'll cross that bridge when I get to it.

"This will be fun, right?" I ask, grinning when I stand, cringing when my binder pushes in on my bruise.

Damn you, Brutus. I'm going to remember you for as long as I live. Or for as long as I'm here. Which, hopefully, isn't long. I'm not sure how much more torture I can take by being in Greenwood and surrounded by them. Every time I see them, I swear they chip away a piece of me. Haven't they gotten enough with my death? Apparently, not. Not that they have any clue I'm the one they murdered.

"Yeah, if you can last all night," he tsks at me, shaking his head. "You give me the signal, and we'll come back and do this." He points to the bed. "It's been a hot minute since I've been able to curl up in bed and just relax with Buffy," he sighs, dreamily.

"I'll be fine," I say, waving a hand.

"Well, if you're not. Just say fried pickles or something, and that'll be our cue to vacate the party."

"Fried pickles it is," I snort.

"Then, let's roll out." He waves me on, and I follow him out of our dorm and through the window into the night.

OLIVIA

Loud thumping music is the first indication that we're getting close to the party. The second is everyone walking around us dressed in short dresses and nice shirts, whispering to each other excitedly about what's to come—something I haven't prepared for. I'm not sure what I'm expecting at a party set in the middle of a graveyard with booze and food. But I guess I'm about to find out.

"So, a graveyard party?" I cringe at the thought of who in their right mind would want to spend their night drinking, eating, and being merry at a damn cemetery. Partying over dead bodies isn't my idea of a good time. Especially since my name sits on one of those gravestones.

My dead body, specifically. Did they do this to gloat about their evil ways? Show everyone who they really are? Fuck, I need to keep my wits about me tonight and not drink so much. Even though my body calls for the numbing effects of the alcohol. It's a bad crutch to have. I know that. But my vices are mine to carry.

Also, I think I'll have to babysit Simon. From what little I know about him, he's a lush. With junk food, alcohol, and binge-watching our favorite shows. He can't get enough. Plus, I kind of want to keep him safe. He's my ally, after all. And I can't lose my newest best friend. *Take that, Jordy.*

"They do it every year," Simon snorts, lifting his chin with a grin, looking over the heads of the people slowly walking before us toward the guarded gates of the graveyard. "It's a tradition for them or something. They throw another one around Halloween. Right before everyone leaves for a week's break. Hell, they do it whenever they want, really. But this is the important one."

"Every year, huh?" I question as we march through the grass. "Why's this one so important?" Even though I already know the answer.

Because it's the initiation party where they try to convince the people on campus to join their frat. *Pick me!* I need in. I need to figure out how they're streamlining their frat members into becoming gang members, too. The question for me is: how? How is that fucking happening? And why doesn't anyone else talk about it? Do their frat members run jobs for them?

It's the burning questions I need to figure out before I jump headfirst into their damn frat. But I can't if no one knows the answers on the outside of it all. Damn it, this is going to be harder than I initially thought. My only worry was facing them again and again, which I'd rather not do. Give me an acid bath or something, rather than seeing them daily.

Simon grins. "It's their initiation party. Drink, fuck, and be merry. Also, drop your name into their little sorting jar of destiny." Jar of destiny? What an interesting way to bring people into your gang. A jar. It used to be proving yourself to Franco by taking a life or bloodying someone up.

"And what happens when they pick your name?" We come to a halt in the grass just outside the iron fence surrounding the booming graveyard. He wasn't kidding when he said they had an all-out party. There are people everywhere with drinks in their hands. Food tables are set up around the perimeter. How the hell aren't people falling over their feet on the gravestones? Especially the drunk ones.

Simon snorts. "Oh, they're very selective with who they pick. Some years, they don't pick anyone." He rolls his eyes. "Have to have connections. Daddy's in all the right places. Moms, too. If your parents can further their dad's pockets, then count yourself in." Well, fuck. I don't have parents who can further Franco's pockets. Not anymore.

"Have you tried?"

Simon eyes me and frowns. "Twice. But I was never selected. But that's okay. My dad wanted me in for the connections and shit, but..." He waves a hand at that. "I'd rather not have to go through their initiations."

I shiver. "What kind of initiations?"

"They're not allowed to talk about them. But I've heard rumors of kidnappings, deadly paintballs..." he trails off, taking in the crowd with a gleam in his eyes. Yes. This is where Simon flourishes. Within the crowds of his peers. He's an extrovert, thriving off them to reenergize his soul. And as for me? I'd rather not. But I'm pretending. Being someone else is quite exhausting. And annoying. I can't wait to go home and be in regular clothes with my normal personality.

Unfortunately, with the size of this massive party—I don't see us leaving for a few hours. So, I take a deep breath and press on as Oliver, who just loves socializing and showing his face at events, when my bed is beckoning me back home.

"That's weird... Kidnappings, though?" All the more reason I have to join. If their initiations are deadly, then I need to keep track of them and what they're doing. Maybe send their asses to Devil Head Island, where they can rot with the worst of the worst.

Simon side-eyes me and nods. "I had a friend get in there. He had daddy connections and all that fun stuff. He told me about the initiation night. They snuck into his room, tied his hands behind his back, and then dropped his ass out in the middle of nowhere... Naked..." he hisses, shaking his head. "Poor guy had to find his way back to campus without getting arrested. Oh, there he is!" He nods toward a large guy standing by a food table. He has a black shirt with a large snake wrapping around a golden sword with EN etched on the back, incorporating the college's motto printed around it. He's tall, muscular, but very unassuming.

I blanch. "Naked?" I swallow hard. If that's true, I can't let them undress me. They'll see my goods. Probably my tattoo, too, and their suspicions will rise. Once I've collected myself out of my thoughts, I shake my head. "What kind of connections does your friend have?"

My eyes scan the crowd as we wait in the long line, hoping to get into the party. I only count about six guys with the same shirt on, indicating they're a part of the frat.

"His dad's the president." Simon shrugs.

"I thought Wade's mom was the one in charge?" I ask, continuing to search the crowd for anything suspicious or out of the ordinary. There's nothing suspicious, though. Well, if you don't count having a party at a cemetery. Now, that's awfully fucking suspicious in my eyes.

"The President, Oli. You know, of this country," he says in a low voice. I startle, turning to look at Simon with a twisted expression that he must read. He laughs at me, leaning in. "If you notice, there are a few Secret Service guys around the perimeter, watching for any threats against him." Now that he mentions it, there are plain-clothed Secret Service members next to him with guns on their hips and eyeing the crowd. Well, some of them. A few stuff their faces with food, looking more relaxed than they should.

What's the president's son doing at Greenwood University and in a gang? Why didn't Jonathan mention this?

"Why is the president's son here?" I blurt out before I can bite my tongue.

Irritation simmers under my skin, spreading like a wildfire. Until the rage fully consumes me. I've stepped into a battlefield blindfolded. Only told half-truths and misinformation.

How didn't I know the president's son was here? Why wasn't it in my paperwork before I stepped foot on campus?

Everything should have been presented to me on a silver platter. People here with those types of connections should have been named with details, so I knew who I was dealing with. Hell, even having roommates should have been in my main briefing.

Jonathan basically threw me into the deep end with an unknown amount of sharks lurking around and ready to bite my feet off. And there's a lot of goddamn sharks around me with sharp teeth.

Immediately, I roll my lips together. I shouldn't have said that out loud. I can't bring attention to myself with all those questions. Although I don't think Simon really minds. Or notices that I can't keep my questions to myself. He seems happy to explain it all.

"He got recruited to the Water Polo team," Simon says with a dreamy grin. "You should see them play," he sighs, staring off at the man in question. "He plays, too." He fans himself slightly, nodding toward—Oh, God.

"Mack?" I question, earning a nod in return.

Macklyn Owens? How strange. The baseball-loving little boy with a backwards Cubs hat, grinning as he raised his baseball bat in the air and hit a ball over the fence.

A grin would light up his face as Hux huffed on the pitcher's mound, complaining about the hit. Mack soared around the bases, touching home with a whoop.

Baseball bled through his veins. He wanted to play in high school, but Franco denied him the chance. So, he settled for playing on his own time.

I'd bet a million dollars that Mack didn't get to choose water polo. No. In fact, I'm sure he was placed there intentionally by Franco.

"So, do all the frat members live together?"

It's something I've been wondering about. Mack, Hux, and JJ don't seem like the type of guys who would live in a giant party house with other members. Not with Franco on their asses. He'd never let them off their leashes that easily.

He'd want to isolate them in their own home and keep his eyes on them. Like always.

"Yup. Well, except for the kings. They live in that mansion on the hill. All alone. It's poetic, if you ask me." He waves his hand toward Franco's mansion—the home I'm all too familiar with.

"Alone?" I quirk a brow, hoping Franco is as far away as possible.

Simon shrugs again. "No one is really allowed there. Very secretive and exclusive. Last year there was a rumor about a couple of guys going up there to fuck with the kings and they vanished! Poof!"

"Vanished?" I ask, needing more information.

Simon shrugs. "It was a rumor." He grins again. "Or is it? You never know with the kings and the others."

Finally after what seems like an eternity, we make it to the front of the long ass line leading into the cemetery. The music gets louder. Laughs grow. Conversations flow. And alcohol is in every student's hand as they mingle. My eyes widen at the sight of the party. Who knew a party in such a dismal place could look so enticing.

Not to me, though.

My stomach swoops. Lead rests heavily there, threatening to send everything in either direction. Those nachos I had earlier? They're about to make their escape.

Fuck.

Being back here is throwing me off my axis and threatening to put my ass in the dirt. I'm barely surviving surrounded by my past. Some days are better than most. But today? Looking over my final resting place with a fake smile, has me wanting to say fuck it and call Jordy to kidnap me. The last time I stepped foot in this graveyard, I wrecked my headstone and wanted to run off into the woods and never emerge.

If only…

I'm still knee-deep in this fucking job with no end in sight. I was really crossing my fingers and toes, hoping for a quick turnaround.

But nothing good ever comes my way. It's bad break after bad break. Over and over again.

One day, Olivia Viotto will come out on top. But today is not that day.

I peer around us with a sigh, taking in the massive line behind us. Damn. Who knew so many fucking people went to the university. I mean, I've read the numbers on paper. In person, though? It's mind-bending.

Thankfully, the people around us in line have been too busy pregaming with their own bottles of booze and getting lost in their conversations to notice me being too nosey for my own good. But I have to ask all these questions without suspicion, and Simon is the perfect person to facilitate them.

The people ahead of us walk through the gates of the cemetery while laughing and brushing past the two burly security guards with mustaches and bald heads. They look like twins with their matching—I don't want to be at a college party—expressions. I wonder if Franco hires them for these types of jobs. He does practically own the university, according to Jonathan.

"IDs?" one of them asks in a gruff voice, looking us up and down. His lip curls at me, like he's not quite sure I'm old enough to enter the party.

Simon hesitates for a second, turning to look at me as I pull out my new wallet that houses my Oliver ID in it and hand it over to the guy. Simon physically relaxes and then hands him his.

The guards nod, handing us back our IDs, and then let us enter through the gates as they stop the people behind us and check theirs.

"That was weird," I mumble as we walk away from the guards checking everyone's IDs.

"They had an incident the first year. Some underage high schoolers found their way here and almost died of alcohol poisoning," he mutters, grabbing himself a bottle of beer and me a margarita in a can from a cooler. Right. I have to make it look like I'm here to have a good time. Not for any sort of reason. Besides, margaritas in a can? Never had those before. It can't be as good as the freshly made concoctions, but I'll give it a go. It beats beer any day. "So, they made sure it'd never happen again and added guards the next time around." He shrugs, taking a long pull of his drink and smacks his lips. "Delicious."

Sure. Criminals not wanting to get into criminal activities. I guess the deaths of minors from town wouldn't look too great on their resumes.

"Simon!" a frantic voice cries out over the crowd with urgency.

Simon's brows furrow as he looks around, finally catching sight of a very familiar brunette frantically rushing toward us with a frown etched into her face. Her green eyes mist over with worry, and her fingers tremble when she tucks a lock of hair behind her ear.

"Hey, Gemma," he says with a slight smile. "You okay?"

"Have you seen Dane?" she asks, searching around the party, but brings her worried gaze back to us. "Please tell me you've seen him and he's just mad at me." Tears form in her eyes, begging Simon for a positive answer.

"Dane?" I interject, furrowing my brows.

She whips her gaze to me with wide eyes. "Oh! You're his roommate, aren't you?" There's a hint of desperation in her tone, and her eyes glisten more, threatening to spill tears down her cheeks.

"Yeah. But he's usually not there." I sip my margarita drink, relishing in the sweet strawberry flavor.

Gemma nods at my answer. You know, now that I think about it, I haven't seen Dane in a while. Not since the store incident where he made fun of my tampons for my nonexistent girlfriend. If he only knew they were for me. Man, I'd pay to see the look on his face.

"He went to the store the other night and took his car. But... I haven't seen him since. I thought maybe..." She sucks in a breath, holding her fingers to her lips. "I thought maybe he got cold feet or something and went back to your dorm."

Things just got interesting.

"He didn't come home after he went to the store?" I don't tell her I saw him there or that I know he was buying her supplies like a good boyfriend should. Most men don't know the difference between supers and regulars. Not to mention, he's always with her around campus, sucking her damn face or squeezing her ass like a territorial alpha male, marking his territory.

So, I didn't blink an eye when he hadn't come back to our dorm room for days on end, because he never does. If you don't count that one time, he graced me with his presence and morning wood. Ugh. It's etched into my mind forever now. Other than that? Dane is a ghost.

"No. I texted him, and he said that he went home! His car is missing. I even called his mom, and she hasn't seen him. I..."

"Have you told anyone else?" I ask, cocking my head.

Please say the police or someone else besides just looking for him. If he's been gone for that long, it's already been over sixteen hours. He could be anywhere by now, especially with the history of this place and missing people. My heart rate bounces high when her lip quivers, giving me the answer.

"I thought he'd come home," she whispers. "Or I thought... I thought he'd be with you guys. I..."

"Tell the police," I say quickly, grabbing her forearm softly. "You need to tell someone." I don't want to scare her more than she already is, but something needs to be done. He couldn't have disappeared off the face of the earth for no reason. Fuck. My gut lurches at the possibilities. I don't want to scream at his girlfriend that he could lose his life for whatever reason.

But something about this stinks. Majorly.

"Oli's right, Gem. You need to go and tell campus police or make a report. At least they'll have it on file. I'm sure he's fine, but just to be sure," Simon softly says with reassurance.

He can offer her all the reassurance, but I don't think Dane is going to be okay. I've got a funny, sinking feeling in the pit of my stomach that something bad has happened. My agent senses tingle and the hairs on my neck stand on end. I'll have to keep my eyes peeled and include this in my daily notes.

Something evil is making its presence known.

"Yeah," she sniffles, gently pulling away from us. "I'll go talk to them now. I just... If something happened to him. I wouldn't be able to live with myself. I sent him out." Tears track down her cheeks, but she swipes them away. "He was only supposed to be gone for five minutes."

Gemma charges away from us and marches through the entrance of the graveyard, losing herself in the darkness of the night. My shoulders stiffen at her words. Dane is out there some-where. Possibly hurt. Or maybe he walked away. He is a grown man. The police would most likely tell her they were not concerned. Adults leave town without telling a soul all the time. But this? It's too fucking suspicious for me.

"He didn't come back, did he?" Simon asks, twisting his expression. Worry mars his face, and he heaves a breath.

I shake my head. "No. I would have known if he had. You think Wade has seen him?"

"He could have." Simon pulls out his phone and types out a message. "I'll ask him. I don't think he's here tonight. He had something to do at the shelter downtown."

"Volunteering, right?"

Simon nods in response, putting his phone away. "Yeah. He's a good guy like that. Always helping out with the animals or volunteering for the homeless shelter downtown." He sips his drink again.

"Hopefully, she finds Dane." I'm not too optimistic, though. I saw him at the store, but he never came home. When I exited the store, the parking lot was dark and devoid of life. Who has the power to do that? There's something so weird happening here; I just can't put my finger on it. It's something I need to talk to Jonathan about tonight. I'll find a secluded spot, call him, and debrief about everything happening. He'll know what to do.

"I fucking hope so. I've known him since freshman year," he says, shaking his head. "We may not run in the same crowds, but the three of us have always bunked together. Cool guys." He plucks his phone out of his pocket and frowns. "Wade says he hasn't seen him either but will be here later tonight. He says he hasn't seen him since last night when he ran into him at the store. He says you were there, too." His eyes dart to me, but there's no suspicion in them.

"Tampons," I grumble, taking a large drink as my cheeks heat.

"Oh, OH!" Simon said in surprise, tucking his phone away. "So, you saw him last night?"

"He was getting the same thing for his girlfriend and some ice cream. But I saw him walk out of the store before I…" I trail off, remembering I stepped into the bathroom before walking out of the store. Anything could have happened between then and when I left. Giving whoever plenty of time to kidnap Dane and…do what with him? I'm not sure. "And that's the last I saw of him."

"So weird," Simon mumbles, crinkling his nose. "Let's keep our eyes out for him." He nods with determination. "But in the meantime, we've got a party to try and enjoy." He rubs at his chest like it's an impossible feat for him, but he plasters on his smile, and we mingle throughout the party, where he introduces me to more people as Oliver.

"This is Victoria and Blane," Simon says, gesturing to two people resting beneath a tree with drinks in their hands.

"Hi," I say, offering a small wave. "Nice to meet you."

Victoria grins in response. "You're new here, aren't you? Simon's roommate, the one he won't shut up about," she chuckles into her glass bottle.

"Shut it," Simon quips, slightly pushing her shoulder. "This is my sister," Simon says, gesturing to her.

"His twin, to be more exact. But I'm older and wiser," Victoria smiles. "This is my husband, Blane."

"Husband?" I ask, furrowing my brows without meaning to.

She laughs at my stunned expression. "I know. My parents begged me to wait, but I wouldn't let them set me up with someone. So, I married the first guy I could get my grubby hands on."

Blane rolls his eyes. A smirk playing on his lips. "Grubby is right, but I chased you for at least two years." He softly kisses her head, and Simon playfully gags.

"You're going to ruin the party with that." He gestures to their PDA.

Sometimes, I think arranged marriages are way more common than people like to believe. Well, in certain societies, that is. In the mafia and mob world, arranged marriages are more than a way of life. It's how they breed alliances and stay in each other's good favor. Even if they hate one another, they have to play nice if their kids are married and their businesses depend on it.

"Oh, look," Victoria whispers, tilting her beer bottle. "Their dog has arrived."

"Their dog?" I question dumbly. My heart beats in my throat when Waffles, whom I have successfully avoided for this long, strolls into the party. I swallow hard, trying to attempt like I know nothing about him.

Waffles? Waffles who? I don't know him.

"He shows up for every party. Honestly, I think he follows them around campus." She shakes her head. "It's adorable."

"It's their guard dog," Blane smirks. "It's always around."

"But, God. Don't touch him..." Simon trails off, wrinkling his nose.

"Yeah, I think he bit a guy last year and took his fingers off," Blane adds dramatically.

That doesn't seem like Waffles at all. He's a watchdog, for sure. Always on the lookout for me and the guys. He'd fight off any bad guy if they got too close. Not that many did. I don't doubt that Waffles sticks up for the guys, but imagining him biting off someone's finger has my stomach twisting into knots.

Not my Waffles.

"Vicious dog," Victoria chuckles, gulping down the rest of her beer. "And to think, his name is fucking Waffles."

They continue their conversation. Not noticing when I don't join in. I can't. Not with my tongue tied into knots as memories assault me. Again. It's been a never-ending cycle since I stepped foot back in Greenwood. I swallow a gulp of my half-finished drink I've been babying.

I'm unable to take my eyes off Waffles. His golden coat hasn't changed. Looking shiny and freshly washed in the bright moonlight. I wonder if JJ still gives him weekly baths to ward off his allergy to dogs. Or if Mack still insists on taking him for walks every morning. Only the two of them. Or Huxley. Does he still measure out Waffle's food, meticulously making sure he doesn't overfeed him, convinced he'd make him obese and hurt his joints?

I don't know anymore. To me, Waffles was an essential companion to us all. He roamed the woods, going to and from each of our houses. Almost always showing up when I needed him most. He crawled through my window and lay in bed with me as my parents argued a room away, letting me snuggle into his fur like a pillow to comfort me.

"Waffles," her husband says with a snort. "He hates everyone. He doesn't let anyone ever touch him. Only those three." And me. Or, at least, he used to. If there's one innocent in all this, it's Waffles.

"Their guard dog?" I ask without thinking.

No matter what, I want to run to him and throw my arms around his neck. The memories associated with him were always happy ones. Some days it was just him and me, wandering through the woods and getting into trouble. All to avoid home. Waffles was my safe space beyond the guys. And now, my only good memory of Greenwood. Everything else is associated with them, tied to them in ways my mind still can't comprehend, despite the truth.

My connection to JJ, Hux, and Mack is complicated. Like a knot in a string, stuck tightly together. There's no way to unwind what was done or what our memories hold.

"That dog follows them to every party. I think he's like extra security or something," Simon snorts, gulping down the rest of his beer. "I'd love to pet him but..."

"God, don't do that, Si. You'll lose your fingers," Victoria scoffs. "Besides, he never gets close to anyone but them." She nods her head toward the three supposed kings of campus.

There they are standing beneath a large tree, a few feet from my grave. My stomach knots when Mack looks longingly at my marker and frowns more, returning to discussing something with JJ and Hux. If only I could read their lips from here, I can't. Maybe my glasses will catch it, but I doubt it. It's a hazy night. The moon shines brightly down on us, but no stars rest in the night sky. Clouds hang in the distance. And if I didn't know any better, I'd say it's going to storm within the next few hours.

"Parties over," Victoria murmurs sarcastically. "Amanda and the bitch squad just showed up." She groans, gesturing to Amanda.

"Oh, fun. Here comes the dramaaaaa," Simon snorts, joining the Amanda hate club. Well, count me in. I've been in the Amanda hate club for longer than anyone here combined.

"I can't believe he's going to marry her," Victoria says, pouting when she gets to the bottom of her beer.

"Marry her?" Blane asks obliviously. "When did this happen?"

Right. She's got that massive diamond ring sitting pretty on her finger. I shake my head in disgust, my heart wanting to tear in two at the thoughts of them kissing in front of a preacher as they happily walk hand-in-hand as man and wife.

That was mine at one point. My life.

I suck in a breath, rubbing my left ring finger.

Simon clears his throat. "Unfortunately. Happened not too long ago, from what I heard."

"Yeah, well I heard it's a bullshit marriage," Victoria says, rolling her eyes. "Some business arrangement. You know how those mafia types are." She scoffs at that.

Something that feels like relief slams into my gut. Why? I haven't a damn clue. No part of me should feel anything for them anymore. They betrayed me. Murdered me, for fuck's sake! So, why is my skin crawling at the sight of Hux peering down at Amanda? Do the others join in, too? Like they did with me?

Hux flexes his muscles, and irritation passes over his face when Amanda and her posse come in for the kill. I swallow hard when Amanda wraps her arms around Hux and hugs him tightly. Something in my chest cracks. She's living my fucking life. The one I was supposed to live before I died. Those were my friends. My companions. Fuck, my lovers. Not anymore, though. I know that. But it's still an odd sensation to me.

I loved them. Now, I hate them. But I can't hate them so much that I let it cloud my investigation. This is who I am now. Apparently, who I was supposed to be all along. Comfort should wrap me in a warm blanket at night, knowing I escaped the fate I dreaded from childhood. I should feel something like relief. I guess I did for a little while. I had to look on the bright side when I lay in the hospital, miserable after the fire had torn through my skin, and I was left to rot.

My fingers curl into fists as I continue to watch the two canoodle against the tree. Amanda looks like she's victoriously won. A smile tilting up her lips. The way her hair hangs over her shoulders as she lifts her chin. Huxley, on the other hand? He looks downright miserable. He's not touching her the way she's touching him. But he can't seem to shake her off. Not that he's trying very hard to stop her hands from roaming over his bare, tattooed chest. He takes it. Every touch. Every caress. Every fucking thing she does to him.

He hates her.

It sits there, slithering in his gaze and clenched jaw.

And how fitting is that? A man who murdered his best friend, for whatever reason I've never deduced, is being forced to marry the woman he claimed to hate in high school. But did he? Everything I knew about him, JJ, and Mack was obviously lies. They cared for me, sure. But did they feel the same bone-deep love I felt for the three of them?

Or was it all a charade to get to their endgame of holding a knife to my throat while wearing dark masks and ending me so cruelly? The only indication I had of them was the color of their eyes staring back at me. Like they were strangers.

Gasoline fumes fill the air as Hux, JJ, and Mack work around the corners of my living room, dousing every inch with the flammable liquid.

"Please," I gasp out, reaching for them with bloodied hands that once held the oozing wound on my throat. "Please don't leave me like this. I love you!" I shout, my voice falling flat from the cut along my throat.

I swear, the world spins when they stand tall, looking down at me with those venom-filled eyes. Moss green. Golden brown. Blue.

"Yeah? Well, we don't, " Hux says in a deep, raspy voice and clears his throat. "Die knowing we used you."

Used me?

My head thunks to the floor. All my strength leeches out of me when the flames start, roaring to life and taking everything hostage. My world goes black, pulling me into the nothingness I want to belong in.

"Hey, Oli?" Simon murmurs in my ear, drawing me back to the damn present.

Moisture blooms in my eyes, but I quickly blink it away. The last thing I need is to be the guy having flashbacks in the middle of the graveyard and crying. So not good for my disguise. Even though everyone cries, damn it. Even men. And me.

"Yeah?" I ask, clearing my throat.

He offers me a soft smile. Almost like he knows what's going through my head, but he doesn't. No one does. Because no one else was there except me, the three of them, and Franco.

"Was just going to see if you wanted another drink? I was going to grab one over here." Simon points to the coolers filled with beer bottles and more margaritas in a can. A large keg sits off to the side, too. People fill their cups, laughing and slightly spilling them like they're already feeling the effects.

"Yeah, thanks." He takes my empty can that I don't remember drinking and takes it to the recycling bin next to the bottles. I wonder if they have to be careful throwing parties here? Probably. I mean, who lets college kids throw a big bash at the cemetery?

I take this moment to drift off to the sidelines. Simon follows my movements before he bends down and grabs two more drinks. Another guy I've never seen before approaches him with a shy smile, and they begin an animated conversation, breaking through the awkwardness that had been there. That's alright. I don't mind him getting distracted one bit. It gives me time to take everything in and examine the party as a whole.

I swallow hard when I drift closer to my grave, sitting beside my sister, Sophia, and my mother, Espie—two more innocent souls who didn't make it out alive at the hands of Franco. I shake my head, trying not to lose myself like I did the first night I was back. The marks of my attack still sit on the headstone, scratching out the numbers that seem to mean so much to Huxley. But I can't figure out why he's clung to the numbers for so many years. I'm dead to him. Forever. I'm never coming back.

My gaze strays to him. They've moved to a more secure corner, away from my grave. They're huddled together, deep in another conversation. Determination settles on their faces, and they nod a few times. If only I could hear what they're saying. It would clue me in to whatever is going on here. An overwhelming feeling takes me over. What if I don't succeed here? Was this all for naught?

Ugh.

I rub my temple, squeezing my eyes shut. I need to stop spiraling down the drain. It's not good for my health. Especially here. So, I force my eyes open, seeking out the one companion I hope to reconnect with. I nearly startle when a four-legged figure moves through the shadows and comes up beside me with apprehension. His warm brown eyes take me in from head to toe, inspecting who I am now.

"Waffles," I murmur, holding out my hand for him to sniff.

The wetness of his nose nudges against my hand, and a deep whine breaks free from his throat. His long, blond tail wags, ruffling the leaves littering the graveyard. He whines more, getting more desperate to lick my face.

Kneeling, I run my hand down his head and onto his neck, gently petting him. "How are you, boy?" I whisper, earning a lick to my cheek and a harder thump of his tail. "That good, huh? I can't believe you're still wandering around." A genuine grin spreads across my cheeks at the memories I have with Waffles. He was always there, following us around. Even when Franco caught on to the dog we found and adopted as our own, he didn't bother him. Waffles proved his loyalty to the family time and time again, snuffing out the bad guys. "Such a good boy," I coo, earning another lick and an excited yip. I chuckle lowly, trying to keep our reunion concealed, but it doesn't last long.

"Waffles," JJ hums, snapping his fingers repeatedly until he stops dead in his tracks and his eyes widen at the sight of us. I swear his breath catches in his throat when his lips flap.

"Waffles?" I ask, continuing to pet the dog everyone deemed as a guard dog. Of course, they don't have the history I do with Waffles. And it seems, dogs don't forget. Even the people who have died. "You know they serve waffles at the diner all day?" I say without thinking, remembering what JJ said to me when I declared the dog's name was waffles.

Waffles John Owens Jones Crewes Viotto. His full name in honor of each of us. Named after my favorite breakfast, because his fur is the same color as Waffles. Long blond, almost looking like a mix between a golden retriever and a yellow lab, maybe some Chow mixed in. Whatever he was, Waffles was the best dog I have ever encountered. Even now. He clearly recognizes me. His big, brown eyes inspect my face, and he whines again, nudging at my hand.

"Waffles." I swear if JJ's eyes get any bigger than they are right now, they might pop out of his head. He shakes his head,

turning his gaze to me. "What did you do to him? He's usually...
growly," he murmurs, tilting his head.

Growly? Waffles? Not here. Definitely not from my memories of him either. Of course, he was a happier puppy back then. He's all grown up and big. Probably at least ninety pounds of pure muscly dog.

"Nothing," I say with a shrug, patting Waffles one last time and getting to my feet. "He just came up to me." I smirk at the perplexed look on JJ's face.

That's right, asshole. If you're not careful, I'll steal my fucking dog back. You know what? That doesn't sound like a bad idea. *Operation steal Waffles and take him home* is on.

"He doesn't do that," JJ says matter-of-factly. "And never has." Ah, he's suspicious. I need to turn this conversation around before he starts asking all the right questions I can't answer.

"So, this is an initiation party?" I ask out of the blue, hoping to steer this conversation in the opposite direction. "And you're in charge?"

He blinks several times. "Yes. It is," he says slowly with furrowed brows. He continuously looks between Waffles—who now sits at my feet, leaning his body against my legs. I brush my fingers through his fur, taking comfort in the only old friend who didn't offer me up on the chopping block. "You can put your name in the jar over there." He slightly cringes when a group of girls loudly laughs a few feet away from us. He shakes his head with a sigh. "You want in?"

I shrug. "It's a possibility. What are the perks?" I raise a brow when he looks me dead in the eyes again.

If I didn't have my colored contacts in, I'd be screwed. Because if anyone were to figure out who I was, it would be JJ. He's the master of figuring puzzles out, and right now, that's what I am to him. Whoever put together my backstory did a shit job. I bet it was Dave. Fucking Dave. The loser intern from IT who barely knows how to type in code. Well, same buddy. But still, this is his damn job.

I push my glasses up my nose, making sure to capture his expression. I can examine it later when I can rewatch every single moment of our interaction with a bag of popcorn while laughing my ass off. It's moments like these that make me forget the anguish bubbling inside me.

"The perks?" Simon laughs, coming to stand close to me, but backs up when Waffles growls protectively. "Whoa! The guard dog?" He chuckles lightly, swaying on his feet.

Jesus. How much did he have to drink while he was away? He seems to make a habit of drowning himself in alcohol the moment he steps away to grab us some drinks.

"Waffles, heel," JJ says, pointing toward the ground in front of him.

Waffles whines, hanging his head slightly, but he side-eyes me, looking me up and down until I give a subtle nod. He slowly moves away from my feet and plops in front of JJ like a chastised dog.

"He was comfortable, you know?" I ask, taking the drink Simon offers me.

"So, odd," JJ mumbles, shaking his head. "He doesn't like anyone." He says it again with a perplexed sigh.

Well, chew on that, pal. Waffles always liked me. I wonder how I can lure him away from the guys for good. Does he still love freshly cooked steak? I bet he does. Now, I have to find the perfect moment to lure him into my dorm without getting caught. Fat chance at that. Everyone seems to know him. If he suddenly started following me around, someone would tell on me.

"I must be different," I grumble, sipping my drink.

"Yeah," JJ trails off, checking me over again.

Look all you want, Jasper Jeremiah, but you won't find anything but Oliver on the outside. I will never be your Olivia ever again. Especially after I leave this fucking place with my life intact and them behind bars. Hope you like islands, because that's where we house criminals like you.

Oh, and I'm taking the dog, too, dumbass.

"Look at those tattoos," Simon says, slurring his words. "He's so hot. It's too bad he's attached to-to that." He sighs heavily.

I follow his gaze as he watches a shirtless Hux walk through the cemetery with a frown etched on his lips. Amanda yaps his ear off at his side, throwing her arms all around. They stop suddenly when Hux turns to face her with a thunderous glare, showing off the right side of his body, giving me a glimpse of a necklace hanging around his neck. Something shines in the moonlight, but I can't tell what it is.

"Mhmm," I mumble, sipping my drink again so I don't say anything stupid.

"I wonder if they hurt," Simon ponders, rubbing at his chin. Then, he tosses back the drink in his hand and finishes it. Crap. I am going to have to babysit. How did he survive before this?

"Only in certain places," I sigh, looking Huxley up and down and stopping on the tattoo we got together. There it is again, taunting me from far away.

"Like the ribs?" Simon chortles. "Oh look, he has one just like you do. What does yours say? Always?" He slurs the last part so hard, I'm hoping JJ doesn't take notice even. Even when I feel the heat of his stare. "Yeah. Right there," he chuckles, poking me right in the rib where my tattoo rests.

I stiffen at his drunken words and bat him away. Right. He saw me naked. In all my womanly glory. If I don't get him out of here, he's going to spill all my damn secrets. Simon and booze should never mix again.

"Yeah, just like that. Ribs hurt. But it wasn't too bad," I say placatingly, finishing off my drink. "Hey, Simon?" I question, feeling JJ's intense gaze eating me alive. And the last thing I need is his eyes on me. He's undressing me and making my skin crawl just being in his presence.

"Yup?" he questions with a watery grin.

"Fried Pickles," I say.

"Fried pickles, those sound delicious. You know, we could get some later and OH!" He stops suddenly like my phrase smacked him in the damn face. "Right! Well, it was nice to hang." Simon suddenly grabs my arm and drags me along. Well, stumbles is more like it.

"You can slow down," I say breathily, digging my feet into the grass until he stops.

My ribs ache from the sudden movement. The bruise on my jaw pulsates with my damn heart rate. My head still aches from my graceful attempt to cover up earlier. And my period. Fuck. I'm a hot mess, and I need to just go to bed. The alcohol isn't helping to numb anything for me. If I had more of it in my system then maybe I wouldn't feel so miserable. But seeing JJ and Waffles all at once, has my fight or flight kicking in. And right now? I'm choosing flight.

"Are you okay? Is it..." His eyes travel toward my crotch area and then back up at me with fear wide in his eyes. Fuck. Right. My period. It has calmed since we came here, but I can feel the cramps building back up and the agony waiting for me later tonight.

I rub a hand over my stomach, feeling the small cramps that are coming through the pain meds.

"Yeah," I say with a nod, twisting my face.

Simon slumps. "Back to our little nest then. We shouldn't have come," he tuts, shaking his head. "We should have just stayed with Buffy and not moved an inch."

"I..." my words trail off when I take in the lone glass jar sitting on a table under the large Magnolia tree.

"You want to join?" Simon whispers frantically.

"Maybe. Is it a bad thing?" I shrug, looking at him.

"I mean, no. But then you wouldn't be my roommate anymore," he pouts with a sniff. "But you'd get a lot of leeway on campus. Never get in trouble. Have perks of missing classes and well, damn... There really aren't any downsides." He shrugs, thinking it over. "Maybe I'll put my name in there again, too." He drunkenly grins at that, stumbling over his feet again. I catch him before he falls, grunting at the sensation rocking through my damn ribs. Pain ricochets everywhere, but I don't show it. I simply grit my teeth as we make our way to the jar.

A few names on pieces of paper sit folded at the bottom of the large jar. None that I can see, but they obviously have interest in their frat. Something I need to investigate more. But no one seems to have the answers I'm seeking.

"Don't many people sign up for this?" I question, righting Simon so he's standing tall and not weaving back and forth.

He shrugs. "There are rumors, too. Like... they're involved with illegal things. They can get you off a murder charge." He leans in closer. "Their dad is like... super important around here. He even helps fund the university." He hiccups slightly. "So, let's do this." Right. Let's do this. Let's sign our lives away. "But don't get your hopes up. They never pick people," he hiccups again, swaying to the right, until he stumbles over his feet and lands on his ass. He barks out a drunken laugh, making a smile spread across my face.

"Noted," I chuckle, offering him a hand and pulling him to his feet. No matter how much it hurts my ribs. The second I get into our dorm, I'm removing the binder and not putting it on until Sunday. If anyone needs me, I'm one with my bed.

"You're a good friend, Oli." Simon grins, picking up two pens and two slips of paper, offering a set to me.

Here it goes. I'm signing my life away to the very people whom I escaped from.

If I get in, I guess. From what Simon has said, they're very selective in who they accept into their frat. It seems very private.

With a deep breath, I print my name. Oliver Davenport. And then, we drop them in the jar together. Simon lets out a squeal of delight and turns to me.

"No turning back now, Oli," Simon snorts, putting his arm over my shoulders. "Now, let's go snuggle."

"Don't say that out loud," I huff, shaking my head as we make our way and exit the booming party, heading to our dorm where we plan to get into bed and do nothing but eat and relax.

MACK

"WHY'RE YOU LOOKING OFF LIKE THAT?" I ASK JJ, NARROWING my eyes when his gaze snaps back to me with a frown.

Really fucking suspect, if you ask me. He's always been a little in his own head and quiet. Maybe too quiet. He's like a devious little mouse with a knife in his hand and on the attack.

But right now? He's suspect as hell.

"No reason," he huffs, gazing toward the cemetery's opening and losing focus on me. Again.

Rude.

"Well, stop it. We've got a party to host and all that shit." I take a chug of my beer, peering around our annual party.

It's a celebration of us. Our frat. Our lifestyle. So many of these suckers wish they could be us and live in our skin. Wait. That's weird as fuck. But the truth. They look at Hux, JJ, and me and see our lucrative lifestyle. The cars. The mansion. The casinos we'll inherit one day. Okay, Huxley will inherit one day. He's the only one Franco signed his name on the dotted line for, adopting him officially.

Me and JJ were just the spares. Bogus, if you ask me. We're equally as important in the grand scheme of things. Maybe JJ more than me. I'm just the muscle. JJ is the brains, and Hux is the leader.

So tonight, with booze running through the partygoers' veins, they'll drop their names into a little jar and seal their fates. Some of them, anyway. They'll be lucky if we choose them. Only the ones who will enhance our organization get brought into the mix. But first, they have to go through my favorite part. Initiation tests, where we put them through tasks they need to succeed in, or they're out for good.

"You really want to bring more people into this?" JJ mutters, twisting his expression.

"Pfft," I sputter, waving a hand. "Why wouldn't I?" My shoulders square, and I lift my chin. "It's the greatest organization of all time."

Sarcasm drips from every word I spout. If it were up to me, I'd bolt in the opposite direction and never come back. But my brothers are here, and I can't leave them to fend for themselves. We're in this together. The Three Musketeers and all that jazz. Besides, I kind of like them at my side and not against me.

JJ rolls his eyes. "Greatest of all time? So great, we have to make a run tomorrow even though we're here."

Obviously, my brother, JJ, didn't understand the sarcasm in my voice. But wait–he said a run? Ugh.

I deflate. "A run? Really? Why am I just now hearing about this?"

It's probably because I'm forced into two-a-day practices in the water, on land, and everything in between. Only a few more months to go, and the season will be over. Fuck. I'm half delighted to be out for good and half terrified I'll be bored. Oh well. There's always the damn gym. Or maybe even baseball. No matter how much Franco hates the simplicity of the sport. I fucking love it. It's grueling in the summer months and much more enjoyable than Water Polo. Maybe I'll be able to find a way out of this damn mess and get us out of here forever. Far, far away from the man who brought us into his home and turned us into weapons.

"If you stuck around more, you'd see the messages..." JJ trails off in his all-knowing tone.

But he knows I can't sit still. Like ever. I'm always on the go. A puppy with a damn treat to chase. I guess that's why Franco insisted I go into Water Polo. Rigorous workouts. Pre-training. You name it; we're doing it. All in the name of going to the championships.

"You could text me..." I grumble.

He sends me a scathing look. "I did. Individually. In the group text. I even left a note on the fridge." I should feel properly chastised, but I don't. I'm sure JJ tried his hardest to get a hold of me.

Oh. Well, fuck. I dig out my phone and slide through the millions of notifications I have—a lot from social media and a few texts from JJ and Hux. And even one Franco sent to us all.

Oops.

"My bad." I quickly drink, enjoying the bitter beer rolling down my throat.

"Don't complain next time," JJ quips, shaking his head. "And answer your damn phone once in a while."

"I would if I wasn't so fucking busy," I grumble. "The school year has barely started, and my schedule is so packed I barely have time to..." I make a hand motion near my poor, neglected cock, ready to spill all the beans on my lack of self-care, but JJ puts a stop to that. What? Like he doesn't care about my well-being? Fucker.

"Don't even finish that sentence. I know it's going to involve your dick somehow." JJ takes a step back, putting a hand between us.

Well, he's not wrong. But what gave me away? The hand motion? Or the desperate lust in my eyes?

I grin. "Aw, you don't want to hear about big Macklyn and his proud sails?" I jostle myself a little.

"What are you, a fucking sailboat now?" JJ quips, attempting to hide his smile.

"He is," I cackle, pointing toward my dick.

"You're an idiot."

"Eh, you kind of like me." I shrug, drinking again.

"Macklyn." I almost choke on my beer when Amanda's sweet voice pierces the air.

And there goes the good vibes.

You know, when I said her voice was sweet, I really meant it's bitter and nasty. Like week old laundry mixed with vomit and shit sitting in the hot summer sun. So, yeah. Nasty and fucking awful. Just like her. She may look like a beautiful girl on the outside with her long blonde hair and sparkling blue eyes. But a manipulative demon lives deep inside her and always has. Even back in high school when she pushed Livy around and tried to act innocent.

She was never innocent. Livy was, though. My girl. She was always so tough and tried not to let us know what had been happening between the two. But we always knew. I tried to let her take care of it on her own, but I couldn't help myself in getting retribution. Even now, despite the fucked-up circumstances, my buttercup will always be the damn queen of this roost.

Not Amanda, the girl I'd love to strangle.

But murder is frowned upon. Especially at parties. Or in public. Fuck. When is murder acceptable?

I eye the snake in the grass with physical indifference. We're obligated to be friendly and cordial to her. Actually, I don't know why *we* have to be. She's Hux's problem. He's the one who was strong-armed into this deal with her and her father. Thanks, Franco. Ya, asshole. You fucked all three of us. Took away our lives. Again and again.

But I digress.

If I go down that rabbit hole, I'll never emerge. So, I bury all my hatred, rage, and whatever else is testing inside me and throw it into the deepest crevice of my mind.

Is it healthy to avoid my problems and feelings? Absolutely not. Do I do it anyway to stay sane? You betcha.

Besides, I take care of those pesky feelings plotting against me daily with my Livy. She may be unable to talk back and offer me advice, but she listens well. And being so close to her, even though she's so far away, settles my aching bones and mind.

If only she were here with me now. In the flesh to soothe my brows and tell me she loves the rock I found her. Or that my kiss took away all her worries. My chest aches. I miss Livy with all my fucking heart. She was my girl. Our girl. The day I had to put her in the ground without tears was the worst day of my life.

And it was all Franco's fault. I'm fucking sure of it.

Just an accidental house fire? Yeah, fucking right. House fire my ass. If the guys and I hadn't been on a damn run that day, working our asses off for Franco, we'd have marched through those flames, laid down in the fire, and sacrificed ourselves with her.

A life without Olivia Viotto isn't a life worth living. I'm barely hanging on to the shreds of sanity I have left. One more minor inconvenience, I'll be a goner for sure.

I quickly peek over my shoulder, zoning in on Livy's grave. The chips in the stone are the first thing I see whenever I look at her now. Rage boils again at the thought of someone messing with her gravestone. Fuckers. JJ better find them quickly and tell me who they are so I can beat their asses and commit that murder I shouldn't, deep in our basement with sharpened knives and lots of blood. Whoever hurts my Livy, even when she's in an eternal slumber, has to come through me first.

I reluctantly take my eyes off the only girl who will ever be allowed to consume me again and glare at Amanda. Or Mandy. Or whatever she wants us to call her. It's whatever. She's still the same basic mean girl from high school. Only now she has bigger tits and a bigger entitlement to our time.

I lie awake some nights, trying to figure out how this all happened. Franco. He did this to torture us for eternity instead of giving us the good life. It'll be a cold day in Hell when Huxley is forced to meet her at the altar. If I can switch her out for someone more bearable, I would.

Amanda saunters up to me with the same grin she wore in high school when she was trying to seduce us to the dark side. That's a *no fucking thank you* from me.

"Mandy." My voice comes out monotone when she runs her fingers over my chest, and I step back out of reach.

Ugh. My skin crawls whenever she tries to entice me into a three-way with her and Hux. I don't mind that guy's dick. I've seen it plenty of times in the past. But her? No, thanks. She can keep her repulsiveness away from me and mine. Besides, her and Hux don't even do the nasty. Never have. He's forcing her to wait until their wedding night. AKA, he's biding his time so JJ can figure out a way out of the contract. Also, so he doesn't have to fucking touch her. Maybe that's why she's throwing herself at us and trying to get knocked up so we can never leave her.

Jokes on her, though. We wouldn't touch her with a million-foot pole.

"What are you boys up to tonight? Hux says you're too busy," she says with a fake pout and baby voice.

Yuck. I think my ears are bleeding from the sound of her.

"We are. Now, leave," JJ grumbles, waving his hand so she'll saunter on by and find another victim to sink her teeth into. She already got exactly what she was gunning for all those years ago. Huxley. And the power of marrying the gang leader's son brings her.

Her future with Hux is as bright as the daisies Livy loved to pick. Fuck. Now, I've made myself sad all over again. Focus, Mack.

I shake my head. Maybe I need to lay off the drinks and focus on the present. On second thought... Nah, that's too serious for me. I'd rather drink myself into oblivion and go on a run for Franco with a hangover from Hell tomorrow than listen to her incessant blabbering and pouting. Seriously, where are the cotton balls when you need to shove them in your bleeding ears?

"You don't look very busy," she pouts again, puffing out her bottom lip and drooping her eyes.

Reminder—murder at a party is hella frowned upon. Franco would gladly get me out of jail. No, wait. He might let me rot if I take her out. She's way too important to the future of his empire and alliance.

I take a step back and finish off my beer. If I don't, I might wrap my hands around her throat and laugh as she expires. Shit. See? Too damn dark again. I need my therapy session with Livy. I didn't have time today. Fucking Water Polo practice. Visiting her is becoming a later and later kind of thing lately. It happens when the sun goes down and the moon is high in the sky. There's usually no one around—just how I like it—but about a week ago, someone else was here, but I didn't get a good look at them.

I probably should have, though. They're probably the ones responsible for the damage to her grave. If I had confronted them like I thought about, that wouldn't have happened. Fuck. JJ needs to invent a time machine so I can go back in time to that night and ream their asses for being too close to Livy's grave. But alas, I can't do that shit, and JJ isn't that smart. Besides, if we had a time machine, I'd go back to the night that everything fell apart.

"We were just leaving," I say, nudging JJ over and forcing him to walk away from her. "Fuckkkk," I draw out softly once we're away from her.

"You can say that again," JJ mutters irritably, peeking over his shoulder. "You're lucky she just got distracted." He rolls his dark eyes toward the stars in the sky.

"I could kill her," I proudly boast, puffing out my chest.

"You and your threats of murder," JJ quips, shaking his head as we move ourselves to an isolated corner of the cemetery and far the fuck away from Mandy. "Come on, Boy," JJ says, softly gesturing to Waffles as he approaches us and follows.

"They aren't threats. They're promises. Because I swear... One day..." I'm going to lose my fucking mind on someone. He knows it. I know it. Fuck, even Hux knows it. With a sigh, I lean down and pet the top of Waffle's head, soothing some of the pesky feelings I'm having.

I guess that's why I'm in sports. It occupies me away from the murderous thoughts plaguing me. Something that hadn't occurred to me until after the love of my fucking life ceased to exist.

Since she's been gone, a black hole has lived in my chest, pumping poison through my veins. Hate. Rage. Pain. I've become the angrier, more unsettled version of myself. And I kinda don't like the guy I give the world.

Olivia Viotto was the sunshine in the sky. She warmed me. Made me a better fucking person. Without her, life isn't worth living.

If I died tomorrow, my brothers would mourn. But Franco? That asshole would replace me within minutes without a second thought.

I just want to reunite with my girl. Sooner rather than later.

I look to the stars. Somewhere up there, my girl is smiling down at me. Or probably frowning. Yeah. She'd have a lot to say about my attitude and wouldn't let it go like JJ and Hux do.

Whatever.

I sigh when Amanda shouts her goodbyes. Thankfully, she doesn't follow us, which means she's set her sights on someone else. More than likely Hux. He's around here somewhere. Parading around with his shirt off and a scowl on his face. Perpetually in Hell, like we are.

"Soooooooo," I sing-song. "Find any loopholes for that yet?" I raise my brows.

"There are no loopholes," JJ says matter-of-factly, staring at two people stumbling through the exit.

I snap my fingers in front of his face several times. "There has to beeee," I whine, slumping my shoulders. "We can't live with that every day for the next million years."

"You're welcome to try," he says in a low voice, unable to take his eyes off the front gate again.

He's locked in on that asshole who provoked Hux in the administration building. Impressive, as fuck. No matter how much it pisses me off that he took Brutus down with a few punches. How, though? He should have been crushed into the mat, bruised and broken. It was a lesson he needed to learn. Don't fuck with us; we're the kings of this fucking castle.

But what did he learn? Absolutely nothing.

I'll have to think of something bigger and better for next time. Shit, I should probably remind the guy, too. Now, JJ is enthralled with this asshole and trying to get to the bottom of... whoever he really is. He's suspicious of him. I can't quite figure him out or put my finger on what makes him so strange. Maybe it's the looks he gives us when we're near. Shit. Maybe he's in love with us.

I shake my head.

I need some more booze and a nap. I've been going all damn day. My body is desperate for anything but this. And tomorrow, Sunday—my only fucking day off from workouts, practice and school—we have to go on a run, doing whatever Franco wants us to do. AKA keeping us occupied and our eyes on the prize—our future empire.

"Ugh. There has to be. There's no way he can be tied to that... that..." I gesture toward Amanda's retreating back, at a loss for words when she saunters to more people at the party and makes her rounds like a hostess in our line of work would. All she needs is a teeny tiny dress, drinks, and Hux by her side, and she'll fill the shoes perfectly.

Or so she thinks.

She'll have a rude awakening when she moves into the mansion with us and realizes we don't fucking care about her or this business. If she moves in with us, that is. That's the plan the moment they say I do.

"It's an ironclad contract," JJ says emotionlessly. "Unless you want Franco's entire operation to cease and our heads on a damn platter."

Well, yeah. Of course, I want that. Then Franco could fuck off to somewhere far from here and leave us alone to create our own world. But then again, if our heads will be served on a shiny silver platter... I rub at the back of my neck with a cringe. I like my head intact, thank you very much. It keeps me alive to see another day. We'd run away, but Franco possesses so much power throughout the country now that we'd never get a fresh start anywhere. We're stuck.

Unlike...

A rogue sense of sadness hits me out of nowhere, and my eyes flit to Livy's ruined grave. Again. Whoever did that will pay for their crimes against her. And me. And JJ. And, well, not Hux. That asshole doesn't come here to visit her. Ever. He planted flowers in memory of her, but that's it. Bastard. She was the most important person in our lives. Well, mine at least. I leaned on her for everything.

She lit up my life and then took the sun with her when she perished.

It's unfair.

"You ever find out who did that?" I ask, pointing to the cracks on the 224.

My ribs ache and the memory. My tattoo practically pulsates at the thought of someone damaging her.

JJ frowns, rubbing at his brow. "Footage was too grainy. I'm currently following their vehicle through town on surveillance videos from different shops. But it takes a bit to hack into those systems. Once we get home, I'll look into it more. But it probably won't be until Monday when I find anything." He shakes his head, running a finger over his temple. "If we didn't have the job tomorrow, I'd find out who they are."

"Then we can take them the fuck out." Murder is back on the table.

"Whoever they are."

"So, there's a possibility they're from here?" A grin spreads across my face. The need for bloodshed and murder crawls through my mind, aching to be free.

"It's a possibility. If not, I can track their license plate wherever they're from..." he trails off, watching my expression morph. "Don't get too excited," he huffs.

"And then we'll pay them a fun little visit," I chuckle, cracking my neck with anticipation.

I live for the fight—especially this one.

"Your definition of fun and mine are completely different," JJ mutters.

"You like attacking from behind firewalls and dismantling shit that way. That's your fun, Bro. I'd rather cause bleeding and the loss of life." Maybe not so much the loss of life. They can live. But I'll make them regret ever stepping foot here in Greenwood. More specifically, in this graveyard. And the best part? They won't see it coming.

JJ sighs. "Do we need to organize another fight?"

Aw, he knows me so well.

"You could have a fight set for every night of the week, and it wouldn't satisfy this..." I tap a hand over my chest. Nothing satisfies my need for revenge. Especially since Livy was taken so cruelly away from us. One second, she was here laughing, and the next... I ball my fingers into fists, throwing my beer bottle against a tree.

"Mack," JJ grits out.

"I'll send a fucking pledge to clean it up," I grunt, rolling my shoulders back.

A few of our frat brothers look in our direction, their black shirts giving them away. They understand immediately when their gazes drift toward the shards of glass lying in the grass. Oops. That's my bad. I'm not someone who believes in littering, but my rage got the best of me.

Maybe another fight so soon isn't such a bad idea.

I snap my fingers in the air as one of our frat brothers runs forward. He's still trying to prove himself to us so he can win Franco's favor in the future. Fucking sucker.

"Clean that shit up," I say, lifting my nose in the air.

"Yes, Sir." His face scrunches when he says those words, but he's a good boy, jogging off toward a trash can and dragging it forward.

"Looking for another fight, Macky?"

My shoulders tense at the sound of his voice mocking me. Malic the goddamn maniac. What the fuck is he doing here? And how did he and my brother get into the party? It's not a place for them. They're the enemy, working for some mysterious asshole who never does his own work. I don't think anyone has ever seen the guy before. Probably not even Malic, who happens to have a boner for the guy.

"Oh, if it isn't Maniac and his peon," I quip, cracking my neck. "Back to ask me for a rematch?"

It's awfully cocky of me, but whatever. Cocky and me go hand in hand. Wilder won. Malic almost beat Hux, but it was a draw. He got lucky there. Hux is aching to beat his ass again in the rematch they're going to discuss at a later date. Or, probably tonight, with the way Huxley emerges from the shadows and hustles in our direction. Where the fuck has he been? Probably hiding from Amanda.

"You mean you want to lose again?" my brother asks with a slight smirk on his stupid face. I don't know why he hates me so goddamn much, but the feeling is mutual. We used to be tight and then bam! He hated me and showed it. So, I returned the favor. Gonna hate me? Well, I'll hate you too, big bro. "How're you at this party, anyway? Aren't you breaking the rules? You're a pariah now, Loser."

Right. Pariah status if you lose a fight. Too bad we're the ones who came up with the rules. Ha. Ha. Haaaa. The Coliseum is ours, anyway. Of course, anyone can call out anyone for a fight on the SlamApp. Or in person. Like we did with that Oliver guy. Poor idiot. I hope he learned his lesson and doesn't come sniffing around again. He's not welcome in my book.

The others might have something different to say. They were mighty impressed. But not me.

Maybe, next time, I should call him out directly.

"I invented the rules, asshole. So, no. This is my party, anyway." I spread my hands, gesturing to the raging party. No chance in hell would I walk away from this all because I lost. Besides, the partygoers are here for the three of us. Not anyone else. They want to be in our gang. Not these guys'.

"So, because you invented them, you can't stand by them?" my stupid brother asks with a cigarette between his lips. Not lit, though. He doesn't do that shit. Not anymore. He has it with him everywhere he goes. For some reason. Whatever. I don't give a shit about him. Or his stupid habits. He hates me. I hate him. Can I punch him in the face yet and make him bleed? Again?

"Oh, I stand by them for everyone else." I grin, to piss him off.

It seems to do the trick. Wilder's jaw tics. His beady eyes narrow in on me as his fingers curl into fists. That's right. Hit me. Strike me down right here in front of everyone so they can see how unfairly you fight. I'll prove to everyone that Jackson Wilder is a joke.

"You're a sore loser, Macky," Malic says with that unusual grin. He pats me on the shoulder a few times. "And an idiot." His eyes scan the party, and he slumps with some sort of disappointment. "When you realize what you did, you might cry." He chuckles at that, releasing my shoulder. "And I can't wait to see that. I'll bring the popcorn!"

Me? Cry? Not in front of them. I'm not ashamed to say I cry from time to time. It's healthy. A release. Something everyone should do to regulate their emotions. Especially that fucker Hux. He's so pent up that he looks constipated. Hmmm. Maybe he needs some chocolate laxative brownies. Again. That'll slow him down and take that expression off his face.

Yeah, yeah. That's what I'll do, whenever I have the damn time.

I smirk at the thought and then realize where I am and who I'm with.

I step out of Malic's reach. "Don't touch me again. Unless it's in the ring."

"Oh, is that a call out?" Malic asks, leaning in slowly. "Because I'd take you up on that. Your brother beat you. I can murder you in the ring."

I grin. "Bring it, Maniac." I snort out his nickname. The one everyone shouts when he steps into the ring. He goes from nonchalant to this crazy fucker. But I'm all for crazy. The more there is, the more blood that's spilled.

"Damn it, Malic," Wilder mumbles, pulling the big guy back with a huff.

Right. He's his keeper. Just like he is with our mom. Her keeper. He's in everyone's business and hasn't learned how to mind his own damn business. Fucker. He even shoved our mom in a home, which she deserves. I don't know why Wilder constantly takes care of her. She never did the same for us. Franco was the only adult in my entire fucking life to take me in, feed me, put me to bed, and make me feel safe. He may be my prison guard now, holding tight to the reign he has over us, but he'll never be like my mom's neglectful ass. At least I have a better chance at life. If only Wilder had come with me back then when I gave him the opportunity, he'd be in a better place.

"You afraid he's going to hurt me? How noble of you," I quip with a snort.

Wilder levels me with that stare. He'd never make a move in public, only in the ring. He has more control over himself than anyone else I've ever known.

"That's not what I'm afraid of," Wilder says, shaking his head. "You're an idiot."

An idiot? That's all he's got for me. I puff out my chest, ready to spout something else, but Malic cuts me off. Asshole.

"You seen your leader? He and I have some fun things to discuss." Malic rubs his hands together menacingly, eyeing the crowds until his eyes light up.

"I'm right here," Hux grits out, stepping up to Malic. All the rage he's feeling oozes out of him. Yes. I'll have to take him into the basement to vent out frustrations on the hanging bag. Bloodied fists, here I come. Hell, maybe Hux will want to do a sparring session. That would be even better. It'd sate this massive black hole consuming me from the inside out.

Violence is the answer. Always. And forever.

"Oh, goody!" Malic grins so widely that I swear it will split his face open. "How about we schedule that rematch?"

"You got so lucky last time," Hux says, narrowing his eyes at Mal.

"Yup. There won't be a win next time," I say tauntingly.

"Do you ever shut your fucking mouth?" Wilder grits out, stepping up to me like he's changed his mind and has decided that we need to fight again. Right here. Right now.

"Not around you." I want to shout in his face or knock him down a peg, but I don't. Being nose to nose with the brother who hates me has my blood pumping and rage boiling deep inside.

"Leave it for the ring," JJ grunts, pulling me back. "Not here."

"Why not?" Wilder asks, shoving the cigarette behind his ear. "We could make this quick and painless. Show my brother how a real man hits. Again." He cracks his knuckles a few times and loosens his muscles, preparing for a battle. "You still got the bruises lining your face."

"I've already seen how you hit, Pussy," I grit out, attempting to claw my way out of JJ's hold, but the little fucker is too strong.

"He said leave it, Keeper," Malic pipes up, putting a heavy hand on Wilder's shoulder.

That's right. Let your best friend keep you in line.

"Leave it, man," JJ whispers in my ear. "Another time. Not around other people."

Another time. It's always another time bullshit. I need this now. More than ever. I need people to leave this fucking cemetery and leave me with Livy alone. Her and I need to have some words.

"Fine," I grunt, shrugging JJ off again and stepping back, removing myself from the equation. "Go back to JJ," I huff to Waffles, who follows me at a slower pace. He cocks his head like he's listening and turns right back around to sit at JJ's feet.

If I stand here any longer, I'll punch Wilder just for being here. The frat brother who is cleaning up the glass from my beer bottle blows out a breath when I step away from everyone. He must have been on the edge of his seat, waiting for a fight to happen. Not today, asshole. My friends say no.

I heave a breath as I stand over Livy's grave. A rock from my run the day before sits on top, shiny and black. Something that she would have loved if she were still here. I can almost see the smile on her pristine face. It brings butterflies to my stomach and rage through my veins. She should be here. We should have been there for her...

I shake my head. Before I can think, I leave it all behind. Forgetting about my duties for one second in my life. I just need to breathe. To live. To feel what I'm feeling deep inside. I want to shout into the trees and let my voice roar to fix the pain festering beneath my flesh. If I had a choice, I would run away. Run to the tallest mountain, find a cabin, and hide for eternity. I'd get a new name and face. Like an undercover agent. Or a ninja. Or something. Fuck. I run my fingers through my hair, pulling at the ends, sucking in several deep breaths meant to calm me. I squeeze my eyes shut and step through the cemetery's back gate. The party booms behind me, leaving the remnants of what I once enjoyed.

But I'm no longer that person.

I'm different.

And it all changed the moment the girl I loved stopped breathing, and I watched as her body was lowered into the damn ground.

"Fuck," I grunt, stumbling over my feet and falling forward. My only saving grace is my hands instinctively coming out and cushioning my fall. "Fuck," I groan, lying on my back and staring up at the trees swaying in the wind. The stars aren't viewable from here.

"Help," a muffled voice says from somewhere around me.

I squint my eyes, jolting upright. Some fucker must have stumbled out here from the party. Idiot. Don't they know ghosts live in these woods, haunting anyone who waltzes through. Or at least, that's the rumor: Greenwood Cemetery and Hell's Hollow possess the most ghosts in the county. Not sure if I believe it or not, but I might see a real-life ghost for the first time ever.

Or not.

I stiffen when my eyes adjust to the darkness of the forest. The moon doesn't break through the tops of the trees, leaving me in a dim world. Only when I'm able to pull my phone out and turn on my flashlight do I see what's happening. It's not a party-goer dying from alcohol poisoning or a person who just saw a ghost. Nope.

It's a dude, covered in blood, lying on the forest floor.

MACK

"WHAT THE FUCKING HELL?" I SHOUT, CRAWLING ON MY HANDS and knees to the man lying on his back between a few large trees. I can't make out his clothing or his face. Not until I get to him.

"Help me," he rasps, his eyes rolling into the back of his head like he's ten seconds away from expiring. Shit! I'm a medical student; I should know how to fix this.

"Shit fuck!" I shout, pressing my fingers into the side of his neck. "Weak pulse," I say to myself, dialing 911 and explaining the situation as best I can. The dude needs help. "Help is on the way, man," I say, looking him over with my flashlight, trying to save the dude's life. I don't know what the hell he got into, but someone tore him up. I turn pale at the sight of stitches working up both sides of his body. My mind goes to dark places. Especially after what happened to the kid last year and all his missing organs. Something the authorities have yet to solve. Not that they want to. But that's beside the point. "What the hell happened to you?" Remain calm. Don't show him how freaked out you are right now. He's just a dude who got hurt in the woods. Nothing more.

"It was them..." he trails off through a gurgle in his throat.

Oh, hell no. That better not be the death gurgle bubbling up his throat. This asshole needs to live so we can get some clues as to what is happening.

"Them? Who the fuck is them? What's your name?" I illuminate his body again, trying to memorize the details of his injuries, and fuck, I almost wish I hadn't. "How the fuck are you still alive?" I sit back on my heels, taking in the massive amounts of blood around him. It stains the leaves and the dirt.

"D-dane..." he gasps out one last time before his body goes limp.

"Well fuck..." I breathe, watching as he dies right before my eyes.

I'm no stranger to death. I wish I was, though. So, this isn't the first time something like this has happened. It won't be the last in my line of work. But fuck. Why did it have to be me? I swear the stars fucking hate me. I dig through his pockets, not caring about my damn fingerprints and take out his driver's license and school ID. Dane Moore. He was a senior at Greenwood.

I need to get the fuck out of here before the cops show. They have my number. They'll track me down if they'd like. But I'm in a much better position being at the mansion with Franco a call away than here in the woods with bloodthirsty cops ready to pin this on me. Ain't no way that's happening to me. Even if Franco has them in his pocket, there's always one cop who wants to show the world the bad guys and try to come out on top. Me and the authorities? We don't mix. I'd rather have Franco take care of it all.

I step back, leaving all his identification on his body, and bring my phone to my ear. "Dude," I say, slowly walking through the woods toward our house, attempting to move quickly but not run. "There's a body in the fucking woods. Call off the party and meet me at home. We need to talk about what the fuck I just found."

"Fuck you talking about?" Hux grunts through the phone, with noise infiltrating from the background.

"It happened again. Senior. Tell JJ. Meet me at home." I repeat my words, hoping he understands why I'm so cryptic. He should. We've been best friends and brothers for years now. I know everything about the fucker. Like his nose twitches before he sneezes. Or when his lids droop right before he tells a lie. I know Huxley better than I know myself sometimes. And that says a lot.

"Fuck. Brief me at home." Hux hangs up on me as I make my way, weaving between the tall trees and finally up the path to our home. The sight of the daisies in the bright moonlight brings me one small ounce of joy. Something that won't happen over the next few hours.

The music in the graveyard abruptly ends, and voices rise as Hux sends everyone home for the night. The echoes of their displeasure ring through the air. Too bad. So sad. Go back to your dorm rooms and pout about it. We've got a real issue at hand.

Fucking murder.

MACK

"A BODY? A STUDENT?" HUX ASKS, PACING THE KITCHEN WITH A beer in his hand. Quickly, he sips it before slamming it on the countertop, nearly cracking it in half. How it hasn't shattered, I don't fucking know. "Fuck! It's already all over the damn Slam-App!" He thrusts his fist into the fridge, grunting when it rocks hard several times. His back heaves until he turns around, looking calmer than he was ten seconds ago.

I frown, staring at my hands. The moment I came inside, I washed the blood from them and watched it go down the drain, staining it red.

"How?" I groan, throwing my head back. "I was the only one there. How could anyone know?" I narrow my eyes when Hux's shoulders heave, and he turns back to me.

"Obviously, you weren't alone. Or they posted a picture of the crime scene after they dumped his body." He shakes his head. "Who does that?"

Not us, I can tell you that. We've seen a lot of bodies. Some alive. Mostly dead. Blood. Guts. Chopping arms off? Yup. We've seen it. Not that we wanted to. But in the gang life, that's what it all comes to when you cross the boss. Death. Destruction.

I blow out a breath and force my mind back to the present. I can't allow the images of my past to haunt me any more than they already do. Time to bring my A-game and stuff it all down again. That's what I'm good at, anyway.

"He said his name was Dane, but you should have seen it... It was like the Miles kid all the fucking over again." Miles. That kid from last year who showed up with nothing left in his body on the steps of the administrative building, bleeding out and barely alive. I didn't know the kid, but I know he went to Greenwood. He was a scholarship student, living in the dorms. But that's as far as we got on researching him. The cops locked that case up tight, and we haven't heard a damn thing since, assuming it was handled.

Clearly, we were wrong.

Dane may still have a brain and heart, but the rest of him? Fuck. He was torn up like a butcher took his insides, and then dumped him in the woods to die a slow and miserable death. How the fuck did his body sustain him for that long? Probably some sort of drug.

Poor dude. What a miserable ass way to die.

"And you still haven't heard from Meredith?" JJ asks abruptly, looking up from his computer screen again. When we arrived, he immediately dove into work mode, accessing the camera systems around town, trying to catch anyone who looked suspicious. So far, he hasn't found a damn thing. Now, that's suspicious in my fucking book. You can't just conveniently bypass every single camera in the damn city.

"No," Hux says, shaking his head. "And the problem is only getting worse. It makes me think..." He shakes his head, turning slightly pale. "What if she got caught up in it? What if she's next? He's going to fucking murder me when he finds out." Yes. *He* definitely will.

I swallow hard at the implications. We hadn't started an alliance with her for very long. She came to us with the information instead of going to the people closest to her. Not that she didn't trust them. But with what she was accusing, she needed people who would take her seriously and not dismiss her claims. She knew they were in too deep with the assholes on her radar and wanted to prove something. But proving that something has resulted in her going missing.

"I haven't been able to find anything on the surveillance videos. Except for your brief meeting with her outside the bar." JJ doesn't bother to look up from his computer this time; he continues tapping and clicking away. Doing God knows what. Whatever it is, I know he's trying to figure out why all this shit is happening and attempting to pinpoint the culprit.

"Yeah?" Hux sighs, plopping onto the bar stool beside me. "After that, she went home. And then... Poof." His fingers run wildly through his hair in frustration. A buzzing comes from his phone, and he frowns. "Franco is on his way."

"Wonderful," I grunt, standing and grabbing a beer from the fridge. If I'm going to face him, I need more liquid of the alcohol variety running through my veins.

"You can't be so sure she actually made it home," JJ says offhandedly. "All surveillance footage around her apartment was looped."

"So, you're saying?" Hux waves a hand.

"We don't speak geek," I quip, leaning on the island with a sigh.

"Meaning, whoever took her knew where to grab her and how. Either in her apartment, where her keys and purse remained. Or, they staged everything and took her."

"The question still stands. Where the fuck is she now?" Hux growls through gritted teeth, heaving a breath. "She was onto something." Yeah, she was.

"Let's discuss it later. It seems our guest has arrived," JJ mumbles, closing his laptop as the front door opens and shuts.

"Boys," Franco says, waltzing into his former home with a soft smile.

Good. That means he's not pissed off at us. If there's one

thing I know about that man, it is that he wears his emotions on his sleeve. Something he should learn to control, but never has. In this business, it's imperative to keep your cool and not let the other fucker know what you're about to do. That's what he's taught us all these years, anyway.

Franco saunters into the kitchen, continuing to smile at each of us. There's an easiness about him. Something that disarms people. Well, until they get to know the real him. His dark suit clings to his toned body. Letting me know he came straight from the casino he owns. For a sixty-year-old dude, he's not doing too bad for himself. He's still pulling in the ladies left and right. But discarding them even quicker. He's a playboy.

"Franco," Hux greets, standing from the stool. "What's the word?"

Franco rubs the dark stubble of his chin, looking pensive. "You're in the clear," he says, peering around the room. "I assured them my boys wouldn't have anything to do with that." And just like that, the cops wrote us off like I knew they would after seeing Franco. If I had stayed, they'd have put me in cuffs until Franco got there. The cops aren't in our pockets. Only Franco's.

"And what is that, exactly?" I ask, sipping my beer.

Franco's eyes snap to mine. Usually, I'd feel a slight fear creeping down my spine at the sight of him. But not tonight. Not after seeing that fucker with stitches on his body and dying right before my eyes. Nothing can scare me now.

Well, that's a lie.

There's a lot in this world that terrifies me. Like losing the family I have. JJ and Hux. They're my true brothers. Not fucking Wilder. Or Franco. Or anyone else.

"Seems we have someone in our territory stirring up trouble," he says smoothly, running his fingers across his chin. "And have been for some time."

Hux licks his lips. "Like stealing internal organs trouble? Because this isn't the first incident at school."

Franco nods. "It seems to be that way. Although pinpointing who it is will be difficult. But seeing how they're picking off students, you boys should keep an eye out and tabs on your peers and administrators. You never know what wolf is hiding with the sheep."

Something in the back of my mind wonders if it's him. Could he be responsible for this? It's a possibility. If someone is stealing internal organs and what... selling them on the black market for a profit? Then Franco would be all over that. He'd love to tell you he has a moral compass and he doesn't get into the flesh trade—AKA—human trafficking, but that would be a lie. Franco will do anything to earn a quick buck and expand his empire.

So, is this out of his league?

"Will do," I say, tipping my beer in his direction like I didn't just fully accuse him of the crime in my mind. I have to have proof. And with how relaxed and off-putting he's being right now, he's my number one suspect. I mean, he employs escorts in his casino/hotel for the purpose of entertainment. They're will-ing, of course. He wouldn't force them to do it. But what if they say no?

My trust in Nathanial Franco is nearly at zero. It wasn't always like that. Franco was the man who rescued me from the Hell I was in. He tried to save my brother, but Wilder turned his nose up at that. Idiot. Or maybe not. Maybe he was on to some-thing, but I'd never tell that asshole that. Not when he's constantly scowling and sneering in my direction.

Fuck my brother. Fuck Franco.

Over the years, Franco has been spiraling higher and higher, becoming way too powerful for his own good. Like a king with too much wealth and power over his subjects, expecting everyone to bend at the knee. The only thing I can count on with him is the paycheck he gives me and the funding for school. That's all I want from him.

The day we can disappear as planned can't come soon enough.

"Anything specific we should keep an eye out for?" JJ asks stoically, folding his hands on the island.

Franco slowly moves until he's standing in front of us all. "Anyone sneaking around at night?"

I snort. "Everyone sneaks out of the dorms. Fight night. Parties. You name it, they're doing it."

Franco nods a few times. "So, no one is abiding by the curfews meant to protect them."

"No," Hux answers before I can. "But most of them didn't see the carnage last year. Or throughout the summer." Two more bodies showed up during our summer break. Of course, we're here at all times. We have our eyes on the city. But we were busy with jobs and all that good shit to keep our eyes peeled for an ax-murderer running the streets.

"Any insights on the cameras?" He turns to JJ, cocking his head.

"Nothing," JJ retorts with a frown. "It's odd. It's like the entire security system at every store throughout the city was down at the same time."

"Very strange, indeed. It seems someone within the shadows is playing a very dangerous game with my citizens and the students of this university that I've heavily invested in."

"It appears that way," JJ says in a formal manner, matching Franco's light tone.

"I expect answers, boys. We can't have this shit hanging out in our territory. We need to eliminate the threat before..." He lifts his chin.

"Before he becomes too big," Hux finishes his sentence with a stoic nod filled with understanding.

"Exactly. Now, enjoy your night. I have gamblers to watch

over. And remember, tomorrow we're going to East Point, up north to engage in conversation with the Blue Spiders to form an alliance and all that fun stuff. It seems the Briar Cove chapter has already locked in with the fucking Viotto's." He practically spits the Viotto name, sending a spear through my heart.

I wish I could go a day without hearing it and thinking about her.

It hurts way too damn much.

I blink several times. "Conversation? Are we hauling?"

Franco grins, turning to gaze at me. "It wouldn't be a conversation without a little tit for tat, now would it? You three are responsible for packing the goods."

"Of course, Sir," JJ retorts quickly.

"Then, see you at nine A.M." He stares each of us down before leaving the mansion.

I slump my shoulders and chug the rest of my beer. "What exactly are we hauling to meet these new fuckers? And in East Point? Isn't that like five hours away?" I groan. I hate car rides. But I know JJ does, too, especially. Especially after what happened when he was a kid. He practically freezes inside the vehicle until he takes his meds and calms down.

"You good?" Hux asks each of us with a pointed brow.

"No. I'm not fucking good. I need to beat the shit out of a punching bag before I can even think about sleeping," I grumble, downing the rest of my beer and throwing the bottle in the recycling. "You coming?"

Huxley shifts when his phone vibrates again. He peers down at it, but gives nothing away.

"Who is it?" I quip, crossing my arms.

Huxley's eyelids droop slightly, and he sighs. "Amanda. She's fucking exhausting. *Huxley come over. Huxley fuck me.*" He scowls, clicking his screen a few times, and puts his phone into his pocket. "The sooner I get out of that, the better off we'll be. She wants to move fucking in before the damn wedding date."

"Uh, fuck no. There are three of us and one of her. No way."
I cross my arms like a child.

"I'll keep digging," JJ grumbles, opening his laptop again
with a sigh. "You two go kill each other. I'll take care of everything else."

"You got an alarm set for tomorrow?" I ask as I reach the
door to the basement.

JJ sends me a glare, his golden brown eyes basically telling
me to fuck all the way off. "I'm not waking you up. You're an
adult."

So he says. I don't feel like a damn adult.

"Whatever." I shrug and disappear into the fully finished
basement that we converted into our own private gym. Because
we'll be fucked if we use the one on campus or the only one
downtown.

Who knew gyms wouldn't be a lucrative business here in
Greenwood? Not me.

"So, shall we start with each other?" I grin, cracking my
knuckles when Hux comes down the stairs.

"I'll even give you a free hit," he grits out, tapping his cheek
a few times.

"Well, then. This is Christmas to me!" I shout as we begin
our match, and I ram my fist into my best friend's face.

Ah, the good life.

OLIVIA

"FUN PARTY?" WADE ASKS, THROUGH A MOUTHFUL OF ICE cream, as Simon and I enter the dorm room.

He lounges on the couch with his shirt off, exposing his tanned and toned body. Damn. Who knew the dude who wore three shirts at a time could be so buff? Maybe the volunteer life is good for the body and soul.

I shake my head, focusing on the delicious ice cream entering his mouth. My mouth waters. My cramps intensify. Fuck. He's got the right idea. Ice cream. Shirt off. Man-spreading on the couch.

I'm sold.

I peek at the freezer. My ice cream beckons me. *Come to me, Olivia. Eat me!* You don't have to ask me twice. I'm itching to get my fingers on the cold, delicious treat I've been salivating for since I bought it.

I grimace when a twinge of pain burrows further into my stomach. I swear my damn ovaries are shouting in pain. Add ibuprofen to the list of needs before I go to bed and curl up with my heating pad.

But first on the list? Rocky Road ice cream.

"You guys look like you had fun," Wade comments with a euphoric smile, pulling at his ice-cream-stained lips.

There's something about him. Something lighter floating around him, giving him a joyful aura.

"Funnnn!" Simon sings, spreading his arms wide. "You missed out. Where were youuuu?" He puffs out his bottom lip. "Did you work too much again, Wadey? You have to stoppppp."

I cover my mouth with my hand at Simon's antics.

Wade shakes his head with a laugh. "I can see that. Yeah, I had too much to do at the shelter before I could leave." He sighs heavily, but it doesn't match the energy wafting off him. "Too tired to socialize at a big party." He shoves another bite into his mouth, noticing me practically salivating at the ice cream. I'm in need. "I got more in there, if you want some." He points toward the kitchen as I narrow my eyes at the ice cream. "Picked up some extra after I got off work. Thought you might want some more."

I cock my head. "Thanks, man," I say, clearing my throat. "I still have some I got."

Is this typical of dudes? Sitting around and eating ice cream together with their shirts off? I mean, I can't participate in the taking off your clothes part, but I'm down for sitting around and eating until I can't feel my period anymore.

Simon sighs, plopping next to Wade, and leans his head back. "It was a fun, fun night. Lots of booze and girls and guys and ohhh, I got a number. He was hot with a capital T!" He fumbles for his phone in his pocket, but gives up with a huff when he can't slide it out. "F-fuck I drank too much," he groans, rubbing his forehead and, lifts his head. "You know their dog likes Oli. Like... came-came up to him and let him pet him!" He hiccups slightly, collapsing back into the couch with a grin. "It's impressive," he slurs.

Lord. He's drunker than I thought. How much did he have in the short time we were there mingling? Seriously, he's like a toddler. I can't take my eyes off Simon for a second or he'll suck down an entire keg of whatever they're offering.

Wade momentarily stops eating, and his brows furrow. "Their dog? Waffles? Likes you? That's weird. That dog doesn't like anyone. I swear he growls at me every time he sees me."

If I'm going to make it through the rest of the night without slipping up, I need my crutch. My cold, delicious crutch of goodness that will help me bite my tongue on the subject of Waffles and why he likes me. And then after I've had my fill, this binder is on the chopping block. Sweatpants will be mandatory. Ice cream in my face. Comforter tucked around my body, and the TV on with nothing but Buffy or Dexter, with plans of not moving for two days.

I can't fucking wait.

But for now, I have to keep up pretenses as Oli. A dude. Who doesn't get periods or pains from it.

I roll my eyes and grab a carton of ice cream from the freezer, pop the lid, grab a spoon, and sit on the couch next to Simon.

Fuck bowls. Tonight is a—eat straight out of the carton—kind of night.

"Why is everyone surprised by that?" I quip, taking a large bite of my favorite ice cream and humming my approval.

"Because their dog doesn't like anyone," Wade says, taking another large bite of ice cream. "Especially since…" Wade trails off, swallowing his bite. "Well, you know." He gestures toward the window overlooking the graveyard, and my spidey-senses tingle.

"Don't leave us in suspense," Simon whines, nudging his shoulder into Wade. "We know nothing…"

Wade snorts, putting the lid back on his ice cream and licking the spoon clean. "Something happened before the kings ruled Greenwood U. Something tragic back when they were in high school or something. I don't know the whole story."

The hairs on the back of my neck prickle and awaken,

standing on end when Wade's gaze surveys our small shared space.

Simon peeks an eye open, looking at Wade. "You're shit at gossip," he quips. "What was the tragic event? Did they eat pizza and mess up their perfect abs?" Simon laughs, waggling his brows.

Wade chuckles softly, but a sobering expression tightens his features. "It was a house fire on their property. They lost someone or something." His gaze sweeps over the two of us. "Or at least, that's what I've heard. The remnants of that house is still there. Somewhere. Some big mystery in town. I remember my mom talking about it, but she didn't know either. Their dad kept everything tight-lipped. But what do I know? That happened before I came to town." He shrugs one shoulder nonchalantly.

A home on their property. My house. The small prison my father kept us in. We were his birds in a cage. Whenever he saw fit, he'd take us out and torture us.

We were never free. Only in death. But Raphael Viotto is still at large.

And I'm not fucking dead or free.

Sweat glistens on my skin when I shove more ice cream into my mouth, swallowing not only the cold substance, but forcing my emotions back in.

My home is still there. The remnants, anyway. After five years, Franco hasn't bothered to tear it down. I wonder why? Why keep such a piece of history around? Maybe to look at whenever he's feeling sentimental with the guys.

Maybe it's time I face my demons. I could traipse through those woods and find it easily. Do I want to? That's the question of the hour.

Maybe when I'm brave enough, I will.

The last time I glanced at my home, it was engulfed in flames with me lying on the floor, bleeding uncontrollably. Good memories rest in the ashes, probably blown to sea by the breeze.

What remains? The structure? Our burnt-up possessions? Memories of days past.

"Whoa! Wait! You're tell-telling me the gods of Greenwood have baggage and a past?" Simon mock gasps. "A fire? Losing someone? Tell me more." He bats his eyelashes at Wade, who snorts.

"It's all rumors, bro. I don't even know if that shit is real. What do you think, Oli?" Wade's gaze connects with mine, sparkling with mischief.

"No idea," I blurt. "I don't know much about this place." I shrug it off, tamping down the panic growing inside me at the mention of my past. Especially by someone I don't know.

"Everyone's got a past. What they do with it matters to the future. Those assholes are crypts of secrets and bullshit." Wade rolls his eyes, disdain flowing through every word. "One day, their past and shit will come back to haunt them."

I lick my lips before shoving more ice cream into my face again. It's the only defense I have right now, so I don't end up saying–*oh, hi. Hello. It's me. Their past! Nice to meet you.*

"Facts!" Simon says with a groan as his phone buzzes incessantly in his pocket. "SlamApp must be popping off."

"You have alerts for SlamApp?" Wade snorts, sitting back on the couch and rubbing his temples.

"Daily gossip, duh," Simon slurs. His tongue pokes out when he finally fetches his phone from his pocket. "Let's see the drama. The…" Simon turns rigid, sitting up straight. All the color drains from his face, and his lips pop open.

"What's happening?" Wade asks as we both lean over and look at Simon's phone.

Alert! Death on Campus. Again!
Graphic Pictures included

"Jesus," Simon croaks, shaking his head. Wade takes the phone from him with a twisted expression, scrolling through the many images of the body lying on the forest floor.

Bloodied.

Bruised.

Pleading with his eyes for help, reaching with bloodied fingers, aching to be saved. Darkness seeps into the photo.

My breaths kick up at the sight of him. Dane. In one picture, he's alive and pleading. Next, he's dead. Alone. Not breathing.

A snake coils at your feet but smiles like a friend.

I swallow hard at the caption sitting below the pictures. A snake? A friend? My breaths shudder. What the fuck does that mean? Who took the pictures of Dane hurting and didn't help?

"How the fuck ..." Wade shakily says with nostrils flaring. "How does this get online? Dane..." He tosses the phone back to Simon, getting up from the couch. "Dane is dead?" he breathes, barely audible in shock. "Dane...." He longingly looks off toward our shared room, swallowing hard.

"Dane..." Simon breathes rapidly, tears streaming down his cheeks. "What the fuck is happening?" He whines, getting up from the couch and dumping his phone. He paces the room, running his hands through his jet-black hair and pulling at the ends. Wade and Simon exchange a few murmured words of grief, embracing each other in a tight hug.

I swallow hard, taking in the pictures with a critical eye. Blood haunts me. The look in his glazed-over eyes reaches through the screen, clutches my heart, and shudders my breaths.

My roommate is dead. He was an asshole, sure. Rude as fuck. But no one deserves to die with a camera in their face.

Now, the question stands—who the hell did this? And why? From what I've come to understand, scholarship students are the ones in danger. Not Dane.

I continue scrolling through the thirty or so photos of the crime scene, looking for anything remotely suspicious. Fuck. I'll have to save all those photos and examine them on my Veritas laptop. Maybe have Carter help me. He's bored all the time right now.

Setting Simon's phone down, I get mine out, save the pictures, and open secure texting with Jonathan. This isn't something that can wait. Dane's death is too suspicious to sleep on.

OLI

> There's been a major issue. **Pictures attached** My roommate is dead. It's suspicious. I want to meet and debrief about similar cases to his.

JONATHAN

> Wednesday. 2pm. 1212 Hubbard Rd. Warehouse 9.

OLI

> I'll be there.

I stare at my screen until it goes black. He never responds. Maybe he's been too busy with new recruits and solving more cases. Veritas has slowly been upping its agents in the past year, recruiting more ghosts like me.

I take a bite of my ice cream, centering myself in the present. Something super fucky is happening at Greenwood. Kids are dying.

And I don't know why.

"I need to go talk to my mom," Wade says, wiping his cheeks. "I need to find out what the fuck is happening."

"The police are canvassing the woods..." Simon's brows furrow.

Wade blows out a breath. "I'll find out shit, okay?" Wade quickly gets dressed, grabs his keys, and hightails it out of our dorm.

"Si?" I question, moving toward him and putting a hand on his shoulder.

"He was an asshole, Oli. But he had a good heart." Simon runs a hand over his blotchy skin.

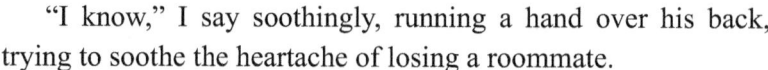

"I know," I say soothingly, running a hand over his back, trying to soothe the heartache of losing a roommate.

They were friends for years. Roommates for the same amount of time. No one would have suspected them to be friends with their vastly different personalities.

"Do you want to have a movie marathon? Eat ice cream?"

Simon licks his lips. "Order pizza, too?"

"Of course," I softly say, leading him into my bedroom and shutting the door. "You think Wade will find anything out?"

Simon plops onto my bed and lies back. "If anyone can find out anything, it'll be him. His mom always tells him what's going on."

I can only hope he's right. It's too fucking suspicious that Dane is gone. Shit. My eyes slide over Dane's belongings. He hadn't fully moved in, but he had at least put his things away into his dresser. I swallow hard.

It's so strange when someone passes. All their belongings stay behind while their soul departs and they're no longer a part of this world. But their things are. They'll stay here and fall into another's hands, becoming theirs.

My fingers run over the blood drive shirt Dane has on his dresser. Greenwood University Blood Drive.

"It happens every year," Simon says mournfully, coming to my side. "All students usually participate."

Right. My advisor had said as much. In fact, she encouraged me to go, stating I'd get a credit from my professors for participating.

"Have you?"

Simon cringes. "I hate needles. Dane did it last year to get an A in one of his classes. Wade did, too. But me? I can't even walk into that room without puking and passing out. Me and needles? No, thank you." He waves his hands around. "But if you can take it, you totally should. We even have a competition with another college. Whoever collects the most blood gets a prize."

"Interesting," I mumble, reading over the shirt.

There's a gut feeling there. On what? I have no fucking clue. But I think I need to check out the blood drive in a few weeks when it comes to town to glimpse why it's such a big deal here.

MALIC

"YOU'RE READY FOR THIS?" WILDER ASKS, ROLLING A FRESH, unlit cigarette between his lips.

"I was born ready." Wilder's bright eyes take in my expression, and he frowns, causing frown lines. "Turn that frown upside down, Old Chap!" I chirp, patting him hard on the back. "Today is a good day."

And you know what? Today is a good day. I feel it deep in my bones, rattling me with an odd sense of anxiety. Or maybe it's anticipation. Exhilaration. Today, I finally get my hands on the footage I've been aching for. Begging for. Anything regarding my sister and who she was with the night before she completely disappeared off the face of the earth.

Wilder's gaze latches onto my grin after looking at the voracious crowd. They're everywhere. Loud. Excited. Whooping every time they win a bet. Fucking tourists. Lining the casino and gambling away their money like they have nothing to lose. Five years ago, this place was a dream for my boss. Then, he brought in Bobby, who manages the casino while Boss stays in the shadows and cooks up more business.

It's a win-win for all of us.

And soon, our kingdom will come to fruition. But first, I need to find my goddamn sister and make sure she's okay. I've continued to stalk her apartment building, looking for anything suspicious. But there's nada. Only the usual tenants coming and going. The bar across the street where she was last seen has maintained their innocence time and time again.

One day, I'll torture that bartender into giving me the answers I seek. He knows something. It's why I keep going back and studying him. Even following him wherever he goes. The only place I can't manage to sneak into is his elusive apartment in the basement. The place he propositioned my little ghost into visiting. Fat chance. I would have stopped that the second he put his hands on her.

He wouldn't have hands left to touch her with.

I knew from the moment I walked through the doors of *X Marks the Spot* that she was mine. My girl. My Little Ghost. The girl I watched getting carried out of that house fire, clinging to life and barely conscious.

I knew it was her by the look in her eyes. The way her long brown hair swished against her back. Her laugh. Her voice. Everything about her, I know all too well. Five years of separation did nothing to tamp down my obsession with her.

Olivia Viotto was always meant to be mine.

And now, she will be.

Ah, my Little Ghost.

She thinks she's hiding so well in the skin of a man, wearing baggy clothes and cutting her hair. But I'd recognize those deep brown eyes anywhere. Even hidden beneath contacts and thick glasses. She can't hide from me. Ever. No one can hide from me forever. I expertly conceal myself in the shadows at every turn. Even Huxley and his idiot friends have caught my eyes. So, I watch their comings and goings when they think no one can see. Even their cameras can't catch a glimpse of me.

My boss taught me well.

They have no clue their old best friend lurks behind them, watching their every move. Doing what, though? And why? I haven't quite figured that out. I think it's high time I lurk straight into her dorm room and find all the secrets she's hiding. Hopefully panties. Or other goodies I can take home and keep until I have her as mine.

Only next time, my tracker won't be leaving her.

I grin again, sending Wilder into a panicked state. He straightens his spine, staring up at me. He goes to open his mouth, but I quickly silence him. I don't need to hear his pish-posh attitude about my scary smile and what I'm plotting.

It's none of his damn business. For now, at least.

"I have a good feeling about this little meeting, Old Chap," I say, slapping him on the shoulder again and knocking him forward with a grunt.

"Malic," he grits out, straightening to his full height.

His forehead comes to my chin. I'd call him short, but I'm taller than everyone else. It has its advantages. Like when I need to intimidate the assholes who end up in my basement, strapped to a chair. They always look so offended when I turn up naked. But what can I say? I'd rather not get blood on my outfit.

"You're fucking grinning again. I told you to knock that shit off, you're scaring the children," Wilder hisses.

"The children?" I ask, peering around.

Oh.

Right.

We're in the casino. Not lost in my damn memories.

"Exactly. There are no fucking children. Only scared as fuck tourists staring at the tall asshole standing in the middle of the casino with that face..." He gestures to my smile again, causing me to frown.

"Rude," I huff, stepping away from him.

"Just trying to keep you and your low profile out of sight. If you happen to strangle Bobby for whatever we're about to see, I'd rather not have witnesses placing you." He shakes his head, rolling the unlit cigarette between his lips.

"You're my keeper, Wilder. You're supposed to keep my fingers from necks." Unless it's my little ghost; I'll choke her within an inch of her life. With my dick. Oh, and my fingers, too. She liked it the first and only time we made love. In fact, she came all over my cock and... Down, boy. Now is not the time to get hard at the thought of her. Later. When we have time for self-care.

"I am. But I'm also supposed to help you not scare people. You have a way about you," he scoffs, nearly running into my back when I stop dead outside of Bobby's office.

"And that means?" I grin again when he narrows his eyes.

He seems to be the only fool not scared of my antics.

"It means, your vibe is fucking frightening. Save it for fighting or something..." he trails off, rolling the cigarette again before he plucks it from his lips and puts it behind his ear. "Are you ready for the rescheduled event with that fuckwit?"

Ah. The fuckwit Huxley. The motherfucker who thought he could beat me. He was so close, I'll give him that. But alas, it was a draw. It seems the little psycho has been training to face off against me.

"More than ready," I say. "Now, let's go see where the fuck my sister is." I nod toward the door before charging in.

"Damn it, Malic," Wilder grunts behind me.

The thing about my keeper is, he's not a very good one. Sure, he keeps me from murdering people on a daily basis. But in this instance? Not a chance. No one can truly stop me from getting to what I want. And what I want is for Bobby to show me the surveillance video of my long-lost sister.

"Bobby!" I shout, throwing my arms out wide.

The balding fuck startles behind his desk as his eyes grow wide in a cartoonish manner. Quickly, he covers something up, slides it off his desk, and puts it into his drawer.

Very interesting.

I'll have to pick the lock later and find out what he's hiding.

All for Boss, of course. He would want to know what the man in charge of his biggest money maker is up to behind closed doors.

"Malic," Bobby gasps out nervously. "Wilder."

"Bobby." Wilder nods respectfully, staring him down. "You said you'd see us today. That you have some footage for us regarding Meredith." He raises a knowing brow as his hand drifts to the pocket of his jeans for the small pocket knife he hides away.

My keeper likes blood, too. He's just not as vocal about it.

"Yes! Of course. Sorry, boys. I forgot you were showing up here tonight. Let me pull it up." The entire time he speaks, there's a nervousness to his tone. Something shaky and off-putting.

Yup. He's hiding something.

And I'll find out what it is because he can't hide anything from my watchful eyes.

"Can we see it then?" Wilder asks impatiently, holding out his phone. He shakes his head, grumbling under his breath. That can only mean one thing. Our boss has summoned us to another meeting.

"Yes. It's right here," Bobby squeaks, sweating hard as he rolls his chair back and gestures for us to watch. I'm the first to jump into action, coming around the desk and hovering above Bobby. I could probably knock him out with one punch and find everything he's hiding. But Boss would disapprove of my violence against his most-trusted man. It's a real bummer. Because I yearn for the violence coursing through my veins. Especially when he presses play on the black and white security footage. "So, this was the night in question. It, um, got Mere walking with someone across the street as she was leaving the bar. There isn't sound or anything, but..." he trails off.

All my emotions--or lack thereof--click off instantly at the sight of her in her nursing scrubs, standing just outside *X Marks the Spot*. Her back is to the building as she looks up and down the street. She brings her phone out of her front pocket and taps it a few times before bringing it to her ear. If I could only hear what she's saying on the phone. Maybe I'd know who she's speaking with and what about. Her lips move a mile a minute, but I can't read them. Not with the camera zoomed so far out. She's almost an inky dot.

My fingers bunch, forming a fist when another figure meanders onto the screen with his hands in his pockets. He walks right up to her. Like he's comfortable being that fucking close to her. That motherfucker has no right. I stand tall, narrowing my eyes at the screen. I will not punch it. I will not fucking punch it!

I slam my fist into the wall above Bobby's head, making him yell and cover his skull. "M-mal!" he stutters, trembling in his damn loafers.

I take several breaths, shaking the drywall off my fist before I look at the screen which Bobby paused. "Play it again," I say with an odd sense of calm. Maybe it's because I know the fucker talking to her and leaning in when she hands him something, and he takes it discreetly, shoving it into his back pocket.

"Motherfucker!" Wilder shouts, balling his fists at his side. "Huxley!" he shouts again, filling the room with his disbelief. "That's who she met with?" And possibly left with. I guess we'll see if they ventured off together.

First things first, chop off Huxley's appendages.

"Motherfucker, indeed," I hum, leaning in closer and examining the video again until it finishes. "Play it again."

Bobby blinks at me several times and nods, playing the video a total of ten times for me. Over and over again, I watch them interact. They're familiar. Friendly, even. Huxley leans close to her like a lover, preparing for a kiss. But I know that's all wrong. Huxley hasn't touched anyone since my little ghost disappeared.

"That's the guy?" Wilder grits out, letting all his emotions out on display.

Fool. He knows he needs to hide those pesky feelings when others are involved. But that's the thing about anger, it's hard to hide behind a mask of indifference. I send him a glare, begging him to school his features in front of Bobby.

Everyone knows Meredith is my sister and that I care for her. But no one needs to know how much I want her in my life. She's the only family I have left. Well, the only one that counts, that is. My birth-giver doesn't deserve any sort of title. Or to be in my damn life.

Besides, when I find out where she went, I have exciting things to introduce her to. Like my favorite knife and torture chamber.

"It appears that way, Old Chap," I say, standing tall and grinning at him.

Wilder immediately frowns, shaking off his agitation. "Can you copy that for us?" he asks, gritting his teeth hard.

"Of-Of course," Bobby sputters, typing in something quickly and handing Wilder a USB. "It's all on there." He nods several times, sweat trickling down his forehead and onto his keyboard.

I wrinkle my nose. Disgust is taking me over as all my feelings click on again. It's an instant wave of rage and hate, fueling me to push past Wilder. My chest heaves as I stand in the hallway, looking at the crowd beyond the set of stairs separating the offices from the gambling.

The people around me buzz with life, on slot machines and card games, gambling their lives away. I've never understood the appeal or gotten the high from giving my money away. My money is mine. But to each their own. I'd rather soak in the blood of my enemies than ever hand over free money to Bobby. Maybe that's why he's so nervous. I wonder if he's skimming off the top.

My thrills come from the hunts. My prey running from me, begging me not to take their lives.

It's music to my fucking ears.

"Mal," Wilder grunts, grabbing my shoulder. I swing my

gaze to him, narrowing my eyes. "We need to go straight home. Okay? Watch this again and reevaluate the situation."

Reevaluate? Oh, no. Who needs to do that? Huxley Crewes was caught on camera with my missing sister on the fucking night she disappeared. The fucking enemy talked to her with a smile on his face. Easily pushed past her defenses and moved in for the kill.

He needs to die.

Or better yet...

I have an even better idea.

MALIC

EVERY GREAT IDEA STARTS WITH TIME ON MY SIDE. AFTER THE casino, I let Wilder guide me home under the guise that I wasn't going to do anything drastic. Drastic? Me? I never!

I grin again when Wilder picks up the glass of whiskey I poured him from the kitchen. It's innocent. Just a glass of unassuming amber liquid. There's nothing in there that would make him sleepy. Nope. Not one bit.

I bite my lip with anticipation. Then, quickly wipe the expression away. He always says I give my feelings away with my expression. Well, not today, Keeper.

"You're doing that thing again." He lazily waves at me, narrowing his eyes.

Immediately, my face falls again. Okay, so I wasn't that great at hiding what I did. Fine. He might suspect something. Like the three sleeping pills I put in his drink—so he doesn't follow me out of the house and figure out my plan.

"What thing?" I ask innocently. I'd bat my eyelashes, but with the way he's staring into the amber liquid sloshing around in his glass, he's heavily suspicious of me.

"The smiling thing. Like you're up to something. Listen…" he trails off, taking a large gulp of the drink. Sorry, Old Chap. You should never trust a bloodthirsty maniac with your drinks. I bet he'll never forget this. It's not like I usually drug my friends to make them sleep. But tonight is vital. He won't leave me alone to plot my vengeance against an annoying gang leader's son. And I need the alone time to achieve my goals. "You can't go after Huxley."

Well. Here I thought he'd not try to talk me out of it.

"Why not?" I reach for my drink and down it in one gulp. Luckily for me, I didn't drug myself. Can't have that. Although, some nights, it would be nice to actually lie in bed and sleep. Or dream. Or anything but stare at the ceiling and wonder how my life ended up here.

Wilder sighs, pinching the bridge of his nose. "Mal, it's Huxley. You can't do anything drastic. It could cause a fucking war or some shit. The last thing Boss needs is fucking Franco trying to track his ass down." He raises a brow. "Especially now when we're so close."

Right. No wars. Booo! I want war. Then, I can skin those three assholes alive without repercussions. Oh, well. Too bad, so sad. The plan is already in motion. No stopping me now. Wilder, my poor, poor keeper, has already ingested part of my plan. The next step? Well, I'll be a gentleman and put my bestie to bed with a warm blanket.

Then I'll go hunting.

Regardless of the consequences of my actions. Huxley will pay for speaking to my sister. Being near her. Handing her some-thing. Even fucking looking at her. Meredith has always been off-limits to the people in the gang life. She's stable. A nurse, working hard to get where she was. I've protected her as much as I could. Boss even gave her secret guards to follow her around and protect her from everyone.

But they failed, too.

They're next on my shit list. But they claimed they didn't see a damn thing that night. Not when she got off the late shift. Not when she went to the bar with friends and then left for home.

Huxley will pay for doing something to her. If he did, I guess. That's the point of this adventure, though. Figure out what Huxley knows and what he potentially did to her. I'll starve, stab, and bleed the answers from his mouth.

I just have to wait for my keeper to fall asleep. Any minute now, the drugs will rush through his system, and I'll be free.

"You don't even know if that asshole had anything to do with her disappearance..." Wilder trails off, looking my expression over.

"I'm aware, Old Chap," I quip, sitting back in my chair with a sigh. "But they know each other." And that's enough for me.

"Meredith is a nurse. She knows everyone—even the doctors in town. She probably met him at the hospital or something." He shrugs.

"Seems like you're making excuses for the fucker." I smirk when Wilder reels back.

"Fuck no. Fuck them. I'm just talking sense, okay? Because fuck knows you need it right now," he grunts, tossing a hand in my direction. "You're ready to storm the fucking castle with a half-cocked gun and no bullets. You do something to that fucker, then war will come. Mark my fucking words, Malic." Oh, he full-named me. He means business. Poor guy. He doesn't realize what's yet to come.

"It's a possibility," I say, stroking my chin. "I solemnly swear." I put up a hand, grinning.

I'm a very convincing guy when I want to be.

His face falls. Okay, maybe I'm not as convincing as I think I am. The fucker has no faith in me. It's rude. In reality, he knows me too well. The second I get something stuck in my head, I hyperfocus until I achieve my goals.

"That's it. I'm tying you to your fucking bed or putting a tracker on you. I swear to God, Mal. You can't..." He sighs, slumping back into his seat. His head droops slightly, and his eyelids threaten to close with a huff. Exhaustion seems to suddenly pull him under.

"Sleepy, Wilder?" I hum, leaning forward so my elbows rest on my knees. "It's all right, you can sleep now."

Wilder eyes me up and down, narrowing his eyes to slits, barely able to hold them open. "Yes," he slurs a little bit until his eyes close. "Fuck you do?" he groans, slumping into the chair further.

"Sorry, Old Chap," I mutter, grabbing a blanket and tossing it on him as he lets out the first of many soft snores. Aw. He looks so peaceful and less defiant when he's in the throes of sleep. Channel that feeling for later, Wilder. Because the moment you open your eyes and discover I'm gone, you'll be on my ass quicker than... Well, anything.

I step back, taking the empty glass from his fingers. I almost feel bad for leaving him in this vulnerable position. Almost being the key word.

Once I set the glass in the sink and wipe my hands down my jeans, something like excitement takes me over.

I'm about to go hunting.

MALIC

My entire life has dealt with sneaking around in the shadows. It's something Boss instilled in me from the second he rescued me from that hotel room of Hell that formed my childhood. Actually, I think it formed me. I am the Malic of today, because of my mother and because of Boss. They molded me into… well, me.

"Malic, you be a good boy and watch Mommy," she whispers, putting her fingers between the black wire in front of my face.

A dog cage. Meant for an animal. Not me. I tried to work the lock on each of the exits, but I need a key. A key that my mother has dangling from a chain around her neck.

"Mommy," I whisper in a panic, recoiling when she attempts to brush her fingers through my hair. "Why am I in here?" I blink several times as her grin widens.

There's something in her eyes—something I can't place. The black part of her iris expands when a knock sounds at the door of the hotel room we've been living in for the past month.

That's when everything fell apart. Meredith left to live with her biological father. Thankfully, my mom knew who he was. Unlike me. We've always been just the three of us. Meredith,

Mom, and me living together. Unless Mere went to visit her daddy on the weekends.

But then we lost our house after Mom lost her job and Mere. And it's spiraled from there. Leading us to this point. In a dark, damp hotel room and me in a cramped dog cage. She was never like this before.

"Be a good boy." My stomach turns when a man enters the room and removes his tie first thing. There's a familiarity there. Him and my mom. Like they've known each other for a very long time. But I have no clue who he is. His eyes find mine. Evil wafts from the depths of his fucking soul, making goosebumps spread across my flesh. I want to scamper away. Leave this cage and run for the hills. Maybe if I ran to the police, they'd help me. Arrest my mom. Or something.

He holds my gaze for the longest time and tilts his head. A big smile spreads across his lips.

I shake myself from the taunting memories of my birth giver and the hold she had on me. Had, being the key word. That woman no longer ruins my days and nights. She's just a fleeting memory of my fucked-up past. Sometimes I wish I could bleach my brain and never recall those horrid times she locked me away in a dog cage for hours at a time. Mostly, it was so she could leave and do her new job. Other times, I was an unlucky bastard.

But no matter.

That was long ago, before Boss swooped in, stole me from my cage, and set me free to work for him. He raised me into the man I am today—tough, loyal, sometimes obedient. Sometimes being the key word here.

Like right now. If Boss had any say in this, he'd tell me to walk away and not engage. That *my revenge* is a dish best served cold after many nights of deep thoughts and careful planning.

But not tonight.

I don't have time to reel myself back in. Absolutely not. Now is the time to unleash the monster lurking beneath my skin and let him have free rein. Someone wronged Meredith, and Huxley fucking Crewes is the key to that. My monster knows it. I know it. So, I set him free. He encompasses every inch of me, taking away my feelings and replacing them with a numbness hellbent on revenge.

Here I come.

I hum from the shadows of the forest as a large SUV pulls into the driveway next to the historic mansion. It sits on a hill, dark and surrounded by the forest. It has its advantages, like concealing me in the shadows of the night. I am one with the darkness. It feeds my body, mind, and soul. Taking a deep breath, I let it overtake me again, stealing every distracting thought and pushing it out of the way.

I'm sure that if the boys did their due diligence and checked their surveillance cameras, they'd see me sitting here twiddling my thumbs and waiting for them to show up. Too bad they're too cocky and egotistical for their own good. They won't check anything. They'll meander through their unlocked front door, walk up to their rooms on the second floor, plop into bed, and not emerge until the morning.

Their lazy, uncaring ways are about to get one of them kidnapped.

Sure, I could have walked through their front door twenty minutes ago and hid in Huxley's closet, waiting for him to appear so I could jump him. Then he'd scream, calling the others to his side. Could that still happen? Yes. Do I want to hear his screams for help? You betcha. But I don't want it to happen until I have him strapped to the metal chair in my secret lair.

Besides, where's the fun in that? That's too easy, even for me. I like challenges. Look at my little ghost. She'll be my greatest challenge yet. But you know what? I'm going to lock her down. Someway. Somehow. Like I should have done five years ago.

Fuck. A giddy feeling soars through me, and my scary smile

breaks free. If Wilder were here, he'd tell me to stop it and think about what I'm doing. Oh, my keeper, I have. I've thoroughly thought out every little detail of this plan. The tips of my fingers tingle. This is it. I feel it in my fucking bones.

I'm about to get answers to the questions I've had for weeks now. Where in the fucking world is Meredith? Huxley knows. He was up to something. But what? Well, I'm about to find out. One way or another. And if Huxley has to perish under my hands, then so be it. Bye, bye Huxley Crewes. You didn't deserve a life anyway.

I don't hold my breath as Huxley, JJ, and Mack emerge from their fancy vehicle and make their way up the stairs toward their front door. Clueless idiots. They don't examine their surroundings. Hell, they barely look up from the ground they're staring at.

Exhaustion pulls at them with every step. Making me wonder what the hell they got up to tonight. Just as my boss does to Wilder and me, they probably went out on some sort of mission, doing... Well, I don't have a fucking clue. It's the one thing I've never been able to pinpoint. What does Nathaniel Franco have his foster sons do? Gun runs? Drug runs? Killing the traitors?

Not everything, that's for sure. Yet, anyway. He's putting them through college, much like Boss is for Wilder and me, giving us a legit degree, so we can step into his businesses and help to run them. All of them.

All in due time—as he likes to remind me.

Silence descends on the three fuckwits when they enter through the front door, none the wiser I'm lurking just outside, ready to attack—or not attack. But take what I need to take. More specifically—who.

I have my sights set on you, Huxley. You'll never see me coming. Well, unless they check the cameras. Then, they'll see me coming from a mile away.

Whatever. I love a good fight. Besides, I'd see them coming

for me, too. Being in the bushes, lying in wait, does have its advantages.

I grin when all the lights in the mansion turn off downstairs, and the lights upstairs turn on in each of their bedrooms. Well, the two that look out over the front of the mansion, that is. JJ and Mack. They're probably getting ready to go night-night, all snug in their respective beds.

Good.

It only takes them fifteen minutes for their lights to cease, letting me know the fuckers are tucked into their beds and ready for a pleasant night's sleep. Two out of the three will get their wishes. The third? Well, he's fucking mine to deal with tonight.

I check my watch with a frown. It's been three hours since I slipped my best friend a sleeping pill or three. Wilder should be awake in the next hour or two. Maybe longer. I'm crossing my fingers for longer. I didn't want to drug him to make him sleep. But desperate times call for desperate measures. He thinks kidnapping Hux is a bad idea.

I think it's the best idea I've had all week. Besides, the asshole deserves it. For many things. But fucking with my sister? Well, that's a whole new level of fucked up I never thought he'd stoop to.

He belongs to Franco, though. And I belong to my boss. Both are enemies. So, naturally, Hux is my enemy. JJ is my enemy. Mack is my enemy. They're all on the wrong side of things. They'd say the same about me, but they don't know who owns me. No one really does. My boss is a shadow of a man, running things through the army he's built to take down Franco and his boys.

And what a pleasure that will be.

I hum as I make my way through the brush surrounding their home as quietly as I can. There's an advantage to them living on top of a hill in the middle of the woods, with nothing but the trees surrounding them and the graveyard below. No one is here.

No one but virtual eyes are recording my steps as I sneak around. Or it would be if I didn't know every fucking blind spot it has.

That's the perks of being one with the shadows and knowing my surroundings.

Like their home being outfitted with the world's best cameras and motion detectors, or they would be the best if I didn't know how to avoid their capture. I grin to myself as I sneak around the outside of their house, ducking the camera's view of me.

Like many times before, I walk straight through their unlocked front door, quietly closing it behind me. What the fuck goes through their heads? Obviously nothing if they're leaving someone the opportunity to sneak up on them. Idiots. Some would call me nosy. But I'm not. I'm observant. How's that phrase go? Know your enemies and all that good stuff. So, yeah. I sneak in here a few times a month, looking for any obvious signs of their activities. There usually isn't much. Mostly their schoolwork or whatever. But it doesn't hurt to try. Boss would be so proud of me. Especially if I found information pertaining to him and what Franco might know. Which isn't much from what I understand. That's the way Boss likes it, though, for now. One day, he'll walk out in the open with his army and take this town back from the clutches of Franco.

I smirk when the nothingness takes over my ears. They're so comfortable with their status on campus that they don't think any of us peons can infiltrate their space. The joke's on them, though. Here I am, ready to take your leader.

Reaching into my pocket, I take out the medication and flick the syringe a few times, moving the air bubbles around. My grin spreads. It never hurts to break into the medical supplies either and take what I need. Like this knock out drug used by the students. Never this dosage, though. It's a mere twilight experience when used correctly.

Huxley Crewes doesn't know what's coming for him.

It's me. I'm coming for him. I hope he's unprepared for that.

With every step I take, my grin grows wider. I could steal from them. Take the files that they have in their office and snoop more than I already do.

As I pass the kitchen, I rearrange things so that when they wake up, they realize someone has been in their house. Maybe they'll notice Hux isn't coming down for breakfast. Or probably not. I grin more when Waffles lifts his head from his dog bed and yawns at my presence. With an exaggerated stretch, he gets to his feet and slowly makes his way to me.

"Hello, boy," I murmur, offering their loyal dog a handful of leftover steak. "Enjoy your snack while I enjoy a little B and E." I grin more when Waffles takes the steak from my hand and goes back over to his dog bed.

Who knew bribing a dog could be so easy? And they say the fluff ball hates everyone. Not everyone. Not me. Or a certain someone roaming this campus. Of course, that's for a completely different reason.

Every morning, Mack jogs through campus for over an hour. Eventually, he ends up at my little ghost's grave with a sad look on his face and tears in his eyes. He'll lay a rock on the top of her headstone and whisper words of love. I shiver, having listened to his therapy sessions with her. I think he needs a fucking therapist and not a ghost to deal with his issues. Eh, whatever. Hope he's miserable and all that. He's made Wilder's life hell for all the shit he used to pull.

JJ will meander down to the kitchen with his laptop and do whatever work he has on the net, forgetting the world for hours. And Hux? Well, the little bastard is slippery. You never know what he's going to do. Sometimes he's up early and away from the house.

Other times, he doesn't emerge for hours, opting to stay in bed and sleep off the alcohol he guiltily consumes to quiet the demons in his head. Or I can only assume he feels guilty. He should, though. For a lot of things that's happened as a direct effect of him being… well, him and who he associates with.

If they only knew how much I lurk outside, watching their every move. I always anticipate their next activity.

Because that's the thing about me. I was brought up to observe the world around me as I was locked in my cage. So, I use it in real life too. With the help of my boss, he directed me on how to turn it into a good thing.

So, here I am. And oh, the things I've seen.

Slowly, I make my way up the stairs, counting the steps beneath my feet. The first room I pass is Mack's. His door is shut, but I hear the muffled sound of music blasting in his ears. He won't hear a thing from the outside world besides the music lulling him to sleep.

The next room I pass is JJ's. His door is wide open. Peeking in, I note his hearing aids are on their charger. I grin. That's another person who won't hear what I'm up to as I tiptoe past his room and make it to Huxley's. Usually, he's sound asleep, but the frantic sound of footsteps pacing back and forth has my spine stiffening.

I lean in, putting my ear to the wood. But there's nothing but muffled voices coming through. Hmm. I tilt my head, observing. There's only one set of footsteps. So, whoever he is speaking with is on the damn phone.

Once I hear Hux's footsteps stop and the sound of his bed creaking, I know it's my time to move.

As soon as the lights in his room go out, I pop open the door and stand in the doorway with my needle in my hands.

"What the fuck?" Huxley grumbles, rearranging his blankets and getting to his feet.

Fuck yes.

This.

My heart pumps when his eyes widen and he takes in my massive shadow. He can't see me yet.

It's when he reaches for the gun in his drawer that I step forward and plunge the needle into his neck.

He never saw it coming. Probably thought I was Mack or JJ coming for a midnight talky-talk. Not so much, buddy. It's me. The boogeyman living in your bushes, aching to get his hands on you.

"You and I have a lot to discuss," I whisper in his ear as his body goes limp in a matter of seconds.

This was way too easy. Or they're way too comfortable in their home.

I hum as I put Hux over my shoulder, confidently walking out of his room into the darkened hallway. I grin when the other two are right where they should be in their rooms and none the wiser. I quietly close Hux's door and march away with him on my shoulder. When I emerge onto the main floor, Waffles continues to chomp on his piece of steak and doesn't even lift an ear when I walk straight through the front door and close it tightly behind me.

Huxley and I have a lot to discuss. In my basement. With the bright lights on and him tied up.

It'll be a hell of a good time.

For me, at least.

Him? Well, he's going to bleed for me tonight.

MALIC

"HELLO, SUNSHINE." I SING-SONG JOYFULLY AND GRIN WHEN Huxley's moss-green eyes slowly pop open and he takes in his surroundings, which isn't much. But you know what? It's my damn paradise.

The basement. It's my favorite place to break free of everything. It eats away at the pesky feelings gnawing in the back of my mind, muting them so I become the best man I can become. The man my boss molded me to be. His soldier. Loyal to a fault and eager to please. I owe him everything, after all. He saved me from my birth giver and sent her on her way.

Despite resembling a dungeon, my basement is a brightly lit, carefully concealed space under the gym that we help run for our boss. No one knows it's down here. Well, except Wilder and me. Fuck. I bet this will be the first place my keeper searches for me. I eye Huxley as he eyes me back suspiciously. Yeah, I need to get this show on the road and make the big, bad future gang leader sing to me a beautiful tune of information.

I grin more as Huxley sets his sights on the knives with narrowed eyes and an annoyed huff. Am I really not entertaining enough for him? This entire gesture seems like an inconvenience for him and nothing more. There's no fear in his eyes. No piss in his pants, which is usually the best part. Minus the terrible odor, of course. But that's when I know I truly have them shaking in their boots.

He's lucky I didn't strip him down before strapping him to his seat. That's even better. Threaten a man's manhood, and he wails like a baby. It's music to my ears.

Huxley licks his lips, while quickly testing the straps around his wrists and legs that are keeping him to the metal chair sitting in the middle of the room. Sorry, Pal. There's no escaping me. Even if he had the chance to run, I'd cut him off before he stepped foot through the secret door leading to the first floor.

The fluorescent lights flicker and shine down on us, haunting us with their ominous buzz.

Hux takes me in with a sigh. Not looking the least bit concerned. Well, until he looks me over inch by inch.

"Why are you naked?" he grunts, testing the restraints again and never taking his eyes off me.

Aw, my dick is hypnotizing him. How fucking cute. Maybe I should make my dick flex a few times for him. He'd probably like it or something.

I look down at my naked body, taking in the tattoos across my flesh with a happy grin.

"Why ruin my best pair of shoes?"

He blinks several times at my answer but still doesn't look alarmed.

"You snuck into my house." Not a question. A statement.

"Not the first time, Old Chap," I quip, grabbing a knife from the shelf. "Hmm, someone didn't do a very good cleaning job." I frown at the dried blood on the tip of the knife. Damn it, Keeper. You're supposed to sanitize our precious weapons after using them on traitors. Not only do I not want their blood staining my best weapons, but how gross.

"Not the first time? Jesus." He hangs his head, slightly shaking it in disbelief. "What exactly is this about, Malic?" He sighs, exhaustion seeming to pull him down as he peers up at me.

It's the effects of the medication. Making him drowsy and compliant. Maybe it's a little bit of a truth serum, too. Hopefully. I need him to spill his guts before I actually spill his guts on the concrete floor. I'm tired of tiptoeing around these assholes. The kings of fucking campus. Yeah right. There are new kings in town, and it's time to step on toes. His, specifically. Tonight. Maybe stabby stab him a little. Or a lot. Or however much I feel like.

Because tonight is the night I throw everything out the window and end Huxley Crewe.

"You know exactly what this is about," I say, pointing the knife at him.

"You want to discuss *her,* don't you?" Tension strains his face, and he grunts several times.

"The binds are too tight, Huxley," I taunt. "You can't escape this conversation." I grin again.

"Leave her alone. She's…"

"You're right, this is about my sister, Meredith." I pull out my phone, ignoring his words, eager to show him the footage I was gifted of him interacting with her.

He sits up straighter, a stranger expression crossing his features, and I cock my head. Wait. What did he say? I shake my head. Whatever. Nothing matters except Meredith and where the hell she is.

"Where is she?" I ask, holding the phone in front of his face.

The footage we captured from Bobby plays across the screen. It's all the evidence I needed to bring him here and force him to watch it again and again. Until his tongue loosens and he tells me everything I want to hear.

Everything I need to hear.

He can't deny he was there. Or the interaction.

Huxley's features tighten again. "I don't know," he breathes, almost with sincerity.

But do I believe him? Fuck no.

His entire life, he learned to lie, steal, and manipulate his way out of situations. Including torture sessions. Nathanial Franco wouldn't raise these boys with his own two hands without making them feel the edge of a knife blade and order them to hold their tongues. He knows his organization well. Too bad I know it better.

They're trained. Smart. And prepared for this sort of thing. It's almost too bad I don't have time on my side to thoroughly drag this out.

I take the knife and hold it to his throat. "Where the fuck is my sister?" I snarl. My patience snaps like rubber bands. One by one, breaking apart until they're nothing but a pile on the ground, and the monster swarming through my veins breaks free, taking control of me.

He swallows thickly against the sharp edge of the knife. Panic doesn't reside in his eyes. Neither does fear. It's acceptance. He knew this was coming. Somehow. Maybe he knew the cameras were there, and that I was looking. But who wouldn't be?

"Where is she?" I say as calmly as I can. But in my defense, there is nothing calm living in my soul right now. Chaos swirls in my mind, aching to make this fucker bleed more, riding me hard, wanting to rip through his throat and watch as all his blood drips to the floor like paint.

It's a fucking art.

"That was the last time I spoke to her," he says calmly, looking straight into my eyes without flinching or missing a beat. "We went our separate ways that night after that conversation. I went home to the mansion. She went to her apartment. Or not." He cocks his head, gauging my hardened expression.

Oh, if looks could kill. He'd be roadkill by now. Actually, that's not a bad idea. I could chop him to bits. Huxley Crewes, who? Never heard of him. Or met him.

Too bad his death would create a mess of epic proportions.

Do I want to create a bigger mess? Yes. I absolutely do. The temptation tingles at the tips of my fingers, currently holding tight to the knife I wish I could use. Over and over again.

Sorry, Boss. He ran into my knife twenty-nine times. It wasn't my fault.

Like that would work.

Fuck, focus!

I shake my head, coming back to the present. I can't let murder infiltrate my mind and take over. Not right now. I've fallen prey to that way too many times to count. The way it consumes me. It's freeing. Liberating, even.

Huxley watches me with a blank stare, taking me in. They say the eyes are the windows to the soul. Sometimes I like to agree. Maybe even right now. There's a sincerity in his gaze peeking through, begging me to understand that he's telling the truth.

But my rationality is all out the window as I dig the knife deeper into the flesh of his throat. All I see is the video playing in my mind on repeat, and screaming—Huxley did this! Blood trickles from the wound, splashing over the sharpened edges of the blade, dirtying it more. But it's my kind of fucking dirty. I could bathe in the blood of my enemies and come out stronger than before.

"You sure about that?" I hiss, leaning in and staring directly into his eyes more. "Give me the truth, asshole. Where the fuck is Meredith, and what did you do to her? Speak to her about? Give me all the fucking answers or you won't walk out of here intact." That's a fucking promise. I'll rip him apart piece by piece until he gives me the answers I seek.

"Are you ready for this conversation, Malic?" he asks calmly again, tilting his head so his throat is at an angle. "Are you ready to learn the fucking truth of what's happening in Greenwood?" He raises a confident brow like he's about to blow my fucking socks off. "Learn the truth of what Meredith was after?" After? What the hell is he even talking about?

"I know everything that's happening in Greenwood, asshole. I know every heartbeat. Everything that makes this place tick. Now, what did you give my fucking sister?" That's the question of the hour. Why was my sister in his vicinity? It's alarming at fucking best and makes me want to rip his eyeballs out. Actually, he doesn't need those, does he?

"Money," Huxley says with a slight shrug, pushing against the binds on his wrists.

I blink. "The fuck she need money for? She's providing for herself." She's a nurse, living on her own and working her ass off to accomplish what she had. How her and I came from the same mother, I'll never fucking know.

Huxley's deep chuckle fills the space. "Yes. She does. Quite well, too. She's a badass nurse and a badass person."

I rear back, blinking at him several times before putting the knife back against his throat, heavier than last time. "You can't compliment your way out of this," I growl, gnashing my teeth together violently.

I'm losing the strands of myself unraveling before him. If he's not careful, he'll be at the end of my murderous rage.

Huxley watches me intently as I retreat and pace in front of him. My fingers work through my long blond strands as I suck in breaths. I'm in way too fucking deep to keep this up. I'm going to end up murdering him. And don't tell fucking Wilder, but he's right. If I kill this motherfucker right now, war will happen. Franco will know exactly who killed his prized son.

"She ever tell you about her missing coworker?" he asks abruptly, his words cutting through the air like a knife.

I stop dead. Turning on my heels, I stare at him, blinking several times. "No."

"She ever tell you about the shit she overheard with said

coworker when she was standing outside a patient's room?" He raises a knowing brow, pissing me off more.

"No," I reply shortly again, taking a step toward him with gritted teeth.

There's no way I'll ever believe that he knows something about her that I don't.

"Or that she thinks your boss is responsible for it all?" Huxley smirks, earning a swift punch to his face.

"Shut the fuck up about shit you don't know," I grunt, punching him in the gut. "Why would she..." I trail off, my expression falling.

"Why would she come to me and not you?" Huxley wheezes, spitting blood on the ground. "That's what you were going to ask, isn't it?" He cocks a brow. "Why would your sister not come to you, her big, bad brother, for the help she needed? Instead, she sought me out." Now, he's poking the fucking bear and pressing the exact buttons to get a response out of me.

He's winning.

I'm losing.

Except he'll be the real loser in this situation.

"Yes," I snarl. "Tell me why the fuck she'd do that."

Huxley smirks again, blood dripping from his nose, over his lips, and dripping off his chin. It's a beautiful sight of red, making my hair stand on end. The monster in the back of my mind roars with delight, begging me to finish off the scum that's obviously lying to me.

"Because she doesn't trust you."

That's it.

That does it.

Red takes over my vision, and my fists fly, pounding heavily into flesh. Everything ceases to exist. This place. Huxley. The door fucking opening in the background. Footsteps coming toward me. Another presence in the room that shouldn't be here.

That should be enough to pull me back. But it isn't. Not until he speaks, gaining ground on me.

"God damn it, Malic!" Wilder shouts, bringing me out of the haze taking over. "You really fucking did it this time, didn't you?" he shouts, stomping up to me. His muscular arms pull me back, and I heave several breaths. "You're a goddamn idiot, sometimes," he grunts as I push against him.

"It had to be him!" I grit out.

"It wasn't me, asshole," Huxley wheezes, dribbling blood down his chin. "I told you everything I know."

Wilder pushes me behind him, and he scowls. "Stay the fuck away from him," he grits out, shaking his head.

Aw. He's not mad, he's disappointed in me. Oh well, this had to be done. Huxley needed to learn his lesson for taking my sister from me. In fact, I don't think I'm quite done with him. I take a step forward, but Wilder puts a hand on my chest.

"We'll discuss more about what the fuck you did to me later." His jaw tics several times until he turns away from me and faces the enemy strapped to our chair.

Huxley lazily grins, losing himself to the delirium running through him. Blood coats his cheeks. Swelling forms around his left eye. He's a goddamn mess. All at the hands of me. My chest puffs out.

"Would you put some fucking clothes on?" Wilder asks, running a hand over his near-bald head.

Rude. He knows how I torture. Sans clothes and all. If blood gets on my clothing, then I have to throw it out. It's a shame, really. And now, he's here to rain on my parade. AKA, stopping my torture session altogether.

"Did you have a nice nap, Old Chap?" I grin, putting on my boxers.

Wilder flips me off. "No. Now, what the hell did you find out?" Oh, so he wants the information. Interesting. Maybe I should make him work for it. Considering I did all this by my lonesome. Not that I needed him, anyway. He frowns at me, shaking his head. "Malic," he says with exasperation. "Just tell me what he told you already. I'm sure his little friends are wondering where he is. They'll be suspicious, and who are the first people they're going to suspect?" He raises a brow.

Fine. He makes sense. Although I could take all three of them at once. Well, minus the tech genius. He could probably hack my phone or something. Too bad he couldn't find anything. I may be impulsive, but I'm not an idiot.

"It seems our prisoner is innocent. Or so he claims." I pull my jeans up with a huff, noting how unfair this treatment is. I should be able to stay in my birthday suit for as long as I want.

"That was the last time I fucking saw her," Huxley chimes in, wincing when his tongue runs over the split in his lip.

"And why the fuck were you even speaking to her?" Wilder asks, looking between the two of us with narrowing eyes.

"Weird, right? He claims she doesn't trust us with certain information he hasn't given up yet." I take a step forward, leaving my shirt, socks, and shoes behind. Fuck it. If I get blood on my jeans, I'll burn them to a crisp.

Huxley chuckles. "Two weeks ago, Eleanor Steele, twenty-four, went missing. Ring any bells?"

"No. Should it?" I question, narrowing my eyes at him.

Huxley huffs. "Yeah, it fucking should. It was her coworker. They overheard some shady shit at work. Eleanor went to the cops. And guess what? She's fucking missing now. Coincidence?"

Wilder throws up a finger, processing the information. "So, her coworker overheard something at the hospital alongside Mer?"

"Isn't that what I fucking said?" Huxley spits, rage consuming him. "Eleanor went missing twenty hours after stepping foot into the fucking police station. And now? Meredith is gone, too. You understand now?"

"What did they overhear?" Wilder cuts him off, taking a step toward him. He's not one to want to get bloodied up, but he'll do it if he needs to.

No. I don't fucking understand.

"That's a question you'll have to ask her. Because I don't fucking know for sure." Something in my chest tugs hard.

"But why you?" I ask again. "Why not me or him?"

"I don't fucking know," Huxley says. "It was two weeks ago. She found me at the casino while I was doing my rounds. She was in her fucking scrubs, pale, and fucking shaking. I asked her the same thing..." he trails off, brows furrowing. "Why aren't you seeking your brother? You know what she said?"

"What did she say?" Wilder asks in a deadly tone.

"That we were the only people she trusted with the situation. That was it. Nothing more. She didn't tell me what the fuck she overheard. She didn't say shit. But she needed my help because she thought she had a lead on something that was happening around town. Something that involved whatever the fuck she overheard."

"And what the hell did you do for her? If she didn't tell you shit..." Wilder asks, shaking his head. "You have to be fucking lying about all this."

Huxley rolls his eyes. "She was fucking afraid to tell anyone what happened or what she heard. She saw that Eleanor fucking disappeared for whatever she told the cops. So, do you think your sister wanted to tell me anything? Not a chance in hell. She only came to me because of my connections in Greenwood."

"So, my sister, who didn't fucking trust me... came to you. Another untrustworthy asshole?" This doesn't make any goddamn sense.

"She came to ask JJ for help, digging into medical records at Greenwood Memorial. She needed information on five patients who had come into surgery and were under the care of Dr. Adriane Lohr."

Silence eats up the space between us.

"And this Dr. Lohr? What was so interesting about these patients she was looking into?" I ask, cocking my head when he wheezes again.

"JJ pulled the files from the hospital's server. All five patients had a few things in common. One, they were under his care. Two, they each went in for a routine appendectomy. Three, they all died within three days of going home. Despite requests, no one performed autopsies. Five accidental cremations? Yeah fucking right. Something more went on in those surgeries that scared the shit out of those two nurses." He shakes his head. "I never hurt fucking Meredith. She's an innocent in town..."

"Damn fucking right she is!" I growl, clenching my fists.

"Any leads on who would have done this to her?" Wilder asks patiently. "Any clue where she could fucking be?"

I hold my breath when Huxley gives us a genuinely apologetic look and shakes his head. "I'd start with the doctor. Maybe bring his ass down here and show him your knife collection. The last thing she said to me was..." Huxley sucks in a breath and blows it out. "She was fucking scared that she was getting too fucking close to something big."

"And you let her walk home alone," I say, gritting my teeth tightly.

"Something I'll live with for the rest of my fucking life. I could have made sure she made it safely there. But she was fucking convinced if she were seen with me, all hell would break loose. But it was the goddamn opposite."

"Go cool the fuck off," Wilder grunts at me. "You got your fucking answers."

"We didn't get shit!" I shout. "Meredith is still nowhere to be fucking found, and now, we have to track down this goddamn doctor."

"I'll fucking help you," Huxley pipes up, sighing when he places his unbound wrists in his lap.

"What the fuck? How..." I trail off, scrunching my brows when his legs break free from the bindings I put on them.

Huxley smirks, standing from the chair and slightly wavering. "It was fun, asshole. But I need to crash. Expect retaliation." He takes a few stumbling steps and rights himself on the wall. "I'll let you know if I find anything out. I'm not giving up on this shit. There's too much happening around here not to be suspicious. I'd look into the loyalties the good doctor has."

With that, Huxley marches up the stairs of my lair and leaves like he owns the place.

"How the fuck did he get out!?" I shout, turning to Wilder, whose gaze is set on the chair.

"Who the fuck cares? You've created a world of fucking problems for us," he groans, gripping his hair.

"If I had killed him, no one would have ever known, Old Chap." But then Wilder came down here and interrupted our playtime. Spoilsport.

"Everyone would have fucking known, Malic. He's going to waltz back into that mansion with the evidence on his face, and they're going to know exactly what psycho did that to him. Ugh." He rubs his temples. "Get dressed. We're going home and..."

"Researching a doctor?" I question with a grin.

"That..." he trails off, throwing my socks and shoes at me with a stern look. "I'm not letting you out of my goddamn sights for at least a year. Boss would have lost his shit if you managed to kill the golden boy of Greenwood. Fuck's sake."

"Golden boy? Pffft," I wave a hand as I continue to get fully dressed. "You feel it, Wild? You feel how close we are to tracking her down?" I question with a slight hint of vulnerability edging into my tone.

Wilder stops, turning his gaze to me. "Yeah, Mal," he whispers with a head nod. "We're one step closer to finding her. I fucking hope." He whispers the last part, abruptly looking away from me.

"She was supposed to be protected at the hospital," I say, walking up the stairs behind him. "She was safe. A good profession." If anyone should have died, it should have been me.

"She obviously found something bad," Wilder says, shutting the secret basement door behind us and locking it tight. "And..." He rolls his lips together, anxiety taking over his features. "We should prepare for the fucking worst."

"Fuck you say?" I grit out.

My sane mind reminds me that, statistically, she's probably gone. Her soul is in Heaven or the ether or wherever we go when we die. But I have to hang onto the tiny strands of her survival.

She's still out there somewhere.

And I will find her. No matter the cost.

JJ

THE MOMENT I WAKE UP AND PUT MY HEARING AIDS IN, I SIGH AT the soundless house. Nothing but static greets my ears. And for once, I'm glad. Some moments deserve to be felt in the nothingness the world has to offer.

Like right now. No one seems to be home. Or they're both sleeping off our late-night mission with the Blue Spider Gang where we tightened our alliance with them and shook on a new deal. I don't blame them. The run we had last night wasn't as difficult as it could have been, but it was still tiring. It's a song and dance with other mob families. Meals. Drinks. Talking. It's endless until we get down to business.

A yawn takes me over as I peer out the window near the edge of my mattress. The sun shines bright in the sky, highlighting the grounds below our home, gleaming off the headstones lining the slightly hilly terrain. Growing up here, the graveyard was our playground. A pang explodes in my chest as the ghosts of us dances over the graves, laughing at each other's jokes. I rub my chest, alleviating the guilty pangs bouncing around inside my chest.

Olivia should be here.

We should have saved her from the damnation that was her life. If only Franco had stepped in and saved her from her father's abuse. Or the fucking fire that consumed their home and took her and her family. We should have been there to protect her.

"We'll always protect you, Liv," Hux murmurs into her hair, pulling her tight as we sprawl on the treehouse floor, listening to the trees creak with the wind. The windows let in the cooler air of the September night as the full moon watches from the shadows of the clouds.

"One day, I'll protect myself, thank you very much," she sasses with a snort, turning to look at Mack and me on her other side. A blanket keeps us all covered and our clothes are crumpled in the corner.

"No, absolutely not, Livy. We're your men. Your protectors. We slay the dragons. You just..."

"Just what?" she asks with a false seriousness, pursing her lips. "Continue that statement."

I hide my grin behind my hand. Mack's such an idiot when he runs his macho mouth.

"Well... You know...." He waves a hand.

"No, Macklyn. I don't think I know. Because if you were going to say..."

"I wasn't!" Mack huffs, leaning down to take her lips with his. "Now, shut up and kiss me."

I roll my eyes. "You can't just kiss her every time you want to change the subject."

Olivia moans into his mouth, moving to straddle his lap. The blanket falls off her bare skin, and I harden watching her grind against Mack's erection.

"Why not?" Hux quips, watching the show with lust filling his eyes. "It seems to work."

I squeeze my eyes shut, hanging my head. Today is one of those days when the memories chase me no matter where I go. Every piece of this land. This fucking town. Holds the ghost of the girl I lost forever. There's no traveling to see her. No phone

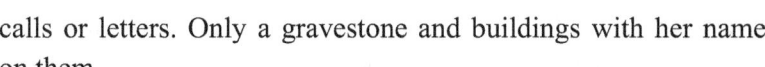

calls or letters. Only a gravestone and buildings with her name on them.

The real Olivia Viotto is gone. Body and soul. The only sign she ever existed hangs in my mind. The images I have of the woman she was. Growing up with her. Loving her. Now, she's just a name etched into a marble headstone, staring back at me. She can't speak or eat, or even react to our lives. Sometimes, I wish I could build a time machine and erase the grief of losing her and bring her back from the brink of death.

If only she were here now. If only she had lived with us instead of in that home. Maybe she wouldn't have suffered under the cruel flames of a faulty electric system. The day I lost her, I lost myself and my brothers in the process.

We're not the same people we were five years ago.

How could we be? It's like the heart of us stopped beating and pumping blood to the rest of the extremities. From that point, we've barely survived. Barely figured out how to put one foot in front of the other one without her.

Every day is hell without Olivia. Some days we can drink away the pain of not having her here and numb the grief sticking to us like fucking glue. But most days, we're the shell of who we used to be.

Like today.

Grief is a fucking rotten existence. Some days you're fine or appear to be okay. You walk through life, laugh, and exist. Others, you're unable to get out of bed, holding onto the memories of the person who left you without warning.

With one last lingering look out the window, I peel my eyes away and force myself to move. Before my class later in the day, I need to spend some time on my laptop and continue following the black SUV through the town's various camera systems.

Whoever they are, they're responsible for cracking Olivia's grave. I promised Mack I'd find the culprits. I also made a promise to myself. Find the people responsible for destroying a piece of us. And I'm so damn close to exposing them. It takes too much time to hack into each business's surveillance systems. Time I don't fucking have. I wish I could speed this process up and find them already, but I have to be careful and take my time. Or I might miss something important.

I yawn again when I stand tall next to my bed and stretch my arms over my head. With a sigh, I check the time on my phone and nod. Yeah. Mack's out on his run, and Huxley? Well, he's probably still in bed, sleeping off the night's events. We aren't strangers to taking out the competition in Greenwood. The only red light we've ever gotten is that fucker Malic and Wilder. Franco refuses to let us take out the trash and eliminate them. The guys have fun fighting them, but it's something I'll never understand.

"As long as they aren't stealing our shit, they're harmless," Franco says from behind his desk, waving a hand. *"Leave them be. Have fun punching their faces in and excelling at school like they can't,"* he scoffs, picking up the newspaper for the day.

There's something there. Something Franco has decided not to tell us. It's a mystery who they work for. We know their boss owns a gym in town and pays his dues around the city. What we don't know is who the fuck he is. The only two people who have met him face-to-face are our enemies.

Whatever.

Another problem for another day.

I quickly grab my laptop and shove my feet into my house slippers, and make my way down the stairs toward the kitchen. After setting my laptop on the kitchen island, I make myself a fresh cup of coffee and sit.

I click a few times, going over the map, and follow the black SUV by several more businesses. Unfortunately, I can't make out their damn faces. The footage is too grainy, and the SUV's windows are too tinted for a clear picture. I curl my fist, hacking into an ATM camera that's next on the route, following it down the long stretch of road running through the heart of Greenwood. By the casinos, over the bridge, over the lake, and through more of the town. For the next two hours, I sip multiple cups of coffee and lose myself in the trail of the SUV. At some point, Mack comes back and goes straight into the basement gym, grunting something about being pissed off at her grave being ruined among other things. But I don't pay any attention to his mumblings or the loud music echoing through the house. It's the same thing every morning.

"JJ, find those pricks so I can hunt them down and disembowel them for sport." Yeah, okay, fucking psychopath. That's what I think every time he looks at me. I'm almost positive he would do just that—end their lives. I want to make them pay, too. No one destroys that grave without consequence. But Franco's influence can only get us so fucking far.

I blow the steam off my newest cup of coffee and sigh when the bitter taste hits my taste buds. They rejoice in the caffeine keeping me awake and the taste of the nectar doing it. My brows furrow when the SUV pulls into a hotel's parking lot. Greenwood Grand Hotel. It's a newer building in Greenwood. A hotel built for the wealthier visitors coming to town and visiting the casinos in their spare time. It's in the heart of the city. Downtown. And perfect for walking to your destination. Restaurants line the road, and a casino is on almost every corner, lighting up the space.

I lean in, my heart pounding hard, when a man emerges from the driver's seat. My eyes narrow, taking him in. He's on the shorter side—maybe five-feet six-inches, wearing black pants and a black shirt. His hair is almost buzzed, looking light in the grainy photo. The trunk of the SUV pops open, and he removes two suitcases and then stands beside the passenger's side door.

"Fuck," I grunt, clicking a few times until I find a second camera to give me a better angle of the two of them.

The passenger door swings open, and a woman emerges with long, dark hair. Her eyes immediately drop to the ground as she grabs her suitcase and walks behind the man, straight into the lobby of the hotel.

My heart pounds as I hit the keys, breaking into the hotel's camera system. My mouth goes dry when the lobby of the hotel comes into view, and the two of them hang by the front desk, getting their keys. The woman nervously looks around the lobby, licking her lips and checking over her shoulder. There's a nervous tilt to her as her breaths come in heavily, heaving her chest.

Tears burn the back of my eyes the moment she lifts her head, exposing the marks on her face. The mark on her throat. The things that weren't there before. No.

"No, no, no," I hiss, backing away from my laptop. My heart slams into my ribs and tears roll down my fucking cheeks. "NO!" I shout, pulling at the ends of my hair. Heaving a few breaths, I force myself back to my computer and follow them to their suite.

I don't know who the fuck he is. But her...

Her...

It can't be her. I have to be seeing shit. She's dead. She's in the ground, in the cemetery just twenty feet away. I visit her fucking grave. I watched as she was lowered into the ground.

No.

It absolutely can't be her. It has to be someone who looks exactly like she did. Or a little different. She's older. More mature than Olivia would have been. Her face is... I swallow the lump in my throat, zooming in on the woman in the lobby. The woman who absolutely can't be fucking Olivia. No. She's a lookalike. That's all there is to it. No matter how many similarities I find as she walks with the mysterious man to their room, dragging her suitcase behind her.

My heart drops when I lose them to their room on the top floor. The video continues, displaying their hallway. Time ticks by. This is them. They came from the SUV that damaged Livy's grave. I followed it from the dark graveyard all through town, never losing sight of it.

It's them.

And...

I cock my head when breakfast comes on a cart and the man answers the door, wheeling it inside. His head stays down, so I can't make him out. The cameras on the inside of the hotel are of way better quality than the ones on the outside. Now that I've pinpointed the people who occupied the SUV, I can watch their moves and hack into the hotel's registry to hopefully get a name for them. From there, I can easily track them down.

On a separate window, still giving me a view of the hotel room, I hack into the hotel's guest list, checking through the room numbers.

Jonathan Viotto.

I sit back in my chair. Bile rises in my throat. Viotto? I shake my head. No. This has to be a goddamn trick of the mind. But how common is that last name? Viotto. I hang my head, shaking it. Nope. This is a mistake. I'm missing something. Bringing my gaze back to the computer screen, I reread the name assigned to that room. Two guests. One name. Jonathan Viotto.

Something rattles in my chest. Something that feels like the depths of hope, overpowering the despair I've felt for years. We've always been in the dark about the day Olivia died. Maybe her family is back in town to... to...

My thoughts trail off when she comes out of the room, rage contorting her face. I pause the footage and take her in. She doesn't bother to hide her gaze as she looks straight ahead. Her familiar brown eyes narrowing down the hall. Her fingers curl into fists like she's ready to take someone down. I keep her image there, staring and staring until my eyes play tricks on me.

It can't be. I just... I can't believe it.

She looks... She looks so much like Olivia. Yet, slightly different. There are scars lining her face. They're faded, like whatever happened was a long time ago and not recently. There's tension there. Anguish. Every emotion swirling in her eyes. The same eyes I used to stare into under the stars.

I press play on the video, following her everywhere and keeping my eyes on her. She travels down the sidewalk, lost in thought, until she lands at a bar—*X Marks the Spot*. I snort when her nose wrinkles, and I don't even register more tears falling down my cheeks when she goes inside. From there, I watch her carefully from their surveillance footage, recoiling when fucking Malic Monroe shows his fucking face and takes her down a hallway that has no cameras. I'm fuming by the time she emerges, blissed out, and holding a piece of paper.

Fuck.

I continue to watch as she makes her way back to the hotel.

And I watch when she emerges again as someone I've seen around campus. Someone I've had a suspicion of. Someone with short hair and baggy clothes.

Oliver Davenport.

And if the feeling in my gut is telling me anything, it's that I need to have a long discussion with the person behind the Oliver mask.

Could it be Olivia? Could it have all been a lie…

Well, I guess I'll see.

Quickly, I close my laptop, run up the stairs to get dressed, and dash out the door. There's only one way to find out if all the hope building inside me is true. I head to Oliver's dorm room like my ass is on fire. Nothing can stop me now. Not the people calling my name or attempting to gain my attention. Not Amanda waving me down and jogging toward me.

Nothing.

If Olivia is really out there. If my eyes are playing tricks on me and the grainy footage is nothing more than a mirage, then I'll find out. If anything comes of this, I know Oliver is not the man he says he is. He's a woman, dressing up to attend this college. He went into that hotel room as a woman and came out in baggy clothes, a suitcase, and a friend escorting him here.

My chest aches when I throw open the dorm entrance and run up the stairs until I make it to his room.

I swallow hard, pounding on the wood urgently. My heart explodes in my chest when footsteps come from the other side and the door swings open.

"JJ?" Wade asks, contorting his facial expression. "Er, can I help you, man?" He nervously shifts from side to side and cocks his head.

"Oliver. I need to speak to him." Only, I don't wait for an invitation, I barge into their dorm.

"Dude," Wade groans, shutting the front door. "Rooms over there." He waves a hand in that direction. I don't hear what he says or does afterwards. Nothing matters when I open Oliver's door, and it slams into the drywall.

"Whoa!" Simon shrieks, tossing the popcorn bowl that's sitting on his lap. His eyes widen at the sight of me standing there with sweat dripping down my temples and my chest heaving.

After overexerting myself last night on our mission, I shouldn't be running through campus like this. Not only will it draw attention to myself and whatever I potentially find, but my body aches and curses me for having the audacity to run so quickly to get here.

But there wasn't time to waste. I already did that this morning.

Oliver is here for a reason. He's in disguise.

I swallow the lump in my throat when my eyes connect with Oliver's. They're wide, watching my every move. But there's pain there, too. Something deeper that I can't dissect from here.

"I need a word with Oliver." My gaze darts to Simon, and I glare into his eyes when he stiffens. It doesn't take long for him to jump out of Oliver's bed and grin.

"Oh!" Simon jumps up. "Is this initiation stuff? Oh my God, Oli." He turns to grin at him, excitedly waving a hand. "This is it!" he whispers hoarsely and then peeks over his shoulder. "But uh, he looks a little murdery. Do you want me to stay?"

Murdery? I loosen my shoulders, which rise to my ears, and take a deep breath.

"No murder, I promise." I study Oliver again. Taking in the faint scars I noticed on the cameras. More specifically, the slash across his throat.

Moisture leaves my tongue a dry desert as I take in the familiar freckles dotting his nose and cheeks. Fuck.

"I'm not getting it this time!" Wade shouts frustratedly from outside the door as someone else knocks on their front door.

"Probably our food. I'll take it to the living room. Meet me there and we can devour our lunch and sip on some piping hot tea." Simon grins at that, nudging Oliver slightly when I reluctantly nod.

"Yeah, it's fine," Oliver says, clearing his throat. I hear the hint of softness in his voice. A familiar one I almost erased from my mind. "You go eat, and I'll deal with this..." This time, Oliver's voice dips low, like it had been all the other times we had interacted. He shoots me a wary look, like he's not quite sure how to take this.

Honestly, I don't know either.

Now that I'm here. Now that I'm staring at a ghost I should have recognized the moment she walked on campus.

Simon brushes past me and stops. "Can I be in your initiation, too?" he asks with a grin, batting his eyelashes.

"Uh, sure," I say absentmindedly. Not bothering to pay attention to his words properly. I'm sure I'll regret it later. But right now?

I'm too damn distracted from the sight in front of me.

Simon leaves with an excited clap, leaving me and Oliver alone. My heart pounds so rapidly, I swear it's the only thing I hear in my ears when I close the bedroom door behind Simon. It's a shame the school doesn't add locks to these dorm rooms. I could use one right now. Then, no one would disturb me and the ghost of my past.

I lick my lips and turn around, facing the girl I thought was dead for five years. The love of my life. The girl I ache for every night when I lie in bed. I know for a fact that when she stands, holding a knife in her hand, my gut feeling was right. Rage burns in her eyes, mixing with something I can't place. She stands tall, despite the slight twinge on her expression. Something is eating her up.

Maybe the guilt from hiding from us for so long when she's clearly alive.

Whatever it is, we're going to squash it right here and now.

Because the girl I thought was dead is alive, and she's standing in the same room with me. Breathing the same air as me. Proving to me that we were lied to, and she ran away.

And she better have a good fucking reason for faking her death.

"Spitfire," I manage to whisper through my closing throat. "You're alive."

Eager to find out what happens next with JJ and Olivia? And with the rest of the guys?
Preorder The Unravelings
Or
Join me on Ream to read as I write book 2!
***
Also, don't forget to come hang out in Aly Beck's Readers on

Facebook to get sneak peeks, discuss theories, and so much more!

***

Do you want more Olivia? More Veritas? More Jordy? Well, you're in luck! Welcome to Aly's Universe! Where every book has familiar characters. Some of their stories have been told, and some...well, they're patiently waiting their turn. Olivia has been a recurring character in my universe for five years now. Yes, that means every series I've written...she's been in.

Want to read more of Olivia as an undercover agent? And meet her grumpy partner, Carter?

*Check out—Web of Lies—where it all began for her (And my entire universe)

Want to meet Olivia's future best friend? And get more glimpses of her life in the future?

*Check out Second Sets Omnibus

Do you want more insight on Olivia's family—The Viottos?

—

*Check out **Twisted in Obsession**

Afterword

Behind every great writer, is a team of people who make this possible.
I literally, could not do this without my amazing people!
Huge shoutout to my teams for helping me prepare The Deceptions. Writing can be such a lonely journey but having you all by my side makes everything better and less lonely.

My Alphas. My dedicated Betas. Thank you all for taking the time out of your days to help me bring this to life. I appreciate you more than words can say.

Thank you to my amazing editor, Jenni, for making sure my commas were commaing LOL and for catching the little things and big things. All the things! As always, you're amazing and I love you! <3

Thank you to Steph for your dedication as my dev editor and for helping me more than you could imagine.

Thank you to Renee for plotting with me and listening to me ramble and spiral and for grounding me when needed. You're an amazing human being!

Thank you to Tamara for being an amazing PA and making my life so much easier.

Thank you to my Ream readers who followed me into a new journey and read as I wrote, you too, encouraged me to keep going!

Let's give a round of applause for all these amazing people.

ALSO BY ALY BECK

The Apocalypse Society Series:

Web of Lies | Book 1

Tangled Truths | Book 2

Wicked Deceit | Book 3

Second Sets Duet:

Bitter Notes | Book 1

Sweet Strings | Book 2

Destructive Devastation Duet:

Twisted in Obsession | Book 1

Twisted in Chaos | Book 2

The Scorned Series:

The Deceptions | Book 1

The Unravelings | Book 2

Standalone:

Four Simple Rules